"IF YOU DEMAND A BATTLE, CAT, I INTEND TO MAKE IT SWEET."

As Nicholas pulled Cat roughly toward him, she fought to break free. But his lips savaged hers with a delicious heat, burning away all thought of protest, and her moan was lost in the melting sweetness of his assault. The warmth of his body surged into hers, bringing with it a rush of elemental longing. His mouth drifted from hers to a path of kisses down to the moist hollow of her throat, leaving her lips to burn in the cold night air.

"Tell me to stop," he murmured. "Tell me you don't want this, and I'll let you go."

Cat shivered. "No, I don't want you to stop."

"A riveting historical romance filled with suspense, passion, heart-stopping adventure, and characters with unshakable spirit and determination."
—*Rendezvous*

Harper
Monogram

Lord of Misrule

STEPHANIE MAYNARD

HarperPaperbacks
A Division of HarperCollinsPublishers

HarperPaperbacks   *A Division of* HarperCollins*Publishers*
10 East 53rd Street, New York, N.Y. 10022

Copyright © 1996 by Stephanie Maynard
All rights reserved. No part of this book may be used or reproduced in any manner whatsoever without written permission of the publisher, except in the case of brief quotations embodied in critical articles and reviews. For information address HarperCollins*Publishers,*
10 East 53rd Street, New York, N.Y. 10022.

Cover illustration by Rick Johnson

First printing: April 1996

Printed in the United States of America

HarperPaperbacks, HarperMonogram, and colophon are trademarks of HarperCollins*Publishers*

❖ 10 9 8 7 6 5 4 3 2 1

For Craig

VERY SPECIAL THANKS TO:

Becky Wyatt and Beth Manz for encouraging me to pursue the original idea.

Cherilyn Angell, Christine Jones, and Trish McLaughlin for suffering through the many drafts.

Terry Tallent and her sister Connie for going above and beyond the call of friendship by listening to my worries and offering both literary and culinary support. Without you I'd still be unpublished and defrosting my frozen pizzas before cooking them.

Joan Domning and her merciless pen.

Susan Wiggs for telling me it was good just when I most needed to hear it.

The many members of the Detroit and Phoenix chapters of RWA and Genie RomEx, who offered their continual encouragement, support, and chocolate.

The Barony of SunDragon for teaching me just how much I still don't know about rapier fighting.

My husband for his countless hours of untold suffering (and a few of those he made sure I knew about).

And last, but certainly not least, to Shelly Thacker for forging the path and graciously lighting the way for the dreamers that followed.

Down the broad way do I go
Young and unregretting,
Wrap me in my vices up,
Virtue all forgetting.
Greedier for all delight
Than heaven to enter in
Since the soul in me is dead
Better save the skin.

—*CATULLUS*

I grieve, and dare not show my discontent.
I love, and yet am forced to seem to hate.
I do, yet dare not say I ever meant.
I seem stark mute, but inwardly do prate.
I am, and not: I freeze and yet am burned
Since from myself, my other self turned.

My care is like my shadow in the sun,
Following me flying, flies when I pursue it:
Stand and lies by me, doth what I have done:
This too familiar care doth make me rue it.
Nor means I find to rid him from my breast
Till by end of things it be suppressed.
Or let me live with some more sweet content
Or die, and so forget what love e'er meant.

—*"On Monsieur's Departure"* BY *ELIZABETH I*

1

London, 1594

'Twas said that anything, absolutely anything, could be bought or sold at St. Paul's Church. But Catrienne Lyly intended to steal what she sought. Even if she'd possessed the vast sums of coin necessary to entice the bookseller, the man would never betray Laurence Heyward. No one putting value on their life would risk the displeasure of the new alderman, magistrate of Southwark. No one except Cat.

But what she meant to steal hadn't arrived. Soon, she told herself silently. Heyward's man will be here soon. You'll finally have your chance for revenge.

The chant had lost its power to convince. She leaned back against the timeworn stone wall that formed the east end of the church's south aisle. Every muscle in her body ached from tension and cold. Chilling wind blew through the arched doorway, rustling tattered fliers posted on the wall, ruffling her long, unbound hair, and cutting through her drab, scratchy clothes. The light that drifted from the enormous rose-colored window overhead provided little warmth with November fast approaching.

She'd already waited more than two hours. Had her enemy found a new way to conduct his illegal dealings? Ruffin, she hoped not. The whore who slept with Heyward's liveryman had demanded almost all her coin in exchange for the secret information that Heyward was using the bookseller as a courier. Cat credited her enemy with cleverness. The merchant hardly looked the criminal, and he was in a good position to transfer messages not safe for the post.

Outside, her lookout, Rafe MacTavish, still crouched beneath the square stone tower where the four Jesus' Bells hung. Undaunted by the gilded statue of St. Paul that glowered down from the summit of the structure's wooden spire, the tow-headed boy had struck up a noisy game of rattling cheats with a group of loitering apprentices. He seemed even thinner than usual beneath his threadbare clothes. Collecting his winnings from the round and scooping up the dice, Rafe met Cat's gaze from across the way with eyebrows raised, silently voicing the same doubts she harbored.

She tried to smile, as if this were but a simple nip and foist, a purse-cutting like all the others, but her throat tightened and she had to fight back bitter tears of frustration. Sweet Mary, it had taken her twelve years to get this far. Was it all for naught?

Trying to distract herself from her worries, Cat studied her surroundings through bleary eyes. Like most places in the City, St. Paul's was a world of contrasts. The sweet voices of the rehearsing choir blended with the sounds of cant and gossip echoing off the colossal vaulted ceiling. The booksellers' stalls encompassing the south churchyard did a thriving business while many books which met the Bishop of London's displeasure left the yard only as acrid smoke issuing from the stationer's hall. Foppish courtiers and satin-garbed ladies moved amongst hungry paupers and thieves to the price of many lightened purses. It had been that way since she'd come here as a child of eight. Since the murder of her family.

Rafe's low whistle penetrated her brooding. A man in Laurence Heyward's livery, carrying a heavy tome, made his way across the churchyard from the east gate. It was finally happening. Cat flexed her slim, wind-chapped hands. Superstitiously, she checked the position of the razor-sharp cuttle beneath her cloak and said the closest thing to a prayer she could remember anymore. Then she fell in step behind Heyward's man.

This would be the most important theft of her life.

Nicholas D'Avenant shifted once again on his uncomfortable perch just inside the south transept of the church and sorely wished that Laurence Heyward valued punctuality more in his servants. So far, guarding his purse and watching the sable-haired beauty who lurked in the south aisle were all there'd been to occupy his morning.

He had first noticed the woman when she'd passed down Paul's Walk with an indolent grace. 'Twas impossible not to notice. Her finely proportioned curves and skin that had been caressed by the sun brought a sudden, fierce ache to his loins. Strangely, despite her plain gray dress and primly starched collar, which spoke of conservative leanings, she'd come unescorted. And the brazen calls from some of London's finest cutthroats and apple-squires, surrounded by their women for sale, had left her undaunted. Rather, a smile played at the corners of her generous lips. That was unusual enough. But it had been the rapacious glitter in her wide, green eyes—set in the quiet, heart-shaped face like precious emeralds—that had riveted his attention. 'Twas the raw, unguarded expression of one driven, obsessed.

He knew that look. By Christ, he ought to. He'd seen it often enough in his own eyes reflected back by half-empty glasses in the taverns he frequented. Spotting it for the first time on the face of another, however, struck a primal chord of recognition inside him. He took a step toward her before he knew it.

Nicholas gritted his teeth and forced himself to return to his post against the wall. Driven and beautiful, he thought. She can be nothing but the foulest trouble . . .

Studying the woman in the ensuing hours had only confirmed his worst fears—she was watching the same stall as he. God's blood! It had taken him the better part of a month to discover the warhawks' illicit communications with the North. Now someone else was onto them, too. Worse still, he had no idea who she worked for. If she'd been one of Burghley's spies, Nicholas would have ensured he'd received an introduction long afore now. What was she doing here?

The foul-smelling beggar to his right began to hack and wheeze again, drawing him from his thoughts.

Nicholas had already given the man a golden angel. Yet—possibly because of his generosity—the man had the damned annoying habit of sidling up to him and trying to strike up a conversation.

"Won't be long now, cove, to the masques at Placentia, eh?" the beggar began again, the stench of sour ale heavy on his breath.

The man asked the damnedest questions. Nicholas managed a vague nod, not wanting to be rude. Why would this poor soul be concerned with the entertainments at Court?

As the answer came to him, Nicholas cursed himself for a fool. Scowling, he turned to fully face the man. Sure enough, the beggar's eyes were hidden beneath scarecrow hair and the abomination of a hat.

Nicholas snatched away the hat and wig, revealing hair as black as a raven's wing and a leather eye patch. "Damn it, Savage! Don't you have better things to occupy your time?"

The vehemence in his tone surprised them both and won a one-eyed blink from his friend.

"Well, cry you mercy, cove." The actor took back his hat and wig from Nicholas and returned them to his head with good humor. "'Haps I'm merely trying out a new costume from the Revels Office."

Nicholas slanted his friend a dubious glance and considered the explanation. During their friendship, Jasper Savage had tested a multitude of disguises on him with more than a little success. If the actor hadn't lost his right eye, Nicholas doubted he would have uncovered as many as he did. Still, if it wasn't for that loss, he doubted Savage would feel compelled to apply his talent beyond the realm of the stage. Since the unfortunate duel that had cost him an eye, Savage was permitted only to play the occasional black-hearted villain. Apparently, Nicholas thought with a grimace, anyone with a physical deformity could not have purer motives.

"And what are you really doing here?" Nicholas replied archly.

Savage's wry half-smile disappeared. "Checking up on a friend who's been rather occupied alate." He cocked his head and trained his one-eyed stare on Nicholas, reminding him of a wizened, old crow.

Trying to ease the ache in his bad leg, Nicholas shifted again. Then he rubbed one of the many scars on his hand and hoped Savage would let the subject drop. He didn't.

"This has to do with Burghley and Essex, doesn't it?"

Nicholas rubbed at his brow with callused fingers. Aye, it had everything to do with the queen's states-man and the earl of Essex, and now he was tangled in the middle of it, too. But he'd be damned if he'd let Savage get drawn in. His mouth tightened in a grim line. Nicholas looked down at his battle-scarred hands. Christ, when had he got the hands of an old man? Finally, he murmured, "I thought you preferred not to hear about the 'Machiavellian manipulations of court.'"

"Well, yes, I prefer not to be privileged with any knowledge that might threaten my neck," Savage replied. "But this is different." His voice lowered. "I haven't seen you like this in a long time. I thought you were through working for Burghley."

"This isn't for him."

"Then why are you here, man?"

Because I have no other choice, Nicholas thought. Because lives and souls are at stake—especially mine.

But how could he share such foolishness with Savage? The actor would take him straight to Bedlam and rightly so. Searching for a distraction, Nicholas surveyed the churchyard just outside the archway. What he saw, however, did nothing to ease his discomfort.

Heyward's liveryman had finally decided to make an appearance, and the woman spy was right on his heels. "'Sblood! What the hell does she think she's about?"

"What? Who?" Savage also straightened. He scanned the St. Paul's traffic. He must have located the source of trouble because he asked, "You don't mean the girl in gray, do you?" He sounded incredulous. "I hate to tell you this, Nick, but the last I heard it wasn't a crime to enter a bookseller's stall."

"Believe me, it's not a book she's after. By Christ, I can't believe she'd be so reckless." His hand convulsed on the hilt of his rapier. The woman could ruin weeks of careful work just when time was running out. "I'll kill her. I swear I'll kill her!"

Savage placed a restraining hand across Nicholas's chest. "I wouldn't be so quick with your word," he said, a silken thread of warning in his voice. "If you raise a hand against Cat, I'd be obliged to try to stop you. And that," he added with a crooked smile, "is not a quarrel I would relish."

"Cat?" Nicholas looked back at his friend blankly. Cat. The nickname brought a fleeting memory of a dark-haired urchin who darted through the alleys like an underfed field mouse. He could remember no features, just a skittish flurry of motion. Only the actor had held her trust.

Nicholas weighed the full implication of Savage's

words and then groaned. "'Sdeath, you don't mean to tell me that woman over there"—he jabbed a finger at the source of his frustration—"is your precious Cat? The one you used to borrow money to buy sweetmeats for?"

"Not so little anymore is she?" Savage's countenance softened into a grin. "Turned into quite a beauty. But I don't suppose I can take all the credit." His grin vanished as quickly as it had appeared. "Pray, what do you want with her? I don't fancy her having the attention of Lord Burghley and his errand boys."

Nicholas scowled at Savage's slur but decided to ignore it. "It looks as though your precious Cat, my friend, is about to involve herself in treason."

Cat, careful to keep her steps unhurried, proceeded toward the bookseller. Out of the corner of her eye, she saw Rafe hastily end his game, to more than one apprentice's protest.

She reached the open stall a few moments after Heyward's servant. She met the merchant's speculative glance with a slight nod and what she hoped was a modest look toward the floor, trying her best to appear the solemn Protestant.

She browsed through the books and folios close to where the merchant stood and waited for her target to act. The pockmarked liveryman took his time, apparently searching for anything awry in the bookstall. His hesitancy renewed her conviction that all was not as it seemed.

The ruddy-faced bookseller nodded at Cat. "The religious tracts be further to the back, mistress." Then his attention darted back to the press of people who passed in front of his stall.

Cat's pulse pounded in her ears. Her mouth went dry. She hadn't been this nervous since she'd spent her first hollow coin.

A copy of Philip Sidney's *Astrophel and Stella* caught her attention, and her hand, seemingly of its own volition, reached out to pick it up. Desperate for a distraction with which to keep herself calm, she traced the rough edge of the paper with a trembling fingertip.

The merchant coughed at her immodest choice of reading material, and heat rose up the back of her neck. She was grateful that it was at that moment Heyward's servant decided to act.

"Good morrow, sirrah." The liveryman frowned and his gaze went immediately to the two occupants in the stall other than Cat and the merchant. Yet she stood close enough to smell the reek of his unwashed body and the tobacco smoke clinging to his clothes. For perhaps the hundredth time in her life, Cat was dismissed as a potential threat because of her sex. 'Twas one of the very few blessings of being female.

The merchant grunted something inaudible and then added, "You were to be here 'fore noon."

"I was delayed. Sir Laurence had an unexpected visitor."

Sir. Cat wanted to spit at the sound of the title.

When the bookseller turned to deal with his patron's man, Cat noted a suspicious bulk beneath the side of his doublet. From its size, she guessed the purse held a generous sum of coin. This was not a man who kept wealth behind concealed panels, and for that, she was grateful. It made her task far easier.

One of the two male customers made his way to the front of the stall. Darting a lecherous glance at her, he exited. One more to go, Cat thought.

Almost hidden behind a wagon that creaked across the cobblestones, Rafe crossed in front of the stall, doubled back from the west, and assumed his position. When Cat was able to catch his eye, she signed the position of the merchant's purse with a quick hand gesture. Rafe nodded and signed back, "I'm ready. Your move." Then he winked at her. To him this was just a game. But she trusted no one more.

"My master requests that you repair this volume . . ." The pockmarked liveryman hesitated and glanced at Cat for the first time.

Casually, she turned to study a display of folios with great interest.

"I fear its binding warrants attention."

A moment's silence passed as the book changed hands. Cat watched out of the corner of her eye as the merchant hefted the volume, studied its side, and then looked back at Heyward's servant. An unspoken message seemed to pass between the two men, and a frisson of certainty shot up her spine. Something was definitely hidden in the book. Her palms itched to grab the damning evidence against Heyward, whatever it might be.

The other male customer moved to the display where she stood. Cat took advantage of the opportunity to "accidentally" step on his foot in hopes of making him leave. It didn't work.

The merchant coughed into a filthy rag. Eyes watering, he was finally able to speak again. "The folio your master requested is ready."

"Good," Heyward's man replied. "He's been waiting for it with much anticipation."

With another precisely misjudged footstep, Cat won the other patron's scowling departure.

The merchant crouched in front of a heavy trunk and withdrew a key from beneath his doublet. The lock he inserted it into was sophisticated. If the chest was where he intended to put the volume, she and Rafe would have to act before it was locked away.

Locating what he wanted within, the bookseller hoisted himself back up with a grunt and handed the folio to the man. Then a staggering amount of coin passed across the counter from the liveryman to him. That done, Heyward's servant hastily made his goodbyes and disappeared back into the crowd.

A trail of sweat trickled down the back of Cat's neck beneath the strangling collar of her disguise. She granted the bookseller a few seconds to scoop up his coin into his pouch. When he went toward the chest with the volume, she grabbed a leather-bound book in front of her and dropped it, pages first. It landed with a satisfying swoosh. The speed with which the merchant waddled to her side confirmed her suspicions about the book's value.

"Oh!" Cat gasped in almost sincere dismay. "I cry you mercy! I had no idea 'twas so heavy."

She dropped to her knees beside the horror-struck man. He waved her back when she made to reach for the book. Almost daintily, he picked up the book and cradled it to his chest.

Always faithful, Rafe stepped behind the merchant and lifted the back of the man's padded doublet with an angel's touch.

"Have you—" the merchant gasped. "Have you any idea of what you've just done, mistress?"

Cat was forced to bite the inside of her cheek to fight back a smile. Not wanting to betray her copesmate's activity, she held the man's glare and stammered an apology.

Rafe cut the purse from its strings with his cuttle.

The merchant continued to splutter in indignation. "There must be amends, of that, mistress, there is no question!"

With another wink at Cat, Rafe verified the bag's contents. Then he tweaked the purse strings that still dangled from the man's belt and took off running down the south churchyard toward the west gate.

"This is a most outrageous—"

After a second's hesitation, the bookseller reached to where his purse should have been and noted its absence with an inarticulate squeak. Spotting Rafe dodging through the flow of traffic with his booty held high, the merchant lumbered after him.

"Thief! Stay that thief! Clubs! Clubs!"

The man's cry drew only passing attention.

"He . . . has . . . my purse!" the merchant wheezed. "He . . . stole . . . purse!"

Rafe slowed to a trot so as not to lose his winded pursuer. When the man finally was able to grab the back of the boy's jerkin, Rafe stumbled to one knee, and the contents of the purse were flung far and wide across the churchyard. Cat, however, would wager a week's earnings that the little lifter held back at least a portion of the purse for himself.

An eerie moment of silence followed as all activity at St. Paul's froze at the golden sound of falling coin.

Then absolute bedlam broke loose.

A costard monger's cart was overturned by the desperate press of people. Several horses screamed as their masters turned savage. Grandames and children alike fought to be the first to the pile. Cat could hardly blame them. More coin lay on the cobblestone than many would see in a lifetime. It felt good to know some of what they scrabbled for was Heyward's gold.

Rafe deftly lost himself in the madness.

Cat moved to the counter, then studied the perimeter of the stall and judged it safe to act. Unable to breathe, so desperate was her hope, she drew the leather volume in her arms, and lowered it behind the counter into the dark folds of her dress. With practiced hands, she searched the length of the volume but kept her eyes on the denizens of the churchyard.

Most of the local thieves had abandoned their languor if not to actively participate in the free-for-all, at least to take advantage of the distraction to make a hasty bet or lighten an unguarded purse. The more world-weary merely cracked a sleepy eye to observe the unusual. Few recognized Cat as the real center of activity. One richly dressed knave, however, watched her with fiendish intensity from the south transept. 'Twas as if he dared her to have the audacity to commit the theft before his very eyes. Raising her chin a notch, she glared back until she was certain he would not actively interfere. Then, with a shiver, she looked away and continued her search.

Uneasy moments passed, marked by the heavy pounding of her heart. "Where is it?" Cat hissed in frustration. Her hands began to shake again as she retraced what she'd already examined. Jesu! Would she have to take the whole damn book? Desperate for any clue of where the missive might be concealed, Cat riffed through the pages. Nothing but choking dust. And there wasn't time to check every bleedin' page.

The hair on the nape of her neck rose. She could feel someone's gaze like a brand on her skin. Instinctively she knew it was the man in the pews. Cat fought to control her growing hysteria and the natural instinct to run before she was caught by the bailiffs. Oh Lord, not again. She couldn't afford to be caught by the bandogs again. Not now.

Heyward's man had mentioned the binding.

Cat tugged her cuttle out from under her cloak. Repeating her half-remembered prayer, she sliced away one edge of the leather. Time was running out. Digging beneath the leather, Cat's finger made contact with something foreign. Using her ragged nails, she pulled out a thin fold of paper, its edge oddly torn. Turning it over with a trembling hand, she found a crimson stain of sealing wax. She had it! It took the length of a few heartbeats to believe that she'd found what she sought, something incriminating.

I have him. I finally have the murdering bastard!

Now she could blackmail Heyward into admitting her family's innocence. Cat longed to open the letter right there, but the crowd was turning ugly. The stall two away had been set ablaze, and a few of the more desperate ruffians had set upon the owner next door. It was only a matter of time before the bandogs appeared.

Cat tucked the letter into her bodice. Hastily, she threw the damaged book into the trunk. She turned the key, then pocketed it. That should buy her some time. Nimbly evading the hysteria, she strode toward the Great Cemetery. It was difficult to stay calm when what she wanted to do was crow in triumph. In an attempt to distract herself, she mentally mapped out her plan of escape. She would take the Cheap Gate to the market and Gracechurch Street back to the White Hart.

So pleased was Cat of her success that she walked right into the path of her enemy, Griffin, before she noticed him.

The leather-clad rogue raised a gauntleted hand, stopping her in her tracks. He looked down at her with a wide, predatory smile and asked, "Going somewhere, sweetmeat?"

"'Sbones, of all the rotten fortune! Nick, that's John Griffin over there." Savage crumpled his hat into further absurdity with his hands. "We've got to help Cat!"

"We?" Nicholas asked, a bitter taste in his mouth. Some small part of him regretted that his instincts about Cat had been right. Not only was she beautiful, her carefully orchestrated feat proved her cunning and courageous as well. But Savage's pet or not, she had just ruined weeks of careful work. Because of her addlepated stunt, the traitors would know they were being watched. They'd be more cautious now, and time was running short if he meant to catch them before England was lured by their treachery into a land battle with Spain. By Christ, there couldn't be another such fight! A cold, sick fury writhed in Nicholas's belly. If the woman had won the displeasure of some petty rogue, he thought, all the better.

Savage began to pace the aisle. "Have you no idea what that man is capable of?"

"Well, he's not someone I'd want to trust with my sword in a dark alley," Nicholas replied dryly.

"Nick, no love is lost between him and the girl. My God, do you know what he can demand of her? He's Southwark's new leader of thieves, their upright-man!"

"I don't care if that's Satan himself," Nicholas said. "In case you've forgotten, your little friend over there just picked up a letter intended for the Scottish rebels. She's a cursed spy."

"You're wrong." Savage drew his rapier.

At that moment, Cat's cry drew Nicholas's attention. The bristling uprightman had hauled her off her feet by her cloak. Realizing Savage would intervene, Nicholas turned to stop him. But the actor was already halfway across the churchyard. "Curse it all, Savage, get back here!"

Only the defiant twitch of the man's shoulders told Nicholas that he'd heard the order. Sword in hand, the actor swooped down on the struggling pair like a giant carrion bird.

Swearing with enough creativity to draw the attention and nodding approval of the local inhabitants, Nicholas drew his blade and stalked after his one remaining friend.

"Going somewhere?" Cat echoed the uprightman's question with loathing. "Aye, I feel the need for some cleaner haunt. Some of the patrons of St. Paul's are not to my liking." She looked pointedly at him.

Griffin raised an eyebrow, but said nothing. Only

the faint twitch of his pale lips hinted at the anger he restrained. Cat began to regret her rash words. Griffin already hated her for being a favorite of his former enemy, Skinner. Now, as the new acknowledged leader of the Southwark underworld, Griffin had the right to demand her unquestioning loyalty and servitude. It was the unwritten law. They both knew that if she mocked it, she would die.

Griffin stared down at her, knowing full well the power of his physical presence. With his fine blonde, almost white, hair and chiseled features, he could serve as the definition of a golden lad. Cat still found it strange that so handsome a visage could conceal so foul a heart. Perhaps, she thought, the man's depravity was the Devil's price for so perfect a countenance.

"A cleaner haunt?" Griffin queried, breaking the silence. "But surely ye jest. My people tell me you've been here often alate." He reached out with an immaculate hand and forced her chin none too gently upward. "Isn't that so, my pretty little Cat?"

"'Tis where the purses be."

"I'faith, it's long past time for ye to be a simple nip and foist," Griffin said. He traced the line of her jaw with a fingertip. Cat was unable to suppress the shudder that ran through her. "A woman—yea, you've certainly become a woman, my pretty little Cat—can be put to better use than as a petty thief. 'Tis far too long you've remained a dell."

"Nay, I am hardly a vir—"

"*Cut bene whids, mort.* Tell me no more lies," Griffin snapped. His calm demeanor had disappeared in an instant.

Cat froze at the sound of the thieves' cant. He'd switched to the language of their trade. This was not a chance encounter. This was a deliberate meeting intended to make her finally acknowledge his supremacy. If she wanted to live long enough to see Heyward pay for his sins, she'd have to play the game. But, Ruffin, at what cost?

"Yea, I've heard the tales," Griffin continued. "And I am curious to discover if ye truly carry the French Welcome."

"Take your chance and find out, you bloodsucking whoreson," Cat sneered, somehow finding her courage. She'd started the rumor of carrying a venereal disease two years ago in hopes of being left alone. Griffin wouldn't easily play the dupe, but she had to try. She took a step forward, and Griffin took an involuntary step back. Good, Cat thought, you worry about your pretty face, cove. "'Twas one of your own men, Glover, who did it," she improvised. "I'd be more than happy to return the favor."

She saw the flicker of concern in the rogue's eyes and felt the first moment of hope. Although it was not widely known, Glover had died from the French Welcome two months ago. There was no way now to ask the man if he'd usurped Skinner's rights by sleeping with her. It was not uncommon for a man's fist to convince a woman to reconsider her loyalties. And none of Griffin's men were known for their gentleness.

Cat's confidence died when Griffin grabbed her by the front of her cloak and hauled her upward until she danced on tiptoes.

"'Slid! If ye lie to me, wench, there won't be enough of ye left for the rats to feast on!"

"The Devil take you, man! Let her go!"

Cat and Griffin both turned their heads to see

Jasper Savage with sword in hand raging across the churchyard. The crowd hastily cleared a path for the furious, patch-eyed madman.

Jasper, you fool, Cat thought. You have but one eye left, and Griffin will be more than happy to take it!

Gasping for breath, she forced herself to wait until the actor was close enough to hear her. "Jasper, 'tis none of your affair. Let us be," Cat warned. Inwardly she cursed her poor luck. Years ago he'd become her self-appointed protector. There was little hope that Jasper would leave her alone if he thought her to be in danger.

Griffin released Cat and reached to draw his blade. "If it ain't Misrule's prick-me-dainty!"

As if conjured by his name, a black-cloaked demon of a man rent his way through the crowd. Cat's heartbeat drummed a quicker, more reckless pace at the aura of tightly coiled strength and deadly skill emanating from the man. 'Twas the cool, confident approach of a trained killer. Moreover, she realized with a start, he was the same man who had watched her earlier.

The duelist stood out as a foreigner in the London crowd of peasants and prettified courtiers. Dressed in conservative black, he moved with a distinctive grace and a costly, gold-hilted blade hung at his side, at his right side.

"Oh, sweet Jesu!" Cat swore as she realized the identity of the man who moved to Jasper's aid.

Griffin froze in the act of drawing his blade. Cat could tell from his puzzled expression that he hadn't placed the newcomer. But she had. 'Twas Nicholas D'Avenant, Lord Dacre of the North. The queen's Misrule. For someone who had become a legend of the Court, he wasn't seen much in person. Obviously Griffin had never had the misfortune.

Misrule. The nickname was whispered in fearful awe at the back of taverns and over men left for dead in the London streets. In the past when he'd appeared with Jasper, Cat, having heard the tales, had always fled.

"Damn you! Draw your blade, man!" Jasper ordered, seemingly unaware of the shadow lurking on his heels. So tight was the actor's grip on the rapier he held toward Griffin's throat, that the blood had drained from his hand.

Griffin returned his gaze to Jasper and drew his own blade with a snarl.

"Nay, Jasper! 'Twas but a harmless exchange of words. Leave be," Cat said with a measured stare at her friend. Although she'd love nothing better than to see Griffin drown in his own blood, she would not risk Jasper in order to see it done. Arms outstretched, she slipped between the actor's and the uprightman's blades, to the ire of them both. It was a stupid thing to do, but she wouldn't be the cause of another loved one's death. Ever.

Griffin's face contorted with fury. "I shall hide behind no woman's skirts!" He shoved her roughly aside.

Cat tumbled painfully to the ground. Out of the corner of her eye she saw a blur of black, then heard a hiss of steel.

"Rogue, if you lay a hand on either of them again, 'twill be me you fight." The voice was as cold and hard and deadly as the Toledo blade Lord Dacre held ready above her.

Cat rose cautiously to her feet, meeting the assessing gaze of her unlikely protector, the Lord of Misrule. His eyes were a blue so dark and cold as to be gray. She willed herself to step back to a safer distance from his blade—and she hoped from his attention—but her feet did not cooperate. Every muscle of her body tensed. Unable to break free from his stare, Cat was forced to respond to the man who stood before her.

By the standards of the day, he wasn't a handsome man. Rather than the cultivated looks of London's courtiers, he had the savage, unconscious beauty of one of the wild cats that roamed the grounds of the Tower. He'd forgone the short hair traditionally preferred by courtiers in favor of a wild brown mane that passed his shoulders. Lord Dacre had also ignored the requirement of a carefully trimmed beard. Instead, his bare chin jutted in a stark line of determination. From one ear, a golden earring still swung, disturbed by the speed with which he'd moved to protect her.

Like Jasper, Nicholas D'Avenant had an acrobat's body, but his muscles were carved from steel. In faith, everything about the man bespoke a deadly strength. The potential danger looming before her broke the trance and spurred Cat to step from between the two antagonists.

Griffin, too, seemed to assess the new threat. He noted the rapier Lord Dacre held in his left hand, and the sneer faded from his face. He must have realized his challenger's identity. Everyone knew that Misrule, touched by the Devil, preferred to fight with his left hand.

Still, Cat had to credit Griffin with not being a man easily frightened, even by Lord Dacre's reputation as a killer. After all, Griffin had trafficked with killers his entire life. "This be none of yer affair, coves," Griffin snapped. "The girl is mine by rights. Ye should know that, Savage. Wasn't there some whore ye meant to take to wife?"

Nicholas D'Avenant's tall, black-clad figure stiffened. He growled a warning. Cat was unsure whom he meant to caution.

"You heartless whoreson," Jasper rasped.

"Lord Dacre, Jasper, I pray you let this be," Cat said, glancing at each of her self-appointed protectors. "'Tis no concern of yours what passes between myself and this man." The words were bitter on her tongue. She hated, nay loathed, to beg for favors, but by challenging Griffin, Lord Dacre and Jasper ensured she'd be found floating in the Thames by the end of a fortnight. The code of thieves would demand no less.

Lord Dacre's blade rose a fraction of an inch. His lips parted, baring even, white teeth. "Faith," he murmured, "it's certainly my concern if a rogue is troubling a gentlewoman."

Cat didn't like the stress he'd put on the word *my*. The uprightman would have to challenge Lord Dacre's possessiveness if he meant to keep his newly won power. And she'd been so close to convincing him to let her be . . . Curse it all!

"Gentlewoman?" Griffin sneered. "Know ye not what she is? Little more than a petty thief and whore."

"By Christ, I won't hear any more of this!" Jasper cried. "Put up your sword, man!" The actor crouched for an opening lunge. "No one, no one, says aught about Cat without answering to me!"

"Jasper, no!" Cat cried, not willing to risk her friend's life despite the prick to her pride. What did she have to be ashamed of? she asked herself angrily. She had done only what she needed to survive. That's what she was—a survivor. And she would never become the uprightman's whore.

Griffin's face was a stone mask of contempt, but he didn't immediately accept the challenge. Instead, he darted a look at Lord Dacre, one predator wary of another's strength.

"Nay, friend," Lord Dacre said. Keeping his attention focused on Griffin, he rested his right hand on Jasper's shoulder. "A man of so little honor is not worth the fight."

Jasper shrugged away Dacre's hand but lowered his rapier a few inches.

"What would you know about honor, Misrule?" Griffin's words dripped venom.

"'Tis something I've been studying much alate," Dacre replied. "And by my word, rogue," he warned, "if you cause this gentlewoman any more harm, I will teach you how I honor my promises." His eyes turned an even colder shade of steel. "I will take my blade, slit your gut wide, and leave you to watch your own slow death. Do I make myself clear?"

"Oh, that ye do, m'lord," Griffin sneered.

Long moments passed with both men unmoving. The taste of fear was sharp in Cat's mouth. People crossing St. Paul's granted the opponents wide berth. A cart, however, passed dangerously close, its wooden wheels clacking on the cobblestones.

Griffin looked away first, his grasp on his rapier shaking with impotent fury. Stiffly, he turned to her. "Till we meet again, *mort*." He made a mock bow, his look lethal. Then he turned with a billow of his cloak and stalked toward the church where several of his men lounged.

Cat began to tremble with fear now that the immediate danger had passed. "Curse you, Jas! What d'you think you were doing?" The unspoken message Griffin had communicated to her was clear. She would be made to pay for this grave insult to his pride.

Jasper opened his mouth to speak, but for once he had to grope for words. After a moment he sputtered and rallied. "Saving your bloody life, you ungrateful wretch!"

"Looked more to me like you were trying to lose your own. Damn it! I'd almost worked things out so that he'd leave me alone. Then you come flying in like all Hades . . . "

"It didn't look that way to me," the actor grumbled. "I thought—"

"Thought? Thought! You know the rules of the street. If he'd demanded me right here on the cobblestones, I'd have no right to refuse."

The lines around Jasper's mouth hardened. "Aye, but you would."

"Perhaps. But then perhaps I don't hold much value on my skin," Cat snapped. "And you!" She turned to face Lord Dacre. "You might as well hand me my winding sheet for all the good you've done me. He'll kill me now if I don't obey him."

"That scoundrel is the least of your concerns, dearling." Casually, confidently, Lord Dacre extended a strong, long-fingered hand. "I believe you have something for me."

The ground beneath Cat seemed to disappear. She drew her cloak closer, wishing it could afford her protection from more than the cold. "What do you mean?"

"You know exactly what I mean, Catrienne," Lord Dacre said, caressing her name. "Give me the letter."

"L-letter?" she stuttered lamely. "I'm afraid there's been some sort of mistake." But there wasn't. He'd watched her take the note, and they both knew it. Sweet Mary, she couldn't lose the letter. Slowly, she reached for her cuttle.

"Don't," Lord Dacre snapped.

Cat's hand froze inside her cloak. Her heart skipped several beats.

Nicholas D'Avenant noted her dilemma with a raised brow. Then he laughed.

A shudder ran down Cat's back at the dry, humorless sound.

"Now are you going to give me the letter or"—a wry smile twisted at the corner of his mouth—"would you rather have me take it from you?"

Cat followed his gaze to her chest. The small scrap of parchment tucked in her bodice seemed ready to burn its way through the cloth. Suddenly, she was furious. First Misrule had brought Griffin's wrath down on her. Now he meant to humiliate her and destroy twelve years of work.

"I'm going to leave now, Dacre," she managed through chattering teeth. "And you're not going to stop me." She gave Jasper a pointed look which he accepted meekly. "Nor you." Squaring her shoulders, Cat turned on her heel and made to go.

Lord Dacre moved behind her with the speed of a viper. As his enormous hand clamped down on her forearm, she gasped in surprise. "The hell I won't stop you."

His grip was like a manacle. Cat fought not to wince. "Let me go right this second, or I'll scream for help at the top of my lungs."

His grip tightened. "Do that," he whispered, "and I'll tell them you're a thief."

Cat suspected he'd hand her over to the bailiffs without so much as a blink. "And I'll tell them you mean to have my virtue."

His features hardened to slate. "You wouldn't dare."

"Try me," she ground out. "Who do you think they'll believe, hmm?" She looked pointedly at her demure garb. "A modest young Protestant?" A slow, mocking smile spread over her face. "Or Misrule, debaucher of women?"

With a curse, Nicholas D'Avenant thrust her away.

Cat rubbed her arm and turned warily to face him.

His body was tight as a coil of steel, the lines of his face sharp with fury. "All right, you're free to go. But have a care, dearling. You've chosen to play a game with very high stakes." His voice was cold and lashing. "I'll just take it from you in a more convenient location."

"Don't be so sure," she answered recklessly.

"Very well, Savage and I will take our leave."

Lord Dacre smiled down at her, Mephistopheles considering a new soul to torment. He drew her hand from within her cloak before Cat realized what he intended. Enveloping her hand in his, he half-knelt, stiff-legged yet graceful in a peculiar way. His whispered kiss on the top of her hand evoked a tingle in the pit of her stomach. "I'll see you soon, mistress."

Turning away, he cut a path through the crowd with the mere threat of his presence.

Jasper fixed her with a long, puzzled look, held his hands palms upward in apology, opened his mouth as if to say something, closed it abruptly, then trotted after his friend.

Cat could make no sense of the turbulent flood of emotions inside her. She scrubbed at the kissed spot on her hand, trying to erase the memory of his touch, the brush of his velvet lips. With a shudder, she tore free of the sudden lassitude that had enveloped her. She was still close enough that the bookseller might spot her so she hurried through the crowd.

She didn't slow her pace until she reached the Bridge. There the traffic and her aching lungs forced her to walk. Gasping for breath, she brought her hand up to her bodice to reassure herself that the letter was still there. It was. The impulse to read it immediately was overwhelming. But she dare not take the chance until she was alone and safe. Still, she'd done it!

Cat indulged herself in a moment's euphoria before she considered her current dilemma. Aye, she'd accomplished her task, but she'd insulted Griffin in the process. Thanks to the cursed Lord Dacre, she thought sourly. Moreover, the duelist had meant to take what she'd rightfully stolen. The rogue.

'Twas a shame, she thought as she wound her way through the Bridge traffic, that Griffin had rejected the opportunity to fight Dacre. She wouldn't begrudge Dacre the uprightman's death. It would alleviate at least one of her problems. Yet, when it came to swordplay, Misrule seemed destined to forever frustrate her dreams rather than fulfill them.

Only once had Nicholas D'Avenant been bested in a duel. To Cat's deep regret, the man who held that honor was Laurence Heyward. 'Twas how Lord Dacre had earned his nickname. Cat's mortal enemy had made a fool of him during the Christmas season of 1586.

Somehow, since Cat had found Skinner close to death in a muddy alley four months ago, the White Hart alehouse seemed even smaller and more run-down than ever. None of the White Hart thieves, all too busy barely scraping by since Griffin had claimed the position of uprightman, had gotten around to correcting the multitude of minor disrepairs that now tumbled the place into ruin. The building's thatched roof was bald in several spots. Its timber showed the beginnings of dry rot, the drinking bench had long ago gone to kindling, and a fresh coat of paint would scarcely improve the pitted placard out front.

Hands in her pockets, shoulders hunched forward, Cat opened the front door and stepped into the firelit dimness of the alehouse's drinking room. Only two of the White Hart's most steadfast thieves, Egan and Declan, sat at one of the rough-hewn tables nursing blackjacks of beer.

Joan Cashel, better known as Jug, poked her head past the rickety swinging door that led to the kitchen. Her weathered face, usually aglow with maternal pride, was crinkled into a frown. Slinging her greasy dishcloth over her shoulder, the woman bustled toward Cat, looking anything but pleased.

"My customers 'aven't been saying good things 'bout ye, lass," Jug complained.

Bristling, Cat straightened slightly. The last thing she wanted was another confrontation after just having tangled with both Griffin and Lord Dacre. "Where's Rafe?" she asked, hoping it would serve as a diversion.

"In the kitchen eatin' all my mutton," Jug grumbled. She bustled closer to Cat and squinted up at her, somehow looking imperious despite the three handsbreadths' difference in their heights. "Now s'pose you tell me 'bout the trouble with Griffin."

"Ah, Jug, when have I ever been a source of trouble for you?" With a rueful smile, Cat wiped away a smudge of wheat meal from the woman's cheek, ignoring her growl of protest.

Without Jug, she would have died on the London streets before her tenth year. After the murder of her family, loyal Lyly servants had secured a job for Cat with the tippler of the new White Hart alehouse. The man had meant for the business to cater to weary travelers who made their way to the City from Dover and Croydon, but few had been willing to stop in dubious Southwark when there were safer establishments just beyond the Bridge. The alehouse went out of business in less than a year, and the owner, believing Cat to be a commoner, left her behind when he returned to his native Oxford. Cat thanked fortune when Jug and Skinner, her mate, and their eccentric band of thieves had adopted her along with the abandoned building. With a new, more earthy clientele—who appreciated the discreetly placed back door and the convenience of paying their bills with stolen wares—the White Hart prospered.

Cat had practiced looting purses tagged with razors and bells at the feet of London's finest pickpockets. Wanting someone who could blend in with the upper classes, the White Hart thieves had Egan, a former student from Oxford who had the enormous bad sense to be openly Catholic, continue her education in reading and manners. They'd given her shelter, street sense, and a trade. It was more than she could ever repay.

"You've been trouble, dear Cat, more times than any of us would like to remember," quipped Egan from the one well-lit corner of the common room. His blonde head was bowed low over the passport he was painstakingly forging.

"Not that we haven't encouraged her, mind you," added Declan. Leaning backward on a joined stool, the gray-haired picklock probed disinterestedly under his fingernails with the edge of his knife. He must have jarred the table, for Egan shot him a baleful glare before returning to his work.

"Out with it, lass. Is Griffin comin' after you?" Jug asked, as single-minded as a terrier after a rat.

"Aye, I'm afraid so," Cat answered with a sigh. She summarized her encounter with the uprightman. "Chances are, he'll make me fret and wait for a few days," she concluded. "Just the same, I'd feel better if you spent the night at Declan's."

"You're more than welcome to share my humble quarters, Jug." Declan winked at the aging proprietress. "Mayhap then you'll stop nagging me to pay my bill."

"Jackanape!" Jug tossed her dishcloth at the man, then returned her attention to Cat. "Nay, girl, I 'aven't taken care of you this long to turn you over to that rogue now. You ain't some *wapping-mort*, some whore Griffin can just help himself to. You come from good blood!"

"Aye, well, I doubt if my good blood would have anything to do with me now." Pausing, she took the woman's rough hands in hers. "I don't want you here when he comes for me, Jug," she pleaded. "He'll just use you to force me to cooperate. You know that."

Jug stared at Cat. Her square jaw raised stubbornly. "I'll not be leavin' you alone."

"Love, I'll keep an eye on your Cat and the place tonight," Declan offered. "Chances are she's right about Griffin making us all sweat awhile first. And if it does come down to it, I think I can remember how to use this rusty ol' piece of metal," he added, using his short sword to stoke the pitiful fire that burned in the hearth. "Go stay at my place and keep it warm for me."

"Please, Jug," Cat begged. "Go. If I were to put you in danger, I'd never forgive myself."

Jug's eyes bordered with tears. She pulled her hands from Cat's to twist the edge of her stained apron agitatedly. "I know not what else I can do!" She reached for Cat and pulled her into her immense, trembling bosom.

"Have faith, dear one," Cat whispered. "I'll be ready for him when he comes. This will all be past us in a day or two." She pulled back from Jug's hold as soon as she could.

"Cat, you ain't capable of killin' a man. You—"

"I am if he tries to rape me," Cat snapped.

Her sudden anger shocked them both. Still, the unspoken question hung in the air. Could she really kill someone if she had to? Rough as her life had been in Southwark, she'd never been forced to make that discovery. Until, possibly, now.

"Don't worry so, Jug. I may still be able to talk my way out of it. If not, I'll try to buy him off."

Lowering her gaze, Jug continued to fret with her apron. "Take care of yourself, girl."

"You too, Jug," Cat said, her throat uncomfortably tight. Disliking her weakness, Cat blinked back her tears and forced herself to smile. If she were to survive, she couldn't afford to be soft. "Now," she added gruffly, "I'd better check on my partner, eh?"

Jug didn't meet her eyes when Cat brushed by her and headed for the kitchen door. Cat was grateful the woman chose not to make their parting any more awkward, since she'd never had a chance to learn how to say good-bye—people had always left her life too abruptly for farewells. She could only pray she would see Jug again.

Declan's words, however, slipped through the kitchen door before it wobbled closed at Cat's back. "You knew you were going to lose her sometime, darling Jug."

*   *   *

As Cat entered the kitchen, the smell of the warm mash from which Jug made her beer assailed her nose. Slouched on the rush-strewn floor, Rafe gnawed at a joint of mutton clutched in both hands. The fabric of the boy's wool stocking was ripped over his right knee, and Cat could see the raw skin beneath.

"Jesu, Rafe, what happened to you?"

Rafe scrubbed at the drippings of fat on his face with the back of his hand.

Cat crouched beside the boy and pushed the over-long, tawny hair out of his eyes. "Rafe? Answer me."

"The cony got a better 'old on the back of me than I meant 'im to," he muttered, still not looking up.

Cat could sense the boy's embarrassment. She knew all too well a thief's cunning and skills were often his only source of pride. "Yes, well, I bet you made a decent day's catch off that cony's extra coin."

Although he still didn't meet her gaze, Rafe suddenly looked more than a little smug.

The faint smile tracing his lips tugged at Cat's heart. If only he had reason to smile more often . . .

"How about if you come up to my room?" Cat suggested. She stood up and offered the boy her hand. "We'll get that wound cleaned up, and I'll pay you for your work."

He regarded her suspiciously. "Are you gonna put that stuff on me that 'urts?"

"I can't afford to let my partner lose a leg can I?" Cat asked, careful to keep a straight face.

Rafe seemed to mull over her answer for a long moment. "Guess not."

Since his mother, a whore, had died two years ago from the pox, Rafe had been forced to survive on the streets. 'Twas no life for a child. She cared far too much for the boy's welfare, Cat told herself sternly. Caring only led to a broken heart. But he reminded her so much of someone who had been special to her in another time, another place . . . Ruffin, in another life.

Keeping Rafe's greasy hand trapped in hers, Cat searched through the pantry until she found a clean bit of cloth and Jug's precious bottle of aqua vitae. The strong spirits were laced with egg yolk and rose oil. It was the recipe a local barber-surgeon had given her to clean the poisons out of wounds, which were all too common at the alehouse.

"'Sfoot," Rafe muttered. He hunched into himself. "Well, you ain't givin' me a bath."

"No bath."

"Cut bene whids?"

"I'm telling the truth, copesmate." She smiled and led him back through the door into the common room. Jug had already left. Declan and Egan were now busy with a game of maw, the forger's project drying on the corner of the table. Ascending the narrow stairway, Cat looked back over her shoulder. "Make sure to give me some warning, Dek, if Griffin shows. And if so, no heroics."

The picklock looked up from his cards and smiled. "Cat, m'dear, I'm incapable of such things."

Knowing he half spoke the truth, Cat smiled wanly, then coaxed Rafe the rest of the way up the flight of stairs and into her chamber.

The room was so small it barely contained the wooden frame and straw pallet that served as her bed, and the timbers that supported the ceiling hung low overhead. A battered trunk, a stool, and a tattered painted canvas she had nicked provided the only ornamentation.

Cat hurried to her meager pile of kindling and started a fire in the open hearth. Then she made Rafe sit down on the pallet so she could tend to his knee. For all his prior complaining, she couldn't tell from Rafe's solemn countenance if he felt any pain from her ministrations. After she'd soaked the wound in alcohol and satisfied herself it wouldn't turn bad, she recorked the bottle and set it down in the rushes where she kneeled.

"Welladay," Cat murmured, drying her hands with her skirts, "I suppose we ought to render our accounts."

Going to where the chest sat in the far corner, she pulled it away from the wall, revealing the small hole she used for her hiding nook. Rafe and Jug were the only people who knew where she kept her few treasures. Carefully, Cat stuck her hand into the hole, disarmed the trap she'd set, and took out the precious wooden box that had once belonged to her father.

Bringing it over to the pallet, she opened it and withdrew the amount of coin she'd offered Rafe for his help.

Rafe took the coins from her and counted them. He tested each one with his teeth. As he finished the task, his brows puckered with displeasure. "There's one more shilling than there oughta be."

"'Tis for helping me successfully get what I'd hoped for. Faith, I couldn't have done it without you."

He cocked his head. "You got what you needed to hurt the alderman?"

"I hope so," she replied fervently. Again curiosity of what the letter contained rose to the forefront of her thoughts.

Rafe startled Cat with his next question. "Will you be going away?"

Sweet Mary, why did the boy have to be so keen-witted? Cat gnawed her lip and wondered how to answer him. She didn't want to hurt their friendship with a lie, but she also didn't want to add to Rafe's worries. He already had far too many things in his short life to fear. "Well," she began, choosing her words carefully, "Griffin's none too happy with me right now. I think it all depends on whether or not I'm able to make amends."

"He's no friend of mine," Rafe muttered. "He'll be answerin' to me if he's causin' you 'arm."

"Rafe . . ." Cat waited until he peered at her through the cover of his bangs. "I want you to do your best to stay off the streets for at least a se'nnight."

Rafe looked back down at the coverlet that covered Cat's pallet.

"Will you do that for me, Rafe?" Cat demanded. *"Cut bene whids?"* She chucked him awkwardly under the chin.

"Aye," Rafe answered finally, his voice naught but a whisper.

"Good." Cat sighed in relief. That was one less thing she had to worry about. "Now, why don't you get out of here before any of your more disreputable cohorts come looking for you?"

Rafe made as if to go, but turned back and wrapped his arms around her waist in a fierce hug. She felt him deftly slide the extra shilling into her pocket but decided not to make an issue of it. Then, without another word, he fled the room.

Cat wanted to cry out for him to come back but didn't. She'd be doing him no favor by taking him under her wing. Griffin would ensure all of her friends suffered dearly under his reign.

Cat couldn't help but feel wherever she went misfortune followed in her wake. *Mayhap we are not so different you and I, Misrule*, she mused, thinking of the mantle of tragedy and scandal that gossip had hung around her strange protector's shoulders.

She hovered at the door for a long moment and stared at the empty staircase, hoping Rafe would come back on the instinct that she needed someone, anyone, to stay with her for a few minutes while she shook off the terrors of the day.

He didn't.

By now, she should be used to the bitter sting of loneliness, but she wasn't. Cat shut the door and turned the rusted key in the lock. Flopping down on the pallet, she withdrew the stolen letter from her bodice. With unsteady hands she broke the sealing wax and unfolded the ragged-edged parchment. In an elegant hand, it read:

> *Lord Huntly,*
> *As arranged per our mutual servant, the supplies and arms will be in Larkryn the first day of the new month. Your men must honor the signal we discussed, or the boat shall not approach. Moreover, the craft must be back at sea afore dawn. Now it's up to you to fulfill your end of the promise. Dare not disappoint me.*
>
> *Yrs.*

Cat read the words twice more to make certain she understood their intent. She could have cried for the pure joy of it. Heyward was smuggling goods to the rebel earls in Scotland who sought to claim King James's throne! Everyone knew they were desperate for arms and supplies now that they'd been in open revolt for almost a year. Cat puzzled for a moment. Had her enemy returned to his Catholic upbringing? Nay, far more likely he couldn't resist an easy profit. Whatever his motives, she'd caught him smack in the middle of treason.

She clutched the letter to her chest. The straw mattress rustled beneath her as she kicked her feet in delight. Until this moment, some small part of her had doubted she'd be able to catch her enemy in the midst of something foul. But, Sweet Mary, she'd done it. She'd found something more incriminating than she'd dared to dream!

Cat studied the letter again. There was no signature at the bottom, but that was no surprise. She'd heard that conspirators would often tear a large piece of parchment into smaller scraps and use those for their subversive communications. The pattern of the tears along each scrap served as the proof of the letter's authenticity. Even without the other pieces, Cat suspected she could easily establish Heyward to be the author. The handwriting would surely match what was known to be his, and the note had been taken from one of his servants. With a faint smile, she traced the scrawl of letters with her fingertip, taking pleasure in every letter that sealed his fate.

She would use this letter to blackmail Heyward into clearing her family's name. He should be more than willing to confess the wrongs committed against her family—provided he could attribute them to the local constable who had also been present that fateful night and had died two years ago. Certainly he'd do that small thing in the hopes of protecting his name.

Once that was done, she would ensure Heyward paid in full for the torment he had caused her family. She'd turn the letter over to the queen. What more fitting way was there for the whoreson to die than a traitor's death? God's blood, she would relish every second of his torture.

Cat tucked the letter inside the box along with her other treasures. She paused briefly to touch the ivory comb that had been her mother's. Once it had been a talisman that brought her comfort. But she was no longer a child, and the trinket wouldn't protect her from an uprightman's displeasure. Instead, she counted on her cuttle. Trying to shrug off the dark mood that had overtaken her, Cat put the box back in the hole, reset the trap, and pushed the heavy chest back in place.

She walked over to the window. The fairly bright light filtering through the grease-paper told her it was still a few hours before sunset. She'd better rest. If Griffin came tonight, she'd need every ounce of cunning and strength she possessed.

Unfastening her cloak, she lay down on the pallet. She checked the position of her cuttle in the pocket of her skirt, then drew the cloak over herself for warmth.

A confusing jumble of images from the afternoon drifted through Cat's mind. The bookseller overrun by the greedy crowd, Griffin grabbing her, Jasper's fury, Lord Dacre's kiss.

Oddly, as she lingered on the last image—recalling the brush of his lips, the warmth of his callused hand, the spark of pleasure in his haunting, gray eyes, the odd tremor his kiss had started in her limbs—her body slowly surrendered to the fatigue it had struggled against for the past two sleepless nights.

Cat knew she must have slept for longer than she'd intended. For when she awoke to the sound of the key to her door clattering to the floor, the only light came from the few flames still flickering in the hearth. With a start, she realized someone outside was trying to pick the lock to her room.

3

Losing control of his temper, Laurence Heyward slammed his fist down on the costly marble table he'd just had imported from Italy to grace his study. *"What do you mean the letter's been stolen?"* The outburst rent the air between him and the ruddy-faced bookseller, Burfet.

The man blanched and shifted uneasily from one foot to the other. "Er, exactly that, Sir Laurence."

Inside Laurence seethed a quickly growing mixture of rage and fear. God's mercy, the letter to the rebel earls had been stolen! Not only could it be the end of his carefully laid plans for advancement, if the letter fell into the wrong hands, *it could mean his life.* He did not relish the thought of a traitor's death. First they hung you—carefully though, so you would not break your neck. Rather, they wanted you to be slowly suffocating when they took a knife to your . . .

No! He closed his mind to that thought. If he meant to avert disaster, he'd need to stay cool-headed. He'd need to gather all the facts. "Pray tell me," he said through gritted teeth, "how you managed this amazing feat?"

The merchant crumpled his velvet hat in his hands. "Well, sir, there was this boy—"

"A boy?" Laurence snarled, before he could stop himself.

The man nodded his head vigorously, causing the wattle along his neck to jiggle. "Aye, there was this boy, and he grabbed my purse. It had all the coin I'd just been paid, you see . . ." Gesturing with his hands in appellation, he trailed off helplessly.

Laurence forced himself to inhale deeply before speaking. "Do go on."

"Well, I went after him o'course." The merchant spared him a brief, uneasy glance before continuing. "I left the book on the counter. 'Twas only a second— really—but by the time I came back the damage had been done," he concluded miserably.

Although he felt the overwhelming urge to strangle the man who had failed him so miserably, Laurence kept his sweaty palms flat on the cool slab of marble before him. "By damage, you mean the . . . my corre- spondence . . . was gone."

The wattle of fat renewed its jiggling. "Aye, the binding had been sliced right through."

Whoever the thief had been, Laurence thought, he'd had a well thought-out plan. And he'd known where to look . . . A sudden suspicion flared in his mind. Like an alchemist analyzing a foreign object, Laurence mentally turned the sudden thought one way, then another, in cold-blooded examination. Could the bookseller have betrayed him? "Who have you been talking to, Burfet?" He murmured the question conversationally, hoping to catch the man off guard.

He did, but the reaction he won wasn't that of a guilty man. Instead the bookseller's eyes rounded, and he gasped in horror. "I've said naught to anyone, sir! Not even to my wife—and that is no small feat."

So the thief had not had the merchant's assistance. That was something . . . "Well then," Laurence continued irritably, "who was near your shop at the time?"

Burfet scrubbed his double chin. "There were two men, but they both left just 'fore the boy snatched my purse—"

They could have easily come back, Laurence mused.

"—and, of course, there was this woman . . . "

That snared Laurence's interest. "A woman? Describe her."

"Well, uh, small and dark. I guess you could say she was pretty—if you didn't put too much mind to the horrible gray thing she wore."

Laurence's eyes narrowed. He didn't like what he was hearing. "Conservative garb?" Just what he needed . . . the letter in the hands of a rabid Protestant.

"Aye, that."

Could she be working for Lord Burghley, the queen's new master of spies? The statesman wasn't overly fond of employing women, but he might do it if he thought it'd be to the country's advantage. God, he prayed his suspicions were wrong! No love was lost between him and the statesman.

What was he to do? Should he tell the other conspirators what had happened? Nay, if the missive was already in enemy hands, there'd be little they could do. And if it wasn't, he'd be a fool to tell them of his mistake. That would destroy all the favor he'd worked so hard to garner. Better to try to catch the culprit himself and hope the rebel earls could intercept the shipment anyway.

The bookseller's restless stirring jarred Laurence from his thoughts. "Er, sir, I'd just like to say again how sorry I am about all this trouble. You know how much I value your . . . patronage."

Laurence plastered on what he thought was his most sincere and encouraging smile. "Nay, Burfet," he soothed. "Don't trouble yourself with it."

"I'm glad to hear that, sir. Is it all right if I'm on my way then?"

Already deep in thought, Laurence granted permission with an absent brush of his hand. By the time the door to the study clicked shut, he'd already made up his mind. Burfet would have to be dispatched sooner than planned. 'Twas inconvenient if there were to be any further communications with the rebels but also very necessary. And he'd long ago learned the value of doing whatever was necessary.

Cat's first thought at seeing the door handle move was that Lord Dacre had followed through with his threat to come for the letter and somehow, with his shadowy grace, had slipped past Declan. Even though she knew she'd have to fight him to keep what she'd stolen, the hair rose at the nape of her neck and she shivered with a strange eagerness. But when the lock finally clicked and the door opened, it wasn't Nicholas D'Avenant's face that appeared but Griffin's.

"It's been far too long a wait to have you, sweet-meat," the uprightman purred. He scooped the key off the floor and locked the door behind him.

Cat sat bolt upright on the pallet. "What did you do to Declan?" she asked hoarsely.

"Merely had some fun," Griffin said. "Oh, don't look so sad. My dagger caught him in the back as he bolted for the door. Disloyal, that." His smile gleamed white as newly exposed bone in the darkened room.

Cat's thoughts stumbled over one another. Declan had run and now he was dead? No. It couldn't be. But slowly, the horrible truth began to sink in.

As Griffin stepped toward the pallet, his shadow writhed and capered along the wall. Flames from the hearth reflected off his white hair. Every instinct screamed for Cat to pull her cuttle free of her skirts. But at the thought of bloodshed, her stomach lurched. Sweet Mary, she was already partially to blame for one man's death tonight.

When his thigh brushed the edge of the pallet, Cat scuttled to the other side of the small frame.

"My, such a show of reluctance. I begin to wonder if you don't welcome my touch." The uprightman caressed the faded coverlet with the back of his gloved hand. "'Tis enough to give a man less than myself pause to consider."

"Nay, it isn't that, milord," she choked past the tight knot of terror in her throat. "But if I dared to share the pleasure of your touch, you would be victim to my dread disease."

Griffin nodded and, lowering his head as if considering their predicament, he paced to the foot of the pallet. Without warning, he backhanded her, sending her flying into the crude headboard.

"Snigger swears Glover never touched you," he snarled.

Cat held a hand to her aching jaw. "And you believe him?"

"Aye," he snapped. "I do."

Cat cursed silently over her failed ruse and glanced desperately at the window.

Griffin sidled around the far edge of the bed and caught her arm in a tight grasp. Slowly, he eased her other hand away from her face and traced the tender flesh of her jaw where he'd just struck her.

"You know, sweetmeat"—with an iron grip, he dragged her across the tangled covers toward him—"you're a great subject of talk on the streets, what with your fancy talk, haughty manners, an' all. Some might even say you think yourself better than the rest of us. But that isn't so, now, is it? Just because John Skinner chose you, out of all the rabble, to be his precious little poppet doesn't give you right to treat the rest of us like nothin'. Does it?"

The venom in his tone stunned her. Did Griffin hate her so much for the attention she'd received from Skinner? They had been children at the time. She suspected it had only been for childless Jug's sake that the uprightman had taken her into his protection. And even if she hadn't attracted Skinner's favor, Griffin would not have been the one to take her place. Even as a boy, Griffin's cruelty toward those more helpless had been plainly evident. For all his faults, cruelty without purpose was one of the few things old Skinner couldn't stomach.

"No, Griffin, Skinner's favor didn't entitle me to consider anyone less than myself. Nor did I ever try to

treat them as such." She tried to wrench her left arm
free from his implacable grasp. Jesu, how was she
going to reach her cuttle?

Griffin shook his head disparagingly and laughed.
"Oh, but you did, Cat. You certainly did. You
thought you were so much better than the rest of us.
You thought you were safe. But are you safe now?"
He dragged her off the pallet and crushed her to his
chest, pinning her arms between them.

He savaged her mouth with his in a long, sickening
kiss that tasted of liquor and rancid meat. Cat pushed
against him with her hands, the gorge rising in her
throat. She tried to cry for help, but his mouth over
hers choked the sound. After long, unhinging
moments, he permitted her to draw back a few scant
inches.

He coldly scanned her face. Her revulsion and horror must have been plain to see because he threw
back his head and laughed.

"You . . . you can't do this!" she protested. "Jasper
will come after you!"

Griffin's features lost some of their beauty. "And
he'll die."

She planted a kick to his shin. He cursed in pain
and loosened his grip. She pulled herself free but
didn't get far. Griffin had her trapped in the corner of
the room and she pressed herself into the wall.
"Misrule will kill you. You heard him!"

"'Sdeath, do you really think Misrule gives a damn
what happens to a trugging whore like yerself?" he
sneered. "'Twas a promise lightly made. Nothing
more."

Slowly, Cat edged her left hand into the folds of
her skirt. Cutting her fingertips on the edge of her

cuttle, she stifled a gasp, then closed her hand around the handle of the small blade.

The uprightman took a step toward her.

Cat lost her nerve. "I have something that may be of use to you, Griffin," she offered recklessly.

"Aye, you certainly do have something of use, sweetmeat," he purred, mocking her.

"I-I have something on the alderman of Southwark, something you could use to your advantage . . ." If she could provide Griffin with some influence over the man who legally governed their territory, there was a small chance he might let her be.

Griffin placed his arms on either side of her against the wall. The heat of his sour breath burned against her throat. "Heyward?" he asked. "What could you possibly have on Heyward that would be of use to me?"

This time Cat sensed something more than simple amusement in his tone. Griffin was always searching for new power. She could trade the letter for her escape! But could she give up her plans of seeing her family avenged?

"I c-cannot tell you right now," she stuttered. "I have need of the information first, but I give you my word—"

"Do you know what I think, sweetmeat? I think you're just making up things in your pretty little head to stall for time."

"But I have a letter," she protested. "I—"

Griffin silenced her by placing a hand over the lower half of her face. "There've been far too many games between us, *mort*. Do you know what I'm going to do about that? Do you?"

Cat shook her head as much as she was able,

pressed further back against the wall, and stared wildly into his pale eyes, not wanting to hear his answer.

"I am going to have my rights with you, sweetmeat. Then," he continued, "I'm going to carve you a new smile right here." He traced a line just above her collarbone with his finger. "And I'm going to leave you in the alley for your friends—provided you have any left—to find in the morning."

His hand tightened around her mouth, muffling her cry and blocking off her air. Just when the room seemed about to disappear entirely into darkness, he let her breathe again.

"Dying scares you, doesn't it?" he coaxed. "That's good. Because I want you very, very frightened when I take you, Cat. I want to hear you beg to live."

Desperate, unthinking, Cat pulled the cuttle free of her skirts and slashed it across the uprightman's face, leaving a crimson streak of blood across his brow.

She'd hoped to hurt him badly enough to buy time to escape, but the uprightman reacted instinctively. With a roar of rage, he tried to wrench the small blade from her grasp, twisting her left hand into an impossible angle. She felt something snap, then a white-hot jolt of pain. Her grip loosened and the blade went clattering to the ground.

"No bit o' flesh is worth this much grief!" The uprightman used the edge of his boot to send it skittering out of reach. "Ye'r baggage, darlin'."

Cat scrambled headlong across the bed, unable to cry out so great was her fear. Just as her feet touched the rush-strewn floor on the other side, however, he grabbed a massive handful of her hair. Mercilessly, he dragged her back onto the bed. Suddenly, Cat remembered how to scream. The sound was pure animal terror.

But it was cut off abruptly when her captor crushed her windpipe with both hands. Cat pounded her right fist ineffectually against his chest. Warm drops of blood fell on her, its musky, metallic scent robbing what little sanity she had left.

"Catrienne?" someone shouted from behind the door.

She would have loved to cry out, but her throat felt as if it would collapse at any moment. The very life was draining from her. She groped along the edge of the pallet for something, anything, she could use as a weapon.

Her hand connected with the aqua vitae she'd used to clean Rafe's wound that afternoon. With every bit of her strength remaining, she brought the bottle crashing across Griffin's head. He howled at the impact and tumbled to the floor.

Cat rolled off the bed, stumbled to the door, and wrenched the handle furiously. It was locked. Sweet Jesu, she'd forgotten that he'd locked it!

"What the hell is going on in there?" a voice from outside roared.

She pounded the door in terror. "Help me! Please help me!"

"Get away from the door. I'm going to break it down!"

Before she could step back, Griffin lifted her off her feet. The overwhelming stench of aqua vitae engulfed her. Cat clawed at him and twisted back and forth.

Arching backward in his grasp, Cat brought all of her weight down on the arch of his right foot. 'Twas a trick Skinner had taught her years ago to deal with unruly patrons. She was rewarded by the satisfying sound of another howl from Griffin.

A moment later, she was unceremoniously dropped to the floor. She tried to rise to her feet, but her legs didn't want to hold her. Someone was hurling himself against the door. The pounding of body against wood, the creak of the leather hinges, echoed the frantic beat of her heart.

"You bitch!" Griffin crawled toward her. "No one hurts John Griffin like this. No one!"

She could barely hear his words, so loud was the sound of her own heartbeat in her ears. Half-leaning against the wooden frame that supported the pallet, Cat grabbed the small stool. Her hands shook so badly she could barely hold it.

When Griffin lunged for her, she brought the stool crashing across his head. He pitched backward, his right arm flailing into the open hearth.

A trail of flame shot up Griffin's sleeve and collar, feeding on the aqua vitae. He screamed. Within seconds his head and shoulders were engulfed in flame.

Just then, the door crashed inward, and Lord Dacre barreled into the room. In the middle of reaching for his sword, he froze to stare in astonishment at the scene before him.

Griffin howled and tottered to his feet. He batted at his face with his hands, and they too began to burn. He stumbled into the corner.

Cat looked wildly at Dacre. "Do something! Help him!"

A trail of flame licked its way up the wall toward the bone-dry timbers supporting the ceiling. By the time Lord Dacre had his cloak off, the crackling fire had spread to half of the tiny room, shocking Cat into motion. The letter. She had to get the letter!

The blaze that was Griffin no longer seemed human in its struggles, but it stood between her and her hiding hole. She grabbed one of the remaining legs of the stool hoping to use it to prod the upright-man out of her path.

"What the hell are you doing?" Dacre roared.

"My belongings," she choked. "I have to get my belongings!"

Griffin lunged for her. In a blur of black, Lord Dacre intercepted him. They both slammed to the floor in a tangle of limbs and cloak. Smoke, heavy with the sickening smell of burnt hair and flesh, curled toward the ceiling.

The wall where the chest stood was almost a solid sheet of flame, but, unthinking, Cat crawled toward it. One of the large beams in the ceiling near the door-way gave way and crashed to the floor, raining plaster and debris. Ignoring the flames lapping the chest, Cat reached for the handle.

Her hand never made it. Dacre wrapped an arm about her waist and hauled her backward toward the window.

"No! Let me go! What are you doing?" Cat cried, fighting him just as hard as she had Griffin.

"Saving your wretched—"

The rest of his answer was drowned out when another beam came crashing to the floor, pinning Griffin, only feet from them, beneath it.

The corner where her chest stood was an inferno, and the air scorched her lungs with every breath. But Cat knew if Dacre would just give her a chance, she could still find a way to reach the letter. Somehow.

But he pulled her inexorably toward the window.

"No. Please don't do this!" she begged. "Let me go!"

Bunching his powerful legs, he hurled them both into the window. The thin strips of wood and grease-paper gave way with a rip and a crack.

Then they were falling.

Nicholas's chest ached and the side on which he landed felt as if it'd been bludgeoned with an enormous club. Across the street from where he and Catrienne sat slumped, the fire roared on, engulfing the second story of the White Hart despite the best efforts of the Southwark residents armed with leather buckets of water.

The minute he'd entered the tippling den he'd known there was trouble. Some poor soul lay dead and two disreputable-looking ruffians were stealing the hard spirits. He'd had to kill the first man. The second took the hint and ran. Nicholas pounded up the steps, his concern for the lady spy growing by leaps and bounds. His fear had proven well-founded when he'd discovered her door locked and a struggle obviously ensuing in the room beyond. At that moment, he'd gone temporarily mad. The primal instinct to protect Catrienne—as he'd pledged on his honor that afternoon—had obliterated all thought of his original reason for being there. That is, until now.

"The letter's up there, isn't it?" he asked, his voice gruff from the smoke.

The miserable look Catrienne shot him from where she huddled on the boarding house landing confirmed his worse fears. "Aye, thanks to you." A single tear ran down her smoky cheek. She angrily brushed it away just as Nicholas's hand involuntarily reached out to do it for her.

He grimaced. The woman was probably working for Spain or the Holy Roman Emperor, and all he could think about was that she was hurting and that he wanted to comfort her. If he had one whit of sense, he'd already be home nursing his wounds and questioning her in an attempt to salvage what little he could. But the entire day had been a rotten farce, and it didn't look as if it were about to get any better. Catrienne seemed intent to sit and watch until her former home was entirely engulfed in flames, so he was stuck there, too. Somehow he felt he owed her at least that much before hauling her away.

She glared at him with burning, reproachful eyes. "If you wanted the letter so badly, why didn't you let me get it?"

"Because it wasn't worth your life."

"You think not?"

It took just one look at her face, so ravaged by the pain of failure, for him to know that something more than he'd originally suspected was going on here, something intensely personal. It was one thing to care deeply for a cause, something entirely else to hold it more dear than one's life.

Only fools became martyrs. Yet, Nicholas wondered, who was the greater fool this night? She'd at least tried to salvage the letter. He'd been too busy with heroics. Disconcerted, he looked away.

Behind them, Savage paced worriedly. The actor had insisted on coming with him. Only threats of death by impalement on Nicholas's sword had kept Savage outside. But apparently his self-restraint was exhausted, because he scowled and snapped. "Forget the cursed letter!" He crouched beside Catrienne. "Are you all right?"

When she didn't look up, he reached toward her shoulder.

She sent him rocking back on his heels with a shove. "Don't touch me! Just don't touch me!"

Her trembling increased as she hugged her legs closer to her chest and buried her head against her knees in defeat. Slowly, so as not to alarm her further, Nicholas moved closer to her, ignoring the fierce protest from his bad leg.

"Shh, Cat," Savage soothed. "We just want to help you."

Catrienne chuckled bitterly, her mood seeming to shift as unpredictably as the drafts of wind issuing from the fire. "Don't you two think you've done enough for one day, Jas?"

Nicholas blanched as he and Savage got their first close look at the woman's face.

"Christ, Cat," Savage said softly. "Was this Griffin's doing?" He tentatively touched the lump forming on her left cheek, causing her to wince.

"His and mine—with more than a little help from you two."

"Where is he? I'll kill him."

"Not if I get there first," Nicholas growled.

Catrienne slanted the two of them a sly, mocking glance and emitted another humorless laugh. "I would thank you both to do me no more favors. Besides," she whispered, "I think he may already be dead."

"Is he still in there, Cat?" Savage demanded.

"I think so."

A thought came to Savage. "Jug, she's not—"

"No. She should be at Declan's place at St. Mary's. I made sure she wouldn't—" Catrienne choked off abruptly. She turned to watch the silhouettes of the men battling the fire. "I didn't want her here when Griffin came," she said, finally.

Another tear ran down her cheek. "Jas," she said. "I want you to give Jug the coin I left with you. I know it's not much, but 'tis all I have left. Tell her . . . tell her to go to her sister's in Newington Butts."

"If Griffin's dead, she should be safe here," Savage protested.

"Just do it, Jas."

Pushing the hair out of her eyes, she looked silently at the flames for a long moment. Then she turned back to Nicholas, her expression inscrutable. "He would have left me alone, you know. That is, until you threatened him. After that, I knew I didn't have a chance."

Nicholas wondered how he'd gotten involved in such a sordid affair. "I'm sorry. I never meant . . . God, I never meant for anything like this to happen."

She kept him locked in her wide green gaze which bespoke several lifetimes' worth of pain and bitterness. Nicholas cursed himself, knowing he'd contributed to that pain. All he'd meant to do at St. Paul's was claim the letter and scare her away from her folly. Not send the uprightman after her. He rubbed the scars on his palm uncertainly. "Catrienne, if there's anything I can do for you . . ." His offer trailed off at her venomous stare.

"You have nothing that I want," she said coldly.

When she began to struggle to her feet, Nicholas offered her a hand. She ignored it.

"Let my physician look at you," he pressed. "You can stay at Dacre House until you heal."

"Just leave me alone, Misrule."

The shouts and screams across the street suddenly grew more frantic. What was left of the frame for the second story of the White Hart groaned loudly, then collapsed. The wreckage of pitched timber, plaster, and lath quickly caught fire. One man began using his hook to press the wreckage back away from the brewer-house. Others followed his lead.

A man, almost entirely black from the smoke, shambled toward them. Stopping to rest his arms on his knees and inhale deeply, he asked, "Where's the girl who was just here?"

"The girl?" Nicholas glanced behind him.

Catrienne was gone.

"Savage, check the alley!"

Without a word, the actor disappeared into the shadows of the small side street behind them. Several infuriating minutes passed before he returned, shaking his head. "She's gone," he said. "I went all the way to Main Lane. Jesus, she's quick when she wants to be."

The confirmation of her disappearance left Nicholas with a strange ache of disappointment. The guilt, however, felt more like a mortal wound to the gut. Wearily, he forced himself to look at the soot-covered stranger. "What did you want with Catrienne?"

The man shrugged dismissively. "Just wanted to know if she was certain 'bout there being someone left upstairs. Jonesy over there made it all the way up but couldn't find anyone. Not that it matters now, eh?" He slapped his knee and laughed at his own joke. It was a dry, rasping sound.

Nicholas started. "No one? Are you certain?"

"Aye," the man said, frowning, probably at Nicholas's sudden agitation. "There were but two rooms up there. Both were empty. Figure he musta got out the back door. Just didn't want the pretty lady to worry when there's no need."

"Don't worry about that," Nicholas said, his last hopes for the day dying.

4

Sometime after midnight three days later, Nicholas's eyes refused to cooperate in his attempt to decipher the encrypted letter before him. The message had been intercepted on its way to the earl of Essex from his spy Rolston in Fuentarrabra.

Nicholas arched back in his chair, stretching his cramped lower back. He picked up the blackened ivory comb lying off to the side of the table that served as his desk in the reconfigured parlor. He studied the comb, put it back down with a grimace, and looked out the darkened window. Somewhere out there Catrienne hid.

That is if she still lives, a small voice nagged. If Griffin had survived, he'd certainly hunt the girl down.

Nicholas scrubbed wearily at his eyes, then frowned once again at the letter on his desk.

So far, he'd managed to translate only enough to confirm his fears that the Scottish rebel envoy had indeed reached Spain. Time was quickly running out, and only he and Burghley realized the true danger of the threat—England's being lured into direct confrontation with Spain by some of her most trusted statesmen.

The rebel Catholic earls in Scotland, Huntly, Errol, and Angus, had long meant to overthrow the Scottish king, James. They'd intended to justify their open rebellion by representing themselves as defenders of the Catholic faith protecting the True Religion. The rebel earls were smart enough to realize that however much Elizabeth might dislike James and his maneuverings eventually England would be forced to intervene or risk a Catholic power to the north. Needing an equally powerful alliance, they'd sent emissaries to Madrid to claim assistance from Spain.

Nicholas went back and forth with Burghley on whether Spain would intervene. King Philip was notorious for refusing to commit himself to anything, especially if it involved money. Now, however, would be an excellent opportunity to bring Scotland back into the Catholic fold.

What worried him the most, however, was that several members of the English Government were deliberately provoking the public fear of Spanish invasion in order to gain support for their cause of decisive national war against Spain with the earl of Essex in command. Only someone who'd fought against Spain and served under Essex could know what a catastrophe that would be.

And now, evidence had reached Burghley and Nicholas that someone highly placed in Court was actually sending assistance to the Scottish rebels. They'd discovered Laurence Heyward to be the courier. As much as Nicholas longed to crush Heyward, he knew the man could not be at the heart of the scheme. That would require someone with more influence and power, someone with higher ambitions. Someone like Heyward's sponsor, the earl of Essex.

When Nicholas had finally returned home from Flanders to claim what was his as the heir to the Dacre title, he'd agreed to shepherd this one last project for Burghley. And so, for the first time he found himself acting as a spy—not for the money or the surge of energy that brushing close to death gave a man—but rather, because it was the right thing to do.

Anything, Nicholas was willing to do anything if he could thwart Essex's scheme. If he could prevent it, there wouldn't be the chance for young, idealistic men to go off to the "glory" of battle only to know the degradation of starvation, to witness the barbarism man was capable of, to be hacked or blown to bits. If he was able to do this one noble thing in his life, perhaps it might make amends for but a few of his sins. Perhaps it might make him feel like less of a monster and more of a man.

Perhaps.

But then, Catrienne was out in the dark and cold because of him—yet another barbarity he was responsible for. Nicholas realized with a dread certainty that whether or not he finished the letter he would find no sleep.

Cat decided to gamble and spend the last penny of the shilling Rafe had slipped in her pocket on entrance to the Cross Key Inn's performance of *Titus Andronicus*.

The performances of the Lord Chamberlain's Men were always a good location to make a score. Especially now that the troupe had settled in at their winter quarters, and the audience would be packed together in the inn's gallery.

Using her good hand, Cat gave her only penny to the ugly brute at the door. The press of people behind her propelled her forward. The heat from the sea-coal fire and from the numerous unwashed bodies was a welcome change from the cold streets. Having lost her cloak the night of the struggle, she had been sleeping in the Spitalfield kilns in an attempt to stay warm. The sharp chill of fall had burrowed into her bones, leaving her with a catarrh.

She moved into the center of the room in hopes of losing herself in the crowd. There was a small chance Jasper might be here since he worked for the manager of the Lord Chamberlain's Men. He'd already led Lord Dacre to her once.

As she turned into the gallery, a man shoved impatiently past, bumping her injured hand. Cat cried out.

The man glanced over his shoulder. "Well 'scuse me, princess."

Cradling her swollen hand, she formed a sharp retort. But a racking cough seized her before she could speak. It was several seconds before she could breathe again.

The large crowd pressed Cat closer to the front of the room than she would have liked. The small stage, curtained in garish colors of silk, stood directly before her. She stood only two rows from the small section of chairs reserved for the higher-paying patrons. She wistfully eyed some of the heavy purses they flaunted. Unfortunately, she'd be too visible amongst the wealthy. Better to go for someone like the liveried servant to her right, or one of the unruly students in the row in front of her.

A young lad selling oranges and sweetmeats passed by. When he managed to catch her eye, she sadly shook her head despite the rumble of protest from her stomach.

Trying to distract herself, Cat glanced circumspectly around trying to mark her target. She ached for the familiar weight of her cuttle beneath her cloak. A nip and foist wouldn't be so difficult, but she was going to have to pick a purse. She'd been ten the last time she'd done that successfully. And the only time she ever remembered using her right hand was when Skinner had made her practice as a mere kinchin on a mock-up cony strung with bells. Skinner had insisted she should have skill with both hands in case the bandogs removed her stronger one as punishment for thievery.

She would have to be successful today. 'Twas her only hope for salvaging her plan to destroy Heyward. She'd furtively returned to the White Hart the following night to dig through the ashes. The first floor was all that remained of the tippling den. The letter, her mother's comb, and her father's box were nowhere to be found. Shivering in the fields, she had cursed Lord Dacre. His interference had destroyed in less than a day what had taken her twelve years to accomplish.

She'd developed a desperate plan: if she could gain enough coin, she could pay Egan to make a forgery of Heyward's letter. She remembered the wording and handwriting well enough for a decent copy. She wouldn't be able to exactly replicate the telltale tears, but with the real letter having been stolen and her knowing its contents, her enemy would have no reason to doubt she had the real thing. She'd just have to make sure he didn't get too close to it until it was too late.

But who was to be her mark?

Cat decided her best chance was the burly man directly in front of her. His purse was small, but from the way it hung she felt certain it must hold at least a few shillings. With luck that would be enough to cover the supplies Egan would need to reproduce the letter.

The audience's conversation faded to a murmur as the curtain parted, revealing a crudely painted backdrop showing the balcony of an upper chamber and the Senate beyond the window. A man in a toga stepped forward with several followers. Cat recognized two of the actors as drinking partners of Jasper's who had occasionally slummed at the White Hart.

"Noble patricians," Saturnis began, "patrons of my right, defend the justice of my cause with arms . . . "

Cat edged forward. The people behind her quickly took up the extra room. She was pressed fully against her target now. The stale odor of sweat hung on his clothes. Go slowly, you can't afford to mess this up, she told herself, flexing her right hand.

"Plead my successive title with your swords: I am his first-born son—"

Slowly, Cat reached out and touched the man's purse strings. She fumbled, trying to untie the tight knot with her one hand. It wouldn't budge.

"—that ware the imperial diadem of Rome; then let my father's honors live in me . . . "

Just as Cat began making some progress, the man

shifted. She snatched back her hand just before he
darted a glance backward. Her heartbeat hammered
in her ears. She forced herself to watch the performance for what seemed to be eternally long moments.

The actor who played Marcus Andronicus stepped
forward bearing a crown in his hands. "Princes, that
strive by factions and by friends ambitiously for rule
and empery . . . "

Even after her heart slowed, Cat was too frightened to continue. Was her target suspicious? Mayhap
she should choose another. She glanced to her left
and right. No, there was no hope of changing her
position now. She was wedged in. And she had no
money for another performance.

Slowly she reached out again to the purse strings.
The leather pouch twirled slowly as she fought to
loosen the cord that held it closed. Sweet Mary,
please, Cat whispered silently, all I ask is for this
one . . .

A large hand clamped down around her wrist.

"Lo, there is a thief in our midst!" cried the man.
He held her arm high in the air, almost dragging her
off her feet.

Twisting in the man's grasp, Cat fought desperately to pull herself free. "No, 'tis not so!" she cried.
"I came to watch a play. I'm no thief!"

One of the actors on stage missed a line, then
another. Some of the more unruly members in the
audience started to boo and hiss.

"Please," Cat softly entreated her captor, "I meant
you no harm—"

"This girl tried to steal my purse!" the man continued in a shout, playing now to the audience he knew
he had. "She must be punished!"

"Kill the thief!" came a shrill reply.

"Hear! Hear!"

An overripe tomato hit one of the students just to the left of the man and her.

The actors broke off their performance.

An angry cry picked up around the room: "Thief! Thief! Thief!" The chant grew louder as others joined in.

Cat drew her injured hand to her ear, trying to muffle the sound. "Please, I was desperate for coin. Let me go," she begged.

The man met her eyes for the first time and smiled. "There are other ways to earn coin you know," he murmured.

"Tie her to the stage!" someone yelled.

Having seen other thieves tortured in such a manner for entertainment, Cat screamed and tried to fight her way back against the sea of people who'd suddenly become her enemies. Hands tore at her clothes, her hair, and her face. Relentlessly, they pushed her forward. One of the actors in Roman garb waited grimly on stage. He held a coil of rope.

Casually easing his way into conversation with his employer, John Heminges, about the upcoming holiday season, Jasper Savage walked through the gleaming hall of the Cross Key Inn. Passing by the gallery, Jasper glanced casually at the performance in progress. He froze, scarcely able to credit his limited vision. He and Nicholas had been combing the City for almost a week trying to find Cat, and there she was tied to the edge of the stage, straining desperately against the ropes that bound her.

"Jesu, what do they think they're doing?" he cried.

The actors were just beginning act two of *Titus Andronicus*, but most members of the audience seemed exclusively focused on tormenting Cat. Remains of overripe vegetables and eggs stained her tattered clothes. Part of her skirt had been torn away, and a young man dodged the various missiles in an attempt to coax a kiss from the terrified girl.

"By Christ, I'll kill the bastard." Jasper reached for his rapier and made to enter the gallery, but Heminges blocked the doorway with his large frame.

"Do you know her?" he asked. His look was an equal mixture of disapproval and concern.

"Aye, she's a dear friend of mine," he said, standing toe-to-toe with his employer.

Heminges gaze drifted to the eye patch, then quickly slid away.

Jasper frowned but decided not to comment on the all-too-common reaction old friends still seemed to have when confronted with his marred face. "Let me by, John."

"A friend eh?" Heminges asked casually, ignoring his request. "You know what I think of you trafficking with thieves, Savage."

"You mean other than you and Edward Alleyne?" Jasper jested lightly, hoping humor might lower Heminges's guard.

It didn't. Heminges still refused to budge.

Jasper cursed and paced the small length of the doorway. Over the manager's shoulder, he could see that Cat had managed to pull an arm free from the ropes. The streak of blood circling her wrist didn't escape his notice. "Christ John! What'd she try to do? Nip a purse? Do you think this is just punishment? They're torturing her for God's sake!"

Heminges looked uneasy but remained where he was. "I don't like it much myself," he said. "But the beadles should be here soon. Teasing is a small price to pay if it keeps her alive until then."

"Is that so? And what do you think the law's going to do with Cat?" Jasper demanded. "At the very least they're going to whip her!"

"Savage," Heminges said sternly, "as your employer I order you not to interfere."

Jasper's grip tightened on his hilt.

"You weren't planning to use that on me, were you?" Heminges asked coldly. "Because that's what it's going to take for you to get to her."

Trembling with impotent rage, Jasper forced his hand away from the hilt. He'd lost the immediate battle. But there must be something he could do. How long would it take for him to find Nicholas? Would he be moping around his garden? Christ, he was probably with Lord Burghley again plotting England's grand salvation. "Where will they take her?" he asked finally.

"Has she been caught before?"

"Aye."

Heminges frowned and rubbed his beard. "If she's lucky they will just take a thumb. Otherwise she could hang at Tyburn."

A drench of cold water dragged Cat unwillingly back to consciousness.

"Wake up, thief. We haven't even started with ye yet."

Gone was the inn. In its place stood a new nightmare. She was bound by her hands to the Standard in the center of Cheapside Market. Someone had sliced away the back of her dress, leaving her skin bare to the cold autumn air. A boisterous crowd had formed, circling her and the two bandogs who held her captive. The crowd's jeering faces dodged in and out of focus. Just as Cat realized what was happening, the lash ripped into the bare skin of her back for the first time.

Cat inhaled sharply, biting back a scream. When they'd caught her stealing at thirteen, she hadn't managed to keep quiet. Her cries had only encouraged her captors further, and for more than a fortnight the denizens of the White Hart had called her the "bawling bantling." She would not show such weakness again.

The lash cut into her back again. Flinching, Cat tried to be grateful they used a short lash. 'Twould cut skin but not bone. Right now, though, all she cared about was how many more strokes there would be. There was no magistrate here to tell them when to stop.

The lash struck out again. Spots flashed before her eyes.

"Sweet Mary, how many more?" Cat realized too late that she'd spoken out loud.

"What'd she say?" one of the bandogs asked, sounding surly.

"The trugging thief," said the other man with a guffaw, "wants us to hurry't up so she can be on her way."

"Wouldn't think," said the surly one, "she'd be in such a hurry to dance on the end of a rope." His voice seemed strangely far away.

It was only then that Cat realized they meant to hang her.

*   *   *

"Damn! Get me another bucket of water, will ye, Boil?" one beadle asked the other.

Nicholas arrived with Savage in time to discover Catrienne's limp form hanging from the Standard, her back marked by three crimson trails of blood, obscene against the pale satin of her skin.

"Hell, I'm not goin' up the hill again," the beadle named Boil muttered. "Just cut her down."

Nodding curtly, the other man cut through the ropes with his knife and allowed her to drop to the cobblestone.

Enraged by their callous treatment, Nicholas reached for his rapier. Nothing would please him more than to skewer these two men right here.

Savage grabbed Nicholas's forearm lightly. "I need your title not your sword arm, friend." The actor held his gaze until Nicholas let his blade slide back into its sheath.

Nicholas flexed his empty hand. "Whatever it takes, Savage," he said in a rough voice. It pained him to know that indirectly he'd caused Cat such misfortune.

Catrienne moaned and began to stir, to the renewed interest of the crowd.

"Go see to her," Nicholas ordered softly.

Making his way over to Catrienne, Savage bent and murmured something softly in her ear. The lovely thief mumbled something in return.

Nicholas hadn't realized he'd been holding his breath until then. Uncomfortable, he directed his attention to the two beadles. Apparently, they were arguing over who should take Catrienne to the Clink where she would be held until it was time for the hanging. For a moment it seemed strange they both wanted the honor, but then, in growing outrage, he caught the gist of the conversation.

"But you're a married man and all," grumbled the larger man. "I 'aven't had a pretty one in months."

"Naw, let me take this one, cove," insisted the one named Boil, "an' I'll buy you a pint of ale aft'r."

Nicholas's feet moved of their own volition. "I'm certain that won't be necessary, my *good* men." He shrugged back his cloak revealing both his blades and a heavy purse.

A murmur ran through the crowd.

Although he longed to draw blood, he knew he'd have to be more cunning than that to save Catrienne. Raising his voice in a play to the audience, he said, "By my right as a gentleman, I pledge to make this woman my responsibility, a member of my household."

The crowd went deadly quiet.

Nicholas casually rested his hand on the hilt of the rapier on his right side. "She will not steal again. Release her to me. She is mine by rights of common law."

Both beadles hesitated, their desire for Catrienne warring with their knowledge of tradition. As Lord Dacre, a peer of the realm, Nicholas could save a thief's life by taking responsibility for her further actions.

An idea came to the one called Boil. He eyed Nicholas shrewdly. "By your right as a gentleman, eh?" He nudged his companion. "An' here I thought he was Old Bess's Misrule. But then that couldn't be so, now could it? Misrule's honor"—he twisted the word into an obscenity—"ain't worth a rat's fart."

The crowd broke into laughter. Nicholas tried not to blanch as the taunt struck home.

Noting the shift in the crowd's favor, Boil seemed to stand taller, a hint of challenge gleaming in his eye. His cockiness fled, however, when Nicholas brought the point of his blade to rest just below the beadle's bobbing Adam's apple. The other man hastily backed away.

"By my right as Lord Dacre," Nicholas said through clenched teeth, "and by my word of honor, you shall release the girl to me."

Long moments passed.

"It's quite an intriguing sight, really," Nicholas murmured, "to see a rapier come out the back of a man's spine." He smiled dangerously, making no attempt to conceal his lust to kill.

The color slowly faded from the beadle's face. Out of the corner of his eye, Nicholas noticed the other beadle circling to the side as if he planned to intervene. With a flick of his wrist, he drove his blade slightly forward, nicking Boil's skin. 'Twas only a scratch, but the man shrieked as though he'd just been mortally wounded.

"Take the girl! You can have her!" Boil blubbered.

The other beadle retreated again.

Keeping his blade still in place, Nicholas unfastened his purse with his right hand. The bag jingled as he tossed it at Boil's feet. "If you think that not enough coin to buy your silence," he said with a sneer. "Think again. I can just as easily slice out your tongue"—Nicholas glanced at the crowd—"or that of anyone here."

He'd never really do it, but, hell, if they were going to toss his reputation in his face, Nicholas thought wryly, he might as well use it to his own advantage. Whomever Catrienne worked for, she had stolen something coming from Heyward. Nicholas preferred that the alderman and his cronies didn't turn up at his door afore he was ready for them.

Boil snatched up the money and scuttled backward. "If she's caught again, there'll be no protection for her."

"She won't be caught again."

Nicholas studied the two beadles until he was certain they were not going to turn on him. Keeping his blade out, he made his way to where Savage knelt beside Catrienne. Her bonds had been cut. She was slumped against the Standard, cheeks flushed, eyes glassy.

Nicholas unfastened his cloak and stooped down next to them, draping it as carefully as possible over her raw back. He didn't want to cause her any more pain, but he couldn't bear to leave her so naked and vulnerable before the crowd. "How is she?" he asked Savage, not trusting the girl to tell him the truth.

The actor exhaled angrily and bowed his head. "Well enough, considering what she's been through."

"I'll be fine," snapped the lady thief. "Let's get out of here before—" A fit of coughing overwhelmed the rest of her protest.

Nicholas didn't like the congested sound coming from her chest or the glisten of sweat on her delicate brow. And her left hand was so swollen that he knew it had to be broken. "We need to get you to my physician."

She scowled but said nothing.

"Can you stand?"

"Of course I can." Catrienne rose unsteadily to her feet.

When she began to slump, Savage wrapped a supportive arm around her. "Just a little while longer, Cat," he murmured.

Although growing increasingly pale, Catrienne shot the actor an ugly look. "Jas," she said faintly. "Keep your mealy-mouthed comfits to yourself, you pig-tupping son of a whore."

Nicholas laughed in relief. "I think she's going to be all right."

"O-of course I am. I plan to thrash both of you no good Italianate prick-me-dainties for all the trouble you've—" Another fit of racking coughs seized her.

Slowly, the three of them made their way to where Nicholas's coach waited at the edge of the crowd. Nicholas helped Catrienne inside, despite her muttered protests. Glancing to Savage he asked, "You coming?"

"Nay, Heminges is bound to have noticed my absence . . ." Distracted by something over Nicholas's shoulder, he trailed off.

"What?" Nicholas glanced over his shoulder, curious.

"Never mind," Savage said quickly. "It's nothing."

But it was too late. Nicholas already saw her. Amye. His precious Amye. Now Lady Amye Heyward. She stood only a few feet away, carefully protected by a retinue of servants. She was garbed in the richest fabrics and gems the alderman's gold could buy. When their eyes met, she lowered the velvet mask meant to protect her fair features from the sun. Her hair had faded to a lighter blonde, but it still looked as soft as silk. Some of the freshness of youth had left her skin, but it remained as clear and pure as porcelain. The years, Nicholas realized with a painful ache, had only made her beauty more precious and fragile.

It was clear she was just as startled at the chance meeting as he. After a moment's indecision she came forward, her gaze going to the carriage and then back to him. A sad smile haunted her lips. "Always the man with a cause."

Nicholas's throat went tight. "Always." He would have given his best Toledo blade never to have seen her again. 'Twas one of the reasons he was seldom at Court. Lady Amye's presence still brought with it too much pain, too many demons from the past.

Fearing he might founder if he lingered any longer, he turned his back on her, nodded a curt good-bye to Savage, and climbed inside the coach.

He only wished it could be as easy to leave behind the memories.

5

Nicholas, *lost deep* in his own thoughts, hardly noticed the coach's springing forward.

Would he ever be the fool where women were concerned? The question plagued him as he studied the girl slumped in the seat across from him. Christ, he'd just rescued a suspected traitor to the Crown. His temples began to ache, and he longed for a warm pint of ale to slow the crazy pace of his thoughts.

If he were smart, he'd rid himself of Catrienne and all the mischief that seemed to follow in her path. She was part of the scheme to aid the rebel earls in Scotland. Realizing his fists were clenched, Nicholas commanded himself to relax, but his annoyance only grew as he glared at Catrienne, naught more than a pitiful pile of rags and bruises. Once again arose the overwhelming urge to protect and care for her, the need to wipe away the dirt and blood, and find some way to remind her of what a smile was. Curse it all!

He forced himself to look out the window at the slowly passing stalls and half-timbered houses that comprised Cheapside Market. Seconds later, he realized he was looking at Catrienne again.

Women had always been his weakness. It had been a woman who had led him to Flanders, where he saw more of war than he had stomach for. It had been over a woman that he'd gotten himself expelled from Court eight years ago. It had been a woman who'd slipped a draught of poison into his malmsey wine just before he'd been fool enough to propose marriage. It had been over many a woman that he'd been forced to kill men he'd never known. And still a pretty face never failed to catch his eye.

And for Catrienne, he'd gone so far as to humiliate himself in the public street. Despite Queen Elizabeth's grudgingly taking him back into the fold, it had been clear from the collective reaction of the crowd that he, the fearful Misrule, was just as much a despised outcast as ever. And Amye had been there to witness it. The past seemed destined to forever chase him like a rabid dog on his heels. He scowled down at the costly hilt on his blade.

He was aware of Catrienne shifting again, trying to find some comfortable position. 'Sblood, what would he do with the girl?

"Always the man with a cause . . . "

"Always."

Cat had heard the exchange between Misrule and her enemy's wife. Lady Amye had seemed to know the duelist well enough that Cat couldn't help but wonder if there was still something between the two. After all, 'twas whispered the reason Heyward had challenged Lord Dacre in open court was that he'd discovered his new bride had been pregnant with Dacre's babe.

Cat surreptitiously studied her rescuer from beneath her lashes. He sat across from her in the coach. His large, powerful frame seemed to devour the small amount of space they shared. Scowling, he hunched his broad shoulders inward, as if trying to compensate for his inconvenient size. In faith, confining the baron to the stylish coach seemed absurd. 'Twas like trying to cage a tiger in a crate.

The coach hit a rut in the cobblestone, throwing Cat full against the seat back. She hissed sharply at the pain. Aware that now the baron's unblinking gray gaze was focused on her, Cat awkwardly eased forward.

"I ask your pardon, Catrienne. I'm afraid the timber perch that serves for the running gear doesn't provide for a very comfortable ride." His rich, mellow voice seemed to warm the very air around them.

Until that moment, she'd fancied herself invisible to the baron. But now Cat had the disconcerting intuition that he'd been observing her all along.

"If I thought you had the strength to walk to Dacre House, we would have." As an afterthought, he added, "And I feared horseback might cause you more pain."

The image of sitting snugly in front of the baron on a horse brought a sudden heat to Cat's cheeks. Trying to measure her breathing despite the ache in her ribs, she boldly returned his gaze but found his expression impenetrable. "Don't fret yourself. I'm fine."

"Aye, you've been assuring me of that very thing since our first encounter." Although his voice was matter-of-fact, she'd swear he was laughing at her behind his stoic mask. "Faith," he continued, "I've never met a woman with such overwhelming self-sufficiency, Catrienne Cashel."

Cat deliberately chose not to correct the surname. She doubted if word of the treasonous Lyly family would have reached the ears of a northern baron, but she wasn't about to take any chances in revealing her identity to a Protestant noble known for his devotion to the Crown.

"In the short time that I've known you," he continued, unaware that her thoughts had drifted, "you've made yourself a target to Laurence Heyward and every warhawk in Court, you've set part of Southwark ablaze, and you've gotten yourself taken by thief-catchers."

"No little thanks to you," Cat snapped.

"Aye, that is so."

Despite her best attempts not to, Cat broke down into another fit of coughing that hurt both her chest and back. By the time she'd recovered, the morning events had come back to haunt her with remarkable clarity. What a clumsy little fool she'd been. What would happen to Laurence Heyward if she'd gotten herself hung? Nothing, absolutely nothing. "I was doing just fine until you came along, Misrule," she said, more to reassure herself than to goad a response from him.

"Now that is debatable." Lord Dacre leaned back against the seat, his arms resting on the top of the cushion. "As I recall, one of those beadles mentioned something about Tyburn."

Cat noticed that the dark silk of his shirt had drawn taut against his chest. After a long, mesmerizing moment, she managed to drag her gaze back to his. Now, he was actually smiling at her. 'Twas the smile of a predator at ease.

He attempted to stretch out his long legs in their confined quarters, the booted calf of his good leg brushing against hers. Cat's trembling intensified. Lord Dacre didn't draw his leg away. In faith, he seemed completely ignorant of the contact. The small space they shared suddenly seemed as hot as the inside of one of the Spitalfield kilns at midday.

"Aye, well I did mean to give you thanks for your help just now. I know it could not have been easy . . ." she trailed off awkwardly as he sat back up in his seat and scowled. What had she done now? Misrule had been under no obligation to tolerate the crowd's cruel taunts in order to help her. Yet, out of some misplaced sense of obligation, he had. She owed him her gratitude, as uneasy as it felt to her to be beholden to anyone. "I just wanted to say thank you for saving my—"

"Don't. There's no need to thank me."

Cat made a fist in the folds of her skirt. Her temples throbbed and her back seemed to hurt all the more as she realized that he wasn't going to make this easy for her. "If 'twere not for you," she said through clenched teeth, "I certainly would have hanged."

"A moment's folly for a pretty face," he said indifferently. "Nothing more."

Cat looked at him sharply, then down into the folds of her skirt. "A pretty face? I am hardly that, sirrah," she murmured.

"Faith, you have even less good judgment than I thought."

"And you even less manners," Cat snapped. "Why can't you simply accept my thanks?"

He leaned forward in his seat until his face was

only inches from hers. "Catrienne Cashel, you are a
thief, a liar, and most likely a traitor. Only a raving
fool would have saved your neck. The last thing I
want is your thanks." He drew back abruptly.

"A plague on you, man!" Cat swore, finally losing
check of her anger. "Is it so beneath you to accept my
thanks?"

He stared across the coach at her, his eyes narrowing to dangerous slits. "Dearling, you seem to forget
to whom you speak. I am Queen Elizabeth's Misrule.
Isn't that what you insist on calling me?" He leaned
forward again and studied her intently. "Misrule." He
twisted the nickname into a sneer as he reached out
with his hand and tucked a stray strand of her hair
behind her ear. "The most reprobate and dishonor-
able member of Court."

"I never meant to harm you by the name," Cat
said, realizing for the first time how much he despised
the sobriquet. "'Tis only how I—"

"—remind a man forever of errors he made as a
boy," Nicholas D'Avenant coldly finished for her.
"Tell me, Catrienne, why must I accept your gratitude? I'm surprised you'd think pretty words would
whet my tastes, dearling."

His loosely checked anger was a palpable force
between them. "You would not have saved me if
there were not something you wanted." As she fought
to hold his stare, Cat felt the sharp pain of her nails
digging into her palms.

Surprisingly, he was the one who looked away.
"Ah, you think you know me so well, don't you?"

Casually, he turned back to study her. "Perhaps
there is something I want. You wish to give me
thanks, Catrienne? You wish to reward Misrule for

his chivalrous conduct? If you're so damn grateful, than tell me what was in that cursed letter!"

Cat froze for a long moment, considering. Certainly she owed him something for saving her life. "What would you do with that information?"

He leaned forward, deadly intent. "Stop a war on Scottish soil. If that letter said what I think it did, some of the queen's most trusted advisors are trying to lure us into that very thing. People are going to die, Catrienne. But I can stop it."

Cat was rendered speechless. Apparently, the baron had a soft side he was careful to hide. But reason quickly rallied. Was he mad? Could one person really stop such an enormous thing as English and Spanish forces meeting in battle?

But what if withholding the information guaranteed his failure? Doesn't he at least deserve the chance? a small voice whispered within.

But no, knowing the contents of the letter was the only ammunition she had left against Heyward. She must think first of the debt to her family. "I can't tell you."

"Can't? Or won't?"

"Can't," she said firmly. "I don't know how to read." 'Twas a lie but he'd have no way of knowing. He'd hardly expect a girl off the streets to be literate.

The baron grimaced, almost looking embarrassed. Distracted, he raked a hand through his hair. "Well, you can at least tell me who you're working for, can't you?"

Cat shook her head sadly. "I cannot give you a name."

"You most certainly can."

She swallowed nervously. "I cannot give you a name because there is no one other than myself. Why can't you believe I'm not a spy? I've no interest in intrigue. I'm pursuing Heyward for personal reasons."

"You would have me believe that?" he asked, incredulous.

"It's the truth."

"You're after Heyward because of some quarrel between the two of you? You destroyed all my work . . ." He reached out and grabbed her arm. "You've risked nothing less than thousands of men's lives, Cat! What petty vengeance could be as important as that?"

"I cannot tell you," she choked out.

"You would have innocent youths die on foreign soil, and you cannot say why?" His grasp on her arm tightened. "Tell me, Catrienne. Tell me why!"

Unbidden nightmares from the past tore into Cat's memory yet again. The sound of her mother's screams at Laurence Heyward's touch. Images of little Edmund bleeding to death on the solar floor. Atrocities she could never put into words. Cat shook her head frantically.

"Would it cost you so very much?"

Blinking back unwanted tears, Catrienne turned her head toward the wall. Long moments passed, marked only by the rhythmic creak of the coach's wheels.

"You wish to repay your debt to me, Catrienne?" he asked finally, in a softer voice. "Very well. I will choose something of less consequence. Reward me with a kiss."

"A kiss?" Cat stared at Nicholas in shock.

"What?" He laughed bitterly. "Is that as distasteful as my last request?"

Cat's cheeks warmed. "No . . . yes . . . do you always mean to trap me so with words?"

Something of the real Lord Dacre seemed to slip

out from behind the mask of Misrule. For the briefest of moments, he seemed as wistful and earnest as a young boy.

"'Twas only a foolish whim," he said gruffly. "'Tis not often I do something chivalrous. Even less often am I rewarded." His voice softened. "I don't mean to trap you, Catrienne."

"Yes, you do." Instinct told her it could not be otherwise. Samaritans did not exist in the streets of London, and Cat wouldn't have accepted their help if they had. She considered Nicholas D'Avenant closely. "You're saying that if I kiss you, I can consider my debt to you paid in full?"

"Is everything with you a matter of accounts and balances?"

"Yes."

He smiled again, but his gaze had lost its playful light. "Very well, for a taste of your lips, you may consider my heroic dealings of the day paid in full."

"Do I have your word on that?" she pressed.

"Would it hold any weight with you, if I were to offer it?"

"No," Cat answered, looking down at her hands. "It probably wouldn't."

"Then I shall not offer it," he answered. "Make your choice, Catrienne."

One kiss and she'd be on her way. One simple kiss. God's mercy, why was she so uneasy? Was it always so hard for a woman to kiss a man? Even one as savagely handsome as Nicholas D'Avenant?

The baron raised an eyebrow. "Am I that much a monster, even to a Southwark thief?"

Cat swallowed uncomfortably. "Hardly that." Why did a kiss seem such a daunting task? Was it because

D'Avenant was a noble and a Protestant, not so unlike her sworn enemy, Laurence Heyward? Or was it simply that she had never shared a kiss before?

"Then pray what is wrong, sweet Catrienne?" Again, she'd swear he relished her discomfort.

Not knowing the answer to his question, not certain she wanted an answer, Cat decided it better to be done with the whole uneasy business. Nervously eyeing his wide lips, she forced herself to lean forward. It was unnerving to be so close to him. Close enough to smell the rich musky mixture of finely oiled leather, bitter steel, and the flesh of the man beneath. Close enough to see the pulse of blood in the side of his neck.

To Cat's dismay she realized the difference in their heights was apparent even sitting down. Slowly, he bent his head down toward hers until their eyes were almost level. His expression softened slightly. "I trow," he whispered, "I've never seen a woman give such thought to a kiss."

"I warrant," Cat retorted, "the women you're accustomed to had far more experience."

"Of that, I'm certain," he murmured.

Cat batted a fist at his solid chest. Before she could withdraw her hand, his hand captured it. Keeping his eyes locked on hers, he coaxed open her fingers and slowly caressed the flesh of her palm with his thumb. Her breathing came in uncomfortable bursts as a strange tingling warmth crept from her hand up the full length of her arm. Before she realized it, he had her palm pressed fully against his chest.

"But what you lack in experience, fair Cat, I suspect you can compensate for with sheer instinct. You are nothing if not passionate." A wistful smile touched his lips. "Even if with me it's passionate contempt."

Nay 'twas not contempt, Cat thought. More like fearful regard. Nicholas D'Avenant was a dangerous man who threatened everything she'd worked for. "Mayhap," she whispered, "you state the case too strongly. I—"

His mouth descended over hers, smothering the rest of her protest. In shock at the sudden intimate contact, Cat pushed against his chest with her good hand. Her protest came out as nothing more than a muffled cry. Both gestures were futile. Nicholas D'Avenant met her pleading gaze and did nothing more than bury his large hands in her tangle of hair and intensify his seduction of her lips. It was clear he would not release her until he was fully sated.

Effortlessly, Nicholas D'Avenant pulled her closer until she sat hard atop his lap. Cat's shock intensified as his lips parted hers and his tongue plunged inside her mouth. With each stroke he plundered deeper. Surprisingly, the intrusion was not unpleasant. Some part of herself deep inside was lit aflame by the contact. The lassitude in her limbs increased until she was uncertain if she could pull away from him.

Had she wanted to.

Sweet Mary, what was she doing?

With a gasp, Cat wrenched herself free and retreated to her corner of the coach.

Nicholas D'Avenant drew back stiffly. "What, Catrienne? Is that all there is to be between us?" There was the faintest flicker of disappointment. Then his gray eyes returned to slate.

Cat brought an unsteady hand to her swollen lips and then to the heat of her cheeks. She could feel her heart pounding against the cage of her chest. "You said only a kiss."

"Aye, a kiss is what I asked for." Slowly, he leaned back, lounging against the coach's cushioned seat. But his unconscious grace was gone. Rather, he had the look of forced casualness, the mock ease of a man who'd rather skewer her with his sword than play the polite cavalier.

The coach slowed to a halt. Looking out the window on her side, Cat could see a huge wagon of wooden barrels blocking their way. Nicholas turned in his seat to study the obstacle. "I suppose 'twas better than empty words of thanks," he mused, not turning to look at her. His voice was as flat and cold as a steel blade.

It soon became apparent that the owner of the wagon had no intention of moving anytime soon. A shouting match ensued between Nicholas's driver and the merchant.

The silence in the coach became an unbearable crushing weight. Cat twisted uncomfortably in her seat. Finally, she cleared her throat. "Aye, well I've given you what you asked for," she said weakly, not looking at him. "Since we've stopped, I may as well be on my way." She opened the coach door.

"And where do you think you're going?"

Cat's hand froze on the door's latch. "Does it really matter?" she demanded, anger rising. "You said all I owed you was a kiss, Dacre. I gave you that."

He sprawled against the cushion seat, his expression once again the neutral mask of a duelist.

"I am free to go my own way now," she continued lamely, trying to fill the silence.

"No, you aren't."

"I beg your pardon?"

Languidly, he grinned at her, like a devil pleased with the results of his pranks. "Did I not give my word to the beadles but a half hour ago that I would ensure you came to no more mischief?"

He polished one immaculate boot against the side of his pants and examined the result. When he met her eyes again, Cat sensed something within his proprietary gaze that told her he'd never had any intention of letting her go.

"Faith," he continued, now openly taunting her. "Everything about you, Catrienne, cries of mischief. I fear I must keep you within my sight until I can teach you how the more virtuous members of the City live."

A sour taste rose in Cat's mouth. Dacre had betrayed her. What a fool she'd been to ever think he might let her go. Why should he, she wondered bitterly, when he hadn't been able to coax the contents of the letter or her intentions toward Heyward from her lips?

Unthinkingly, Cat brought her swollen hand to her mouth. The kiss had been naught more than a trick to lower her defenses, another ruse to coax her into trusting him. "And pray what can you possibly teach me about virtue, Misrule?" she demanded, unsuccessfully trying to hide the rage she felt.

"Very little, I fear," Nicholas D'Avenant answered. "You may be a guest of Dacre House for a very long time." He polished his other boot against his leg with slow ease. Then he looked at her insinuatingly. "Not that I mind."

Cat swore, colorfully enough to win another jump of his eyebrow. "No one really takes a thief into their household, D'Avenant! 'Tis merely fancy words to save a life. Everyone knows that! The thief is turned free the moment the bailiff's back is turned. You cannot possibly mean to keep such a promise!"

"I most certainly can," he snapped. "And I most certainly will. I gave my word, and I intend to keep it. You might as well have a seat, dearling, we have a ways yet to go."

Numbly, Cat did as he bade. With cold certainty she realized that Dacre had meant to use her from the very first. The intervention with Griffin, his presence at the alehouse, his rescue at the Standard—they were not out of concern for her welfare but rather to gain the letter or at least learn of its contents.

From across the coach, Dacre studied her beneath hooded eyes. "Mayhap you don't know me as well as you thought, Catrienne."

Cat sighed, unable to ignore the sting of humiliation and betrayal. "That, sirrah, has become painfully clear."

If fate were truly the mercurial woman the poets envisioned, Lady Amye Heyward would wring the deity's lily-white neck for the mockery that had been made of her life.

By all rights she should be a baroness right now instead of the wife of a base-blooded man who'd managed to claw his way only to the position of alderman—of vile Southwark no less. "Lady Dacre," she whispered. The title sounded glorious. She would have been mistress of a grand home, a cherished wife, a mother.

A mother.

Amye stared at her reflection in the tarnished

looking glass above her dresser, checking her profile for the telltale marks of tears. They would smear the cosmetics that required the better part of an hour to apply. But there were no tears. There hadn't been for a very long time.

The haggard look of the woman staring back at her still came as a shock. For all her tricks with the gallipots, her growing age was beginning to show. Her beauty, the one thing that truly belonged to her, was being taken away in slow steps. Her misery as Laurence's wife only accelerated the pace. Considering her reflection, Amye knew there was little left of the young woman Nicholas D'Avenant had once loved. Mercy, what a shock it had been to run into him by accident after almost seven years! She'd headed straight back to the town house. It didn't do to have an old lover see you at anything but your best.

"Am I still beautiful to you, Nicholas?" Her reflection arched a finely groomed eyebrow at the question. "Tell me, why have you never married? Is it some memory of the girl I was? Have you possibly forgiven me?"

Her father, the marquess, had said 'twas better to marry a yeoman's son with prospects, than a cripple with no title and little fortune. Amye had been young enough and scared enough to believe him. Nine years later, she was still paying for her poor judgment. If only she'd known that Nicholas's leg would heal like he'd sworn to her it would. The physicians had said 'twas impossible, and Amye believed them. No one had counted on Nicholas D'Avenant's insane determination. Nor had anyone known Nicholas wouldn't remain a second son forever, thanks to the Black Death's taking his elder brother.

"What could you possibly find in that piece of glass to hold your attention for so long, darling?" A familiar sneer accompanied the endearment. In a blur of motion, the image of her husband loomed behind hers in the mirror.

She noticed her reflection paling but forced herself to meet the eyes of the phantom Laurence in the glass. She'd be wiser to turn around so that she could respond quicker to any attack, but she refused to give him that satisfaction. "I was merely thinking. I did not mean to stare."

"Thinking?" A tight little smile having little to do with humor formed on his lips. "Nothing runs through your head that would merit such a substantial title." Idly he traced a line up the side of her neck with a hand as soft as a young child's. "'Tis a shame, really. If you had any intelligence it might make some small amends for how ugly you've become." He snatched his hand away.

Amye flinched. Why didn't he simply go ahead and hit her? She could recover from a beating, but his cruel words never seemed to leave. Rather, his verbal darts always struck close to the heart and burrowed there to fester.

Taking stock again of her reflection, Amye knew that soon even the few courtiers who weren't disturbed by her tarnished reputation wouldn't bother with her at all. Not that it mattered. Laurence swore that if he ever again discovered her with another man he'd kill her as well as her lover.

Her husband's thoughts must have followed a similar course, for his eyes narrowed. "Do you know what it does to a man of my stature to have a wife who causes him continuous public humiliation? Not only are you unpleasing to the eye, but you're a whore as well. Fancy a marquess's daughter itching to rut with any man at Court. 'Tis a good thing Providence gave you a husband with a firm hand."

He was the one with a bastard child on the way! Events had conspired that she was never to bear her own. Amye bit her lip, however, having long ago learned the price of any angry retort. Besides, she'd been a fool last winter to give Laurence another reason to be provoked. Taking Sir Robert as a lover had been nothing more than an aging woman's vanity. Robert had doted on her, made her feel beautiful again. At least he had until the day he was found dead in the snow outside Bull Inn with a hole through his chest. Since then Laurence's rage went unchecked. He would kill her if she didn't find a way to escape soon.

"Fortunately we won't be having any more of such foolishness, hmm?" Laurence pushed her head aside and perused his reflection in the looking glass. Frowning, he fluffed his enormous lace-edged ruff.

Among his numerous faults, Laurence was the vainest man Amye had ever met. Was it fair for him to accuse her of a fault that was truly his? If only she were free of him! If she'd been smart, she thought bitterly, she would have picked a better duelist to have a liaison with than Robert.

As if God himself had spoken to her, a plan materialized with striking clarity. 'Twas said Lord Dacre was the best duelist in the City, possibly the best in all of England. Little matter that Laurence had beaten him before. Nicholas had been little more than a boy. Now Nicholas was a man and a seasoned killer.

If she were to take Nicholas as a lover again . . .

Certainly there must be some small spark left from the love they had shared in their youth. And she had grown quite talented at manipulating even the slightest opportunity. When her liaison became publicly known—and she'd make certain that happened—Laurence would be forced to call Nicholas out. The Court would hardly be surprised. Everyone already thought that was what had happened nine years before.

This time Nicholas D'Avenant would make Amye Heyward a widow. The Queen's Misrule could set her free.

"Pray what do you find so amusing, you stupid bitch?"

Her husband was glowering at her in the glass. Amye noted with some amusement that her own reflection was smiling.

6

Their transport rattled to a halt. Cat, still brooding over Dacre's treachery, roused to have a look. A crumbling stone stairway ran up to a doorway on the side of the manor, probably to the kitchens. So, the baron chose not to show her through the main door. He meant to sneak her into his house, away from the prying eyes of his all too illustrious neighbors. Griffin's words, "She's naught more than a Southwark thief and whore," came unbidden to mind. Yet, what had she expected, she demanded of herself angrily, a greeting worthy of a baroness? She was nothing but a prisoner, after all. A fool who'd stepped into the baron's snare.

The heavily carved, well-weathered door at the top of the stairs slowly creaked inward. An elderly man, dressed in dour gray, teetered through the doorway. She watched him carefully make his way down the uncertain steps. Could this man be the steward? Nay, he had the look about him of having spent time in the fields.

Dacre didn't wait for the driver to come around and open the door. He pushed it open with an impatient shove and stepped outside. "Jonah." He gave but the briefest nod to the man approaching them. The baron's face had resumed the cold, tight lines Cat was beginning to recognize as signs of discomfiture.

"If you're having second thoughts," Cat murmured, "I can be on my way." She wasn't certain how far she'd be able to walk, but she was willing to find out if only he'd set her free.

"You're going nowhere but inside."

In faith, she almost slumped in relief. Cat shook her head, confused by her reaction. What possible reason could she have to want to stay? Well, possibly for some food and mayhap a bath. Aye, Dacre owed her at least that after all his troublemaking.

"Can you make it down from the coach without my help?"

Clutching the frame of the door with her right hand, she rose on unsteady legs. As she cautiously stepped to the ground, Dacre put a guiding hand on her arm, much to her annoyance. "Don't worry. I hardly think I'll collapse on your doorstep." Then she broke out in another spasm of coughing.

The servant, Jonah, hurried to their side, peering quizzically at her from under tufty brows. "Ah . . ." He seemed to grope for an appropriate comment. "Do you require some assistance, my lord?"

Dacre maintained a steady hold upon her arm. "Aye, Jonah, go rouse Guerau. Also, send Maris to find me when she has a free moment."

The servant nodded in acknowledgment but seemed in no hurry to carry out his orders. "Does the, er, mistress require some assistance to your, er, to wherever she's going?"

"I'll walk to my grave if I have to. Just let me be." She fixed Dacre with an ugly stare, but he didn't so much as blink.

Cat forced one foot in front of the other though her entire body begged for rest. Despite her order to let her be, Dacre stood close enough so that she could feel his breath at the nape of her neck. Was he planning to catch her if she passed out in a dead faint or simply proving that he did not follow a woman's orders? She no longer cared.

A wall of heat bore down on her as she stepped into the kitchen proper, and the smell of fresh bread and cooking meat assailed her senses. A fire raged in the hearth. The kitchen and scullery servants had clustered together in a silent, gaping mass. For the size of the manor, they were surprisingly few in number.

Saying nothing, Dacre propelled Cat with a guiding hand toward the doorway beyond. Jonah lagged behind, issuing a curt order to the skinny boy who perched atop a bread safe hanging from the ceiling. Cat could hardly bear to leave all that food behind but, unwilling to beg even this favor from her captor, she stumbled forward.

They entered a long, dark corridor. Only a single, smoky torch burned to light their way. The planks of the wooden floor seemed to sway in the uncertain light. Biting her lip, Cat forced herself to focus carefully on her steps. Costly portraits hung from the walls, staring down their noses disapprovingly at her. The current baron, she decided, had definitely inherited that ability.

"'Tis not that much further, dear Cat," Nicholas coaxed the second time she stopped to regain her breath.

Squinting blearily in his direction, Cat realized that sometime in their progress, her arm had come around Dacre's well-muscled shoulder. He had a firm grasp on her in case she fell. Even with him crouching slightly, she was pulled almost on tip-toe, and her hand did not fully reach his far shoulder. "Come, this way." He led her past an enormous screen into what must be the Great Hall.

At least, the room had the long, stately proportions belonging to a Great Hall, but that's where the resemblance ended. The huge iron racks of candles that hung from the ceiling were unlit. Cobwebs draped them like a shroud. A single shaft of sunlight fought its way past a heavy, faded velvet curtain on the opposite wall to scatter a faint spray of light across the floor. Wayward tendrils of light traced what few pieces of furniture there were against the walls. The chests and narrow tables, coated with dust, were well-crafted and obviously costly but also more than twenty years out of date. Well-worn suits of armor stood like a phantom army along the closer wall. Above their steel-clad heads hung more than enough weapons to outfit the eerie crew.

Her days in Oxfordshire were not so far gone that she'd forgotten that the Great Hall was the pride of most manors. A mistress of such an estate would spend hours ensuring its visitors were left breathless at its splendor. This one, however, simply made her feel tired and forgotten.

"I hope you did not bring me here to clean house," she managed weakly.

A single, heavy exhalation came from the solid frame beneath her arm. "Dacre House isn't known for her guests."

"One can see why." But, despite his scandalous reputation, she couldn't help wondering at the baron's lack of visitors.

They passed through the far archway into the room beyond. Before them stood the master stair. Time and dust could not disguise its gorgeously carved balustrading and the elaborate newel posts. The wood was dark and gloomy as everything else in the manor but looked sturdy enough to carry giants.

Dacre steered her toward the stairs, and she muffled a groan. If he meant to put her in the servant's quarters, it'd be quite a climb. She might have been better off if he'd left her lying in the muck and mire along the Cheap. Panting, she struggled with the too-steep steps, somehow managing to reach the first landing with his help.

As Cat fought to clear her aching head, she tried to focus on the enormous tapestry hanging along the wall. But instead of the intricate images becoming clearer, the individual threads began to whorl into splotches of gemstone color. She noted that the beautiful carpet had become moth-eaten through lack of care. Then her legs promptly buckled, and the ground rose up to meet her.

Nicholas was almost grateful when Catrienne finally crumpled in his arms. Carrying her, he thought as he lifted her small form into his arms, made it easier to think. What in the name of mercy did he think he was doing? Burghley, his employer and ally, would probably have his head for giving aid to the enemy. Yet, what else could he have done? Let her die, and wonder forever if he were to blame? Nay, he already had too much weighing on his soul.

Reaching the second floor, he paused to consider his dilemma. Dacre House had several guest chambers, but not one of the beds had sheets. Moreover, he doubted any had been aired out or cleaned since his older brother Christopher's death. What little medical knowledge he'd gleaned from his physician, Guerau, suggested that a dirty, stale room was not the place to put a woman who'd just been whipped and was burning up with fever.

It would have to be his own quarters.

That conclusion, although discomfiting, seemed to be the only option. She'd already proven the treachery she was capable of. 'Twould be wise to keep her under watch.

After all, keeping the spy in his chambers was a simple matter of practicality, not the preliminaries to seduction. That bit of whimsy in the carriage had been a foolish mistake. He'd just been too long without a woman, nothing more.

Everything around her was burning. The walls, ceiling, carpets on the chests, even the very air seemed ablaze. And Edmund! Oh God, little Edmund was screaming. He must have survived the sword thrust. The bodies of Mama and Papa burned like dry kindling. And there, in the center of the solar floor, was the letter that would end their suffering. Its corner sparked to life and began to burn. She had to get to it! Now! But something—nay someone—held her back. The harder she fought, the tighter his grasp. His desperate hold was choking her, dragging her unwillingly

*into oblivion. Before her leered the faces of her ene-
mies. Laurence Heyward, imperturbable and arrogant, and Griffin, a golden Lucifer melting into
nothing more than hatred and venom. She could not
let them win! But she couldn't break free.*

"Shh, *mia cara*, 'tis only a dream."

*The letter. She had to get the letter. It burned to
ash a handsbreadth from her grasp. It was too late,
but she couldn't seem to stop trying. A voice inside
her whispered that if she could recover the letter
everything would be all right. But every time she
strained to reach it, she was forced roughly back by
the man that held her.*

"Let me go, you bastard," Cat wailed. "I said, let
me go!"

Her captor gently brushed his thumb along her
cheek and forehead. Sweet Mary, she wondered, how
could he be both gentle and cruel? The kindness must
be a charade, for she'd learned at a young age the
duplicity men were capable of, the duplicity that had
led to the death of her family. But now she was older
and knew how to play the game. She could be just as
hard and cold as those opposing her. The thought
allowed her to relax into the softness of the feather
mattress beneath her.

"That's better, *cara*. 'Twas only a bad dream."

Cat's eyes fluttered open. The flicker of the rush-
light held close to her face made her squint. Misrule.
He loomed over her, the uncertain light skirting over
his weary features making him look all too mortal.
Despite all the trouble he'd caused her, in that
moment, she almost pitied him. What had he lost, Cat
wondered groggily, that could make him look as
though he longed for nothing more than death?

"Nay, do not look so sad, Catrienne. 'Tis over. You're safe here at Dacre House."

Safe? Nay, she'd never be safe. Cat closed her eyes in resignation. Dacre House might protect her from Heyward and Griffin, she thought as she began to drift back to sleep. But there was nothing that could save her from the demons that chased her from within.

Nicholas slouched on the iron folding stool and blearily studied the figure sleeping in his bed. Clothed only in one of his silk shirts, she lay on her stomach sound asleep.

Guerau had dosed her with enough opium to last several days, assuring him that time and rest were what she needed most. He hadn't argued the dosage because he suspected that as soon as Cat awoke they would have another heated argument on the technicalities of rescue etiquette. God, what sort of nightmare could rouse her from so deep a sleep?

But that was one more piece to the unfathomable puzzle she presented. Since Catrienne's disappearance from the White Hart, Nicholas had relentlessly questioned Jasper on what he knew of the girl. Despite the actor's long-standing friendship, he didn't know much about her background. The majority of her life was cloaked in mystery.

What, he wondered, had made Catrienne become a spy? For him, it had been his right hand. He held up the offending member. He stared at it, slowly rotating it palm to back watching the play of the candlelight on flesh. It was crazy to be so damned proud of a hand, to regard it as a token of what he'd endured.

Yet, he was proud of it. His right hand was what Elizabeth had demanded as payment for his shameful encounter with Laurence Heyward. 'Twas the traditional punishment for dueling in open court.

Nicholas, however, had refused to surrender his. When he'd asked for help, his father had rebuffed him, so shamed was he by his younger son's behavior. Rocco Bonetti, Nicholas's dueling instructor, had come to his aid. Bonetti found him a position at the Italian court and doctors who might help correct his leg. As the outcast of London society and of his own home, Nicholas was welcomed into the Italian fold with open arms. It was a little-kept secret that Lady D'Avenant, Nicholas's mother, had been a devout Catholic all of her brief life.

By the time Frances Walsingham, Elizabeth's keeper of spies, contacted Nicholas, what little coin he'd possessed had long been spent. What little scruples remained had departed even before the coin. He became an agent for Walsingham. It wasn't hard to betray a country he'd only fought the year before. If there had been a conscience it was smothered under the wine, women, gambling, and duels. Nicholas was only sober when he ran out of coin, and this he worked hard not to do. He'd almost been too numb to feel pain when news of his father's death reached him. Almost.

Three years later, in 1590, Walsingham died. The flow of money dried up. One night Nicholas regained consciousness and found himself in a dark, muddy alley with a dead boy at his feet. A boy. Somehow, that night provided him with the courage to return to England.

Elizabeth's wrath had moderated to some degree.

Court was under orders to tolerate him. Nicholas found himself in the middle of a hundred petty quibbles over women, all of which demanded satisfaction with the point of a blade.

But Nicholas disappointed everyone, including himself, by surviving the attacks. His reputation as a duelist and a troublemaker, his identity as Misrule, only grew. The one good thing to come out of that time was that he met Jasper—and even that had been at sword-point.

Apparently Elizabeth's tolerance only went so far. William Cecil, Lord Burghley, had appeared on his doorstep one day with a proposition. Burghley wanted him to become a spy again. The amount of coin he offered made it clear the queen wanted Nicholas gone from Court. And so, Nicholas, armed with more tainted money, fled to France and later to Flanders. Even after his brother Christopher's death from the plague in 1592 he refused to return.

He would still be in Flanders, in fact, if he hadn't been fool enough to risk loving someone a second time. Fool enough to believe a Catholic exile from England loved him for himself, deformities and all. Fool enough to drink poison from her very hand. Again, he wished he'd died. Fate, however, hadn't proved so kind. Nicholas had been too weary—of body and heart—to argue with Jasper when the actor arrived to bring him home.

Home to his current dilemma. Home to a tempting spy who lay sleeping as innocently as a babe in his bed. Christ, what had he gotten himself into?

Nicholas continued staring at the delicate figure under the satin coverlet long after the solitary candle burned low, then out.

7

Someone pulled at the bandages on Cat's back. The pain dragged her reluctantly to consciousness.

"She's doing well, *señor*. Her fever's down and her wounds are healing. Her hand should recover fully. God willing, there should be no impairment in use."

From the foot of the bed came Dacre's amused voice. "God willing? If God were to have his say she'd be too crippled to steal again. Not that we've ever honored his wishes, eh Guerau?"

"This is nothing as extreme as your situation, *señor*."

"'Sblood, I hope not," Dacre muttered. "There's no way I could keep her in a rack for two months."

So the rumors were true, Cat thought. Dacre had gone through the same radical treatment as Francis Loyola in an effort to heal his crippled leg.

"Aye, but she must stay abed for a least a fortnight. 'Twill take her at least that long to recover from the catarrh she's caught."

Two weeks? She didn't have two weeks! She'd have to act soon if she were to convince Heyward she had his letter. Still, she forced herself to feign unconsciousness. Lying on her stomach, she couldn't catch a glimpse of her captor. He was watching her, though. The raised hairs on the nape of her neck told her so. She imagined him studying her with those cold, gray eyes, his expression the inscrutable mask behind which he so effortlessly hid his thoughts. She shivered, feeling naked and vulnerable to the unseen threat he posed at her back.

When, after his unbearably long ministrations, the physician clothed her expertly with an enormous silk shirt, Cat was eternally grateful. Her discomfort returned, however, when Dacre, after escorting the physician to the door, returned to kneel at the side of the bed.

"Well," he whispered close to her ear. "Guerau's gone and you're clothed, Catrienne, so you can drop the charade."

Ignoring her throbbing head, she rolled over. She forced herself to meet Dacre's impassive gaze with a steady one of her own. "Charade?" Cat queried, not managing the unruffled tone she'd have preferred. "You, sirrah, have had far more practice at acting alate than I have."

Dacre's hand on the edge of the mattress tightened into a fist. He made as if to speak, then paused to reconsider his words. "'Twould seem that you're well on your way to mending."

She didn't care for his condescending assurances one bit. "Well on my way? Nay, I find myself fully recovered." Meaning to prove her words, she struggled to sit up. It felt as if a cart-load's weight of coal lay on her chest stopping her. Still flat on the feather tick, she glared at him, fuming. "I want out of this limp-wristed, prick-me-dainty thing you call a bed, Misrule. Now!"

Dacre's expression gave way to a full grin. "Then, dare I be so bold as to suggest you get out of it?"

That did it. Cat was going to gain her footing and strangle him, if it killed her. She pushed against the mattress until her hand shook and her arm wobbled. Biting her lip, she strained to sit up. Just as she accomplished that heroic feat, a spasm of coughing seized her. Gasping for air, she closed her eyes and leaned back weakly against the headboard.

"Giving some thought to my suggestion?" he taunted.

Instead of playing the courtier and offering his assistance, he was going to make her ask for it. The thought galled her. Yet, if all it took was a trampling to her pride to get on with her plan, she'd endure it.

"I think I might need . . . "

"Eh? What was that?" Dacre leaned close. "I can't hear when you whisper so."

"I said that I think I might require some assistance to stand up."

"Assistance? Pretty Catrienne requires *my* assistance?" he asked, feigning surprise and delight in equal measure. He subjected her to another of his absurd mock smiles. "The very woman who would have rather been hanged than suffer the embarrassment of my intervention?"

"Stow it, cove," Cat ordered, abandoning any pretension of civility. "And help me out of this damn bed."

"Why would I want to help you do that?" Dacre

asked. He withdrew to the foot of the bed and crossed his arms. "Didn't you hear Guerau? You need to rest. Besides, I don't have time to play chaperone to an ill-tempered, Catholic troublemaker. Nay, you're far less trouble confined to a bed. Granted, 'twould be more convenient if it hadn't been my own. But who am I to complain of the sacrifices a gentleman must make?"

He made a mocking half-bow and then stepped toward the doorway.

There was no point, Cat decided, in trying to coax or wheedle. Dacre wasn't about to help her, and she wasn't strong enough to leave the bed on her own.

She groaned. If spewing court incense wouldn't convince him to help her, doubtlessly voicing her frustration most certainly wouldn't. But she no longer cared. "You mealy-mouthed, pig-tupping, son of a whore!" she hollered at the dark figure retreating through the doorway.

Dacre poked his head back through the portal, the hoop in his ear swinging mischievously as he informed her, "I'll tell Cook you seem recovered enough for a meal."

Soon thereafter a gray-haired, crouched-back male servant as antiquated as Jonah scuttled into the room with a tray bearing food. Cat had hoped that once he'd placed the food on an iron folding stool next to the bed he'd be on his way, but he hovered over her expectantly instead.

"Nay, I'll have no one feed me like a babe. Begone." With an aggrieved sniff, she brushed him away.

The servant drew back as if insulted. "Eh? Is this 'ow ye treats a friend wot comes ta visit ye?"

Arms crossed, Cat scowled at the foot of the bed. "No one in this accursed house is a friend of mine."

"Say you not so!"

An unexpected blur of motion in the corner of her eye made Cat turn toward the servant. The old man had snatched away his mop of gray hair and now clutched it to his chest like a gentleman would his best velvet hat.

"You wound me to the quick, dear Cat, to say I'm no friend." The actor's one blue eye danced mischievously.

"Jas." Cat sank back into the cushions.

Jasper crouched down beside the bed. "Good to see you, too, bantling."

Although she grimaced faintly at the nickname, Cat was glad to see him, too. As both invalid and prisoner, she felt very vulnerable and alone. Taking one of his hands in her good one, she squeezed it and asked, "So what brings you to such humble quarters as these?"

"I wanted to see how you were." He settled himself on the edge of the bed and lightly stroked her cheek. "So tell me how you feel."

She managed a wan smile. "My good hand is broken, my back burns like the furies, and this plagued catarrh makes me feel like I'm being crushed to death. Other than that, I'm in perfect health, thank you."

"You could have come to me, you know."

Cat scowled. "What? And have you lead Dacre to me again?"

Jasper shot off the bed and turned to face her.

"That's not fair. I'm just as much your friend as his!" His chest rose and fell in short, angry breaths. "'Haps my debt to you is even greater."

Cat winced at his sudden reference to the past. Five years ago Jasper had fallen in love with a young prostitute named Lenore. While searching for customers, she'd become entranced by one of his performances. Jasper urged her away from her apple-squire, and for a while they had lived in penniless contentment in the actor's small quarters.

Only a little older than Cat, the two girls became fast friends. In fact, Lenore confided in her first about the baby. That summer Jasper went on the road with a troupe in the hopes of earning extra coin with which to support a wife and raise his child. In the sixth month of her pregnancy, before Jasper had returned, Lenore's former apple-squire tracked her down and had her beaten for her disloyalty.

When Cat found her friend she had the men of the White Hart bring Lenore to her own bed and did everything she knew how to make the two deaths— the babe's and then Lenore's—as painless as possible. That small kindness was the debt of which Jasper spoke.

"Nay, Jasper," Cat murmured finally. "There is nothing to repay. And I should not blame you for bringing Dacre to me," she added. "You were only trying to help."

"Just the same, if you're ever in need of a friend . . ." He quickly signed one of the thieves' gestures she'd taught him long ago on a whim, "I am ready."

Smiling, she extended her hand in an offering of peace.

Jasper took it readily and kissed it. He let it drop gently to her chest. "Poppet, there's something else you should know. We think Griffin might have escaped the fire."

Cat's heart skipped a beat. "What? How? Jas, he was injured and pinned beneath a beam."

"One of the townsmen made it upstairs. He found no one."

Cat stared up at the canopy, allowing the news to sink in. Ruffin, the uprightman had made it out of the alehouse. "He was so badly burned," she murmured to herself. "He cannot have survived. The townsman must have missed the body in all the rubble." Ruffin, she prayed so.

"Aye, there is that." Sensing her uncertainty, Jasper added, "Never fear, if he's alive we'll find him. Nick's a powerful man, Cat. Whatever trouble you're in, he can help you. He's not the blackguard you presume."

"Oh? Is taking prisoners a habit with the baron?" The actor's expression once again clouded, but before he could muster a retort, Cat raised her bandaged hand. "Nay, Jas, I'm too weary for further argument. Could you just pass me some of the lovely bread instead?"

The wistfulness must have been plainly evident in her tone for the actor threw back his head and laughed. "Certainly, my lady." He cut off a generous hunk and spread cheese across it for good measure. Handing it to her he added, "Nicholas told me to tell you that if there's anything else you require all you have to do is ask."

"Oh really?" Cat asked casually, taking a large bite out of the bread. "Anything?" Anything other than my freedom, she thought sourly.

*　　　*　　　*

When Dacre returned later that afternoon to check on her, Cat was too tired to do anything but lay flat on her tender back and glower at him.

"Such an ugly frown," he murmured. "'Twould seem I'd brought you to Bridewell rather than to my home."

"Velvet cushions and a canopied bed don't make it any less a prison," Cat retorted. "You said I'm not free to go, did you not?"

"Aye, that is so." Idly he scratched the faint shadow of a beard along his jaw. "Mayhap if you'd given me a reason, any reason, to trust you it would not have to be so. The person I'm working with will be none too pleased that I've taken in a spy."

"I'm not a—"

"Save it," he snapped. "Yes, you'll be under guard. But without me, Catrienne, you'd have been hanged. You might want to keep that in your pretty head."

"Little do you care if I were to hang. You saved me for your own selfish reasons, you—"

"Everything," he interrupted, "I do is for selfish reasons." Pausing to consider some inner dilemma, he closed his eyes, hiding his impenetrable gaze behind a fan of dusky lashes. "Well," he amended in a lower tone, slowly opening his eyes. "Almost everything."

Dacre leaned forward. "Aye, Cat, I rescued you to know what your scheme is and what was in that letter." Something in his unforgiving eyes seemed to soften. "But 'haps I could also not stomach the thought of such beauty hanging at the end of a noose. Did you ever think of that?"

The quiet intensity in his voice made Cat sink

further back into the pillows. No, she hadn't thought of that.

Dacre withdrew something from within his doublet and tossed it onto the coverlet. 'Twas her mother's ivory comb. Cat stared at it for a moment in disbelief, then returned her gaze to her captor. "H-how . . . ?"

"I found that in the wreckage of the alehouse when I went looking for you," he said.

"How did you—"

"I figured if you were willing to risk your life for such a trinket, you must hold it in high regard."

Cat opened her mouth to say something more, but before she could find the words he cut her off again.

"Nay, do not thank me." A muscle twitched along his lean jaw. "I'm sure you'll discern a darker motive in that small kindness as well."

He turned stiffly and made for the door. Cat could do nothing but watch his rigid back as he exited the room. Rubbing the talisman that was her last surviving token of home, she strained her ears to hear his fading footsteps.

The letter, undoubtedly lost, had been in the same hiding hole. Sinking back into the pillows, she rubbed the comb's spine across her cheek.

Should she thank him? Dare she feel grateful? Wouldn't that just give him more influence over her? Cat couldn't afford to be weak. There was too much she still owed her family, too many debts yet unpaid. By keeping her his prisoner, Dacre threatened her plans. In that regard, he was almost as much an enemy as Heyward himself.

But as much as she'd like it to be otherwise, in her heart she knew he expected nothing for the return of

the comb. Dacre simply had an unexpected streak of
kindness. She'd seen signs of it before although she'd
tried to deny it. He'd intervened with Griffin on her
behalf. He'd saved her from the gallows. Now this.
How could she hate such a man? Cat irritably blew a
tendril of hair away from her face.

Unable to sleep, Cat stared at the canopy overhead. A vague sense of uneasiness plagued her. She'd
foreseen her plan proceeding smoothly. Ruffin, why
did everything seem to grow ever more complicated?

8

"*Therefore let all men* take this caveat." Nicholas raised a finger in pontification. "That when they walk abroad amid any of the forenamed places, or like assemblies, that they take great care for their purse, how they place it, and not leave it careless in their pockets or hose, for the foist is so nimble-handed, that he exceeds the juggler for agility, and hath his legerdemain as perfectly . . . "

He glanced pointedly at the real-life specimen of a foist who sat curled in his favorite sitting room chair. She hugged her delectable legs to her chest beneath the over-large silk shirt. Resting her chin on her knees, a bemused smile lighted her lips at his exaggerated mimicry of his most despised childhood tutor, John Pendergast. He couldn't help but grin in return. Cat's smiles were so rare that each one seemed a small victory.

Considering her rapt attention, Nicholas decided he must have finally found reading material that suited her pleasure. It had taken him the better part of a week. Cat had had no interest whatsoever in his texts of military tactics and human anatomy. Reciting sonnets and verse had made them both uncomfortable. And he certainly wasn't going to read from his collection of erotica—the last thing his increasingly active libido needed was inspiration. Hoping it would entertain his surly captive, he'd picked up one of Robin Green's more colorful pamphlets that in lurid detail presented the London underworld to the unwary. So far it had been a smashing success.

"And?" Cat arched a delicate brow.

"Er . . ." Nicholas searched for his place in the text. "Therefore an exquisite foist must have three properties that a good surgeon should have—"

An exquisite foist. With her cascade of dark, unruly hair, luminous eyes, and pixie nose, the lovely creature that sat before him was certainly that. Damn, but she was going to be his undoing! Yet he couldn't seem to leave her alone. Despite the increasing urgency to catch the traitors, whenever he had a spare moment he seemed drawn to her room. No. *His* room. *His* bed.

" —that is, an eagle's eye, a lady's hand, and a lion's heart; an eagle's eye, to spy out a purchase, to have a quick insight where the bung lies, and then a lion's heart, not to fear what the end will be, and then a lad's—or lady's—hand to be little and nimble, the better and the more easy to dive into any man's pocket."

"Ever so true," Cat conceded. "But he left out the most important traits of all."

"And what might those be, my fair lady?" Nicholas leaned forward in his chair, acting as if he hung on her every word. Rather, it was to get a better view of her delicate feet peeking out from underneath the hem of the nightshirt.

"A stag's speed to elude the chase, and the treachery of a snake to win one's freedom should the speed fail. I seem to be sadly lacking in these last two alate," she concluded mournfully.

Nicholas stared blankly at her. Then he threw back his head and let out a great peal of laughter. His laughter was infectious, and she couldn't help but join in. Fighting to regain her breath, Cat wiped at her watery eyes.

Suddenly, the real humor in the situation became apparent. Her injuries reduced her to this—fraternizing with her captor. Except for the first few lonely days, the baron had spent a surprising amount of time at her side, no doubt to foil her plans to escape. Cat, however, was reluctantly grateful. It was taking far longer to regain her strength than she would have liked. Only yesterday had she managed to reach the chamber pot on her own. Even then Maris, the principal woman servant, had hovered by her side, lest she fall. It was humiliating and frustrating.

Company kept her from brooding. Jasper had visited a few times, but the upcoming masques at Court kept him busy. Thus, even Nicholas's presence was welcome. Originally, their time together lapsed into fits of snipes and accusations, but their venom eventually evolved into a gentler banter.

Still, she couldn't help wondering, was she falling into the same trap her friends had in the City prisons? In the long days of confinement and desperation, it was all too easy to become friends with one's captor. But if it kept her sane until she was strong enough to go to Egan for the forgery was it really so bad? Yes, it was. Especially when her thoughts kept drifting to that foolish kiss in the coach. She couldn't afford to be distracted.

"Why suddenly so solemn, Cat?" Nicholas's grin had transformed into lines of concern. "Have I tired you?"

Unwilling to return to the bedchamber she'd grown to loathe, Cat shook her head. "Do go on! I must discover how such a fragile and innocent lady such as myself can arm herself against so foul of villains as the foist."

He studied her as if to reassure himself she was indeed well. Reluctantly, he returned to the text. They both seemed to sense, however, that the moment's innocent pleasure had passed.

"What? Shall we not play again, sirrah?" Catrienne deftly returned the chess pieces to their opening positions on the board.

She'd vowed she'd beat him at least once. 'Twas her current obsession. Nicholas supposed he ought to be grateful he'd managed to channel her simmering animosity to the confines of a chess board. He much preferred his well-mannered opponent over the screaming banshee he'd rescued from the streets.

The game progressed for the better part of an hour. The fire in the grate had burned low. With only the light of the two guttering candles propped on opposite corners of the chest upon which they played, they were both reduced to hunching forward to discern their pieces. She was proving to be as much a creature of the night as himself. However, despite her continued enthusiasm to see him firmly trounced, dark lines furrowed her brow and betrayed her fatigue. As much as Nicholas was enjoying her company, he knew she needed to rest.

"Do you never sleep, good lady?" he asked.

"As little as is possible," she admitted. She continued to scrutinize the board.

Nicholas wondered if her dreams were as troubled as his own. But now wasn't the time for such morbid thoughts. "You may as well surrender now, mistress," he jested, "and spare yourself hours of futile effort. You have already stepped deep into one of my nefarious traps."

"I kindly beg to differ, sirrah. I am quite pleased with the course of the game thus far." She quickly took his knight with her rook, foiling what he had prided himself in being a subtle offensive.

Nicholas couldn't help but smile. She'd picked up the rudiments of chess far quicker than he'd expected. That basic knowledge combined with a bravado that hid a deeper cunning made Cat an intriguing, if not formidable, opponent. Granted, he'd learned a few days ago the danger of turning his back to the board. In but a heartbeat, the girl had maneuvered the pieces greatly in her favor. When he'd called her trick, she'd acted so honestly offended that he'd had no choice but to play the rest of the match at a severe handicap.

Yea, she'd proven herself a guileful opponent. If he had any sense, Nicholas thought sourly, he would chain her to the bed before she made good her threats to escape. Her hand had mended nicely, and every day she regained more strength. Letting her roam about Dacre House was about as intelligent as inviting an asp to his breast. However, charming—not to mention lovely—companions were in rare supply. He'd discovered he was a markedly lenient guardsman.

His pretty opponent bit her luscious bottom lip as she tried to fathom the logic of Dacre's next move. Deep in concentration, Cat seemed unaware of his lengthy perusal. Sitting atop an oversized pillow from his bed, she distractedly pushed back wayward tendrils of sable hair and frowned. Clothed in another of his loose nightshirts and the pair of leggings she'd insisted on, Nicholas fancied she looked all the world like Scheherazade conjured here for his personal delight.

Meeting his gaze boldly, Cat made a move of equal daring to his own. A thoughtful smile curved her lips. Nicholas suddenly found it hard to breathe. Jesus, what a charming adversary.

What would it be like to take her here on the floor? The thought came unbidden. What would it be like to have her sprawled over that cushion, eager for my touch? He felt the muscles of his stomach tighten. It had been months since he'd wanted a woman so. In fact, Nicholas thought, it hadn't been since Flanders just before he'd been poisoned.

"What, sirrah? Have you found good cause to surrender?" Cat prompted smugly.

Surrender? Nicholas's blood ran from hot to cold. 'Sblood, he was a fool! Did he never fail in choosing his women unwisely? He no sooner proffered his heart then it was promptly stomped upon with an uncaring heel. If he was rattle-brained enough to act on this new, ill-fortuned desire, Catrienne would prove no exception. By risking her own life, she'd made it clear she'd go to any lengths to reach her goal. Why should he think she might develop scruples where he was concerned?

Rather than making her the object of his idiot fantasies, he should be giving her his cautious attention. Yet, here he was playing chess with her rather than subjecting her to the inquisition her actions merited. Winsome or no, she was an enemy. Had she given him any reason to believe otherwise? Aye, if she was anything other than what he had reason to suspect, then let her prove it.

"What was in that letter, Cat?"

"What?" She breathed in sharply and drew away from the board. Suddenly wary, she studied him with wide, unblinking eyes.

Something inside him cringed, knowing he was deliberately destroying the tentative bond that had formed between them in the past week. Nicholas gritted his teeth. He wouldn't stop, couldn't stop. "You heard me. I asked you what was in the letter? Since we've become such good friends alate, Cat, certainly you can tell me that." His words ended in a sneer.

"Is that what all this is about?" Cat gestured wildly at the board. "Getting me to tell you what was in that letter?" He could hear the hurt in her voice.

"I couldn't say. Is that what it's been about, Cat?" They stared at each other for a long moment in silence. Finally, Nicholas looked away.

"I told you I wasn't able to read it."

"But certainly whoever you're working for gave you some clue as to what it might contain."

Cat crossed her arms in front of her and met his gaze with a defiant glare. "What exactly would you do with that information?"

"I suppose," he answered grimly, "that would depend on the contents of the letter."

"That's no answer at all." She turned to study the dying embers of the fire.

Nicholas fidgeted at her continued silence.

Abruptly, she turned and leaned forward. "Can you swear to me that you would tell no one else?"

The question hung in the air. *Yes.* The lie was on the tip of his tongue. Time was running out and he needed the information. Would it be so wrong to betray her trust? "No," Nicholas answered wearily, "I cannot swear. 'Twould depend on what exactly was in the letter. I have sworn to Lord Burghley—"

"Then," she demanded, "will you at least swear to leave Heyward's punishment to me?"

There it was again—that veil of rage that cloaked her features whenever she spoke of the alderman. The candlelight flickering over her twisted face only accentuated her anger and pain. God's wounds, what had the man done to earn such hate? "Has he indeed committed some sort of crime? If he is a part in this treason, I swear to you, Cat, he'll die a traitor's death—"

"No," she answered, her voice void of all emotion. "Heyward's punishment is to be left to me."

"Cat, you're no executioner. Surely a traitor's death could be reparation for whatever he has done—"

"Then," she said. "I cannot tell you."

"But you must!" He slammed his fist down on the board, sending chess pieces flying everywhere.

She did not so much as flinch at his outburst. "Why? Why should I have to tell you anything at all, Nicholas?"

"Why?" Choler surged through his blood. "Because

I'm not the one who attacked you or the one who set your alehouse on fire. Because I have never done anything deliberately to hurt you. Because I saved your bloody life!"

"I did try to say thank you," she replied. "Besides, I thought you'd already claimed your pound of flesh in the carriage." She pressed her lips into a flat, thin line. With an almost-steady hand she reached for the white queen at the edge of the chest and placed her back in the proper position. "Again, Nicholas," she questioned with quiet firmness. "Why should I tell you anything?"

Nicholas rose to his feet and clenched his hands tight with frustration. "Did it ever occur to you," he whispered, "that mayhap I want to understand what you're up to? That I want to know what reason Heyward has given you to hate him so?"

"No," Cat answered coldly. "That never occurred to me."

Her reply stung like a slap. If there had been any degree of trust building between them, Cat's impassive tone made it clear he'd destroyed it. He hovered there, shaken. She stared at him with wide, accusing eyes. With a dark oath, Nicholas stormed from the room.

The smell of dust and the warmth of the afternoon sun drifted toward Cat as she stepped into the musicians' gallery. Desperate for anything with which to occupy her mind, she had been drawn by the sound of friendly shouts and clashing blades coming from the Great Hall below.

The gallery was a small, faded room on the second

floor from where musicians must have at one time entertained the banqueting guests below. Cat pushed back a timeworn curtain.

Jasper and Nicholas, dressed in black hose, close-fitting Venetians, and flowing white shirts, sparred up and down the length of the empty hall that loomed beneath her. The two men lunged and retreated from one another in a strange dance that she knew could mean death if one of them should misstep.

Jasper thrust at Nicholas, pivoting on his heel. Effectively blocked, the actor extended his dagger and circled to his right. "You still haven't confessed what has you so out of sorts, my good friend," he panted.

"Savage," he said with a growl, "I tell you nothing's wrong."

"In sooth, then why is it taking you so long to beat me?" At Nicholas's advance, Jasper was forced to backpedal at ungainly speed.

Nicholas, his face a deadly mask, arced his blade with blurring speed toward his opponent's calf. He pulled the blow at the last second. A good thing too, Cat thought, or he would have hamstrung Jasper. After a short bark of triumph, he lowered his blade and walked away with the sure-footed grace of a swordsman. Cat couldn't help noticing that his shirt, damp with perspiration, clung to his chest. Nicholas glanced back at his friend and smiled crookedly. "You were saying?"

Jasper's laugh floated up to the gallery. "Er, I surrender?"

Nicholas glanced about the room as if considering something. Cat's heart increased its beat, and, for a brief second, she thought he was going to look up at her. When he did not, she felt an odd twinge of disappointment. He was just as elusive and distant as ever.

Since their fight three nights ago, they had exchanged only a handful of words. Nicholas no longer came to visit her in his chambers, and when she finally mustered the strength to explore Dacre House he was nowhere to be found. Cat clasped the railing with her slender hands, and stared at them.

At that moment, Nicholas seemed to perceive her presence and whirled to faced the gallery. Spotting her, the duelist's muscle-corded frame froze except for the steady rise and fall of his chest. It felt as if all his vital energy were directed at her, as if he were gauging her potential threat. Nicholas fixed her with a seething glare that bespoke equally of hurt and rage.

With a contemptuous snort, he whipped back his hair and turned away.

At his dismissal, a pain squeezed Cat's heart. As much as she hated to admit it, she missed Nicholas's truculent company and dark humor. She missed Robin Green's tracts of advice and the late-night games of chess she inevitably lost. She suspected— Sweet Mary help her—she might even miss the pedantic lectures on military strategy.

With a heavy heart, Cat watched Nicholas, shoulders squared, stalk to the east entrance. Pausing only long enough to rest his precious blades on a heavily scarred table, he left the hall.

Jasper stared in puzzlement at the doorway through which his friend had abruptly disappeared. "Nick? Where are you going?" Sheathing his blades, the actor hustled to the same exit and disappeared after his friend. Cat could hear his cries as he moved through the corridor beyond. "What the hell, Nick. I let you win, didn't I?"

Cat sighed at the empty hall. Yea, it was clear. Nicholas once again viewed her as a threat. Yet what could she have done? She stared into the dark recesses of the chamber, as if hoping to find an answer to her problems lurking in the shadow-filled corners. She found none.

A single thought continued to haunt her. If she'd told him what was in the letter they could have found some way to achieve both their goals. But nay, he'd practically assured her 'twas impossible. If Nicholas had evidence of Heyward's treachery, what would stop him from turning the alderman over to the authorities? She needed time to force Heyward to clear her family's name of treason. And, Nicholas would give her no guarantees. She had waited and planned for her revenge for twelve years. She could not abandon her only chance for success.

A moldering pillow rested on one of the rickety chairs beside her. Cat, uncaring of the dust, picked it up and hugged it to her chest. Nicholas thought her a spy for the enemy. If only she could make him believe that Heyward alone was her target. Deep in thought, Cat rubbed her chin against the faded tapestry of the cushion. To do that she would have to tell him what had happened that terrible night twelve years before.

No! The single word that screamed inside her was weighted with finality. She'd never been able to speak of that night, not even to Jug. A maelstrom of images from that dreadful night tore their way to the surface of her memory. The screams. The fire. A wave of ice curled through her belly up into her throat, choking her. She'd rather die than relive that night. No, she couldn't tell Nicholas. Jesu, she couldn't tell anyone.

*   *   *

Jasper found her an hour later hiding within the curtained confines of the four-post bed. Over his arm were draped several richly colored gowns. Maris and another servant woman followed, their arms laden with an assortment of stockings, gloves, foreparts, and sleeves. As if sensing Cat's somber mood, they laid the clothing on a wooden chest across from her and hurried from the room.

Pushing the one half-opened curtain further back, Jasper joined her on the bed and held out a gown of tawny vellat. "I should think you would look quite pretty in this one."

Cat smiled wanly and extended her right hand to trace the double wreath lace that adorned the body and sleeves.

When she failed to exhibit enthusiasm, Jasper patted her leg. "Come. Stand up. Lets see if this is the right length for you."

Cat obeyed with a sigh. Looking down with a critical eye, she was forced to admit it would fit her well. "Aye, I suppose my back is healed enough for gowns again. But Jasper, these are far too rich for me. What should the Revels Office say if one were to be damaged?"

"They are not from the Office. Nicholas had them made for you."

She involuntarily took a step back.

"Come, Cat. You need something to wear." He backed her into one of the bed posts. "You can't spend the rest of your days sulking around in a nightshirt."

"Sulking? Is that what you think I'm doing?"

Laying the gown upon the bed, the actor crossed his arms in front of him. "Aye, sulking like ill-tempered children is what both of you are doing." He rolled his eyes heavenward. "God only knows what's been going on under this roof while I've been away."

"An ill-tempered child?" Cat emphasized her outrage with a kick to the bed. "He holds me prisoner! He calls me a Catholic spy!"

Jasper's impassive, one-eyed stare didn't falter.

"What should he think when you offer him no other explanation for your actions? Cat, you stole a letter he said was en route to the rebel earls. He has good cause to wonder why."

"Jas, you know I—"

He held up a hand, cutting off her protest. "Nay, do not tell me again that you can't explain your motive. You simply won't."

Cat opened her mouth to speak, but words failed her. Tears of frustration welled in her eyes. She angrily blinked them away. "I did not think I'd have to defend myself against you as well."

"Ah, bantling." He drew her into his arms. "I know you're not a spy. But what has you pursuing Heyward? He must have done you some terrible harm to hate him so. No, you do not have to tell me if you don't want. But you *must* tell someone. It's too wearying to try to carry such burdens all alone."

Possibly seeing the defiance in her eyes, Jasper pressed on. "Nicholas is an honorable man, and he cares about you, Cat. He'd help you if he could. But you won't give him the chance. He deserves the truth."

Cat shook her head sadly against her friend's chest. "Jas, you know not what you ask."

"I did not say 'twould be easy. But you must tell him what Heyward has done to you. For yourself and for him."

Knowing they were at an impasse, Cat only nodded mutely.

9

It was with great relief that Cat regained enough strength to abandon the deserted rooms of Dacre House for the estate gardens. There was something immensely comforting in burying her worries amidst the wild roses and sweetbrier, saffron and gillyflowers. Although it was too late in the year for much to be in bloom, the verdant greens and subtle grays were a welcome change from lonesome, moldering rooms. A sharp chill hung in the air, but it was little bother to her. What the gardens lacked in sunlit warmth, Cat compensated for with the overlarge wool cloak Jasper had brought with him on his last visit.

The ground cover of wild strawberries and rosemary dominated the graveled path she followed to her favorite hiding place, a small pond hidden in the center of the garden. She suspected she'd also like the tree house (a current landscaping whim among the aristocrats) she'd found nestled in the orchard, but had yet to risk the climb.

It had come as a shock when Cat discovered the gardens were still beautiful. All the care the house lacked was lavished here instead. The fountains were all running, the fence to the kitchen garden had been recently mended, the flowers were not weed-choked, and the hedges and rosebushes were pruned, though with a much more lenient hand than most would consider proper. The hedges were overlarge, half obscuring the interwoven pattern of the pleached alleys, and an aging orchard shadowed the stone wall separating Dacre House from the Thames. What Cat surmised had once been a sterile, uncreative formal garden of terraces and hedges had been carefully allowed to grow into a wild Eden of colors and smells. It seemed an appropriate garden for the master of the house.

Obviously Lord Dacre could be lenient when he wanted to be. Is that, Cat wondered, pausing to sniff a solitary blossom, what he'd decided to do with her? Although rarely present himself since she'd seen him in the Great Hall four days ago, the baron's servants afforded her a surprising deal of freedom about the estate. It came as a surprise after their last, hostile argument. Mayhap, Nicholas thought her too weak yet to be much nuisance. Little did he know that she was pushing herself further physically each day in an effort to regain her strength.

Cat took a seat on the small stone bench next to the pond. She suspected she was strong enough to make it to Egan's and back. She was ready to procure the forgery. Yet, for some strange reason, she hesitated. A paralyzing reluctance had descended upon her, leaving her unwilling to . . .

Unwilling to what? Cat scuffled a slippered toe into the dirt. There was no reason Heyward's crimes should go unpunished any longer than absolutely necessary. But she couldn't help wishing there was some way she could give Nicholas an explanation for why she could not help him. For all the trouble he'd inadvertently caused her, she still owed him her life.

The bench suddenly seemed very cold and uncomfortable. Cat shifted but was unable to find a better position. Strange, she thought she'd long ago forgotten what it was to feel guilty.

Sighing heavily, she withdrew from beneath her cloak the small stash of brewer's grain she'd nipped from the pantry and carefully wrapped in the folds of one of her new sleeves.

She sank unsteadily to her knees by the edge of the lily-covered pond and released a handful of grain into the water. A dark cloud of carp rose to the surface and gulped down the unexpected treat. Her lips curved into a faint, unbidden smile. There had been a fish pond much like this at Lyly Manor. She remembered hurrying down the hill with little Edmund, arms loaded with the bread chippings they'd begged off Mama.

The heavy snap of a twig down by the river gate abruptly stopped her reminiscence.

Cat glanced toward the direction of the sound and, upon spotting the cause of the noise, suddenly forgot how to breathe. A giant, golden cat stood at the edge of the grove no more than twenty paces from where she knelt. It watched her with unblinking amber eyes. Bobbing its immense head once, it began to slowly approach, padding softly on enormous paws.

Cat was on her feet afore she could even think.

"Don't run." The command came, soft but with

deadly intent, from somewhere close to her back. She didn't need to look behind to know it was Nicholas.

The lion, its tail held in a sharp arc of interest, hastened toward her. Gravel ground beneath her feet as she took an involuntary step backward.

A strong, masculine hand closed about her arm. "If you turn your back on him and run, he'll think you mean to play. Trust me," Nicholas said. "You wouldn't like his idea of playing."

Swallowing against the impossible lump in her throat, Cat whispered, "Oh, is that so?" She tried to mimic his calm but her voice cracked.

A fearsome roar erupted from the beast's throat. With a gasp, she drew back until she was flush against Nicholas's unyielding chest. His arms quickly captured her about the waist, holding her still.

She had blackened more than one man's eye in the past for such familiarity. Now, she was simply grateful she wasn't alone. He was just tall enough to rest his chin on the top of her head. His warm breath ruffled through her hair when he chuckled softly.

"Quick!" she whispered, barely daring to breathe. "What would you have us do?"

His arms tightened about her waist. "I would have us stay just as we are, my sweet," he answered, lazy, seductive.

"I cannot speak for you." She squirmed against his hold. "But I would rather not be that creature's meal."

"Nay, he doesn't want to eat you, Catrienne. Crassus's teeth are too loose even for such a tender morsel as yourself. Although, I suspect he could still break your neck."

Cat would swear she heard affection in his voice.

Crassus? He'd gone to the trouble of naming the monster?

She watched with open-mouthed amazement as the giant animal tentatively approached them. The beast brushed against her captor's bad leg, and Cat could feel Nicholas's body stiffen to prevent them from tipping over. The lion, with an odd rumble in its throat, turned and brushed past them again. Cat's nerves were stretched as taut as a hangman's rope, and she felt the absurd need to laugh. Her close proximity to both the animal and the duelist was too much to bear.

Nicholas withdrew one of his arms from her waist and allowed his open palm to run across the length of the creature's back as it passed. The animal's rhythmic grumble intensified. It turned yet again. When Nicholas's hand apparently found a good place to scratch somewhere within the tangle of its mane, Crassus stopped and sat on his back haunches. "You see," Nicholas coaxed. "He just wants to meet you."

The absurdity of the situation hit. That giant beast was Nicholas's insane idea of a pet. Cat discovered she was suddenly able to breathe again, if somewhat unevenly. "We were doing just fine from the length of the grove. Mayhap you could get your friend to go back to that distance, and then you could introduce us."

Nicholas's laugh was genuine. "I was beginning to think nothing could frighten you."

"Nonsense," Cat admitted gruffly. "Most of London frightens me, as it should frighten anyone with a wit of sense." Realizing his grasp about her had loosened, she pulled away from him and the lion.

Nicholas quickly captured her hand in his and

drew her slowly back. Careful not to lose her again, he shifted her hand into his right and wrapped his other arm about her cloaked shoulders. Cat shuddered, unsure whether Nicholas's touch or the solemn beast before her was the greater threat. "Trust me." He exerted a strong pressure to draw her toward the ground. "You're safe."

He meant for them to kneel before Crassus. Between her stiff-muscled resistance and his bad leg, 'twas an awkward affair, but they finally met the ground. Crassus wriggled closer to them. And then, with what sounded to Cat an almost contented sigh, the lion lowered its enormous head onto his front paws.

When Nicholas tried to guide her hand into the furry tangle of mane, Cat renewed her struggles.

"Wouldn't you like to pet him?"

"Nay," she replied, blood pounding in her ears. "I need my hands to work."

Nicholas laughed. "So do I. If he gets your hand, he'll certainly get mine as well."

Reluctantly, through half-closed eyes, she allowed him to guide her hand into the silky fur.

"He likes to be scratched here." Nicholas guided her to the warm flesh behind Crassus's ear.

The animal's rumble deepened and his eyes narrowed to contented slits. Nicholas slowly withdrew his hand from hers to stroke Crassus's broad forehead. As she continued to scratch, Cat began to relax a bit. Between Nicholas's casual ease and Crassus's encouraging behavior, she could almost believe it natural to be petting a lion in a baron's garden. Almost.

"You've been letting me go into the gardens unescorted with a lion roaming free?"

"You're not usually out until around noon."

And how would he know that? Cat wondered. Had he been watching her?

Seeming to read the question in her expression, he looked down at the cat. "I've been staying with him when he's out of his pen. I wanted to make sure I was here, should there be the need for you two to become acquainted."

"That was very considerate of you," Cat answered dryly. As her thoughts fell into a confusing tumble, she sat back, allowing Nicholas to dote on the beast alone. Puzzled, she studied her captor. The dark, savagely handsome rogue had blackmailed her into granting physical favors, then returned one of her must precious belongings without even expecting thanks. He interrogated her, then bought her costly gowns. He scorned her presence, yet stayed close enough to ensure her safety.

A soft, unguarded smile of pleasure slowly creased Nicholas's face. 'Twas clearly not meant for her eyes, but she was too transfixed by his sudden vulnerability to look politely away. As if sensing her attention, he returned his gaze to her, his expression warm and open. It was as if they were friends instead of adversaries. But Cat knew it could never be so, that she'd only get hurt if she dared to hope for it.

"So," she managed weakly, unable to stand the uncertain silence. "How does a gentry cove like yourself come about owning a lion?"

"Savage insisted upon attending a match in the pits." Cat suspected from his frown that he disliked the pits as much as she. "'Twas the third fight of the day for this poor fellow. His owner let a fresh pack of deer hounds on him. I didn't think he'd survive the match. In fact, I don't think his owner wanted him to. After all," Nicholas asked bitterly, "how much profit is there to make in a half-blind, worn-out cat?"

Taking a better look at the lion, Cat noted the ragged scars that covered his flanks and the many white hairs shot through his coat and muzzle. Moreover, she realized that every time Nicholas leaned close to pet him, Crassus swung his head sideways as if that was the only way he could see past the milky sheen that covered most of his eyes. Nicholas was right. The lion had definitely grown old.

"But he survived," Nicholas continued. "Despite everyone's expectations. Fighting off the hounds left him half-dead. Most of the blood in the pit was his. The crowd was disappointed and the owner wasn't happy to have lost so many prized hounds. It wasn't right." He stopped to slump forward and fondle the lion's silky ears. "The owner was more than willing to part with the useless beast for a handful of coin."

"Didn't he wonder why you'd want a lion?"

"Ah, but you forget, dearling," Nicholas responded. He looked back at her, his gray eyes now dark as a storm, his expression vacant. "'Twas Misrule he was dealing with. God only knows what private perversity he had in mind." His voice lowered to a whisper. "Little matter what he thought, I offered good coin. As far as any one of them were concerned, this poor fellow had outlived his usefulness. As if 'twere enough reason to end a life!"

As she noticed his hand tremble slightly, she realized he was speaking of far more than just the lion. "And so now you have a lion to grace your garden," she finished lightly for him, wanting to end the distress his explanation was causing him.

Glancing up in surprise, the bleak, closed-off expression slowly left his features. "Aye, Crassus is the best protection I ever bought." He managed the lopsided smile she now knew was forced. "No one asks to view the gardens, and it keeps out the thieves. Most of them, anyway." For once the carefully schooled mask failed him. He was unable to hide his hurt behind the weak attempt at humor. Rather, an age-old sorrow weighed him down.

In that moment, Cat knew with bone-chilling certainty that Nicholas D'Avenant had somehow come to know pain as great as hers. And because of that pain, pain which would have destroyed a lesser soul, she knew she owed him at least the truth of why she could not help him, of why they were meant to be enemies. She had to tell him what Heyward had done.

Cat's heart fluttered like a panicked bird in its cage. She'd never been able to speak of that night twelve years ago. Yet, suddenly, she found herself willing to try.

A chilled wind blew past them. Cat's expression had changed from open-mouthed surprise to something so immeasurably still and solemn that Nicholas knew he'd somehow broken past her defenses. Getting sentimental over an old, battle-scarred lion had achieved what all his prior goading and threats could not. Nicholas didn't know whether to laugh at himself or shout in relief.

When Cat finally spoke, her words came out in a sudden rush. "There was a priest. A Jesuit." She looked up to gauge his reaction.

Nicholas tried to keep his expression neutral, but already his heart felt heavier. Cat's first words confirmed his suspicions that she was a Catholic sympathizer. Still, he wanted—no, *needed*—the truth of what there was to be between them, no matter how hard it might be to hear.

Cat seemed reassured by his lack of outburst. "He was heading north," she continued, her voice flat, "bringing news from Rome to members of the True Faith." The last two words came out in an ugly, embittered sneer. "Papa invited him to stay the night before journeying on. We intended no more than to give him a good supper and a place to sleep. Papa didn't know." Her voice dropped to a fragile whisper. Cat looked down to her hands, fidgeting in her lap. "We couldn't have known . . . "

When she spoke again, her voice was cold and steady. "They came for the priest in the middle of the night—Laurence Heyward and his men. They killed our sentry when he tried to stop them. There'd been barely enough time to conceal the Jesuit in the priest-hole. Old Nan sealed the panel afore I even had a chance to climb back out." She hesitated and then added, "They seized Mama and Papa."

She'd clasped her hands so tightly in her lap that they'd turned white. "Heyward had been Papa's boyhood friend," Cat continued. "But the man that confronted Papa was some perverted creation two years in London had made him. He said . . ." She swallowed with obvious difficulty. "He said the priest was on a mission from Rome, that he plotted against the queen. By helping him, we'd become traitors also. We didn't know. I swear we didn't know."

Her green eyes pleaded for his understanding. Nicholas's growing sense of dread intensified. "When was this?"

"The summer of 1582, when I was eight." Her words were void of feeling, of any sympathy for the eight-year-old child who'd probably been terrified to witness such a confrontation.

1582. The year nagged at him. Leaning back on his heels, Nicholas mulled it over. Reality hit him with sudden clarity. Jesus, the priest must have been part of the 1582 conspiracy to murder the queen! He'd been nineteen at the time, spending his days and nights almost entirely at Blackfriars, learning to duel with London's best. But even as immersed as he'd been in the world of fighting, he'd still shared England's outrage that someone dared to threaten their monarch.

There had been a family, he remembered, somewhere around Oxford . . . But no, they'd all fought to the death.

"Aye," Cat answered, seeing the question in his eyes. "My family's surname is Lyly."

Nicholas winced.

She pressed on. "I couldn't understand why Heyward would betray us so, betray his own faith. And then one of his men mentioned something about one of the queen's men promising him an appointment at court if he could capture the Jesuit. An appointment!

"He ordered his men to search the house. They were so close we dared not breathe. They searched inches from where we hid." Her small frame trembled. "I thought for sure they'd find us, but somehow they didn't.

"Heyward was enraged. He hit Mama and threatened to do worse—things I didn't understand then—if we didn't surrender the priest."

Nicholas fought back the urge to go to her and hold her. He suspected if he did so she might fall apart completely and be unable to finish.

"He threatened my brothers Edmund and Richard, but still Papa wouldn't tell him." A puzzled frown pulled at Cat's features. "I couldn't understand why he said nothing. Aye, the man we hid was a Jesuit, but if any of what Heyward said was true . . ." Her voice lowered to a whisper. "And then I knew." She hugged herself tightly. "They were protecting me."

Nicholas scanned her face, searching for signs of guilt. He knew all too well how that dread emotion could torture and bend a soul until it was no longer recognizable. "If Heyward was a friend of the family, why didn't he realize you were missing?"

Cat shook her head. "It had been two years since he'd seen me, and my servant girl, Merry, was the same age. They thought her to be me." She stared off into the distance.

"What happened?" Nicholas prompted.

Cat glanced back at him absently, as if she'd forgotten his presence. Tearing a strand of gray-green rosemary from the half-frozen ground, she shredded it into bits. "Heyward said if they didn't surrender the priest he'd kill them one by one. Mama begged Papa to tell. But he said Heyward meant to kill them all whether or not he succeeded."

"And?" Nicholas asked, wishing he didn't have to ask.

"He had them murdered, one by one."

"Oh, *cara*." He didn't need to hear the rest, didn't want the torturous details. He buried his face in his hands, but she continued, oblivious to his reaction.

"He started with Edmund. Then Richard. Then

Merry. They made her suffer my fate. I tried to call out, to reveal where we hid and make them stop."

Cat raised an unsteady hand as if pleading for understanding. "But there was this hand, this big hairy hand that covered my mouth. I couldn't yell. I couldn't even breathe. Or even think." A tear ran unheeded down her cheek. "I'd waited too long to cry out because I was afraid. I could have stopped them, and I didn't."

"Nay." The word came out in barely a croak, so badly did he ache for the poor, confused child who held herself partially to blame for her family's deaths.

"I guess I must have passed out. The Jesuit allowed them to kill my family so we . . . no . . . he might live."

Trying to push her past the trance of remorse, he asked hoarsely, "How long were you unconscious?"

"Long enough for Heyward's men to set fire to the house. Long enough for the priest to leave me to die in the flames." Cat stared at him, her face colorless and haggard. "I . . . I wanted to die, right there with my family. God, I wish I had. They were all there. Right there in front of me. Edmund even cried once before . . . I-I curled up on the floor next to him. The smoke grew so thick I could hardly see them, and then I was tired, so awfully tired. I would just go to sleep and everything would be all right. But Thomas, one of the servants from the separate quarters out back, found me." She glared at Nicholas as if he'd been the black-hearted soul so uncaring as to save the life of that eight-year-old girl all those years before.

He refused to flinch or turn away. "And the priest?"

She broke eye contact. "Heyward caught him

fleeing from the fire. I found out later they took him to the Tower. His head was speared on Traitor's Gate by the time Thomas and I reached London."

"That must have been a terrible sight."

"I took great pleasure in it, actually," Cat answered, an uneven smile twisting her lips. "The man paid for his crimes against my family, leaving only two yet to meet justice."

"Two?"

"Heyward and the local constable. Aye," she continued, noting his incredulity. "The law was there as well. The man's since died of plague, God rot his soul. So now there's only Heyward."

"Why did you never go to the crown?"

"Who were they going to believe—the daughter of traitors or a member of Court? Nay, better to be thought dead. At least that way Heyward wouldn't come looking for me before I was ready."

Nicholas suspected she was right. Court would have flatly turned her away. The alderman would have done worse. Slowly the true extent of the disaster began to dawn on him. 'Twas one thing for Cat to oppose his plans for political reasons. He could stop her with little remorse. But this! She wanted justice for what had been done to her family. And she meant to bring retribution to the alderman personally. How could he help her without defeating his own purpose? An idea began to form.

What if he went to Lord Burghley, the queen's statesman and his ally? Burghley was one of the very few men remaining whose integrity Nicholas didn't doubt. Certainly, upon hearing Cat's story, the baron would be willing to go to Elizabeth on Cat's behalf. Catholic or not, the queen would never stomach such

unforgivable treatment of her subjects. Heyward's
position as alderman of Southwark would be little
enough protection against the queen's wrath.
Burghley and he could arrange to take Heyward into
custody just as soon as they were able to trap Essex.
In fact—he realized excitedly—they wouldn't even
have to wait for that!

Bringing Heyward in on charges of murder would
afford them the opportunity to garner some straight
answers they so desperately needed. After what Cat
had told him, Nicholas would feel little remorse in
stretching the man upon a rack.

By the time he surfaced from his ruminations, Cat
had managed to recover most of her composure. "Do
you understand now?" she whispered. "Can you
understand why I hate Heyward so? Can you see why
he must be made to pay, why it must be me who sees
to it?"

Nicholas took her delicate hands in his. "Aye, *cara*,
I see why you hate him so." When he raised her good
hand to his lips, she didn't struggle. "I didn't think
'twas possible to hate the man more," he murmured,
his lips brushing against her tender flesh. "But I do."
Returning her hand to its mate, he cradled them both
gently in his own. "He will pay for what he's done to
you and your family. I swear to you, Cat."

"You will let me continue my plan, unhindered?"
she asked.

"The plan you still don't tell me of?" He sighed.
"No, Cat, I can't let you do that."

"I tell you what Heyward has done and still you
will not let me be?" Cat tried to snatch her hands
away but he wouldn't let her.

"Shhh. There's another way." When she continued

her struggling, he snapped. "Cat, would you listen to me?"

She stilled, but her eyes flicked emerald daggers of rage in his direction. Pretending not to notice, Nicholas recounted his plan to her—of how he could go to Burghley on her behalf.

"Trust me, Catrienne. Elizabeth will clear the dishonor on your family's name. Moreover, I will make Heyward pay in full for his crimes, and I'll take immense pleasure in doing so," he concluded.

As he spoke, her expression had changed from stormy anger to something akin to surprised disbelief. Christ, did she think him so much the monster, Nicholas wondered, that he wouldn't try to help her? At least fate had provided the opportunity to prove her suspicions wrong.

"Why can't you see that it must be me who makes him pay?" she asked angrily.

'Sblood! There it was again, that personal thirst for revenge. "And how do you plan to do that, Cat?" he demanded. He had to fight back the urge to grab hold of her and shake some sense into her. "You've only just begun and you've nearly lost your life. You'll do your family no good if you're found murdered!"

She opened her mouth but then abruptly shut it. Finally, she lowered her head in defeat. "What else can I do?"

"You can trust me, Catrienne." Nicholas felt strong and noble for the first time in many long years. "That's what you can do."

Mutely, she nodded her head.

Nicholas stared at her, unable to breath past the enormous knot that had formed in his throat. Should he draw her into his arms in sheer joy or weep in her lap with gratitude? Cat had just given him a chance he would have thought impossible. He could be her shining white knight. Her hero.

He dare not fail.

10

"*What do you mean* you won't help her?" Nicholas's shout reverberated off the parlor walls.

"Exactly that," Lord Burghley replied dispassionately. Lean and stiff as a scarecrow, the older man laced his deathly pale fingers behind his back. Absorbed by the view the large parlor window provided of Dacre House's front lawn, the statesman didn't spare Nicholas a glance.

Nicholas clenched and unclenched his fist in a futile effort to regain control of his temper. Burghley was a man who valued moderation and logic, not unchecked emotions. Nicholas couldn't help, however, but feel outraged. "'Sblood! William, why won't you help her? That bastard murdered her family!"

Stiffly, Burghley turned around. The afternoon sun winked off the Lesser George he wore about his neck and gave his face the look of fine, wrinkled parchment. "Ah, well," he said, his hand going to his long, white beard with a flutter, "I was the one who sent that bastard to find the Jesuit."

The words hit Nicholas like a blow to the gut, leaving him stunned and unable to speak. Laurence Heyward had worked for Burghley. A bolt of white-hot rage ran the length of his frame. "You were the one who promised him an appointment to Court?"

"The Jesuit was part of a plan to kill the queen. Would any measure be too much to protect her?"

Nicholas shook his head, trying to clear his thoughts. He couldn't believe this was happening. Burghley was his ally, for Christ's sake! "Protect the queen, aye, but there had to have been some other way to—"

"There wasn't." Burghley struggled to control his red-flushed features. "Don't you think I tried? The priest was heading toward Scotland. The only place we knew he'd stop was Lyly Manor. We had to intercept him there."

Burghley's matter-of-fact explanation only heightened Nicholas's shock. "Heyward tortured and killed her family! I would have countenanced it from Walsingham but never from you!"

Although just as ambitious as the former spymaster, Burghley had always been guided by a higher code of ethics than Walsingham. It had been with some relief Nicholas had received news of Walsingham's death and accepted Burghley's offer of employment. He'd never known Burghley to go against what was right.

Burghley's fine brows drew together as he looked thoughtfully at Nicholas. "You should know that I never gave him leave to do what he did to the family."

Somehow that admission renewed a small degree

of Nicholas's faith. "Then go to Elizabeth on Cat's behalf," he implored. "She would never tolerate such treatment of her subjects."

"Nor," Burghley sighed, "the counselor who had permitted it, I fear."

"Why didn't you tell the queen?" Nicholas asked bitterly. "Elizabeth would have never believed you'd been behind such evil."

"I thought the whole family dead," he muttered under his breath. "There would have been nothing served."

"Well, one survived," Nicholas snarled. "She's lost her family and her name, and she wants justice. You have the power to give it to her, William."

The statesman only stared at him, unblinking.

Nicholas realized with a start that Burghley was afraid.

The discomfort of a consummate statesman, however, meant little to Nicholas when compared to the terror of an eight-year-old child. "Go to the queen," he urged softly.

Turning away from Nicholas, Burghley drew his arms across his padded torso and tucked his hands into the long sleeves of his gown. "Nay, I cannot take such a chance"—he slanted Nicholas a glance—"though, I assure you, this weighs heavily on my soul. There is Robert to think of. I cannot suffer a blemish on the family name. Essex's influence waxes strong. One stumble on our part, and he may leap ahead."

Nicholas stared at Burghley in shock. He'd never dreamed the man might willingly sacrifice Cat for fear it might hurt his son's political position. He knew of the animosity between the statesman and the earl, but he hadn't realized it had grown this extreme.

"Very well," Nicholas said. "I'll go to the queen myself."

Snatching up his white staff, Burghley took a menacing step toward Nicholas. "You do that, and this will be the last time we ever speak. Ever."

"I must do what I feel is right."

"You cannot be serious, man," Burghley blustered. "You'd abandon our cause for the sake of a woman, a woman who's little more than a gutter thief?"

Nicholas's hand went to the hilt of his blade. "Don't say another word against Cat."

"By God, I will say more!" The statesman brought his staff down to the hardwood floor with an emphatic rap. "I don't countenance what Heyward did to her family, but the Lylys were hardly what I would call innocents. They willingly harbored a Jesuit!"

Nicholas threw up his hands in exasperation. "They didn't know what he was about!"

"Just the same," Burghley continued. "Harboring a Jesuit is against the law. You know that just as well as I!"

"And so they deserved to be murdered?" Of all the self-righteous, sanctimonious offal he'd heard over the years, this was some of the absolute worst.

Burghley banged his staff again. "I'll speak no more of it." Glowering, he took another step forward. "By the saints, Nicholas, we have a war to stop!"

The statesman had turned the conversation back to Nicholas's point of weakness. Nicholas winced, wishing there was some way he could block out the words before they lulled him into doing what he feared he must.

Seeing he was at a loss for words, Burghley lowered his voice. "You're one of the very best. I need you. Could you live with yourself, Nicholas, if Essex's plan succeeded and you hadn't done all you could to stop it?"

Wearily, Nicholas closed his eyes. Could he live with himself? he wondered. There was already so much shame and remorse, so many burdens on his soul. Would a little more really make a difference?

Yes, it would.

"Damn it, man," he whispered hoarsely. "Why must I have to choose?"

Burghley knew he'd won. "Because, my son," he said, dropping a friendly arm on Nicholas's shoulder, "'tis the way of things."

The statesman, quite the magnanimous winner, gave him a good-natured shake. "We all have to make sacrifices for the greater good."

Then why do I feel so horribly selfish? Nicholas wondered.

The creak of the door opening from beyond the Great Hall's screen drew Cat's uneasy attention. It had to have come from the parlor.

Peering past the musicians' gallery banister, she caught a brief glance of the well-dressed Lord Treasurer, Burghley, as he limped through the corridor. Uncertain whether the queen's statesman would want to help her or, rather, drag her off in chains as a Catholic traitor, she was careful not to let him see her lurking above.

Should she be excited or apprehensive? She could read little in Burghley's expression. Nicholas's slouching gait, several steps behind, however, sent Cat's hopes plummeting. It hadn't gone well.

She drew her knees to her chest and forced herself to wait for Nicholas to escort his guest to the coach that waited discreetly out back. After what seemed an eternity, she heard the mismatched steps of her champion returning. Without so much as a glance about the hall, he looked up to her hiding spot along the railing.

The tortured regret so evident in his features told Cat all she needed to know. "Cat, I'm so sorry."

She let the curtain drop back into place. Her eyes burned fiercely. Cat quickly gained her feet and fled to the master bedroom. Huddling on the edge of the bed, she knew she had only a few moments to gather her composure before Nicholas found her.

Cat shook her head violently. Really, what a fool she was! Why had she expected something good to have come from this? She'd learned long ago never to rely on anyone but herself to get what she needed. Why should this time be any different?

Sensing a shadowed stillness behind her, she turned around.

Nicholas hovered in the doorway. "Burghley will do nothing." He stood there, pale and trembling with impotent rage. "He already knew what Heyward did to your family. He didn't act then, and he won't act now."

"He knew?" The words came out as a hiss.

He nodded. Waiting for him to continue, Cat dug her fingernails into the tender flesh of her palms.

Nicholas spoke, looking sickened by his own words. "He was the official who promised Heyward an appointment at Court if he could gain the priest."

"Oh, God." Cat drew in a ragged breath. Now it made sense.

"Cat—"

"Nay," she interrupted shrilly. "Let me guess! He doesn't believe it would be in the country's best interest to reveal this bit of past."

"That's pretty close," he croaked.

A dark cloud of despair descended over her. Only her feelings of outrage, betrayal, and self-loathing seemed strong enough to cut through the heavy fog. Sweet Mary, it had taken Nicholas three days to gain an audience with Burghley. Instead of going ahead with her own plans, she'd wasted all that time, pinning her hopes on him. By now, she could have been confronting Heyward personally.

"Well, Dacre, I really must compliment you on the friends you keep."

"Cat," Nicholas said. "I won't allow you to give up hope."

"What makes you think I've done that?" She managed a lopsided smile. She'd allowed her unwanted feelings for Nicholas to have sway over her actions. And now she was paying for it. *Fool. Stupid, little fool.*

"Heyward will still suffer. He's working for Essex. All we need is proof that Essex is part of the scheme and then there will be no need to protect Heyward. If only you'd tell me what was in that letter."

Cat stared at him, dumbfounded. "You can't be serious." She'd told him things she'd never thought she could speak of. She'd given him her trust. She'd broken her sacred code of self-reliance only to be let down. Now he expected to be told the contents of the letter she'd stolen?

"Tell me what was said, Cat," he entreated. "There might be something I could use."

"Aye, something you could use." Fury slipped its leash. "What about my family, Nicholas? What about what's right for them?"

"I swear to you—"

Cat shook her head frantically. "No, don't promise me anything else. Your word means nothing to me!"

First pain, then anger registered on Nicholas's face. "Heyward will meet justice."

She rose from the bed. "Whose idea of justice? Yours? Or maybe Lord Burghley's." She allowed her glare to bore into him. "No, I'll be the one to decide when and how much Heyward is made to pay." Turning away, she added, "All deals are off."

"What do you mean by that?" His voice was soft but deadly cold, bringing a shiver to her spine.

Resolute, she brought her arms across her chest and turned again to face him. "What do I mean? Exactly what it sounds like."

"God only knows what you have planned," he raged. "But you're insane! How do you believe that you, a penniless thief, a woman, can prevail over the alderman of Southwark?"

Cat flinched. "I suppose," she answered, closing her eyes so he couldn't see how badly he'd hurt her, "the same way a half-crippled reprobate hopes to single-handedly prevent a war with Spain."

Nicholas's expression went from stunned disbelief to thunderous rage. Menacingly, he closed the small distance between them. "So help me, Cat." He gripped her upper arms. "If you take one step off these grounds, if you even think of it, I'll drag you to the gallows myself."

"Wouldn't that cause you some great inconvenience?" she quipped. "After all, how am I to confess to you what was in Heyward's letter when I'm dead?"

A growl issued from deep within his throat and his iron grasp tightened further. "Don't toy with me, Cat. I mean what I say."

Unblinking, she met his enraged stare. "So do I."

He drew back his right hand, and for a moment Cat thought he meant to strike her. Instead, paling, he let her go, swearing an oath so foul that even she had to blush, and thundered from the room.

Long before sunrise, Cat had already donned two of the sturdiest dresses Nicholas had provided for her, along with a woolen cloak. Her midnight search had uncovered a pouch of coin and a small knife in the letter-writing cabinet located in the sitting room adjoining her chambers. That was all she would take with her.

Crawling into the four-post bed, she stuffed pillows under the coverlet to resemble a sleeping form and drew the curtains. Maris was accustomed to her sleeping late. Cat hoped to buy a few hours with the ruse.

Using the gallipot of sword oil she'd borrowed from the Great Hall the night before, she applied it with a feather quill to the hinges on her door. Holding her breath, she opened the door.

One of the stable boys she didn't know by name lay sprawled on the floor sound asleep. Cat smiled to herself. She'd run the poor child ragged last evening preparing a bath, rearranging furniture, running her meal back to the kitchen three different times. Nicholas had been willing to indulge her whims provided she was kept safely on the grounds.

Silently, Cat hurried down the hall to the servants' stairway, descended to the kitchen, and exited through the side door. "Ruffin," she muttered under her breath, ducking into the garden. "Don't let the lion be out."

The crunch of leaves and her quickened breath were the only sounds in the cold predawn. Locating the tree house, she climbed the ladder and hurried around the balcony to where a limb extended over the gate to the Thames. After struggling with her skirts, she made it over the balcony and began to crawl. The limb bore her weight.

Hands raw and lungs aching, she made it safely over the gate and dropped to the ground. The Thames, smelling of fish and decay, rushed noisily alongside the narrow path.

Cat turned back toward the house. There was no light, no sign that anyone was awake. For a moment she felt something akin to regret. She was sneaking off in the middle of the night just like the lowliest, most ungrateful sort of thief.

"Good-bye, Nicholas," she whispered. Turning east along the bank, she made her way toward the Bridge without another backward glance.

11

The candles around Egan fluttered as he hunched over the piece of parchment and carefully blew his handiwork dry. He scattered sand upon it, then leaned back and exhaled heavily. "I think that's the best we're going to be able to do." He looked up at Cat hovering behind his shoulder. "Do you think 'twill serve your purpose?"

"It's going to have to," she replied grimly. "It's the only weapon I have left." Yet doubts continued to plague her. Had she remembered enough about the original to make a believable replica? Would the tears look similar at a distance?

Her gaze drifted to the trestle table that was still buried under the handwriting samples she and Egan had pored over to find a match close to what she remembered. Thankfully the letter had been short and she had a good memory for words. She could only hope it was a good enough duplicate to fool the alderman. She'd be wise to show him the replica only as a last resort.

Egan rose from his stool, careful not to bang his head on the low timbers overhead. The tiny room in St. Mary Overy was barely tall enough to serve as quarters to the lanky scholar. The forger studied her for a long moment, concern evident in his pale blue eyes. "Cat, I wish you'd tell me what you're about."

Cat took his refined hands in hers and squeezed them reassuringly. "Trust me, you're better off not getting any more involved."

"Aye, I want no part of treason." He stared down at her sternly. "Neither should you. Those be dangerous words in that letter. The original author is bound to come looking for it."

"That's what I'm counting on." Cat took a step back, drawing her hands free. Aye, she wanted Heyward desperate to regain the letter, for it was her only chance at blackmail.

"Cat, all of us have been worried these past few weeks since the fire. We thought you might be dead. And though I discover you're not, I fear you soon could be." He paused, as if considering something, then added softly, "Two of Griffin's men were here looking for you the day before last."

Cat froze. She'd hardly dared to consider the possibility and refused to even discuss it with Nicholas. "He's alive?"

"Although he's yet to make an appearance, that's what I suspect. Who else could marshal that lawless rabble into line?"

Cat cursed softly. Despite Jasper's warning, she'd counted on the fact that the uprightman had been too badly burned to survive. If Griffin was indeed roaming the streets, stalking her, there'd be no safe place to hide in all of Southwark.

"Mayhap Griffin would let you be if you went south to join Jug and her sister."

"I doubt it."

The forger nodded in reluctant agreement.

"Well, no one's seen him yet. Let's just pray the rogue is really dead, eh?" In her heart, however, she knew that wasn't true. She'd have to return to Dacre House. There was still a chance her absence hadn't been discovered yet.

"Isn't there any way I could convince you to abandon this folly?"

For a moment, Cat thought he was referring to facing Nicholas, then she realized he meant the letter. "No, I'm afraid not. I must go through with my plans."

She declined to tell him that a much more determined soul than he had already tried to stop her and failed. And, thinking of her all-too-determined captor, Cat realized she'd best be leaving. "I need to be going. Here," she said, handing him a small pouch of coin. "The loose coins are for your services, great *bene faker of gybes*. There's another pouch within for Jug."

Egan tried to hand the purse back. "Nay, Cat. I don't want your coin. Only leave what's meant for Jug."

Refusing to take back the money, Cat grinned. "Relax. It's not mine." Growing serious again she added, "Besides, we both know that you've put yourself in danger by helping me even this much. Let me at least pay you."

Egan nodded mutely. He rolled up and tied the forged letter, and handed it to her. "Just take care of yourself, all right, bantling?"

Cat tucked the letter safely within her bodice. "I promise." Ignoring the scholar's rigid posture, Cat kissed him lightly on the cheek. She made her way to the door, and drew the voluminous hood of her cloak about her face. Opening the door to leave, she turned to look at him once more. "Thank you again, Egan."

He shrugged, a sheepish smile on his face. "How could I refuse you anything?"

"And where the hell have you been?" The composure Nicholas had meant to keep cracked with his very first words.

Cat, ruddy-faced from being out of doors, turned to where he lurked in the shadows of the hall leading off from the kitchen. Nicholas's eyes narrowed as he realized the treacherous bitch had even gone so far as to help herself to the cloak he'd had made for her before flouting his trust. The way she stared at him, her green eyes wide and bright and her mouth forming an "O" of surprise, told him she was afraid. But it meant nothing to him.

Both of his hands were clenched in white-knuckled fists. Maris had discovered her missing more than two hours ago. He'd been waiting for her return ever since, all the while fretting over how much damage she might be able to do or if she'd return at all. Forget the gallows. He'd rather throttle her on the spot. "Damn it, woman, tell me where you've been!"

Her gaze fluttered to his clenched hands, then back to his face. Slowly she undid the fastenings of the cloak and removed it from her shoulders. She offered it to him with a slightly unsteady hand but drew it back when she realized he didn't mean to take it. "I went to visit a friend. He was worried I might have died in the fire."

She met his stare evenly enough, but it didn't make her any less a liar. Nicholas was learning all too well how good an actor she could be when it suited her. "You would have me believe that?"

"It's the truth."

"Certainly not the whole of it."

When she stood before him silently, refusing to say more, he could taste the bitter gall rising in his mouth. "How dare you stand there so prim and self-righteous! I know you've done something to advance your scheme against Heyward!"

Her full lips pressed into a thin line. "I told you I'd do as much yesterday. You were duly warned."

"As were you! Surely you haven't forgotten a little matter of the gallows?" He advanced, intent on hauling her to Tyburn that very moment.

"Very well then," Cat said, her eyes flashing a challenge. "Take me there."

His belly tightened into an impossible knot. "So help me, Cat. I mean it."

"As do I." Her chin lifted defiantly. "Go ahead and take me to the gallows, Nicholas, because that's what it's going to take to stop me!"

A wave of absolute, blinding rage washed over Nicholas. Slowly, the source of his frustration came back into focus. She tossed back her unruly, sable mane and placed her fists on her hips.

"Do it, Misrule!" she challenged.

With an inarticulate roar, Nicholas reached out and grabbed a heavy handful of the back of Cat's dress. The cloak flew from her hands and drifted to the floor. Starting toward the side door, he dragged

her behind him. She tripped and staggered to keep up
with him. He didn't glance back; he couldn't allow
this single woman to jeopardize England's fate. As he
dragged her down the steps and into the barren yard,
Cat slipped and fell in the mud.

Nicholas noted that she bit her lip deeply and felt a
sudden, uncontrollable pang of regret. He forced
himself to look away before he had second thoughts.

He was grateful to see Jonah hobbling out of the
carriage house. At least, he was until the elderly servant froze to stare at him open-mouthed as if he'd
never before seen such heinous behavior.

"Don't just stand there, man," Nicholas said. "Go
tell them to prepare my coach!"

Stiff-backed, Jonah turned and went for the coach.

Cat lay in a tangle at Nicholas's feet, a fist held to
her mouth, eyes bright with unshed tears. Only once
in all his life had he seen that look before. 'Twas on
the face of a woman who thought she was about to
die.

God's mercy, what was he doing?

Nicholas felt as if he'd been doused with a bucket
of ice water. With sudden clarity, he knew he
couldn't turn her over to Tyburn. Trembling, he
stared down at Cat's crumpled figure. He'd bluffed
and she'd called him on it. Nicholas realized he'd
never felt more wretched in his life. "You win, thief,"
he admitted in a raw-voiced whisper. "I won't be the
cause of your death."

In sinking anguish, he stumbled back into the
house. Spotting a three-legged stool and fearing his
strength would flee him completely, he collapsed
upon it and buried his face in his battle-scarred
hands. 'Sblood, Nicholas wondered, what was he to

do now? He couldn't kill her and she wasn't about to stop pursuing Heyward. An ache of foreboding throbbed through his head.

He had no idea how long he sat there before he heard the whisper of her skirts. Slowly, he lifted his head, bracing himself against the torment of her presence.

She wandered restlessly around the kitchen, glancing at him from time to time. Finally, she cleared her throat. "I suppose I once again owe you my life."

"Not that it will do me any good," he muttered.

"What would you have me do?" She threw the words at him like daggers.

"Stop pursuing Heyward," he said raggedly. "You're going to scare Essex away before I can trap him. Can't you understand that?"

"No, Nicholas, I don't understand!" She advanced toward him. "You want me to forget my family because of a possible confrontation with Spain?" She pointed a rigid finger inches from his face. "I'd hate to destroy your idealistic notions of world order, but we are at war with them!"

"Curse you, woman! You know it's not the same thing!"

"Isn't it?"

He would have to tell her.

The words came out in a cracked whisper. "In 1585, I was young and very stupid," he began. "I thought that Elizabeth's campaign in the Low Countries was my chance to make a name for myself, to build my own wealth. My older brother, Christopher, was still alive then. The barony would be his."

Cat threw her hands up in exasperation. "What

does any of that have to do with myself and Heyward?"

"Would you just shut up and listen?" he roared.

She opened her mouth as if to speak but then shut it again. She crossed her arms in front of her chest and leaned against the shelves in the corner. "Very well."

"I knew the captains made money, but I never thought about how. You wouldn't have believed the corruption. The captains bled their companies dry and the clerks looked the other way. For a price, of course."

Her brows creased in a confused frown. "How could they do that?"

"Men died, Cat. The marsh fevers saw to that. Even more deserted. Most of the companies were down to half-strength. Instead of hiring new men and rebuilding their forces, the captains pocketed the dead men's wages. No one seemed concerned that when they fought it would be at half-strength."

He fought back an involuntary shudder. "God, those poor wretches," he continued, his voice hoarse. "And that wasn't even the worst of it. The captains robbed from the living—their wages, their food, their clothes. The captains sold it off to the locals. It was under market value, but they still made a profit. Everyone was crooked. Even me by the end."

Her words came in a whisper. "No, I can't believe that of you."

Nicholas forced himself to meet her gaze. "I needed money, Cat. There was no point in returning to London without it."

"And this is why there can be no other war? Because of what it can do to a man's character?"

"Nay, that is only the beginning." Gritting his teeth, he tried to gather his resolve. The only person he'd ever told of that day was Jasper, and he'd been very drunk at the time. Nicholas knew, however, he'd have to tell Cat. There was no other way. "I served under the earl of Essex. He was General of the Horse." His voice took on a peculiar note. "It was supposed to be only an honorary title, but he managed to do enough damage with it.

"We were ordered to besiege the town of Zutphen. 'Twas an impossible task. The town had survived a ten-month siege two years earlier, but we were ordered to do it, nonetheless." His expression became pinched and closed off. "Word came that the Duke of Parma was sending a convoy of extra supplies to help Zutphen withstand the siege. Essex decided to intercept it. He took only three hundred horse and one hundred foot soldiers. My company was among them. We found the convoy by the River Yssel. The four hundred of us faced an army of forty-five hundred strong. And do you know what the earl ordered us to do?"

From the way Nicholas's voice broke, the look of torment in his eyes, Cat knew even before he said it, but she shook her head mutely.

"The bloody whoreson told us to attack. Essex led the sally. He was truly without fear and expected everyone else to be just the same. But how could we not be afraid?" His voice broke. "Our men, my men, were dying all around him and still he kept charging."

An inward battle of emotions played itself upon Nicholas's face as he struggled to make himself continue.

"And?" she prompted softly.

His face was pale and bleak. "The Spaniards pushed Essex almost all the way back to the town gates. He could do nothing when a garrison of two thousand came out and escorted the convoy safely inside."

Pushed Essex. There was something odd in the way he'd phrased it, as if he were no longer there. She played her hunch. "Where were you?"

He lifted his head to meet her eyes. She could see the torment behind his gray gaze as he spoke. "A musket ball had hit Excelsior, my horse. I was trapped beneath his body, my leg shattered," he choked. "'Twas almost a day before anyone came for me."

There was a dry ache in the back of Cat's throat. "It must have been horrible for you."

"That's not it!" He leaned forward and grabbed her fiercely by the shoulders. "Don't you get it, Cat? Essex survived that attack! A man with any sense might learn something from the past, but not Essex."

He let go of her, but his voice remained cold and unforgiving. "'Tis his party that now urges England to go to war again with Spain, and the earl who plans to be in command. Jesus, do you have any idea what that would be like?" Nicholas's eyes burned with a mad intensity. "He's Elizabeth's favorite, Cat. He just might be able to get her consent. But, if I can show the queen proof of what treachery he's capable of, mayhap I can stop him!"

"You are but one man. What can you hope to do?"

"I have to at least try!"

"Yes, I understand." How could she not? Nicholas's situation was so much like her own. The odds were overwhelmingly against them both, but they still had an obligation to try. To do otherwise, to forget the horror of the past, would be to go mad.

When Nicholas drew her into his arms in a fierce hug, she didn't resist. Rather, she buried her head into his broad chest, her heart aching for the man that held her. She'd been right. He had known pain as great as hers.

Drawing back slightly to see him better, she reached up with her healed hand to touch his forehead. Slowly, gently, she smoothed the worried lines along his brow. Her eyes welled with tears, and, for once, she didn't fight them. She might not be able to cry for herself, but she could for him.

Nicholas watched the drops wend their way down her cheeks. Cat could feel a shaking start from deep within him. With a strangled sob, he cradled her head in his powerful hands and brushed away a tear with his thumb. He leaned forward and brought his lips to the tender, salty skin.

His kiss began as a whisper, so surprisingly gentle it seemed he meant nothing more than to comfort. Cat drank in his sweetness.

Abruptly, he raised his mouth from hers and gazed into her eyes. Trembling, Cat ran her tongue across her lips. "Sweet Mary," she panted, "why do you—"

Her half-voiced protest changed into a whimper when Nicholas brought his lips to the hollow under her jaw, then proceeded down her neck with slow, shivery kisses. Discovering the other hollow just above her collarbone, he circled it lazily with his tongue. Just when Cat thought she could stand no more, his mouth recaptured hers.

The kitchen seemed to reel oddly about them. His kisses became more urgent, more demanding. As his

tongue began to explore the recesses of her mouth,
she moaned. Her heart thumped erratically, struggling like a wild thing to break free from the confines
of her chest.

Losing herself, Cat kissed back with reckless abandon. Recognizing her surrender, Nicholas groaned.
Cat felt the sound vibrate in her own throat. Gently,
he guided her back against the wall.

'Twas her turn to gasp in sweet agony when he
lowered his mouth to where her breasts strained
against the confining fabric of her bodice. Spanning
her waist with his hands, Nicholas used his tongue to
lave her through the embroidered cloth. She shuddered as her nipples grew swollen and hard.

Murmuring something under his breath, he
reached out to touch her. His fingertip skimmed over
the neckline of her bodice. Cat froze, suddenly
remembering the forged letter she'd tucked there for
safety. She could not let him discover it! What if he
took it from her? With a gasp, she tore free from his
embrace.

"What the . . . ?" Nicholas stared at her, befud-
dled, his handsome face ruddy with passion.

Thunderous rage quickly consumed his features.
Looking toward the ceiling, Nicholas shook his head.
"God, what a fool I've been." He looked back to her,
his eyes narrowing. "Couldn't go through with it, eh?
Tell me, Cat," he said, cradling her jaw in his hand.
"Why did you enter this little charade?"

Cat shivered at the barely restrained menace in his
voice. Yet, that didn't stop her from being indignant.
"Charade?" she demanded. "What the hell do you
think I'm about?"

He said nothing. His expression remained cold and

unrelenting. Slowly it dawned on her that he thought she'd meant to prostitute herself in hopes of some sort of gain. "How dare you!" she raged. "If you think I'd—"

"Save it, dearling, for someone who'll believe your pretty lies. Believe me, if I want a whore I know where to find one!" He snatched his hand away and stalked from the room.

Cat remained where she stood, shaking with fury. Damn him! If Nicholas wanted so badly to believe the worst of her then let him! 'Twould be that much easier for them to remain enemies. However, when she heard the front door slam shut, she flinched. And why, if she cared so little what he thought, did she suddenly feel the overwhelming urge to cry?

12

For someone seeking moral redemption, Nicholas doubted if the Lady Rose, the finest—not to mention the most costly—brothel in Paris Garden, was probably where he should be. But after Catrienne's treachery he no longer cared.

The Lady Rose had superior wine, the most beguiling women, and the highest stake games with which to forget Cat and the burning need she'd set aflame. Unfortunately he hadn't found anyone who could compare with the sable-haired thief who'd stolen his heart.

"Christ, man, you'd think Old Bess had died for all your solemn countenance," Savage chided from across the dining room table. His trained voice was raised just enough to be heard over the laughter of the other patrons, the creak of the stairs, and the rattling of dice in the adjoining room.

"Methinks some pretty thing has made Lord Dacre forget the finer pleasures of a man's existence,"

Augustine purred seductively while she adjusted her position on Savage's lap. It was clear from the woman's exquisitely arched brow that she considered herself one of those pleasures. It was equally clear that she was still miffed at the cool greeting she'd been receiving since Nicholas's return last spring. As gorgeous as any of the paintings of the world's most famous bawds mounted on the walls, Augustine had little personal experience with rejection.

"Indeed, have you learned so much since I've been gone, sweet Gus?" Nicholas quipped irritably. Curse it all, where was Sophie? he wondered. Mayhap he could still salvage something from this day. As the proprietress of the Lady Rose, Sophie had the secrets of the Court, of the queen and her many servants, and of the bedchambers across London. All were within her gentle grasp. If anyone could learn news of Essex's treachery it would be her.

"In faith," Augustine continued caustically. "I think the dread Misrule has lost his heart."

The courtesan Violet, seated at Nicholas's side, giggled. Grimacing, he was forced to fend off her not-so-subtle caresses underneath the table. Hell, Sophie'd probably charge him for it if it went on much longer.

"What Lord Dacre has lost is his sense of humor," Savage said. He gently stroked Augustine's golden hair, his admiration eloquent in the gesture.

Augustine leaned back against him, lulled into complacency. Violet was also beginning to edge her slender form toward the actor. Savage had a true gift for women. They always flocked first to Nicholas, wanting to sample the legend of Misrule, but were quickly lured away by his friend's gilded tongue and

generous attention. *Misrule*. 'Twas the despised nickname of a man who no longer existed. Women grew
quickly bored by the shadow.

"Here, love," Savage said with a wicked gleam in
his eye, reaching for the bottle on the table. "Offer
our friend some of this fine malmsey wine, and mayhap we can win his favor again."

Augustine held out the bottle as a peace offering.
Catching a whiff of the sickly-sweet alcohol, Nicholas
was unable to stop himself from flinching. He drew
rigidly back in his chair. Savage grinned at Nicholas's
unease, but his smile disappeared the minute
Augustine glanced at him in confusion. Violet, observing Nicholas's dismay, stifled a laugh. A sly one she.

"Aye, 'tis time to declare peace, friend," Nicholas
said while he wrestled with his impulse to gag. Never
would he be able to drink that vile concoction again,
which Savage well knew. The mere sight of the stuff
brought the bitter aftertaste of foxglove to his tongue.
His intended wife had come far too close to killing
him in Flanders.

"Aye, cry your apologies, Nicholas. There'll be no
fighting here," Sophie said in her throaty voice, glid-
ing toward their table. Wearing a French gown of rus-
set satin, she cut an elegant figure.

"About time, Sophie." Nicholas stood and kissed
the woman's delicate hand.

"We wondered when you might delight us with
your presence, mistress," Savage said. He smoothly
moved Augustine aside and rose to his feet.

"When I was convinced you'd spent enough coin,
you charming rake," Sophie said, her blue eyes
sparkling. "The two of you have not visited as oft'n as
I'd have you alate."

Taking in Nicholas's mood in a single sweeping glance, she turned to her two women. "Ladies, I believe Lord de Vere is in need of some company. I wouldst have a moment alone with my dear friends."

As soon as Augustine and Violet drifted from the room, Sophie gestured for Nicholas and Savage to have a seat and selected the chair between them for herself. She studied them silently for a minute, irritably pushing back a blonde wisp of hair that had drifted forward.

Sophie's hair was still only chin length. Once again, Nicholas wished he'd been able to buy her freedom sooner from Bridewell. It would be a few years before it totally recovered from having been shaved. Even worse, her time in prison had left her with scars she couldn't completely disguise. Yet, Nicholas thought, Sophie was one of those rare women whose beauty could not be demolished by the cruelty she'd endured. Then he remembered another, darker beauty, one that tempted him far more than the proprietress ever had, and scowled.

Sophie reached for the bottle on the table and examined it. "Malmsey? I warrant you two might actually live to see the end of the decade if you continue to curtail your excesses so strenuously," she jested lightly. "Have you two actually grown tired of the rogue's life?"

She was right, Nicholas thought. He and Savage had met the night of the duel that had cost the actor his eye. Nicholas had found him in the alley and brought him to Guerau for treatment. His and Savage's friendship had been founded on a mutual search for oblivion, a destructive escape from love gone wrong. But slowly, something in the nature of their amusements had changed. Now they both sought a good reason to live.

"Resting, Sophia. Merely regaining our strength for all those fortunate women we've yet to meet," Savage replied. He took back the bottle from her. Snagging Nicholas's untouched glass with a finger, he poured some wine for Sophie and some more for himself.

"In faith, merely waiting for something worthy of our attention," Nicholas added. "I'd hoped you might have found something of merit. Mayhap in the way of news?"

Sophie took a sip of the wine, then leaned back in her chair. She traced the edge of her glass with a fingertip and studied Nicholas uncertainly. "'Haps I've found something that would interest you, Nick. But I doubt if 'tis what you'd hoped for."

"I like very little of what you tell me, Sophie," Nicholas said wearily. "But 'tis all useful."

"Heyward's mistress carries his child."

Savage whistled. "So it truly is Lady Amye who's been barren?"

"Aye," Sophie answered. "I wouldn't put much value on Lady Amye's life. My woman Lilith comes from good blood. Heyward might be inclined to try to make the babe his heir. There have always been questions about his first wife's convenient tumble down the stairs."

"'Haps you two should have given a little more thought to the woman you chose to spy on Heyward," Savage said. "This Lilith may put your interests aside in favor of her own ambitions. God help Amye if she does." For the first time that evening, he sounded serious.

"Amye made her choice. Let her live with the repercussions," Nicholas said, Savage's words weighing heavily on his heart. He was partially to blame for her misery. Christ, would he be to blame for her death? Not that one more sin would truly tip the balance in his life, so far had the scale already tilted, but it pained him just the same.

After his rash words, all three brooded in silence, allowing the laughter and conversation of the other patrons to enfold them.

"What does Lilith say of Heyward's dealings?" Nicholas asked, breaking the silence. "Is it truly Essex he's playing the messenger for?"

"She hasn't been able to find out, Nick," Sophie said. "Heyward is a shrewd one. No man is a hypocrite in his pleasures, but Heyward makes certain to keep his entertainments separate from the rest of his life. It was hard enough to snare him, let alone to find out anything useful."

"Damn it, Sophie!" Nicholas pounded the table with his fist.

Sophie observed Nicholas silently, her expression neutral. Savage merely smiled ruefully, all too accustomed to his friend's sudden temper.

Realizing his outburst had drawn attention from the closer table, Nicholas forced himself to soften his voice. "All that woman's been able to tell us is that Heyward's gone to Essex House often alate. Hell, we already knew he had the earl's patronage!"

"I know that, Nick," Sophie said softly. "Certainly your other sources must have something—"

"Nothing! Absolutely nothing I can use."

"Something will turn up," Sophie countered. "It always has for you."

Nicholas's hand, without thought, tightened in hers. "The one thing I don't have, Sophie, is time. The earl's convoy is already at Philip's court."

Sophie squeezed his hand in return. Her clear blue gaze held his, unwavering. He suspected she was trying to convey her faith in him. But optimism belonged to days long past. All Nicholas felt was old, tired, and beaten.

The conversation about them faded abruptly when a young Italian dressed in rich velvets made his way through the room with a purposeful stride. "*Signore* D'Avenant?"

"Aye?" Nicholas asked, looking up. There was murder in the young Italian's eyes.

"I," said the dark-haired youth, puffing out his chest, "am Don Antonio Carranza." The *r*'s rolled grandly from his tongue. "And I have come on behalf of a noblewoman's honor."

Savage groaned. "Christ, not again!" he said, voicing Nicholas's own thoughts.

Nicholas pushed back his chair. "And what woman would that be?" he asked, sounding callous even to himself. Surreptitiously, he began flexing his bad leg.

"My sister, *Signorína* Margarite DeAnna Carranza."

There was a long moment's pause while Nicholas searched back through his memories until he found the image of a small, willing brunette with a shocking amount of knowledge for her tender years. "Took her long enough to complain," he muttered under his breath.

The boy swore angrily and drew his blade. "I call you out, *signore*!"

"Take it outside, Nick," Sophie ordered, standing up. "There will be no dueling in here."

"Aye, Sophie," Nicholas conceded wearily. "One immoral activity in an establishment is quite enough." He rose to his feet, his right leg aching from the sudden movement. Christ, the youth only came to his shoulders.

"Have you a second, *signore*?" The color began to flee his face. Perhaps he'd just observed the difference in their heights and begun questioning the wisdom of evoking Misrule's ire.

"As always," Savage replied. He, too, rose to his feet, although a little more unsteadily. Before following the young man who had already turned toward the doorway, Savage grabbed the wine bottle and his feather-plumed hat. He bowed toward their hostess with a dramatic flourish. "As much pleasure as ever, Sophia."

Sophie merely tapped her foot and frowned toward the man she obviously blamed as the source of trouble. "Perhaps you haven't changed your ways after all, Nicholas."

Nicholas managed a pained smile. "Will anyone let me?"

Cat tossed in her bed and punched the pillow beside her until feathers flew into the air. Ruffin take it! She couldn't sleep. The strange, fluttery feeling had yet to leave her stomach, and her thoughts kept drifting back to the dizzying embrace in the kitchen.

What was wrong with her? After kissing Nicholas that first time in the coach, she'd discovered how dangerous it could be to capitulate to his dark attraction. Yet today she'd succumbed once again, allowing herself to be consumed by pure, sweet desire. If it hadn't been for Nicholas's almost discovering the letter, she had no idea how far she would have let it go.

There had been an undeniable energy between them since their first meeting. Feminine instinct had told her that sooner or later he'd make another advance. She'd been prepared to ward it off. But she'd never thought she'd have to worry about her own response, that she might welcome his touch and prove to be her own worst enemy.

She closed her eyes and tried to collect her scattered thoughts. The restless, achy feeling that possessed her body made it impossible.

Nicholas had fought so many times in the alley behind the Lady Rose that it was often the setting of his nightmares. The alley was narrow, dark, and, on this rainy night, dangerously slippery. It reeked of the trash pile kept behind the house for the dung masters. From the open window, he could hear the conversation and laughter of Sophie's patrons as the night's entertainments continued on without him.

He studied the grim-faced boy who conferred in quiet Italian with his swarthy companion. He doubted the boy was even twenty-five, the legal age for dueling. That fact, more than his sister's dishonor, was probably why Carranza had pushed him into a *duel alla machia*, a hot-blooded fight with no rules or restrictions.

Coming to the Lady Rose had been a rash stunt, Nicholas reflected sourly. It made him too easy for fools to locate him. He unfastened his long cloak, removed the amulet he wore, and handed both items to Savage. The former item might trip him up on the slippery cobblestones, the contents of the second might break if he were to fall.

"Don't do anything noble, Nick," Savage said softly. "This isn't Paris."

Savage's words evoked the old memory and made Nicholas wince. 'Twas more than two years now, he realized, feeling timeworn. He had been so drunk that night that he hadn't even realized the boy who challenged him was only twelve years old. Not until the child lay dead in the muddy alley. He still couldn't recall what they had fought over.

"No more," Nicholas replied grimly. He tugged on his left leather glove. "I swore there'd be no more killing."

Savage tossed his empty bottle against the wall, winning the momentary attention of the Italians and the scurrying of the rats hiding beneath garbage. "This hothead isn't worth your life."

Nicholas grimaced and flexed his hand. "My life won't be worth a farthing if I live and he doesn't. Not once Old Bess gets through with me. That boy's the Imperial Ambassador's nephew."

Savage groaned. "How do you manage it?"

"It seems to be a talent of mine," Nicholas answered wryly. He took out the rapier he used for his right hand and did a few practice thrusts to warm up his wrist.

Carranza looked at him and frowned. "Do you think me not good enough for your good hand, *signore*?"

No, actually Nicholas didn't. He didn't want the boy confused by fighting a mirror image of what he was used to. "Isn't it my right as *reo* to choose the weapons?"

"Si, ma—"

"Which, if you want to be technical," Nicholas interrupted, "I'm not even yet. As you obviously haven't noticed, I never denied your claim of sullying your sister's honor."

The boy's face reddened and his grasp tightened on the hilt of his rapier. "But you are Lord Dacre. As a gentleman you must defend your honor."

"Ah yes, my precious honor," Nicholas said grimly, hating himself for having changed enough to care about such a thing. It left him a walking target for any hot-blooded member of Court.

"Do you not intend to fight, *signore*?" the boy asked indignantly.

"Aye," Nicholas sighed, "I'll fight. Not that my second here is doing a good job here of protecting my rights, eh, *padrino*?"

"Hell, Nick, what do you want me to do? Fight that behemoth over there?" Savage replied, keeping his tone light. They shared the unspoken belief that as long as they could look at a situation humorously nothing could get the best of them.

Still, Savage's assessment of Carranza's *padrino* was accurate. Nicholas smiled. "Keep an eye on him, will you? I don't like all this talk," he added softly.

Savage gave a subtle nod of his head.

"Shall we get this over with, *signores*?" Nicholas asked much louder.

Carranza conferred with his friend for a moment more, then reached for the amulet around his neck and kissed it. Nicholas would wager his best blade that the pouch probably contained some fool concoction like wormwood and St.-John's-wort, meant to give the boy magic powers in the fight.

Finally the boy stepped forward. "So it will be rapiers and poniards?" He frowned again at the blade in Nicholas's right hand.

"Aye."

Carranza drew his rapier and dagger, his face becoming a grim mask. Nicholas met him at point with his own blade. He flexed the muscles in his bad leg, hoping to dispel some of the ache from the cold.

Then they began to circle.

Cat had just finally drifted off to sleep when it sounded as if an army were bursting into her chambers.

First came the physician Guerau speaking a frenzied stream of Spanish. Jasper, cursing and grunting, half-guided and half-dragged Nicholas's stooped form into the room. Maris and Jonah followed, armed with rushlights.

Cat squinted into the sudden light. The sense of foreboding she'd been fighting ever since Nicholas had stormed away returned full force.

"Here, take this." Maris handed Jonah her light. "He'll be needin' some water and clean cloths." Without another word, she hurried from the room.

Nicholas's physician, too impassioned to issue his directions in English, tore wildly through the chest against the wall. Jasper, however, seemed to discern the general idea of the Spaniard's instructions and lowered his friend onto the other side of the bed where Cat sat in confusion.

Pale-faced, Nicholas slumped against the ornate headboard. Wearily, he turned his gray gaze to meet Cat's. "I'm reclaiming my bed, dearling. Get out."

Despite his apparent weakness, his words came out sharp and fierce.

Cat cut short her retort when she noticed the dark stain of blood on the right side of his doublet and shirt. "Sweet Mary, what happened?"

Nicholas merely closed his eyes. He'd either chosen to ignore her or was too weak to speak.

Jasper answered for him. "One of the other patrons at the Lady Rose didn't take too kindly to his presence."

The Lady Rose. The most renown brothel south of the Thames! Nicholas's angry words came back to haunt Cat. *"Believe me, if I want a whore I know where to find one!"*

She'd known Sophie and her ladies for several years, even counted them as friends, but now a sudden spark of anger flared bright and hot within her. Nicholas had spurned her to go to the Lady Rose? Served the whoreson right to end up in a duel, undoubtedly, she thought with a snort, over the favors of some pretty skirt. Still, despite the sudden disconcerting sense of jealously, something else nagged at her. Who would be skilled enough to land a blow against Misrule? "Who did he fight?"

"A young Italian." Seeing the question in her eyes, Jasper added, "The boy still lives, thanks to Nick. He could have killed him, but he pulled back. That's how he—"

Nicholas's eyes flew open. "Savage, say no more!"

Jasper frowned at the order but pressed his lips shut.

Guerau, arms laden with strange paraphernalia, hurried to the bed. Dropping the supplies on the coverlet, he made as if to unbutton Nicholas's doublet but was quickly swatted back.

"I can manage my own clothes, man," the patient snarled.

Cat watched uneasily as Nicholas fumbled at the buttons with an unsteady hand. It took him far longer than it would have the physician. All the while, the bloodstain continued to spread. Finally, the blood-soaked jacket slid from his shoulders, followed quickly by his shirt, revealing sinewy arms, chest, and muscle-knotted stomach. And an ugly-looking gash across his ribs.

At the sound of her gasp, Nicholas's back muscles stiffened. "Did you forget what my profession is, dearling?" he ground out through clenched teeth.

Aye, Cat thought. He had been so gentle the last few weeks that she'd ignored the fact that he was a duelist. Even if he were lured into a fight, she hadn't really believed he could be hurt. But the bloody gash was painful evidence that the dread Misrule was as fallible and mortal as any man.

A sick feeling curdled in her stomach. In a fit of temper, she'd let him leave the house in a rage. Was she to blame? *Ruffin, what if he'd been killed?*

A gamut of complex emotions massed and raged inside her. Disconcerted, Cat shook her head. Oh God, she wasn't just attracted to him. She cared what happened to him.

Nay, she couldn't think of such things! People died. Things were ever changing. The only thing that remained constant, the only thing she could cling to, was her dream for revenge. But, she realized with sickening shock, she couldn't help herself. She did care what happened to him. Somehow, the impassable defenses she'd built around her heart had been breached by this dangerous, troubled man.

Without thought, Cat reached out and traced lightly with her fingertip across one of his broad, sweaty shoulders.

Nicholas jumped at her touch. "Christ, didn't I say I wanted you gone? Savage, get her out now!"

"No, I want to know what happened! I-I want to make sure he's going to be all right."

Nicholas's raised eyebrow spoke elegantly of his disdain. "Dearling, do I look all right?"

"No, you don't. That's what worries me." Cat's gaze slid to the needle and thread Guerau was preparing. She implored the Spaniard with her eyes to intervene on her behalf. "Please, what can I do to help?"

The physician squinted at her, then smiled kindly. "Take one of the lights from Jonah, *señorita*, and bring it closer to the bed."

Cat got up from the bed and did as she was ordered.

"Don't you think you've done quite enough for one day?"

"Curse it, Nicholas, I'm trying to help!"

"I'd rather have a scorpion in my bed." Gritting his teeth, he rose unsteadily. "'Sblood, if no one else will listen, I'll make you leave the room myself!" Clutching his side, Nicholas staggered toward her looking as if he meant to throttle her on the spot.

When the physician let loose with another torrent of Spanish, Cat began to realize the seriousness of the situation. "Are you mad? Get back in bed 'fore you bleed to death, you fool!"

Jasper, along with the physician, tried to get him to do just that but were sadly unsuccessful. Cat was forced to retreat or be trampled by the three struggling men slowly making their way toward her.

"*Ave Maria*," Guerau muttered, hanging on to his patient's shoulders. "How much has he had to drink?"

"Not enough to warrant this." Jasper's boots scrabbled across the wooden floor as he tried to turn his friend toward the bed.

Nicholas seemed oblivious to the men's efforts. Rather, he continued forward, his lean face twisted in anger, his gray eyes blazing death at Cat. "Get the hell out of here!"

Jasper flashed her a desperate look from over his shoulder. "Do as he says, Cat! There'll be no peace until you're out of sight. You're only hurting him by staying."

With a sinking feeling, Cat knew Jasper was right. Handing the actor her light, she turned and headed for the doorway where Maris hovered with a cistern of water and an armful of cloth.

"Don't be worryin', mistress. The boy has his fits of temper, he does. He'll be over it soon enough."

Cat nodded mutely as she passed into the hall. If only 'twould be that easy.

13

He'd allowed them only a single meager fire in the hearth since he'd claimed the half-burned alehouse as his lair. In the midnight confines of the cramped room, the burning timber provided little warmth and even less light. Griffin's wary minions huddled close to one another in search of protection. Their shadows slunk like wraiths against the sooty walls as he watched them from his throne.

Within his cowled hood, Griffin permitted himself a brief, feral smile. Idly, he stroked the greasy mane of the girl crouched at his feet. She fought to draw away but was jerked back by the chain around her ankle. Aye, he'd reminded them who was the master of Southwark, and they were once again properly submissive.

At any rate, he thought with a sudden frown, all but a half-score of his former followers. And they would soon suffer for their disloyalty. But first must come Cat.

Griffin motioned for Teddar, his right-hand man, to cast the prisoner, frightened and bound, into the vermin-ridden rushes before him.

"So good of you to come, Egan."

A trickle of blood ran down the forger's chin. In his expression was the repulsion Griffin's followers tried so hard to disguise.

The black flesh and half-scabbed wounds only grew worse by the day. Where once he'd been handsome, now he was a monster. Where once he'd been respected and feared, now he was watched like a maddened beast that would be put down at the first sign of weakness. And it was all the whore's fault.

An icy fury writhed and curled in his belly. Griffin permitted the menace he felt to infect his words. "Where's the girl, *faker of loges?*"

"Cat?" the forger asked hoarsely, his face stark with fear.

"Aye," Griffin snapped, "the *wapping mort.*" He leaned forward in his chair.

"No one's seen Cat since the fire."

With a growl, Griffin's man, Teddar, ground his boot into the curve of the prisoner's neck, eliciting a groan. Crouching low, the hunchbacked man hissed in Egan's ear, *"Cut bene whids, cove!* Word on the street is the traffic paid you a call."

"I swear to you," the forger gasped. "I haven't seen her!"

"With or without you, I'll track 'er down," Griffin said. "Tell me where she hides and at least you'll have yer life."

With a shudder, Egan dropped his head into the rushes. "Nay," Egan muttered. "I suspect you mean to kill me either way."

"There be more than one way to die."

The forger gave a choked laugh. "I can't tell you what I don't know."

Griffin glanced sharply at Teddar. "Take off a few of his fingers. 'Haps it will refresh his memory."

The hunchbacked man grunted and, placing a foot firmly on the captive's back, cut away the wrist bindings.

"No!" Egan panted in terror, struggling and flailing. "God, no!"

Griffin nodded for Bodel and Webb, two of his more bloodthirsty men, to hold the forger's hands. Teddar slammed the forger's head roughly to the ground. The other two men splayed the captive's arms out to the side.

Realizing he was pinned, a strangled whimper came from the forger's throat. "Cat didn't tell me where she stayed. Please, make them stop!"

Griffin shifted restlessly in his chair. He didn't want desperate pleas. He wanted information. "On second thought, Teddar, don't take his fingers—"

"Oh thank you! Thank you, my lord."

Griffin stared his captive down. Interruptions were a sign of disrespect. Returning his attention to Teddar, he said, "Take the whole hand. This grows old."

What little color remaining in Egan's face drained away. Inside Griffin, a brief spark of interest began to kindle. If the man knew anything, now should be the time he'd break.

The forger managed to raise his head from the floor. Rushes stuck to his face as he cried, "I don't know where she is! Please, I beg you—"

Teddar's blade came down and a strangled scream

ended the rest of the forger's protest. The girl at Griffin's feet moaned and then retched loudly.

Slowly, Egan's screams faded back to whimpers as he tried unsuccessfully to gain his feet. He gave up the futile effort and slumped back to the floor. "*Ave Maria,*" he panted, "*gratia plena . . .*"

"Finish him," Griffin snarled.

With a curt nod, Teddar kicked the forger over onto his back and drew his rusty blade. Without a blink, the hunchback used it to run the captive through the stomach.

The room went painfully silent. Enraged, Griffin glared balefully at his disloyal subjects. Slowly, an uneasy cheer struck up. It was enough to placate him. Leaning back in his chair, he drank in the applause that was his due. With a few nervous laughs, his followers lapsed back into silence.

"I want the word on the streets. Griffin searches for a girl named Cat. The man who discovers her hiding spot will be well paid." Smiling at the greedy glitter in their gazes, Griffin added, "Very well."

Teddar nudged the body sprawled in the middle of the floor with his toe. "An' what of him?"

"Pry open Old One-Hand Wirral's cage in Chepemans and put the cove's body there. Corpse or not, I ken he'll tell the whore what I mean to do to her when we meet again."

Cat waited with Jasper in the grandeur of the Great Hall of Greenwich Palace. Never had she felt so dismally out of place as here in the monstrous estate better known as *Placentia*. All around them were foreign ministers, councilors of state, court officials, and a

multitude of finely garbed ladies and gentlemen. All
waited for a chance to glimpse the queen on her way
to prayers.

Cat would gladly have abandoned such an honor if
it wasn't for her overwhelming sense of guilt on
Nicholas's behalf. Two days after his injury, a summons from the queen had arrived at Dacre House
ordering him to appear at Court. Even a lowly thief
like Cat knew that Elizabeth was notoriously intoler-
ant of dueling. Since the arrival of the summons, Cat
had spent the better part of the past week worrying
how Nicholas might be punished for the rash actions
to which she had helped drive him.

Although not fully recovered from his injury,
Nicholas had insisted on going alone. When Cat
learned Jasper held enough sway to attend as well,
she'd begged him to take her. Now, she began to
wonder how wise her decision had been. What good
was her support if Nicholas refused to accept it? Pale
and rigid, garbed in a spotted silver satin doublet and
matching hose, he stood several paces away, ignoring
the two of them and the many courtiers who were so
blatantly snubbing him back. He'd tied his dark mane
of hair back, accentuating the dark, brooding lines of
his face.

A sudden rustle of excitement drew her attention
to the other end of the hall where the flame-haired
queen appeared. Exuding raw vitality and power,
Elizabeth, bedecked in white silk, hovered in the
doorway for a moment until all eyes were upon her
and then proceeded up the length of the corridor. She
was followed closely by her ladies of Court, also
dressed in white, and fifty gentlemen pensioners with
gilt battle-axes. Involuntarily, Cat sucked in a breath.

'Twas the very first time she'd seen the monarch up so close.

Elizabeth and her entourage glided toward their adoring throng of courtiers. Turning her back to Cat's side of the hall, the queen gave a regal nod of her red-wigged head. Her subjects along the opposite wall dropped en masse to their knees.

Remarkably, the sixty-one-year-old queen had a figure and waist that could rival that of the most shapely woman. Jewels glinted off her wired head rail. The pearls on her gown were the size of large beans. 'Sbones, Cat thought, she could have paid both Egan and Rafe for their services with one pearl alone!

The queen turned to their side of the hall. When Cat apparently took too long struggling with her far-thingale and skirts in order to kneel, Jasper tugged frantically at her hand. Finally reaching the floor and hoping to go unnoticed, she kept her head bowed.

In the unnaturally quiet hall, the queen's lilting voice switched easily from English, to French, to Italian as she deigned to chat with a few of her ministers and foreign emissaries.

How would this woman receive Nicholas? Her hopes plummeted when Elizabeth spared Nicholas little more than a single, sharp glance. Sweet Mary, Cat thought desperately, the woman could destroy him if she so desired!

That dreadful thought continued to plague her as Jasper coaxed her to rise. She followed on wooden legs as he guided her in the queen's wake to the antechamber that lay beyond the Hall's door.

As was customary, Elizabeth, with great dignity, assumed the ornate chair stationed in the center of

the far wall. She motioned for the first of her petition-
ers to approach.

After the first handful of requests, Cat could hear
nothing over the nervous thrum of her heartbeat in
her ears. Jesu, if she was this nervous, what must
Nicholas be feeling? He stood alone against the far
wall, arms pressed to his side, his expression the careful mask she'd grown to hate.

A sudden rustle of silk drew Cat's attention to her
right where a courtier and his lady stood. Her throat
tightened. 'Twas Heyward and his wife. Her insides
twisted over the casual ease with which the alderman
leaned to murmur something in the woman's ear.
Damn the man. He would not live in such idle comfort for much longer!

Oblivious of her baleful glare, Heyward turned to
speak with a red-haired gentleman to his left. The long-
faced man frowned, seeming annoyed with Heyward's
presumption. Studying the man's fine ginger beard and
mustache and elaborate garb, she began to form a
dreadful suspicion. Could he be Robert Devereux, earl
of Essex? Aye, from the way the queen glanced so
often in his direction, he could easily be her favorite.

What must it be like for Nicholas to stand so close
to his enemies, awaiting his fate? If he was aware of
their presence, he did not show it. Rather, he kept his
attention intently fixed on the queen.

"Now," Elizabeth said. "Where is our Misrule?"

"I am here, your majesty."

As the dread Misrule made his way forward, the
Court drew back amongst itself, shuddering and murmuring words of distaste. It might have been a demon
passing amongst them so loathe were they to be
tainted by his touch.

Yet, as Cat watched Nicholas approach at a measured pace that masked his limp, she noted nothing to earn her disdain. His head was high, his powerful shoulders squared. His gray gaze as he looked at the queen was unblinking. He fully knew the danger of his situation, but he betrayed no outward signs of fear. Dear Nicholas, she mused, you are a fighter to the bitter end.

When the unruly subject finally stood before the throne, the queen leaned forward to peer over her hooked nose like a bird of prey. "Ah, Nicholas, we have been told by our ambassador DeSpes," the queen said, sparing an unfathomable glance toward the Imperial Ambassador, "that you have been giving his good nephew unwarranted trouble alate."

She paused, a pregnant silence adding weight to the charge. Then, with a rustle of silk, she leaned further forward and challenged, "Is this true?"

Nicholas's wide-eyed expression of surprise proved he could feign emotions as easily as he could mask them. He turned to look blankly at Carranza for several seconds. "I have given him trouble? Nay, 'tis not so, my good queen."

An angry hiss of whispers arose among the Imperial Ambassador's retinue, drawing Elizabeth's imperial gaze. She frowned slightly, causing her heavy façade of plaster-colored makeup to crinkle about the brows and forehead. Redirecting her attention to Nicholas, she inquired, "You have been dueling, have you not?"

The Court seemed to hold its collective breath until Nicholas broke the silence with a laugh. "Hardly so! That would be against our law and subject to severe punishment." Nicholas glanced wryly at

Carranza, then to DeSpes. "Why, I'm sure even the Imperial Ambassador will be hasty to assure you 'twas merely an unpleasant exchange of words."

Elizabeth smiled, displaying blackened teeth. "Ah, a mere unpleasant exchange of words, that reassures us greatly."

Carranza started forward. "It was a good deal more than that, *signorína!*"

"What's this?" Elizabeth pierced the young upstart with her gaze, stalling his advance.

DeSpes yanked his nephew back, glancing nervously at the provoked monarch. "What I believe my nephew means to say is that D'Avenant—er, Lord Dacre—is to blame for this disagreement. And, as such, we believe he should be punished for the . . . ah . . . breach in unanimity between our two representative powers."

"You believe?" With dark, hooded eyes, the queen perused the room. "My good ambassador, you have given us reason to wonder if some might require a gentle reminder of who rules England here."

A nervous titter of laughter arose from the Court and quickly died.

DeSpes retreated another step. "Forgive me, your majesty, but there is the matter of a gentlewoman's honor."

"Aye, I suppose there is that." After a moment, she smiled faintly. "Very well. You have asked this Court for a punishment and we shall grant it. Baron, are you ready to hear our sentence?"

After waiting in tense silence, Nicholas cleared his throat and raised his chin almost defiantly. "Aye, your majesty."

Elizabeth straightened in her chair, fully assuming

the mantle of monarch. "Misrule, this is not the first time you've brought trouble to our Court. In faith, 'tis how your nickname arose."

Cat noted the nervous rustle of people around where Laurence Heyward stood. "She speaks of the time Heyward confronted him for his impropriety against his wife," she murmured to herself.

Jasper, apparently having overheard, glanced at Cat sharply. "Lady Amye was not his wife then, and 'twas Nicholas who challenged Heyward."

Nicholas who challenged Heyward? Nay, that made no sense. Before Cat could ask for anything more, Elizabeth's words drew her back to the present dilemma.

"Perhaps, Misrule, 'tis meet you should earn your nickname now." Elizabeth stared down at her wayward subject.

"If that is what you wish, my queen. How would you have me do so?"

"For your slight to a gentlewoman's honor, Nicholas Ashford D'Avenant, Lord Dacre of the North, you will serve as the official Lord of Misrule for our upcoming Christmas season." Seemingly oblivious to the uproar she'd provoked, Elizabeth added, "Perhaps this way, we may benefit from your talent toward mischief. 'Twould be a most pleasant change for our Court."

Nicholas managed a pained grin. "I suppose it would." He bowed, meaning to depart.

Red-faced, DeSpes started forward. "But, your majesty—"

The queen raised a hand. "Enough of this foolishness. I came here for prayer not petty bickering."

The morning's petitions were clearly at an end. As

the musicians struck up the music for the first hymn,
the Court shouted, "Long live Queen Elizabeth!"

Relieved by the queen's merciful judgment, Cat
and Jasper joined in the cheer. However, Nicholas's
thunderous expression as he turned away from the
queen proved that he didn't share the crowd's senti-
ments.

She and Jasper, along with most of the courtiers
who'd appeared out of curiosity, were unable to discreetly escape before the sermon began.

"Relax," Jasper murmured in her ear. "'Twill be little more than a half hour. Elizabeth may be pious, but
she's frugal with her time."

"Did you really mean 'twas Nicholas who challenged Heyward?"

"Aye."

"If that is the truth, then why does the gossip say—"

Jasper's sharp look silenced her. "The truth, my
dear, is determined by the one who wins the duel,"
the actor whispered. "Remember, Cat, he'd just
returned from the war. At full strength, Nicholas
could have easily bested Heyward. As it was, he
barely escaped with his life."

"But what reason would he have to challenge
Heyward?"

Jasper stared at the archbishop, but the intensity of
his expression told Cat he was seeing not the ceremony but something out of the past. "'Haps it was
because he was about to marry the woman Nicholas
had been betrothed to for over a year."

Cat felt her jaw go slack. "Nicholas was engaged to
Lady Amye?"

"Aye, Nicholas was the one wronged, not
Heyward. The scandal drove him all the way to the

continent. In fact, I suspect he'd still be there if there hadn't been an attempt on his life in Flanders."

She could only stare at him. "An attempt on his life?"

Jasper, finally noting her surprise, frowned. "'Sbones! Hasn't Nick told you anything?"

"Apparently," she murmured, "not very much."

Singers joined the music, preventing any further discussion, leaving Cat to her tumultuous thoughts.

Cat found Nicholas in the parlor, a solemn shadow in front of the large window overlooking the front lawn. Before she could lose her nerve she asked the question that had plagued her the whole ride home from Placentia. "Is it true?"

Nicholas turned to look at her, his mouth hardening into a cynical smile. "Probably. But just to make sure, why don't you tell me what you're referring to."

"That you were engaged to Lady Amye."

"Who told you that?"

"Jasper."

Nicholas looked away. "Savage is too enamored with the sound of his own voice."

Her heart contracted painfully inside her chest. Now she understood why he'd been so driven to earn a name and a fortune for himself. 'Twas the only way a second son could hope to marry a marquess's daughter. Then again, how had Heyward, a yeoman's son, managed the honor? "If she was pledged to you, why did she accept Heyward instead?"

"That was the marquess's doing. According to him, I was a cripple without a future, hardly the appropriate match. Unfortunately for the marquess," he said, hunching his shoulders, "Lady Amye was damaged goods. No other peer would touch her after I had."

Cat could only pray he hadn't noted her wince of pain. Oh God, the rumor was true. Nicholas and Amye had been lovers. Were the tales of the alderman's wife's having a miscarriage shortly after their marriage also true? She discovered she didn't have the courage to ask.

"Heyward had a great deal of money from his first wife and a promising future," he said gruffly. "The marquess felt it was the best he could hope for his daughter."

Cat watched as the color left his face, and he closed his eyes. She discovered that focusing on Nicholas's pain lessened some of her own so she forced herself to listen to the heartbreaking truths that had forever changed the course of his life.

"When Amye came to me with the news that she had married Heyward, I went mad. I found that bastard, Heyward, at Court and challenged him to a duel. I think you know how the rest of the story goes. Jasper mentioned Flanders, didn't he?"

"Someone tried to kill you."

"No, not just someone. A lovely Catholic exile I wanted to make my wife. Unfortunately for me, the wine with which we sealed the betrothal was laced with foxglove. Apparently I'd been detected as a spy by her peers. I'd invited Savage to stand with me in the ceremony. Instead he became my nursemaid."

Nicholas looked tired and beaten. When he spoke again, his words were filled with self-loathing. "So you see, one woman chased me from London and another chased me back."

"Oh, Nicholas. I'm so sorry."

"Don't feel sorry." He warded her off with his hand. "You want to help me, is that it?"

"Yes, of course! Anything."

"Then stop tearing me apart! Stop pursuing Heyward. Stop forcing me to relive the past."

He turned back toward the window. "I'm tired of running, Cat."

Although she was almost an hour late, Rafe was still waiting for her beyond the south gate of Dacre House that led to the pier and the wherry-filled Thames beyond. Cat breathed a heavy sigh of relief.

The boy had burrowed himself in a pile of leaves against the ivy-covered wall. Upon spotting her, he rose to his feet, ignoring with a quiet dignity the leaves that still clung to him and made him look like a bush with legs.

Cat could tell from his pale expression that he'd been trying hard to master his fear. Before she could think better of it, she gathered him up in a hug. Surprisingly, Rafe allowed it, though awkward and stiff.

"I was beginnin' to wonder if ye'd come," he grumbled into the folds of her cloak.

"So was I."

For several seconds, she just hugged him and listened to the swans honking and the wherrymen shouting along the river. Slowly, she drew back. "I'm so sorry. Dacre's manservant, Jonah, has been shadowing me all morning. I didn't think he'd be so difficult to shake."

"It sounds like ye'r losin' yer touch."

Cat grinned ruefully. "I'm beginning to think so, too. I had to ply Jonah with drink until he was forced to excuse himself to go to the garderobe."

Her comment almost won a full smile from him. "'Twas good to 'ear from ye, Cat. Was beginnin' to think Griffin had really got ye at the Hart."

"And I was worried he might have found you." She fixed him with a pointed glare. "You weren't that hard to find. I told you to lay low for awhile." He'd refused to abandon what everyone knew to be his favorite haunt, the pantry of the Lady Rose in Paris Garden.

Rafe glowered, the breeze off the water ruffling his matted hair. "Movin' about ain't goin' to do no good. If Griffin wants me, 'e'll find me, sure enough." With an imp's smirk, he added, "Besides been too busy helpin' ye to be hidin'."

A feeling of dread caught in Cat's throat. "Rafe, what have you been up to?"

The boy's eyes danced mischievously. "Watchin' Heyward."

"What?" The breeze cut through her thin dress, causing her to shiver. "God's blood, Rafe, do you know what could have happened if he'd caught you?"

"We done it, Cat! His ol' high-an'-mighty is in a right-good fit. He be hurtin' for that letter, for sure."

Cat's mouth opened and closed several times before she was able to speak. "He's upset about the letter? Tell me how you know!"

"Didn't I just tell ye I been watchin' him?"

"And I'm sure you did a very good job," Cat replied, knowing she'd have to concede a little if she wanted to know anything more.

"The cony we figged, the bookseller"—he added meaningfully, as if he feared she'd already forgotten thieves' cant during her brief stay among the rich—"he went to Heyward. When he 'eard what happened to the letter, his high-an'-mighty just about coughed up his innards."

Unable to contain herself, Cat crowed in delight, little caring that she drew the attention of a wherry passing the Dacre pier. Her hunch had been right. She'd managed to send Heyward into a panic! *Aye cove*, Cat thought, basking in her newfound power, *here your suffering begins.*

Noting her delight, Rafe's face brightened beneath the smudges of coal and dirt. "So when do we act?"

"What?"

"When do we let the cony know ye mean to blackmail 'im?" Rafe studied her shrewdly with his brown eyes. "That is what ye mean to do, isn't it?"

With a reluctant shake of her head, Cat answered. "Aye, that's what I intended. But I may be having second thoughts."

"Second thoughts? Why?"

Cat scrubbed her brow wishing she could push away the confusion within. Glancing at Rafe, she said, "Things have become a lot more complicated."

What if she continued with her plan and England was indeed drawn into another war with Spain? Moreover, could she again betray the trust of the man who had saved her life? The last time she'd done that had resulted in him almost being killed.

"Cat, I 'ope ye won't be takin' no offense when I say that now is not the time to be draggin' yer feet." His brown eyes held hers for a long moment. "Egan's dead." His last words were whispered so faintly they might have been a creation of the wind.

Cat's heart seemed to stop beating. "What? How?"

"Someone lodging at St. Mary Overy swore they saw you there with him."

"Oh God," Cat choked. "I didn't think that by going to Egan's—" The rest of the words were lost in a sob. It was her fault. She'd gone to Egan for help and now her dear friend was dead.

"Use the letter, Cat," he urged. "Make Heyward protect ye from him. It's yer only chance."

"Nay. Griffin won't think to look for me along the Strand. It's far too rich. I'm safe, at least for now."

"Nowhere's safe from 'im. Ye know that, Cat." The trembling of the boy's underfed form bespoke the intensity of his belief.

She knew Rafe was right. Sooner or later, Griffin would find her. They'd both seen it happen too many times afore. Cat could feel her shoulders slump in defeat.

"Then you'll use the letter?"

Aye, Cat thought, she'd use the letter—but not to protect herself. Rather, she would renew her original plan, Nicholas or not. Time was running out. She would have to see her family avenged before Griffin caught up with her. Certainly, there would be no mercy when he did. But by then, Cat thought with grim satisfaction, death would be a welcome peace.

Aye, she would fulfill her obligation to her family, but betraying Nicholas would weigh heavy on her soul.

14

The night air hung heavy with the smell of sea coal and rich dinners being prepared at the estates upriver as Cat and Jasper made their way down the stairs to the private dock along the Thames.

"Relax," the actor coaxed. "Nicholas has almost an hour's lead on us. He's not going to be lingering around the pier."

"I hope you're right." Gathering the heavy layers of her skirts to keep them from trailing in the leaves and dirt, she peered into the darkness of the river, noting a sudden flurry of motion.

With a splash of water, several wherrymen had begun to pole their way toward them. Cat suspected they must have heard about the masque at Court and staked out the Strand, richest hunting ground for prospective passengers. When the boatman closest to the shore seemed comfortable with his lead, he turned back to brandish a fist and let loose with a foul torrent of curses at his lagging competitors. Although she supposed a lady should be offended, Cat couldn't help but smile. 'Twas all part of the etiquette of the Thames.

As Cat stepped onto the wooden dock, Jasper proffered a hand. She took it gratefully for she felt terribly awkward, perched atop wooden pantofles and unbalanced with the heavy weight of her costume. "I feel like such a fright."

Beneath his broad crimson and gold hat, Jasper's one blue eye sparkled in the light of the torch he held. "Nay, my dear friend. You make a gorgeous Greek goddess." Jasper turned to the wherryman who was using his pole to hold himself at the end of the dock. "Come now, my good man, isn't she the most beautiful thing you've ever seen?"

Slapping his knee, the gap-toothed man cackled. "That she is, sir!"

Nodding her head in silent thanks, Cat gazed down at the black velvet and taffeta of her intricately embroidered and bejeweled gown. Maris had been right when she said it flattered her figure, grown all too slender by starvation and recent trauma. "'Haps it suits me," she murmured, trying to hide a secret smile.

In faith, she could not be more appropriately garbed for the night that lay ahead of her. She was dressed as Nemesis, goddess of retribution. Yet she suspected the costume's significance had eluded poor Jasper.

Cat accepted her friend's help onto the bobbing wherry. "I must say, I think you did well in choosing disguises for us both," she said, eyeing his costume of a rather affluent-looking wild Irish kern.

"Aye," Jasper answered casually. He helped the

wherryman shove off from the peer and into the current. "'Tis amazing what variety of garments are donated to the Lord Chamberlain's Men. Let's just pray we don't run into Heminges, shall we?"

Cat mimicked his mock-stern gaze and voice. "By all means." Inside, however, she felt the first twinge of guilt at misusing their friendship. Self-consciously, she began toying with the gilt handle of the mask in her hands.

Jasper obviously didn't understand how deeply the rift had grown between his two friends, for he'd agreed to crash the masque with her in tow. Ever the foolish romantic, he had written off the coolness between them as a mere lover's quarrel, nothing that couldn't be mended when Cat appeared at the masque in all her glory. She, however, had different intentions for the evening. Tonight she would confront Heyward. And if Nicholas caught her, there would be hell to pay on both her and Jasper's parts.

The actor took her free hand in his, trying to cajole her away from her thoughts. "Come now, why so sad, Cat? This is supposed to be an adventure."

"Mayhap I grow tired of adventure," she mused.

The wherryman loomed over Jasper's shoulder. "Did I hear you call the lass Cat?" he whispered.

"Aye," Jasper replied. "'Tis short for Catrienne. What of it?"

"Oh, nothing. Nothing at all." With sudden, absorbing interest, the wherryman returned his attention to guiding the small craft down the Thames. Noting that the dark-haired gentleman continued to watch him strangely, he added, "'Tis only that it's such a lovely name for a lovely lass."

As much as Kerney hated to smile, 'twas easy now,

so pleased was he at his sudden good fortune. Griffin had offered a goodly sum of coin for news of where this girl, Cat, hid. And now he, Kerney Medcalfe Arter, knew the answer. Dacre House.

He'd been invited to the masque but that didn't mean society meant to take him back with any great enthusiasm. Court was indifferent to the fact that he once again held the queen's favor. The courtiers and their ladies were careful to avoid him—just more decorously. Even if he hadn't been so obvious by his choice of costumes, a skull's mask and dueling outfit all in black, Nicholas knew he could be spotted by the limp he could never fully disguise. That defect, along with his tattered honor, marked him for life.

Quickly draining his goblet of spiced wine, Nicholas longingly eyed a doorway he knew led off to the garden. Attending this farce was only the first of several annoying tasks he'd be expected to perform in his newly official role as Misrule. With the warhawks' treasonous scheming, he did not have time to spare for such foolishness! Yet, to disobey the queen could easily mean a far harsher punishment for his crime.

Once again, he cursed himself for tangling with the Imperial Ambassador's nephew. If he'd had his wits about him, he would have found some other way to settle the matter. But no, he'd still been stinging from Cat's treachery. Angry that he'd opened himself and his secrets to her only to be manipulated like a pawn, he'd welcomed the chance to vent his frustration.

Served him right, Nicholas thought bitterly, for ignoring the common sense that had told him to leave Cat to rot at the Standard in Cheapside.

Heroics were well outside the realm of his experience. Rescuing the damn thief had turned into a miserable affair that only seemed to get worse with each passing day.

He placed his empty goblet on the table behind him. An elegant lady, clad in white silk and taffeta, made her way in his direction. 'Sblood, who'd be willing to be seen in his scandalous presence?

Some whimsical creature of fate must have heard his question, for on the woman's next step, her mask dipped slightly. He was rewarded with a glimpse of pale, sculpted features and a wealth of golden lashes. Feeling as if he'd taken a blow to the stomach, Nicholas stiffened. 'Twas Lady Amye Heyward.

Cat had not seen this part of Greenwich on her last visit. Hovering in the doorway, she took in the banqueting hall that gleamed in the light of a wealth of candles and torches. The tapestries that draped the walls were very colorful and undoubtedly even more costly. But even the needlework's vivid hues couldn't begin to compare with the jewel-bright costumes of the courtiers.

Noting the objects of her attention, Jasper murmured, "Lovely, aren't they?" Wagging his brows at her, he added, "Just don't let their pretty plumage fool you, my friend. They have a nasty bite."

Cat laughed nervously. "Why doesn't that surprise me?"

As Jasper led her into the room, she pressed her mask to her face and prayed it would protect her from detection. She must not allow Nicholas to discover her! She knew she was taking an enormous chance by being here, but with Griffin hunting her, time was running out. It was doubtful she'd ever get a better opportunity to confront Heyward.

From behind the screen that obscured the gallery, musicians struck up the opening measures of a new tune. In a flurry of tissue and tinsel, dancers hurried from the four corners of the room to join the lively steps of the coranto.

Cat walked with Jasper around the perimeter of the room. They were forced to stop time and again as friends of Jasper's—mostly female—flurried to their side. Although Jasper repeatedly introduced her as a distant cousin of his from Dover, Cat barely paid any attention. She was too concerned with finding Heyward and avoiding Nicholas.

Why was she having so much trouble? Despite the cloak of a costume, she should at least be able to spot Nicholas. There were very few as tall and imposing as he. And she swore she'd be able to find Heyward in even the darkest black of night.

Sweet Mary, she hadn't expected so many people to be in attendance. The costumes of the courtiers began to dissolve into a blur.

The musicians stopped for their first break, and the dancers fled the floor in favor of the bowls of spiced wine along the far wall. Cat recognized Nicholas looming near the queen's throne. With a quick intake of breath, she clutched the handle of her mask even tighter in her sweaty palm.

Although fearful her gaze might draw his, she couldn't help but study her magnificent adversary. He'd dressed to mimic the demon everyone who'd ever heard tales of Misrule harbored in their darkest thoughts. And, Cat decided as she studied his lean, lethal form, the menace of the reality far outweighed any creation of the imagination.

Apparently, his physical threat hadn't dissuaded everyone from approaching him, for a fair-haired lady in white silk lingered at his side. She stood entirely too close for Cat's taste and something about her teased the beginnings of a memory.

'Twas Heyward's wife! At the realization, Cat momentarily lowered her mask. A sudden irrational fury grabbed hold of her throat. Apparently, she thought sourly, the caution Nicholas had advocated in order not to raise the alderman's suspicions didn't include dallying with the man's wife.

Yet, why should she care if the wife of a murderer had drawn Nicholas's attention? Amye Heyward could serve as a distraction.

As the musicians began their second set, the flock of ladies around Jasper rustled excitedly, drawing her attention back to her immediate surroundings.

"Surely, Mister Savage," cooed a blonde-haired swan, "you wouldn't deny a long-time admirer a dance?"

Jasper placed a black-gloved hand over his heart. "How could I scorn to dance with such a beauty, Julia?" He brought her hand briefly to his lips, then let it go. "I fear, however, I must offer the first dance of the evening to my lovely cousin, here."

Several pairs of feminine eyes directed venom in Cat's direction. Jasper, oblivious to the mounting hostility, beckoned Cat with his hand. "Shall you join me, dear lady?"

"Nay, Jasper, I would be a poor partner. I haven't practiced in many years."

"Well, what a shame." Julia possessively linked her

arm through Jasper's. "Dover must be even more rustic than I thought."

Several of the other ladies tittered behind their masks.

"Go ahead and dance with her, Jasper," Cat said. "I'll be all right on my own."

With a rueful grin, the actor conceded defeat and allowed the determined swan to lead him onto the dance floor. The other ladies, lacking prospective partners, dispersed quickly in search of fresh prey.

Cat renewed her search for Heyward. Curse it all, had the alderman decided not to attend? Nay, his wife was here. Still plastered to Nicholas's side. From the way she fawned over him 'twould seem she found the company of her mate distasteful.

Playing on that hunch, Cat searched the farthest point in the room from where Nicholas and Heyward's wife stood. Sure enough, there, surrounded by surprisingly somber courtiers and deeply entrenched in conversation, was Heyward.

As Cat strolled toward her target, a sudden, excited energy coursed through her limbs. Finally, after all these years, the moment for which she'd lived and schemed was finally here. She was to have her first taste of revenge.

Keeping her mask before her, she wondered if he would recognize her. Nay, she reassured herself silently, Heyward had not seen her in fourteen years, since her father and he had still been friends.

When it became clear to the men surrounding the alderman that she'd sought them out, they stopped talking. The red-haired man she now knew to be Lord Essex boldly perused her with his eyes.

With a sudden start, Cat realized that the arrogant

knave thought she had come to seek him. Cat took great pleasure in squaring her back to the earl in order to face her true target. Her family's murderer stood dressed in the rich garb of Oberon. "Pray, would you favor me with a dance, Sir Laurence?" she purred.

The group of men surrounding Heyward shifted faintly in surprise. A sudden coughing fit seized one man in particular. A nearby companion started to pound heavily on his back. Fighting against a smile, Cat imagined she could feel the earl's stare of displeasure boring through her back. Essex, both handsome and powerful, was accustomed to being the man of choice.

Keeping her attention focused on Heyward, Cat watched as he glanced meaningfully at his companions, undoubtedly promising to return quickly and finish their business. Then the golden-haired devil turned to her and proffered a smile void of any true warmth. "Why, dear mistress, 'twould be my delight."

Placing her hand atop of his, she silently thought, Not for long, cove.

Christ, Nicholas wondered in despair, what could Amye mean by approaching him? 'Twould have every tongue wagging in the room.

"Dare I hope you might have found it within yourself to forgive me?" Amye whispered.

In that moment, the cool façade of resignation Nicholas had spent the last nine years fortifying tumbled into ruins. "My lady, I wouldst ask the same of you."

Uncaring of the curious gazes they were attracting,

Amye drew his hand to her cheek and murmured, "There was never anything to forgive."

"But how can you—"

"Nay," she retorted. "I will not hear of it."

"And, pray," he asked hoarsely, "what would you have us do now?"

A faint flush heightened her cheeks. "Can we not at least talk as friends?"

Could they do that, Nicholas wondered desperately, after all that had passed between them? 'Twould be easier to face Bonetti's entire studio of duelists all at once. Swallowing the lump in his throat, he said finally, "Aye, we can do that."

Amye seized upon his offer and began with a disjointed rendering of the recent events of her life, some of which Nicholas already knew. She and her husband had returned recently from France, and Heyward was quickly appointed the newest alderman in London. Amye made a few tentative inquiries into his life, which Nicholas did his best to answer.

Gradually they shifted to less treacherous matters such as the latest Court gossip. Nicholas doubted if either one of them really heard what the other said. They were each too busy examining the changes time had wrought on one another's face—and the contents of their own hearts. Eventually, they lapsed into awkward silence.

Nicholas scanned the hall for Heyward. The last thing he wanted was a repeat performance of what had happened eight years before.

The musicians concluded the last few measures of a brawl, and several red-faced dancers, struggling to regain their breath, hugged their partners in congratulation. The laughter of more than one woman could be heard drifting through the conversation like a gentle breeze.

There was one laugh in particular that drew Nicholas's attention. Although he hadn't heard it often, he'd know that sound till the day he died. The pained but polite smile he'd so recently achieved quickly fled his face. Locating the source of the laugh, his worst suspicions were confirmed. 'Twas Cat.

By Christ, he'd forbidden her to attend! Yet, here she was in a provocatively low-cut gown being led onto the dance floor by Laurence Heyward. Cold fury began to boil in his blood. "You wench," he muttered. "What are you about?"

Amye, startled by his words, glanced sharply at him, then followed the direction of his stare. Her gentle expression clouded with displeasure. "Pray, who is that young woman dancing with my husband? Do you know her?"

A dry brittle laugh of self-depreciation found its way from his throat. "My dear lady, not only do I know her, I just may have to kill her."

Amye's gaze narrowed. He may have claimed to wish to murder the girl, but Nicholas's eyes followed his target like those of a jealous lover. 'Twas easy to see why, she thought bitterly. The girl's dark hair, as sleek and shiny as the pelt of some woodland animal, fell halfway to her waist. She was young, shapely, and beautiful. Something about the defiant set of her chin tugged at Amye's memory. 'Twas the same girl she'd seen him with at Cheapside, she realized. And from Nicholas's rapt fascination, the girl would obviously prove a rival for his affections.

Nicholas struggled to regain his composure. "Please excuse me." He stalked away, ripping apart the tentative bond of intimacy she'd been so carefully building.

Nicholas cut a straight line through the dancers, to where Amye's husband stood in intense conversation with the girl along the far edge of the room.

She watched the following confrontation avidly, hoping Nicholas would follow through on his unlikely threat. Otherwise, something would have to be done with the girl.

15

Laurence Heyward was a polished dancer. Had the minstrels picked anything other than the stately pavan, Cat would have proved a poor partner. Thankfully, she seemed to be pulling off the role of a decorous lady of Court.

Laurence Heyward's pale blue eyes stared down at her from over his patrician nose. Caressing the top of her hand with his thumb, he murmured, "I don't believe we have had the pleasure of meeting before, young mistress."

Cat permitted herself a private, predatory smile. "Nay, sirrah, I believe you are mistaken."

"Oh?" Ignorant of the impending danger, he turned his attention to peruse the crowd of watchers along the wall.

Cat peered at him over the top of her mask. "I believe you and my father were friends at one time."

The alderman swept her face with a far less cursory gaze, searching for clues. "Forgive me, mistress, but I don't believe I've had the pleasure of your name."

"Why, 'tis Catrienne. Catrienne Lyly." She lowered her mask completely.

He jerked back, breaking his hold on her before he could master his reaction. Glancing at the surrounding dance partners, he reluctantly took her back into his arms. Under his breath, he muttered, "Nay, it cannot be so."

"Think again, cove. Look at me." She closed her hand tightly over his and raised her chin a notch higher. While she favored her father's coloring, she knew she had her mother's look.

Recognition dawned and his face paled.

"So good to see you again, Laurence."

His words came out in a horrified whisper. "How did you . . . "

"You mean, how did I survive the fire you set? I hardly think that matters now. The point, cove, is that I did survive."

Heyward sucked in his breath. The hollow of skin below his cheekbone quivered like the top of a minstrel's drum struck with a light hand. "What do you want?"

"Justice."

Cat concentrated on her steps, forcing him to wait. Moisture from his palms soaked into her expensive gloves. Finally, she gave him a level stare. "You will bring me a written statement of my family's innocence to the Cheapside fountain, noon tomorrow."

His hands tightened around her. "Don't threaten me," he hissed. "'Twould be far easier, and might I add pleasurable, to have you killed."

Cat was no longer the terrified child he'd left behind. And she had something he desperately wanted. "Do that," she said steadily, "and a certain letter of yours will find its way to the queen's hands."

He stiffened.

The pavan drifted to a close.

"I must say, Laurence," Cat purred in the ensuing silence. "It's touching to know you've rediscovered an interest in the True Faith. The Pope would be so pleased."

The alderman gaped at her dumbstruck. Her parting comment drew the attention of a couple nearby, just as she'd intended. Heyward wouldn't dare detain her if they were being watched. But when she turned away, he yanked her back into his grasp and whispered, "Where the hell do you think you're going?"

Stronger arms drew Cat away. A dangerous voice at her back said, "I believe Catrienne is going to dance with the Lord of Misrule. Certainly she owes him at least that one small courtesy."

Heyward's face went a livid white, but he released Cat. She reluctantly turned to face Nicholas.

"Dance with me. Now."

Cat's gaze darted between the enraged alderman and her even more threatening captor. "'Twould be my pleasure, sirrah."

Nicholas ushered her out of the alderman's reach. "Your pleasure?" he asked, shaking with rage. "Rather, Cat, your last mortal act."

Laurence Heyward stumbled through the pairs of dancers back to where his allies lurked, wishing he could head straight for the garderobe. Upon hearing the Lyly bitch's announcement that she had the missing letter, his bowels had run to water.

God's mercy, what misfortune! He'd begun to hope the stolen missive would quietly remain lost, that the drop-off might be successful without anyone being the wiser of his man's bungling. Now there was no hope but to confess to Essex, Raleigh, and the others how the plan had gone awry. Together they could present an unstoppable front. The miserable chit would suffer fully for her foolish schemes.

Catrienne Lyly would have been wise to learn from her parents' example, he thought coldly. No one crossed Laurence Heyward and walked away. No one.

"I distinctly recall forbidding you to attend." Nicholas glowered down at his dance partner.

Cat swallowed nervously. "Jasper invited me."

"I bet he did." He raked her half-clad form with his gaze. The low-cut bodice of the gown drew particular notice. To his great irritation, he felt himself quicken at the tempting show of flesh.

He couldn't help thinking that she looked every inch the vengeful goddess whose role she'd assumed. He could detect a dusting of kohl and rouge about her features. That, combined with a natural flush—no doubt from pursuing Heyward—only heightened the sensuality of her features. The curves of her body shifted beneath the precious wrapper of glittering black silk and taffeta. He fought back a groan as even more blood pooled in his loins.

Aye, she was a beautiful, dangerous Nemesis, he

thought grimly, and she didn't give a damn about anything but her own mindless vengeance.

But Court was no place to break into another rage. As civilly as possible, he said, "Kindly tell me exactly what went on between you and Heyward."

"You'll have to do better than that," she murmured close to his ear, not taking her eyes off her target.

Nicholas turned so she couldn't watch Heyward. Unfortunately, his attention was drawn to the man instead. The agitated alderman huddled Lord Essex and his party. The earl seemed to be issuing orders to his forces.

Curse it, they had to get out of there now! Essex wouldn't dare seize Cat before the queen but nothing would prevent him from ambushing them on the way home. "We're leaving. Now."

"What?" Cat's expression turned sullen and defiant. "I'll leave when I'm ready, not before."

Knowing she respected logic over threats, Nicholas supposed he should explain to her, though he wanted nothing more than to turn her over his knee right there and swat her pretty little rear end half to death. "So help me, Cat," he managed through gritted teeth. "We're leaving now, even if I have to carry you."

Nicholas tightened his gloved grip on her delicate hand and dragged her through the intricate pattern of dancers to the door.

The trip home on the wherry was conducted in silence, for which Nicholas was grudgingly grateful. If the battle of wills had progressed further, they undoubtedly would have both ended up in the water fighting to drag each other down. The unlikely truce ended the moment his wherryman handed Cat to the shore.

In a flounce of taffeta and silk, she marched up the garden path toward the house, preferring to take her chances with the lion rather than with him, which only increased Nicholas's irritation. The shrubs and trees of the garden cast dark silhouettes, the perfect setting for his mood.

He could hear Cat tramping hastily through the leaves up ahead. No doubt she meant to escape to her quarters—nay, his quarters, damn it!—before they could further discuss her treachery. Jonah had locked the side door to the house, however, so she was forced to wait under the overhang for him to let her in.

When Nicholas loomed over her to turn the key in the lock, he noticed she was trembling. That brought him some small measure of satisfaction. Whether or not she'd admit it, Cat was fearful of his displeasure.

Not fearful enough, however, to obey his orders. This night's folly proved that all too well. She swept past him, through the door, and down the hallway. Nicholas closed the door behind him and followed in her wake.

His bootsteps fell heavily on the wooden floor. Hesitating at the foot of the stairs, Cat glanced back. Every rigid line of her body bespoke haughty arrogance and defiance. Despite his threats, she'd approached Heyward. Moreover, 'twas clear she'd do so again if given the opportunity. In that second, Nicholas wanted nothing more than to throttle her.

She raised a sable brow. "What? Was there something more to discuss?"

He studied her in silence, allowing his gaze to

leisurely rove from her elegant coiffure, down her dark, sleek form, to the tiny points of her slippers peeking from beneath the heavy folds of her gown. Hovering at the bottom of the stairs, Cat seemed very much a woman in full mastery of herself and her environment, leaving him to feel like an intruder in his own home.

"I should have taken you to the gallows when I had a chance," he muttered darkly.

The faintest hint of a smile tipped her lips. "Can't you think of a new threat, baron?"

"Damn it, Cat!" Closing the small distance between them, he seized her by the upper arm. "This is going to stop for once and for all!" He gave her a fierce shake. Lush cascades of hair scattered about her bare shoulders. He tried hard to ignore the tantalizing effect, but the muscles of his stomach and groin tightened involuntarily.

The unwanted desire only honed the edge of his anger. "Mayhap, I'm too much the gentleman to be the cause of your death," he raged. "But, as God is my witness, you will not defy my wishes again!"

The skin about her bare shoulders and neck flushed, and heat stole into her cheeks. Remarkably, her voice remained as cool as ice. "And how exactly do you plan to ensure that?"

The challenge issuing from her emerald gaze was as defiant as her tone. But something elusive, other than rage, flickered in her eyes. She shivered beneath his hands, and he realized what he'd just witnessed. Desire.

'Sdeath, Nicholas realized with a start, she was struggling not to give into the deadly attraction just as much as he! "Jesus, Cat, you feel it, too, don't you?"

"Sirrah, the only thing I feel for you is disdain."
Her voice faltered, lacking conviction, and Nicholas's
spirits soared.

Drawing closer still, he murmured, "Nay, I don't
think so. Not seeing the way you react now." He
searched her stubborn features, identifying the clues
he'd missed before. The passion that had passed
between them in the kitchen had been genuine. "Say
it, Cat," he demanded. "Say you want me."

Sweet Mary, why did he have to figure that out
now? Cat wondered, her finely honed instincts beginning to shriek in alarm. She had to get away. Quickly.
Before she made a terrible mistake. "Why should I? I
thought you'd seen through my petty manipulations."

His expression hardened. "You deny me even that
one small truth?"

Her laugh sounded weak even to her own ears.
"'Tis hardly a matter of truth."

"Very well, Cat, you are the one who started this
war. If you demand a battle, then I intend to make it
sweet." He pulled her roughly toward him.

Cat's knees weakened as his mouth descended to
capture hers. Shaking her head and pushing against
his chest, she fought to break free. But his lips savaged hers with a delicious heat and, as he crushed
her close to him, her hands were pinned between
them.

With demanding mastery, he forced her lips open
with his thrusting tongue, and her moan was lost in
the melting of his assault. As his tongue twisted and
entwined with hers, a trembling thrill raced
through her. Her thoughts spun; her emotions skidded out of control. Sweet Mary, Cat thought desperately, she was powerless to muster a defense, for

in this field of battle she'd lost before she'd even begun fighting.

Nicholas renewed his attack, demanding full surrender with his mouth. Cat could do nothing but respond in breathless wonder. Her pulse skittered and her limbs grew heavy. The heat from his body surged into hers, bringing with it a rush of elemental longing. His mouth drifted from hers to graze an earlobe, leaving her lips to burn in the aftermath of his fiery possession.

"Tell me to stop, Cat," he murmured at her ear, the warmth of his breath fanning her overheated skin. "Tell me you don't long for my touch."

She could only close her eyes and groan as the stubble of his beard rasped against the tender flesh of her neck. He left a path of kisses from the edge of her jaw down to the moist hollow of her throat. There, he lingered, doing maddening things with his tongue. The cold metal of his earring brushed the side of her neck, eliciting a shiver.

Finally, Nicholas drew back, allowing her arms to drop limply to her sides. "Tell me you don't want this, and I'll let you go."

She wet her lips with her tongue. "I-I . . . can't."

His look one of burning intent, Nicholas traced a scorching line down her chest to where her breasts swelled beyond the confines of their velvet bodice. The whisper of his callused fingertip over her bare flesh ignited an uncontrollable trembling in her.

Nicholas chuckled softly, then slid his hand beneath her bodice and gently coaxed a pale breast free of its confines. Her nipple tightened in the cold air, growing harder still when an instant later he ran his thumb over the nub. Biting her lower lip, Cat fought back a moan as his feathery touch worked magic over her, causing a queer ache to writhe to life in her belly.

With unbearable slowness he leaned over her and brushed her aching breast with his lips.

He pulled back and his gray eyes smoldered with self-confidence. "What? Aren't you going to remind me who's master, Cat? Aren't you once again going to put the dread Misrule in his place? Tell me to stop, Cat, and I'll set you free."

Cat tried to, but the spot on her skin that was still moist from the touch of his lips began to ache in the coldness of the unheated hall. "No, I don't want you to stop."

She had just enough time to note the delight spreading across his features before he enveloped her fully in the warm velvet of his mouth, obliterating thought of anything other than piercing pleasuring.

Sweet Mary, what was he doing to her? The restless ache in her stomach plunged lower, to her most intimate, private parts. It was a good thing one of his arms encircled the small of her back, supporting her weight, or she would have crumpled to the floor.

For a timeless moment, he continuing his laving caress. Breathing heavily, Nicholas tried to free her other breast. Failing, he cursed under his breath.

Carefully, he eased her down to the floor at the foot of the stairs. He untied the strings of her cloak and smoothed the fabric beneath her so she'd have a place to lie. Then he drew back on his good knee and surveyed her sprawled form with brazen interest. Trembling, Cat returned his fascinated stare.

Never had she seen a more virile-looking man. His nostrils flared and the broad expanse of his chest rose and fell with his quickened breaths. His eyes, normally cold and deadly, had taken on a lazy, half-lidded look. And the proud swell of his manhood strained against his breeches. Dressed in black, his expression deadly earnest in its desire, he could easily be one of the demons said to rob a maiden of her virtues in the night.

Slowly, his hand slipped under the trailing edge of her gown. It snaked its way up the length of her leg, beneath her shift, to circle her quivering belly with shocking intimacy.

When she fought to sit up, his caress turned quickly into a command, pressing her back into the folds of her cloak. "Nay, my sweet Cat, let me show you pleasure."

His hand feathered over her stomach and thighs in dizzying circles, bringing her untried senses to life. Ruffin, she'd never dreamed his hands would feel so warm, so gentle. Or that they could drive her mad with an urgent longing for . . . something . . . more.

His hand drifted lower and, finding the very center of her sensitivity, he rubbed it between callused fingers. The need within Cat reached a screaming pitch. With a whimper, she clutched the fabric beneath her.

Then he did the unthinkable. He touched her there with his mouth.

The pleasure he won from her bespoke a world of new possibilities. His caress drew a sheen of perspiration to her half-clad form. The tremors of pleasure grew so strong that the contractions of her stomach muscles lifted her away from the floor.

And then he plunged inside her with his tongue. Shock racked her body, followed by a growing surge of excitement. This . . . this most intimate of connections . . . was what she'd been longing for. He probed her in a steady thrust of possession, increasing the dizzying passion. She twined her fingers in his hair and clung to him with trembling limbs.

Release came in a fierce wave of pleasure that started at the very core of her being and rippled outward to the furthest extremes of her body. A cry of wonder escaped her throat. She clung to Nicholas as her shudders slowed. "I never knew . . . "

Yet, as blissfully pleased as she already was, she couldn't help wondering if there was to be more. Certainly she wanted Nicholas to share the pleasure she'd just experienced. Breathless, somewhere between disbelief and enchantment, she raised her head to look at him. Her sleepy grin faded immediately.

His pale eyes danced with self-satisfaction. "Who would you say won this confrontation, Cat?"

She stared at him. Sweet Mary, the bastard was gloating. Aye, the lovemaking had begun as a battle of wills but somewhere along the way she thought it had become something intimate and genuine, something from the heart. But for him it had only been a game of conquest.

A hot ache of shame enveloped her. Cat sat up with a jerk, flipped her gown down, and desperately yanked her bodice back in place. Fighting tears, she backed to the edge of the cloak and got up on her feet. "'Twas a single round in the battle, Misrule. It won't happen again." Before she could mortify herself further, she spun on her heel, and bolted up the stairs to the relative safety of her new, smaller chambers.

Watching her flee, Nicholas let out a loud, shuddering breath, and said a silent thank you to God.

He'd meant the seduction to be nothing more than a raw act of dominance and possession. He hadn't meant to get caught up in it. But, for all his single-minded intentions, a ravenous hunger had seized him, and he knew that if she'd lingered one moment longer, he would have been driven to fully consummate what he'd so ruthlessly begun.

Long after she'd gone, he continued to stare into the darkness of the stairs. His pulse pounded out of control, his stomach churned, and his aching member remained rampantly hard. Nicholas scrubbed his forehead in frustration. He could smell her on his hands. Dark, terrifying emotions raked his gut. He swung his head back and forth in denial. A low groan of pure, evil-tempered wretchedness slipped out of him.

He would not go to her.

He could not. He'd finally uncovered her weakness, turned it against her, and asserted his dominance. If he went to her now and gave in to his own staggering longings, he'd be surrendering his newly discovered weapon.

Worse, he knew with dread certainty that she could turn the weapon of desire back on him. And, if she dared to do so, she'd undoubtedly be the victor of any confrontation.

16

Laurence Heyward and six of his most loyal men, stripped of their livery, arrived in West Cheapside an hour before noon the next day. On his command, the men took up positions inconspicuously about the marketplace. There they lurked, waiting for the signal to seize the woman who'd won their employer's wrath.

Blackmail or not, Laurence wasn't about to admit any of his prior misdeeds in writing. After all, Catrienne Lyly would certainly reveal the location of the letter with the right methods of torture.

And he knew them all.

A prickling sensation at the back of her neck whispered she was being followed. But every time Cat glanced at the milling crowd over her shoulder, she saw nothing amiss. Still, the uneasy feeling nagged at her. She couldn't help wondering if Nicholas had followed her.

After last night, Cat thought with a pained grimace, she wouldn't put anything past him. Never had she felt so thoroughly betrayed, so humiliated.

She drew her cloak closer about her. 'Twas one of the first really chill days of December, and the air was choked with the smell of damp wool and burning sea coal. Around her moved all manner of people: black-robed merchants, costly-dressed ladies with retinues of servants, a pockmarked beggar. Her gaze darted nervously from one person to the next. 'Twould be difficult to identify an attacker if he were in disguise.

Gabled houses, huge creations of oak and plaster overhung the broad cobble street on both sides. Beneath them stood stinking, steaming laystalls. Searching for an easy meal, flies and kites hovered thickly overhead. The costard mongers hawked their wares in lilting cries. Wood Street and the Eleanor Cross appeared on the horizon. The well-known landmark indicated one of the spots the body of King Edward's wife had lain on its way to Westminster.

Cat approached cautiously, clutching beneath the folds of her cloak the only protection she had against treachery, a knife she'd taken from Nicholas, the same time she'd helped herself to some of his coin. Surprisingly, no rabid Puritans stood at the base of the cross, condemning the statues that decorated the landmark as idolatry. Rather, only Heyward stood there with his aura of authority that demanded instant obedience.

At the sight of her family's murderer, Cat's muscles tightened and the bitter taste of long-suppressed rage rose in her throat. Raising her head a notch, she walked slowly forward. The day for vengeance—nay, justice—was finally here. He would give her the letter that proclaimed her family innocent of any treason. And as soon as Cat made sure it reached the right hands, she would see personally that this man suffered just as much as her family had.

Heyward watched her closely, his expression a mask of stone. When she drew close, he nodded curtly. "Catrienne."

"Heyward."

He offered a bleak, tight-lipped smile that drew his crepelike skin tight over the stark lines of his skull. "Kindly hand me the letter."

Something moved along the periphery of her vision. She scanned the milling crowd on her right before answering. "First, mine. That was the deal."

"Really?" He raised a disdainful brow. "I don't recall agreeing to that."

"We both know you had no choice but to agree." She extended a gloved hand from beneath her cloak. "Hand over the statement, and I'll tell you where to find your letter."

"I think further negotiations are in order." His voice was low and silvery, causing a shiver of unease to crawl the length of her spine.

He was stalling. It had to be some kind of trap! Throwing her cape wide to reveal her knife, she spun in her tracks.

Heyward's pockmarked servant from St. Paul's, the letter carrier, lunged for her. Cat's blade tore a savage gash through his doublet and the straw used to pad the garment rained out. With a curse, he swept her up in a crushing bear-hug.

The breath knocked out of her, she opened her

mouth to cry for help but no words came out. She writhed and turned, trying to break his hold. Her feet scrabbled desperately for purchase.

From behind Heyward's servant came a wraith-like rasp. "She's mine, cove."

Her captor inhaled sharply. His grip loosened, and he crumpled in a heap at her feet. An evil-looking blade protruded from his back. Gasping for breath, Cat stared at the body in shock. Then she looked up.

Before her towered a cowled figure, rank with the smell of rot and death. The specter clutched a rapier in one leprous hand and extended the other toward her. "'Tis good to finally find you, sweetmeat."

Cat started violently, then staggered backward. Jesu, 'twas Griffin! He must have been the one she sensed following her from the house.

Another of Heyward's men bore down upon them, short sword in hand. After a quick glance at each of them and the man already fallen, the second livery-man opted to deal with Griffin first. Metal rang on metal as their two blades engaged.

Not waiting for the outcome, Cat ran as if the demons of hell were after her.

Heyward watched, furious, as the girl eluded his trap. He whirled on the man who had subdued the cowled figure. "Don't bother with him. Go after the girl!"

His servant leaped up to obey.

Exhaling sharply, Heyward turned his murderous glare on the man who had foiled his carefully wrought plan. "And who the bloody hell are you?"

A deathlike rasp of a laugh came from beneath the cowled hood. "Her worst nightmare, cove."

* * *

Nicholas led his black stallion outside the gates. Maris had only just informed him that Cat was missing. Hoping she'd keep a low profile, at least temporarily, after last night's stormy confrontation, he'd been dismayed. He had to find her!

Before he could close the gate, he heard the pounding of boots. Wide-eyed and gasping for breath, Cat crested the hill just up the road. Three armed men raced at her heels. If there'd originally been more, she'd managed to shake them.

The closest man caught hold of her cloak. She staggered backward, her scream a mixture of outrage and terror. The man wrapped her in his beefy arms.

Merciful God, she could be dead afore he could reach her! The realization hit him like a mortal blow. In a hiss of steel, Nicholas drew his blade. Dropping the reins of his horse, he charged toward Cat's attacker.

Cat fought and clawed like a wild thing, forcing her captor to sway and lurch in order to maintain his hold. From somewhere she managed to produce a knife, but the blade fell when her captor crushed her even tighter. Cat slammed her head back into his with a crack. Howling, he dropped her. She lay on the ground, stunned. Cursing, the man brandished his blade.

Nicholas was still twenty strides away and his bad leg felt like it might give out at any time. *God, don't let her die. Please don't take her, too.*

Just as the sword came crashing down, Cat rolled. The blade screeched off the cobblestones. Carried by his own momentum, her attacker pitched to the right.

She was on her feet and hurrying toward her knife by the time the man reoriented himself.

The distance between Nicholas and Cat seemed impossibly far and the sound of his blood pounded in his ears. When he realized she wouldn't be able to reach the knife in time, his gut tightened into a cold knot. "Run, damn you, run!" he bellowed.

At the sound of his voice, Cat's attention swiveled to him, and she did exactly what he'd ordered.

They exchanged places in a heartbeat, and when the man lunged for Cat he found Nicholas instead. Their two blades met in a bone-jarring clang of steel.

The thickly built man backed away and ran a nervous tongue over his lips. "I don't want to fight ye, Misrule. Just let us have the girl."

"What?" Nicholas trembled in his fury. "So you can murder her before my eyes?"

Not waiting for an answer, Nicholas lunged, skewering him straight through the stomach. The man slid to the ground in a pool of blood. Out of the corner of his eye, Nicholas discovered Cat hovering by his horse, twisting the reins in her hand. "Get inside the gate and lock it behind you!"

"There are more coming," she cried. "You can't hold them all off!"

Nicholas eyed the remaining two men in front of him. They seemed to have reached a consensus that they would strike together in a flanking maneuver. "Cat," he said through gritted teeth, "lock the cursed gate. Do it or we'll both die."

Three more men crested the hill.

Knowing it might very well be his last chance, he glanced back at Cat. Her expression was tortured.

"All right. I'm going for help!" She slammed shut the gate and ran for the house.

Do that, Cat, Nicholas silently implored, lowering into a crouch. Whatever it takes to get you as far away from Heyward's men as possible. By Christ's blood, 'tis far easier to let them kill me than you.

It seemed as if an eternity passed while Cat fretted at the main door waiting for the Dacre servants to reappear. Then she saw Nicholas stumble up the path, one arm slung over a brawny stableman's shoulder.

He had a bloody cut along his cheek and his shirt was slashed in several places, but she couldn't spot any serious wounds. Wearily, he raised his head to look at her. "Christ, Cat, half of London was on your heels. Don't you have any friends?"

Fighting back tears of relief, she managed a wan smile.

After having his wounds tended to, Nicholas dismissed his servant. He took Cat firmly by the arm and ushered her into the parlor. The door closed with a soft click. The look he gave her was sharp, assessing. "What the hell was that? Why were Heyward's men after you?"

He's safe, and now the battle begins again, Cat thought to herself. She swallowed, then answered softly, "The alderman and I had some business to transact."

Nicholas's expression clouded, his voice grew rough. "Business at the end of a blade?"

She looked past him to the rich oak paneling on the walls. "That wasn't how it was supposed to go."

"Cat, this must stop. Now."

"Why? Because I'm endangering your all-important plans?"

"No," he said quietly. "Because you are endangering your life."

At that unexpected answer, her breath caught in her throat. But her wariness returned. "How good of you to care," she said softly. "I'm still standing, aren't I?"

His hands tightened into fists and he whirled back to face her. "Yes, thanks in great part to me."

Cat's gaze kept returning to the slash along his cheek. He was right, of course. But after last night, she was loathe to admit it. Never had someone she cared for hurt her so badly. Even risking his life for her could not completely erase the pain of that betrayal. But it didn't stop her from feeling terrible guilt that he might have died. Not trusting herself to speak in her own defense, she waited, cautious and silent.

"Christ, Cat, you went after Heyward without any protection."

"I had a knife," she muttered.

"And you quickly lost that!"

Remembering the terrifying moment outside the gate, she nodded, chastened.

But instead of being pleased by her submission, his fist tightened further and he cursed under his breath. Regaining some small degree of control, he asked, "What could be so important that it's worth your life?"

"My family, that's what! Heyward was supposed to give me a statement of their innocence."

"You risked an ambush for some fool statement?"

"They didn't deserve to be branded as traitors!"

"And a piece of paper isn't going to bring them back!"

"Don't you think I know that?" she screamed, tossing the words at him like daggers. "No, nothing will bring them back. But I can see their name cleared. I can make sure that bastard"—she spat out the word—"suffers for what he did."

His expression softened and he took a step toward her. "No, you can't." Slowly he took her hand in his. "Heyward is one of the most powerful men in the City. You may have escaped him this time, but you could easily die the next."

"Damn you! I didn't ask for your concern!" Cat cried, snatching back her hand. "I'll die, then. If that's the way it has to be."

"Cat, you have to let go of this obsession for vengeance. It's eating you alive. Believe someone who has been there."

Cat suspected he was remembering Lady Amye and Heyward's treachery and the dark years that had followed. Feeling her resolve begin to weaken, she shook her head. "It isn't the same thing at all. You lost your betrothed. I lost my family, my life."

"Curse it, woman, your life isn't over yet! And it won't be until Heyward puts a blade through your heart. Revenge isn't worth that!"

"Yes, it is." The words came out unbidden, with the fervent conviction of a zealot.

"You cannot mean that!" He stared at her for a long moment. "God's blood, you do." He wearily scrubbed at his forehead. Finally, he looked back at her. "Why, Cat? Tell me why."

Her whisper came out hoarse and thin. "They gave their lives trying to protect me. They would have

given Heyward the Jesuit if I hadn't been hiding with
him, if I hadn't been too slow to leave the priesthole."

"Cat, you can't blame yourself! 'Tis madness!"

"I-I should have cried out. Revealed where we
hid . . ."

"Heyward still would have killed them! And you as
well!"

Trembling uncontrollably, she lowered her head in
defeat. He was wrong. So incredibly wrong. But she
didn't have the faintest idea how to even begin to
explain it to him.

One of Nicholas's broad, callused hands cradled
her chin, raising it so he could snare her eyes with his.
"Cat, listen to me. Nothing can be served by your sac-
rificing your life in some sort of insane penance. Not
then. Not now. My God, stop and think about what
you're doing!"

Raw, primitive grief curled deep within her, threatening to tear away the last shreds of her self-control.
Sweet Mary, she knew what she did was illogical. She
knew they were dead and that nothing could change
that fact. But if she dared to admit it, truly accept it,
she'd be washed away in a torrential wave of despair.
The only thing that still anchored her to sanity was
her dream of revenge. "I don't want to think. I just
want this finished."

Instinctively, Nicholas tried to draw her into his
arms.

She started violently, her spine a rod of ice. There
was no comfort to be found in his arms. Not after last
night. "Don't touch me."

"Cat, I—"

Slowly the ice spread, cooling her tears, numbing
her pain, freezing her heart. 'Twas ironic, but in the

sting of his betrayal she found the strength to rebuild
her defenses. She slowly raised her eyes to his. "Don't
ever touch me again, Nicholas. You lost that right
with your conquest last night."

Sir Laurence and his wife made their regular Sunday
appearance at St. Paul's, sitting prominently up front.

The chaplain had just begun the sermon when tam-
bours, pipes, and whistles struck up in a raucous par-
ody of music from the direction of Paul's Cheap.
Beetling his brows, the clergyman cleared his throat,
then proceeded in a louder voice. Try as he might,
every eye of his congregation drifted past his pulpit
on Paul's Cross to the direction of the noise.

Suddenly, a procession of hobbyhorses burst
through the Cheapside Gate led by a one-eyed jester.
Two ribboned dragons chased close on their heels. A
chaotic crowd of fools, minstrels, prisoners, dancing
gibbets and stocks, and garishly dressed courtiers followed. Next came twenty men dressed in liveries of
green and yellow. Like morris dancers, they had bells
tied to their legs. With tongue-in-cheek solemnity,
they bore their Lord of Misrule on a litter.

The leader of the carefully choreographed fiasco
was decked out in velvet and cloth of gold. Peering
down from his dais, he grinned dangerously at
London's finest like an inmate from Bedlam.

The chaplain halted his sermon midsentence,
dumbstruck. Certainly, the Sunday ceremonies in
small towns and villages had been disrupted by the
Lord of Misrule during the Christmas season, but
never in the City.

A nervous breeze of laughter ran through the

church. Then one rebellious soul—no doubt, a commoner—struck up a cheer. Another joined. The laughter became genuine, and London's Lord of Misrule was greeted with hearty applause.

Encouraged by their reception, the men bearing the livery guided it to Paul's Cross. The minstrels came to a halt and the congregation quieted.

Lord Dacre tilted his head at the chaplain. "What, my good man, have you started without us?" The question came out in a casual, jesting way.

Everyone held their breath, curious to see how he'd be received by one of the City's men of authority.

The clergyman's stoic features softened into a smile. "Cry you mercy, my lord, we did not know to expect you." Then, he offered Misrule a genial salute as was the country tradition.

The congregation cheered and the unlikely minstrels once again struck up their tortured version of music. With great spirit—and even greater noise—the entire procession paraded around the churchyard twice.

Then the litter stopped before the Heywards. The half-familiar one-eyed jester rushed up, produced a velvet step with great ceremony, and helped the Lord of Misrule to the ground.

Regally, Nicholas stood before the couple, assuming the mantle of power and respect that was his due until Twelfth Night. Neither Heyward nor his wife rose to their feet, though Lady Amye seemed pleased by the attention. As the Lord of Misrule continued to boldly stare at her, a flush rose to her cheeks. Continuing to meet his gaze, she finally murmured, "Lord Dacre."

"Amye." With a swagger and a bow, Nicholas took

her proffered hand in his. He caressed it overlong with his lips while slanting a glance at the alderman, who quivered in barely suppressed rage.

Doing his best to look casual for the onlookers, Nicholas issued the warning he'd waited all week to deliver. "Hear me well, Laurence," he whispered against the flesh of the alderman's wife. "If you dare to come after Cat again, there will be another duel." He slid a small piece of paper into Amye's hand and then released it. Then he bared his teeth at Heyward in a mockery of a smile. "And we both know who will win this time."

Heyward stared through the Lord of Misrule, denying his very presence. But a muscle in the hollow of his cheek ticked furiously. Content with what he'd wrought, Nicholas whirled in a flourish of cloak and resumed his litter.

Misrule and his merry band of men circled the congregation twice in a cacophony of blaring noise. Then, with great show, they exited the way they'd come.

"Don't touch me," Cat hissed.

"Cat, I—"

Slowly she raised her eyes to his, making no attempt to mask her hatred. "Don't ever touch me again, Nicholas. You lost that right with your conquest last night."

He winced as her accusation struck home. Aye, he'd hurt her badly, horribly. In faith, he could do nothing but shake in shame and frustration as Cat drew up rigidly and left the parlor.

Slowly, the dreadful truth settled on him like a crushing weight—there would be no stopping her . . .

'Twas four days since Nicholas's confrontation with Cat, and still she hadn't come to her senses. She wouldn't even see him. Cursing loudly, he looked out a mullioned window as if he could find the answer waiting in his front yard. He'd tried his best to make her understand the danger she put England in. But her thirst for vengeance smothered out reason. Force didn't work either. Neither he nor his servants had been able to keep her from going after Heyward. She deftly outwitted all attempts at control.

And after his near fatal encounter with Heyward's men, he'd hoped with quiet desperation that he might be able to reach her by pointing out the self-destructiveness of her pursuit. But, God's blood, she didn't care. Faith, it seemed she relished the thought of death, as if only that could make amends for surviving when the others had not!

Suddenly, he felt the overwhelming urge to punch his fist through the precious glass. How could Cat blame herself for what Heyward had done? 'Twas the twisted logic of an eight-year-old child who had been exposed to horrors no one should ever have to face. But the misplaced guilt was firmly entrenched. And it was about to get her killed.

It was only with a great deal of luck that she'd gotten as far as she had, that he'd been able to reach her in time, that the third wave of attackers had been intimidated by the fallen comrades, and that the Dacre servants had arrived in time to get him back behind the gates. Heyward had no intention of letting Cat live. That had been made clear.

His stomach clenched into a painful knot. The window before him fogged with his furious breaths. Frowning, he rubbed his knuckles against the glass.

There had to be something he could do to change the dread outcome that loomed on the horizon. Something that might alter Cat's headlong flight into destruction. Something that might at least raise the chances of her survival. *By God's teeth, I can teach her how to fight.*

17

Nicholas loomed dangerously in the doorway of her new chambers. Cat was forced to put down the piece of needlework she was mangling and acknowledge his presence. "What do you want?"

He nodded graciously and hastened forward as if she'd just invited him for tea. There was a mischievous light in his eyes. "I've got a proposition for you."

"A proposition? Dacre, that's the last thing I want to hear. Go away."

"But you haven't even heard it yet."

"I told you. I don't want to hear it."

"Very well," he said. "Too bad, though. I thought I could give you an advantage with the alderman." With a heavy sigh, he took a step toward the doorway.

"Advantage?" Cat asked, straightening in her chair. "What do you mean?"

He turned back to face her, confidence drawing bold lines along his body and face. "If there's one thing I know, Cat, it's swords. Let me teach you to fight. Show you how to protect yourself from Heyward."

"But it takes years to master the rapier."

"Aye. There's much you won't have time to learn," he said. "But even a little skill with a blade would be better then what I saw outside the gates the other day."

Cat scowled.

"Jesus, Cat," he exploded, throwing his hands up in exasperation. "You couldn't even hang on to your knife!"

Cat knew Nicholas had a point. "All right, mayhap you could teach me something useful," she conceded. "But why would you do that for me?"

"Why?" Nicholas sputtered the word. Placing a hand on each arm of her chair, he leaned forward until their faces were only inches apart. "Because, dearling, I don't want your blood on my hands. Is that a good enough reason?"

The bluntness of his answer shocked her. Aware that he was scrutinizing her reaction, Cat tried to master her features and collect her turbulent thoughts.

Nicholas shifted restlessly. "So what's it going to be, Cat?" he asked.

Cat looked up at him and smiled. "All right, cove. Teach me how to fight."

Nicholas thrust at Cat with his blade, forcing her to suck in her stomach and retreat. He continued to

stalk her, but his lips curled in approval. "You antici-
pated the move well, but you're off balance. Look at
the position of your feet."

Frowning, Cat corrected her form and exhaled in
irritation. "Is chasing me around the hall with a
sword your idea of teaching me how to fight?"

His expression grew grim. "Yes, to start with. You
need to learn to evade cuts and thrusts gracefully."

Damn it, she'd come here to draw blood! "Let me
show you how well I've mastered the concept of eva-
sion. I'm leaving."

Nicholas's penetrating gray eyes darkened and the
lines around his mouth grew taut. "No you don't.
We're in the middle of a practice session. Turn your
back on me, and I'll save Heyward the trouble of running you through." He thrust at her again.

Cat had no choice but to step to the side. "I've
changed my mind. I don't want to learn how to handle a sword."

Grimly, Nicholas continued to pursue her across
the length of the hall. "You must learn. It very well
may mean your life. You need my help."

"Of all the self-righteous cr—" Her retort ended in
a gasp as a thrust came dangerously close.

Swearing, Nicholas lowered his blade. "You and
your cursed pride! It keeps you from accepting anyone's help! You even push Savage away."

The truth of the accusation lodged in Cat's heart,
stinging like a deadly accurate missile. "I'm doing just
fine on my own, Dacre," she muttered.

"The hell you are."

Cat looked at the man who'd risked his life protecting her from Heyward's men, and realized she could
not deny the truth. She was in serious trouble; they

both knew it. Annoyed that Nicholas was beginning to
know her so well, she shot him an ugly look and asked
caustically, "So when do I get a blade? Next year?"

The swept-hilt rapier was heavier than she'd
expected. The blade's weight tipped it downward,
and she had to fight to keep her wrist straight. Wire
wrapped the handle, but the sweat from her hand,
combined with the coat of oil that had been applied
to keep the rapier from rusting, made it hard to maintain her grip.

Almost reverently, Cat held the rapier before her,
her gaze transfixed on the blade. This was a weapon
that could easily kill a man. Moreover, it was worth a
small fortune. Even Skinner had only possessed a
short sword.

Nicholas watched her carefully. "Move it around
so you can get a feel for its heft and balance."

She swung it back and forth. The blade's momentum gave it a life of its own. She practiced a few awkward thrusts and her confidence grew. Candlelight
played on the rapier as she rotated it back and forth.
Looking closer at the blade, she said suspiciously,
"The point's dulled."

He shot her a dark look. "Aye, so is mine. Would
you like to change that?"

Cat's dreams of bloodshed faded in an instant.
"Never mind."

They devoted the greater part of the second morning
to practicing lunges. Cat had trouble remembering to
lead with her blade, which destroyed the timing

between her sword and footwork. Nicholas hounded her mercilessly on the point.

Pounding his hilt on the floor in steady thumps, he walked her through the paces again and again until Cat thought she would scream. Her legs were cramped and the rapier felt like it had tripled in weight. Her aching muscles cried for rest. She gathered her resolve with a fierce grimace.

Dreaming of the unspeakable things she would like to do to Nicholas and his descendants to be, Cat delivered a thrust simultaneous to the fall of her foot. She had no time, however, to bask in the accomplishment. With the swing of a booted foot, Nicholas kicked her front leg out from under her, and she crashed to the floor.

Cat inhaled sharply. "Curse you, Dacre. What the hell was that for?"

"You forgot to pivot your back heel. You were off balance."

Wincing, she slowly sat up. "*So?*"

"When you are off balance, you are out of control. Being in control is the essence of competence."

The unruffled cool of his tone set her teeth on edge. Dressed in tight-fitting black breeches and a gaping, crisp white shirt free of sweat, the duelist seemed the epitome of control and competence. Again, Cat had to fight back the urge to scream. Damn it, she'd meant to humiliate him not herself! Slowly, not permitting her gaze to wander from his, she gained her feet. "And the dread Misrule is always in control, isn't he?"

His dark, unblinking stare was her only answer.

*   *   *

The morning of the third day, Nicholas strode into the Great Hall, a pair of woman-sized boots dangling from his hand.

"Here. A reward for your hard work. Be careful not to grab them by the heels."

Cat looked at him suspiciously. "What are these for?"

"Keeping you alive." Taking one boot by the toe, he turned it over. "Look carefully at the sole."

At first she didn't notice anything unusual. Then she realized that the part of the heel plate closest to the sole was wider than the base. Someone had honed the jutting metal on the inner and outer edge of the plate to razor sharpness!

"I've never seen anything like this," she murmured, smiling tentatively. "It's even more cunning than the garrote Jasper wears disguised as a bracelet."

"Now you'll be harder to completely disarm. They may search your boots for weapons but I doubt if they'll think to look at the heels."

Her annoyance was back in an instant. "You're assuming they'll be able to get that close."

Raw fear flickered across his features. "Yes. I am."

Cat's eyes watered and the battle between their blades was little more than a blur. Groaning, she held up a hand for Nicholas to stop and lowered her blade.

For once, he didn't have a ready taunt. Frowning with concern, he asked, "What's wrong?"

Stripping off a leather glove, she brought her hand to her sweaty brow. "Ruffin, my head aches!"

He chuckled softly. Stepping forward, he squeezed

her arm lightly. "You're still looking at the blades instead of my gaze."

"That's because the sword poses the greater threat. Looking up into his piercing, gray eyes, however, she had to wonder if that was entirely true. In faith, every time their eyes met—even now—she felt light-headed and awkward.

"Eh?" Her quip won a grin from him. "That may be, but the blades move too fast for your vision to focus on. Keep your attention on me. You'll have a better chance of anticipating my next attack, and you can still see the blades along your periphery."

Lowering her hand, Cat eyed him suspiciously. "This is some sort of test, isn't it? How gullible do I look?"

"It's not a test. I'm being serious. Come on," he said. "Let's try it again with you meeting my eyes."

Suddenly, Cat felt uncomfortably warm. Her heart began to flutter and it had nothing to do with the physical demands of their swordplay. Nicholas gave her a strange look. Then, patting her once more on the arm, he turned around and walked back to fighting distance.

Cat groaned. She felt better now that they weren't standing so close together, but she dreaded the thought of any more practice. "My head's just starting to feel better," she grumbled.

"Just a few more minutes," he coaxed, "and we'll break for supper. From the smells coming from the kitchen, Maris is making up something wonderful for us."

Her stomach rumbled at the mere mention of food. Since they'd begun training, she couldn't seem to get enough to eat. Cat raised her blade. "You drive a hard bargain, Dacre."

"It's part of my charm."

He was careful to hold her with his gaze as they went through their paces again. At first it was a struggle not to look down at his blade when he advanced, but Nicholas slowed down his pace, allowing her time to adjust. After a few minutes of practice, she was surprised to realize she could predict some of his attacks. Her confidence grew, and their speed increased.

Once, she misjudged an attack and their bodies, warm with exertion, collided together. She drew back with a rueful smile and tried again.

They thrust and parried with an uncanny intuitiveness. 'Twas like they were two partners in a dance, she thought. An intimate, dangerous dance. As she continued to stare into his mesmerizing gray eyes, a shudder ran the length of her spine, and the lightheaded feeling she'd been battling returned. Her breathing quickened and a trickle of sweat ran down her temple.

Cat swallowed nervously. One of them needed to do something to diffuse the strange tension that drew them closer and closer together with silken bonds. She opened her mouth to make a jest but couldn't find the words.

He seemed to sense her struggle, his dark brows drawing together. His gaze smoldered like the wick on a cannon about to explode into devastating action. He dropped his blade and took her by the arm, forcing her to do the same. "Cat, I—"

Someone coughed. "Er, my lord?"

Disoriented by the interruption, Cat glanced wildly

from one end of the hall to the other until her attention settled on Jonah. He hunched nervously in the doorway leading to the kitchen.

Nicholas's grip tightened briefly on her arm before letting go. "Jonah, I thought I told you we weren't to be disturbed."

The old man hunched into himself. "Y-yes. I know, my lord. But you have quite an insistent visitor."

"Then show him in."

"Ah—"

"What the poor man means to say, Nicholas," Amye Heyward cooed, floating into the room in a breeze of yellow silk, "is that your visitor isn't a man, and she's already had the temerity to let herself in." At her side was Rafe, trying furtively to free his hand from hers.

Nicholas stared at the woman and the boy in surprise. His voice, however, remained steady as he offered a terse greeting. "Amye."

Cat could only stare at the woman with loathing as Nicholas walked to her side.

He took Lady Amye's hand in his. "How good of you to come."

Rafe took advantage of the woman's distraction to break free and scurry over to Cat.

Amye watched Nicholas through lowered lashes as he brought her hand to his lips. "You couldn't keep me away," she murmured. "I must say you're keeping unusual company these days. First a thief and now a street urchin. I found the little boy lurking out by the carriage house." She laughed lightly.

Both Rafe and Cat bristled.

Straightening, Nicholas glanced back at Cat with a pained look of embarrassment.

Suddenly she was burningly aware that she was sweaty from several hours of practice, half her hair had long since slipped its ribbon, and she was garbed in men's clothes. Heat stole to her cheeks. Yet, what did she have to be ashamed of? she asked herself angrily. Nicholas had suggested that she dress so. Did he now mean to cast her aside for it? The confusion and guilt playing over his features were all the answer she needed.

Amye arched an elegant brow. "Nicholas, you did beg that I come to visit whenever it was convenient. But if I've interrupted something, I suppose I could come back."

Cat met the woman's gaze bravely. "No, you didn't interrupt. My partner and I were just about to get something to eat. You're free to do as you please with milord."

Mockingly, she saluted Nicholas with her blade. Then, squaring her shoulders, she motioned to Rafe and the two of them headed for the kitchen.

Nicholas quietly shut the door behind them and turned to face his guest. His look was guarded. "I was beginning to wonder if you were going to come."

"I had to wait until Laurence would not notice my absence." The lie passed easily from her lips. Amye took the chair he offered, bending slowly so that he had ample time to glimpse the daring cut of her gown and inhale the musky rose scent of the pomander she wore on a golden chain dangling between her breasts.

Nicholas drew back rigidly.

Amye smoothed her skirts, doing her best to mask her annoyance. The ties that bound them seemed to be loosening. Never matter, she'd just have to work that much harder to manipulate him. "I must admit," she murmured, "I was surprised by your request." She looked up at him with feigned concern. "You must have a pressing reason to invite me here."

A strange melange of emotions—guilt, need, and something else—crossed his features, and she began to hope again that he'd brought her here for a liaison.

Finally, without looking at her, he spoke in a low voice. "Amye, I need you to let me see some of your husband's correspondence."

Amye bit the inside of her cheek. Outwardly, she was careful not to show anything but pretty confusion. "What sort of letter?"

He haltingly told her about the scheme between her husband and the rebel earls and where he feared it would lead. Saying nothing, Amye coldly watched the pain and guilt ravage his face. Poor old Nicholas, she thought. You still can't let go of that one pitiful battle, can you?

He went on to explain about the bookseller who had recently disappeared and that there wasn't time to discover the new courier. Any further communications with the rebel earls would have to be taken directly from her husband. He desperately needed proof of the conspiracy. Soon. "Will you help me?" he asked in a low rasp, the velvet stripped from his voice.

Instinct told her it had cost him a great deal to make this request. If she agreed to help, he'd be deeply in her debt. Yet, she was still irritated by the fact that he wanted nothing more from her than to spy for him. She'd do it, of course, but she'd make him work for that favor.

Bringing a delicate hand to her décolletage, she stared at him in wide-eyed shock. "Nicholas, you ask me to betray my husband?"

He shifted uneasily. "I ask you to do what's right for England."

Some of her cynicism must have shown through her careful demeanor because Nicholas tried another tactic. "If not for England," he said, watching her carefully, "can you not at least do it for me?"

She allowed herself to crumple in the chair, slouching into herself. She waited for a long moment, then weakly nodded her head. "Yes, of course," she whispered. "I'll do whatever I can to help."

He let out a great sigh of relief and the tight coil of tension within him seemed to release.

Amye carefully studied him through lashes heavy with fake tears. Oh yes, she'd help him. But not out of some foolish loyalty for England or even out of love. She'd bring the letters to him. If Laurence was involved as Nicholas suspected, it might mean his downfall. Better still, the numerous trips to Dacre House would provide ample opportunities for her husband to catch her secretly meeting with her new "lover." And to ensure that very thing, Amye thought with a small smile, her carelessness was about to grow enormously.

Cat's blade met with Nicholas's with more force than was strictly necessary. He shoved her back without much difficulty. "You're overstepping again."

She exhaled sharply, her breath coming out in a cloud of vapor in the cold, morning air of the Great Hall.

That morning when he'd come to rouse her for practice at their regular time, Nicholas made no mention of Amye's visit the day before. Yet, for some, inexplicable reason, it tore at Cat's nerves like a thorn plunged into tender flesh, leaving her short-tempered and oversensitive.

Cat didn't want to think about form and technique. She wanted to pound her teacher senseless with her blade. So far, though, he hadn't been very obliging. Cat attacked again and again, despite aching muscles and flagging energy. Her opponent's "My, we're a bit high-spirited this morning" was all she needed to spur her on. If only she could draw a single drop of the rogue's blood.

Gritting her teeth, she pressed herself to be more cunning and quicker than she'd ever been. But time and again, Nicholas countered her moves until she wanted to scream in frustration. Finally, uncaring, she lowered her blade and stumbled away.

"What? Surely you don't mean to surrender, *mia cara*?"

My heart. The endearment brought a flush of anger to her cheeks. Cat turned round to face him. "What's the point? You're clearly better than I."

"With a little more practice we shall be better matched. Have a little patience, Cat. You have talent and you're learning quickly."

Cat snorted at the false compliments. "I can barely manage a steady thrust and a scant handful of the tricks you have tried to teach me."

"All the more reason to practice."

She stiffened and her eyes narrowed to suspicious slits. "Faith, how much longer would you have me practice? Until Heyward is safely in his grave?" The accusation came out sharp and vehement. "Nay," she said, squaring her shoulders. "I have already wasted too much time with this foolishness. 'Tis time to finish what that bastard began twelve years ago."

He stared at her, alarmed. "But you're not ready! You—"

She shook her head fiercely. "Nay, say no more! I am done playing the dupe to your silver tongue."

"Silver tongue?" A shadow of annoyance crossed his face. He took a step toward her. "That isn't fair. I've always been honest with you!"

"Oh, have you?" She raised her chin belligerently.

Nicholas took another step toward her, his features dark. "Aye, always."

"Then tell me this. How can you protect that traitor Heyward when he stole your honor and the woman you love? How can you live with yourself when he still breathes?" The minute the accusations left her lips, Cat regretted them, but by then it was too late.

Nicholas stiffened as though she had struck him. His jaw worked violently but there was no sound so deep was his rage.

Part of Cat couldn't blame him. He'd trusted her with private details of his past, and now she turned them back on him as a weapon. But she was also sick to death of his hypocrisy.

Curse it all, Heyward was his enemy, too! The man had done his best to ruin Nicholas's life! But instead of seeking recompense, he denied the fact that he was even angry. Apparently, the mold of the noble and honorable man Nicholas was so busy trying to crush himself into allowed no room for such a base and human thing as a desire for revenge.

He made no effort to retort.

She studied him closely feeling both tired and sad. "The truth hurts, doesn't it?"

Nicholas advanced on her, sword still in hand. "You'd be wise to shut your luscious mouth before it's too late."

"Too late?" Cat eyed him narrowly, sensing triumph. "Why, Nicholas," she drawled. "I dare say your precious control is slipping. And weren't you the one who told me control is the essence of competence?"

"That's it. You go too far." Nostrils flaring, he took a third step toward her. "Prepare to defend yourself, dearling."

"Against what?" Cat backed away, sensing too late the danger she had wooed.

Nicholas raised his blade. "Why, me, Cat. Me."

18

There was a flicker of fear in Cat's eyes, but it was gone in an instant. On instinct she raised her sword. "What are you going to do? Kill me because I have the courage to speak the truth?" Her voice trembled slightly.

It may have been the truth, Nicholas thought, but she'd hardly brought it up in any kind-hearted attempt to enlighten him. Rather, she wanted him angry, enraged enough to join her pursuit of Heyward.

And it had worked.

Her ruthless questions had triggered a white-hot explosion of rage, leaving him blind and breathless. Heyward has done the unthinkable, a voice inside him screamed, and for that he should die. But a single, painful truth brought him teetering back to the edge of sanity—if he destroyed Heyward, he would also destroy his last, tattered shreds of self-respect. No matter what, Nicholas wouldn't sink to cold-blooded murder like that whoreson. Not anymore.

As his sight slowly returned, he stared at Cat in shock, as if seeing her for the first time. There wasn't the faintest flicker of remorse in her gaze.

Not only was she bent on a path of self-destruction, he realized, but she was capable of taking him down with her. He'd entrusted her with private truths about himself, and now she didn't hesitate to wield them against him like a weapon. And with that knowledge, came a fiercer, more immediate source of anger—and it was directed exclusively at Cat. She'd played ruthlessly on his weaknesses. She'd betrayed him.

When Nicholas swung at her with his blade, he no longer pulled the blow. Cat was able to stop it, but it almost brought her to her knees.

He didn't wait for her to recover. Rather, he renewed his assault, driving her toward the west wall of the hall. Realizing her predicament, Cat, in turn, increased the strength of her blows. But her efforts could not match what years of bloody experience and pure rage lent to him.

Finally he had her backed against the wall, her sword half-lowered. "What?" Cat challenged weakly. "You don't have the courage to pursue Heyward, but you mean to kill me?"

"Kill you?" He laugh was a cold bark of denial. "That's not what I have in mind."

She swallowed nervously. "Then what?"

Nicholas felt the muscle in his jaw twitch. "I entrusted my past to you, Cat, and you turn it against me. I want you to know just how that betrayal feels."

Anger blazed in her eyes.

"Nay, do not look so confident, dearling. You've done your best to hide the chinks in your precious emotional armor, but I broke through it once before. And I can do it again."

Her cheeks flushed, but it was impossible to say if her reaction was one of embarrassment or anger. Glowering, she raised her sword slightly. "You set yourself a much more difficult task than a duel, Nicholas. My heart and soul are protected by more than a few fumbling parries. You won't have any part of me I don't want you to have."

Her denial only increased his determination. "Is that so? We'll see just how much of yourself you can defend when I am through with you and you lie naked and spent beneath me."

She inhaled sharply.

There, Nicholas thought, it was said. It was no longer hints and innuendo. He meant to have her.

Her gaze darted to the exit to her left, then back to him. She must have realized he could stop her before she could escape, because the color left her face. Her lower lip trembled. "You will not take me willing."

"Yes, I will." He'd pleasured her once before, and he'd do it again. 'Twould make the betrayal that much sweeter.

She thrust at him with her blade.

With a single sword stroke, he sent her rapier flying into the corner. "Undress."

"No."

"Very well," he said grimly. "I'll help you." With the tip of his rapier, Nicholas flicked away the top button of her shirt. Cat blanched. The button rolled noisily along the wooden floor before coming to rest. He raised an eyebrow. "Do you think you can manage the next?"

Cat spat at him.

Two more buttons went flying, leaving her exposed to the midriff. Nicholas noted, with less detachment than he'd like, that the strip of cloth she'd used to bind her breasts had slipped down some revealing inches. A rivulet of sweat sped down her neck to disappear into the just-visible cleft of her cleavage. At the sight, his reaction was swift and violent. His stomach tightened and his loins ached with blood.

His hot gaze upon her, Cat shivered and he shivered in return. God, she was beautiful—

Stop it. She's a manipulative, treacherous bitch. He didn't bother to ask her to take off her shirt. Rather, he used the tip of his blade to guide it over her shoulders. Gooseflesh appeared where his rapier's steel brushed against her tender skin. But she stood there immobile, her eyes half-closed, shutting away the part of herself he most wanted to reach.

Tossing aside his blade, Nicholas pulled her to him in a fierce, crushing embrace. He buried his hands into the silken tangle of her hair and dragged her mouth to his. Cat's passive lassitude was gone. She struggled to free herself from his arms. Nicholas fought in turn, bringing her back against the wall, meeting every inch of her flesh with his own.

He thrust his tongue into her mouth, but it came hard against her teeth. He insisted with his mouth that she answer his kiss. Cat tried desperately to shut down her instinct to respond, but her body conspired against her, pressing closer to him, opening to his assault.

All of a sudden, Nicholas was lost in the warm velvety textures and tastes of her mouth. As her tongue dueled with his, a groan escaped him. He knew now that he didn't mean to teach her a lesson in betrayal, he simply wanted her, *had* to have her.

His lips traced a hungry path down her neck and shoulders, lingering at the edge of the cloth that bound her breasts.

She shivered, this time—he suspected—more in eagerness than fear. Bringing his hands together, he rent the cloth in two. Her marvelous, full breasts sprung free. Nicholas watched as their rose-colored tips stiffened. His self-restraint crumbled as his male member grew rampantly hard.

As he bowed over her perfect breasts, he was vaguely aware of her shirt sliding to the floor. He took a breast into his mouth, caressing it. With a whimper, Cat arched backward against the paneled wall, her breathing coming hard and fast. Nicholas taunted the nipple with his tongue until it was harder than the best Toledo steel and still he would have continued if it wasn't for the fact Cat was slowly sinking to her heels. Frustration ran through him in a shudder, but he couldn't blame her. His own legs were hardly steady.

Without a word of explanation, he swept her into his arms, and carried her into the parlor. With a single swipe of his arm, he knocked the blotter and papers on his worktable to the floor. He laid Cat's half-clad form on the polished wood.

He used his poniard to cut the length of rope that bound her oversized trunk hose at her tiny waist, then hurled it into the expensive oak paneling. He had just enough control left to pull her pants off before he tore down his own and climbed on top of her, his amulet dangling between her breasts. Thankfully, the desk was long enough to accommodate them.

As his flesh met hers, Nicholas tried to marshal his patience, his self-control, but he failed miserably. Painful need ripped through him. In a primitive act of domination, he thrust his aching member into the cleft between her legs. But he could no sooner stop than he could single-handedly overwhelm the entire Spanish army. "Forgive me, Cat," he pleaded on a half-suffocated breath as he thrust himself into her with greater force.

At the sudden foreign invasion of her body, Cat stared up at Nicholas in shock. There was a sharp, sudden pain but it was quickly replaced by another sort of ache, a languid heat. Sweet Mary, she could no sooner defend herself against his seduction than she could his swordplay. Rather, she welcomed it.

As he felt her body relax to his, Nicholas closed his eyes in tortured pleasure. She was warm and wet for him. With that knowledge fled the last, tattered remnants of his control. Supporting his weight on his muscle-corded arms, Nicholas took one of her perfectly rounded breasts in his mouth and thrust in and out of her in a wild frenzy.

Cat moved beneath him, yielding to his urgent thrusts with first shy, then with growing eagerness. Groaning, he took her mouth with his and roamed one hand downward to massage the satiny delight of a buttock. With every thrust, the pleasure grew, his shudders increased. For an immeasurable moment the sounds of sex were the only reality in the room. Then he was aware of her silken legs entangled with his, her hands pressing into the small of his back, urging him deeper.

And it was over far too soon. His body arching, Nicholas exploded with a savage shout. He lay on top

of her, breathing hard, feeling his blood rush violently
through his limbs. With a grimace, he realized that
Cat's breath wasn't as rushed as his, that she hadn't
climaxed. He'd been mad, selfish, too long frustrated
in his desire to have her. Even now, his body swelled
again in longing. Jesus, what a selfish bastard he was.
Gently, he stroked her cheek. "I'm sorry, Cat. I—"

Cat brought an unsteady hand to his lips. "Shh.
You did nothing I didn't want you to do." She closed
her eyes for a long moment, and when they opened
again their rich, sable lashes were wet with unshed tears. "It appears you were right after all. You
can have any part of me you want."

Regret pierced him like a blade. Aye, he'd succeeded in proving his point, but what a shallow victory it was. He'd turned what should have been an act
of love into one of conquest. And it had been her very
first time. "Cat, what I did was wrong. It doesn't have
to be this way between a man and a"—he swallowed
hard—"between us."

Her lush mouth quirked into a sad smile. "I'll take
your word for it."

Nicholas pushed a sweaty tendril of hair away
from her face. "Nay, *mia cara*, let me show you."

She stared at him, green eyes wide with some
unspoken emotion, then nodded. That was all the
invitation Nicholas needed. This time he would do it
right. Their lovemaking wouldn't be complete until
he shared with her the full pleasure she had given to
him.

He rose from the desk and picked up a cloak that
had been abandoned on a trunk in the corner of the
room. He returned and took her into his arms and its
dusty folds. She struggled at first, but then relaxed.

Not bothering to re-don his breeches, he carried her up the two flights of stairs to his chambers.

Nicholas lowered her onto his bed, then went to the closet. He returned with a wet cloth with which to wipe away the stains of blood that smeared her stomach and his still-engorged member. She squirmed slightly at the first touch of the cold water. Then, managing a weak smile, she watched his ministrations with embarrassed fascination.

Nicholas returned the soiled cloth to the closet. Next, trembling with an unfamiliar nervousness, he lowered his weight onto the bed. Cat watched him warily, as tense as a coiled spring. He needed to be gentle, go slowly, teach her what lovemaking was, but Christ, his body was once again ready to slake its own thirst.

Leaning over her, he cupped her chin in his hand and caressed the tender flesh of her cheek with his thumb. He marveled at the softness. Though life had been hard on her, it had not marred her beauty. The scars were all within. "Ah, Cat, don't be frightened. I want to bring you pleasure. Not more pain."

Cat stretched back into the feather tick, her stomach aflutter, her senses on edge. Nicholas's hand moved slowly from beneath her chin so that he could trace her nose and brows with a fingertip. He continued his gentle caress, stroking her forehead, rubbing lightly at her temple. He threaded the fingers of both hands into her hair and massaged her scalp.

Drowsy with the innocent pleasure, Cat closed her eyes. Slowly, his hands roamed to the back of her neck and kneaded away the tension that had lingered at the base of her skull. Without stopping the caress, he brought his lips to hers in a whispered kiss. Then another. One hand drifted to the tender flesh of an earlobe, stroking it.

When her lips curled in a soft smile, he kissed both corners of her mouth, then trailed kisses under her chin and down her neck, evoking a shivery pleasure. Cat's eyes flew open and she made to sit up.

"Nay," he murmured, gently pushing her back. "Let me. Please."

Capturing her hands with his, he pressed them into the mattress near her shoulders. Boldly, he traced down her breastbone with his mouth and tongue, then licked under the straining flesh of her left breast. As he made lazy spirals with his tongue up the curves of each breast, her desire coalesced into a desperate ache between her legs. Cat weakly raised her head, trying to discover how his mouth could so shock and pleasure her. Her view was obscured by the thick tangle of his unbound hair.

It took a frustrated whimper from her to make him draw a nipple into the warm, wetness of his mouth. What few reservations she had left were lost in the heady, reeling sensation. Dampness flowed between her legs. Her own feminine smell drifted upward to mix with the scent of spilled seed and sweat that was already on them both. Nicholas's nostrils flared; his silver eyes widened. Heat rising to her cheeks, Cat could only bite her lip and nod.

Watching her closely, he released her right hand, bringing his own down to the juncture between her legs. It took only the slightest pressure from him to spread her legs. Then he was seeking her, parting her, tender and gentle.

A rumble of pleasure came from his chest when he discovered how wet she was. He withdrew his hand

and tested the scent that lingered on his hand first with his nose, then his tongue. Longing flashed in his eyes like steel's sharp sheen.

He released her other hand. Carefully, he guided his engorged member past her tender folds. As his breath rasped unsteadily against her throat, he watched her closely, afraid of causing her pain. The faint rawness Cat felt was nothing, however, compared to the need screaming inside her for fulfillment. Bringing her hands to the pale flesh of his well-muscled buttocks, she urged him deeper.

In a long, resolute thrust he plunged all the way inside her. "Oh God," he gasped, "Cat . . . "

His fingers twined deeply in her hair as he apparently fought for control. After going still for a moment, he began to move his hips, thrusting in deep strokes. Jolts of pleasure shot up Cat's spine. Wrapping her legs tightly around him, she pulled him deeper into her. The mattress seemed to have disappeared from beneath them, but she didn't care. She followed him into their own private world of rapture. For a long moment she lingered at the crucial juncture, then the dizzying ecstasy ripped free and she found her climax with a sharp cry.

"Yes. Yes! That's it, *mia cara*." A smile of delight lit his lips, then faded as he increased the speed of his thrusts. With a groan, he jerked inside her and spilled his seed.

This time, instead of collapsing he brushed the hair away from her face and studied her solemnly. "Are you all right?"

Cat could only laugh in tired delight. She drew him into her arms and brought him down to her chest in a hug. "How am I? Happy, Nick. Happy."

*   *   *

The afternoon sun, which darted through the mul-lioned windows and past the fabric curtains into the private abode they shared, roused Cat.

Cracking an eye, she saw that Nicholas drowsed next to her. Sleepily, she ran a hand over the hard lines of his stomach. With a faint growl of pleasure, he awoke. Stretching with all the self-congratulatory grace of one of the Tower cats, he lazily watched her hands play.

The newly discovered intimacy brought a happy blush to Cat's cheeks. Enraged beyond reason, they'd discovered a new way to channel their emotions. Passion. Although she thought at first that they were as liable to kill one another as anything else, their lovemaking had been wonderful, something more than even what she dared to dream possible in her most private of thoughts.

Cat's fingers trailed slowly through the dark curls of his chest, then circled toward the strange neck-lace she'd noted earlier. A battered gold ring and a small pouch hung from a leather cord around his neck. She prodded the pouch lightly with her finger, finding something lumpy. He pushed her hand away.

She rolled over on her stomach. "What is it?" she asked, her curiosity piqued.

He dangled the strange talisman from his fingers. "Some good luck I bought."

Cat's ears honed in on the self-mockery in his tone. "Oh, Misrule is into buying magic now, is he?"

"Something like that." His smile was good-natured but his eyes were a shade more solemn.

She nestled closer. "And the ring?"

His body went taut next to her. "The ring is something from a long time ago. Let it be, Cat."

Her own instincts told her to do just that, but it irked her that, laying naked and blissful after what they'd shared, there could still be secrets between them. In a harder voice, she pressed, "No really, what is it?"

Nicholas's head tilted back as he looked at the hand-carved canopy above them. She could see the muscles work in his jaw. "It belonged to my mother. It was supposed to go to my wife."

Cat felt her heart wither and die within her chest. "You mean Amye Heyward."

"Yes," he said grimly.

"Tell me, was it her you were thinking of when you made love to me?" Her question surprised them both. They stared at each other for a moment in shock. Then Cat brought a hand to her lips.

"What the hell kind of nonsense is that?"

Although knowing she wouldn't like the answer, Cat pressed on. "You do still have feelings for her, don't you?"

"That isn't easy to answer."

"Yes, it is." Her voice was gruff. "You either do or you don't."

He struggled for a response.

She blanched. "Never mind, your face says it all."

"Cat, I—"

Sweet Mary, his passion, his gentleness . . . they had been for someone else. Shame and disillusionment chased Cat from the bed. Thankfully, she was able to take one sheet with her as she fled from the room.

19

Ensconced behind his expensive Italian table, Laurence Heyward smiled to himself. The Cheapside affair might very well have been a disaster, he granted, but in the long run events had played nicely into his hands—in the form of the man who now sat in the chair opposite him.

Except for the modest fire in the hearth, only a single candle lent light to the study. Griffin had quite a distaste for light due to his recent disfigurement.

After plying the rogue with spirits and carefully dropping hints of his own hatred for the Lyly girl, Laurence had coaxed from Griffin the history of his animosity for Catrienne, nodding and frowning in all the right spots.

At the end of the man's muttered testimony, he clucked his tongue and shook his head sadly. 'Twas time to make the rogue see him as an ally. "She deliberately set you on fire?" he asked, brows high. "To think of such treachery! Was there no one to come to your aid, sirrah?"

The fabric of the cowl shifted as its wearer shook his head beneath. "No, it happened in her chambers. There was only her and that whoreson, Misrule. Ye can bet that neither o' them lifted a hand to help me."

Laurence sat up in his chair. "You say the fire was in her chambers?"

The hood raised slightly and the alderman could see the glimmer of the uprightman's suspicious eyes. "Aye, I barely made it out of there with my life."

"Thank fate for that small mercy." Inwardly, Laurence's mind wheeled with irrational hope. Was it possible the letter had burned in the fire? Nay, that would involve too much luck. Better to assume and prepare for the worst. Still, he'd have one of his men look into it. Right now he had more immediate concerns. Laurence forced himself to lean back in his chair.

Fortune had handed him a wonderful opportunity, in the rotting form of this obsessed madman, to capture and torture Catrienne without being directly involved. He meant to make full use of it. Leaning forward, he offered his most sincere smile. "Suppose I make a proposition to you."

"Let's hear it."

Listening to the proposition with half an ear, Griffin watched the alderman closely, careful to mark the silent clues. On the surface the bargain was simple enough. All he had to do was come up with a plan to trap the whore, and his high-and-mighty over there would finance the expedition. Right now, coin would be a welcome thing. A growing number of his people were holding back his share of their gleanings.

But there was one catch; Heyward wanted the girl alone for an hour before Griffin could dispatch with her as he pleased. That was when Griffin smelled the real opportunity.

The gentry cove would have him believe the whore had not returned his affections and that he wanted nothing more than a sexual dalliance with a bit of spice before her unfortunate demise. Griffin knew better. The whore hadn't been bluffing when she'd offered him a shot at blackmailing the alderman. She really had something on him. Whatever it was, Griffin meant to recover it for himself. All in all it was a pretty deal. He'd have influence over the legal head of Southwark and he'd get to murder the whore who'd wrecked his face.

When Heyward's proposition came to a close, Griffin smiled. "Sounds right-fine to me, cove. Here's what I have in mind . . . "

The City sprung into a flurry of activity the day before Christmas. Kitchens swarmed with armies of servants. Precious puddings were put in their clothes and dropped into coppers of boiling water, the kitchen boys taking turns as the stokers. Young members of congregations hurried to-and-fro with holly berries and ladders, decorating their churches. Presents were wrapped and people broke out in spontaneous carols.

Griffin and the liveryman Heyward had loaned him waited in a darkened corner of a Temple Bar tavern, draining their mugs and biding their time. They were careful to be sober by the time the short winter day drew to a close and the sky outside darkened. Griffin paid their bill, and, departing to an alley, they donned the tattered, foul-smelling garments of the two beggars Griffin had rolled the night before.

They waited while a few parties of carolers passed them, then fell in step with a good-natured group of beggars making their way down the Strand. If any noticed the bulk of blades beneath their threadbare cloaks, they wisely chose not to comment.

Beneath his hood, Griffin smiled, congratulating himself on his cunning. On this one day of the year, the poor were welcomed into the houses of London's finest to be served cake and ale. No one would dare to break the tradition. Not even the reclusive Lord Dacre.

Cat watched from the servant's entranceway to the Great Hall as the carolers and beggars made quick work of the cake and ale on garlanded trestle tables. Shunning his role as head of Dacre House, Nicholas stood deep in conversation with Jasper on the far side of the hall. He was pointedly ignoring her presence, just as he had since the morning she'd left his bed.

One of the beggars made his way toward her with an extra cup of ale. "Here now, missy," he said affably. "There's no cause for someone as pretty as you to look so sad."

Cat had just reached for the cup when she met the man's eyes. Her words of thanks fled unspoken. Sweet Mary, 'twas one of Heyward's liveryman who had confronted Nicholas outside the gates. And just behind him stood Griffin.

"Take her," the uprightman rasped. He tossed

back his cloak and drew his blade. "I'll make sure Dacre doesn't interfere."

The two cups of ale clattered to the floor. A woman screamed; Cat wasn't sure if it was due to her spotting the uprightman's naked blade or simply the first clear sight of the man himself.

The liveryman lunged for her. Quick on her feet from her weeks of practice, Cat bolted through the servant's corridor into the kitchen. Panic welled in her throat as she fumbled with the latch. Throwing the door open, she fled into the darkness of the gardens.

Cat raced down the first path she came to. The man's boots crunched on the gravel behind her. Rosebushes caught at her skirts as she wove and ducked through the pleached alleys. When her pursuer drew close, she crouched behind an overgrown hedge next to a fork in the path.

Squinting into the darkness, Cat did her best to become still and silent, but her heart hammered so loudly she feared Heyward's man could find her from the sound alone. Sweet Mary, Griffin had appeared with Heyward's man. Her enemies had joined forces! Moreover, they had eluded Dacre House's security.

Heyward's man came crashing through the greenery, stopping a few feet from where she hid. He turned one way and then the other, moonlight glinting off his blade. Cat could smell the bitter tang of rosemary that was being ground beneath his boots. Cursing, he stomped down the path to the left.

Cat scurried down the path to the right. Thank God the thin layer of snow had melted or he could have easily discovered her tracks. She wound her way through a cove of fig and almond trees, then crouched to listen. The faint sound of carolers rang from the Strand. The hiss of the chill wind cut its way through the barren trees.

Where was she to go? What was she to do? She had no weapon to use against her pursuer. Her best bet was to hide and pray Nicholas or Jasper would be able to reach her. But where was the best place to hide? Before her, half lost in shadows, stood the orchard. She would try to lose herself there.

She just reached the first of the trees, when she once again heard the rapid pounding of boots coming her way from the direction of the carp pond. She fled deeper into the thicket of trees. As she ran she thought she heard a whimper of terror come from somewhere. She realized with an odd sort of detachment that it must have come from her. Then there was no more time to think. Her pursuer was closing the ground between them.

Cat's foot caught a root along the ground and, with a scream, she went down in a panicked tangle. Panting, she scrabbled to her knees. And looked straight into an enormous pair of amber eyes. She screamed again before she could stop herself. In return, Crassus rumbled a greeting and, brushing against her, knocked her back onto the ground. Only now did she remember Nicholas's curt warning, earlier in the day. He'd let the lion out to prowl the grounds before winter set in.

Heyward's man came crashing up behind them. Cat turned to see her pursuer skid to a halt and stare at the lion. Then he turned and fled.

Crassus, always delighted with a game of chase, followed with a hearty roar. The man had just cleared the orchard when the lion brought him down. The strident scream may have been from agony or simply terror; Cat couldn't tell. And as quickly as it came, it was cut short.

Cat's legs gave way and she sank back to the ground. Nicholas was right, she realized sickly. The lion's teeth might be loose, but he still had enough strength left to snap a man's neck.

Nicholas raced through the dark garden, his heart in his throat. Griffin had fled the Great Hall just after Nicholas had scored his second cut upon the rogue. Jasper followed close on the uprightman's heels. Only a few minutes had passed, but Nicholas knew that was more than enough time for the liveryman to reach Cat.

A stark image of Cat sprawled in the gravel, moonlight probing a bloody hole in her chest, ripped through his mind. Ignoring the fiery pain in his bad leg, he raced down one path, then another. A few broken branches were the only clue to where they had been.

Crassus's roar followed by a scream came from the orchard. Nicholas broke through the hedges. Beyond, the lion pawed at the man lying on the ground like a broken toy.

"Cat?" Nicholas shouted.

Cat flew into his arms with enough force to send him rocking back on his heels. He wrapped his arms around her. Trembling violently, she began to sob.

Slowly, he eased them both to the ground, and, leaning back against a tree, he drew her fully into his lap. Holding her too tightly, he looked to the heavens and thanked God she was still alive.

Her muffled words came from somewhere beneath his chin. "Oh my God, I'm so sorry. I forgot about the lion. I didn't mean—" A sob choked off her words. She tilted her head upward and gasped for air. "I didn't want him dead. I just wanted to escape."

Nicholas crushed her to him, his own eyes beginning to water. He couldn't help but feel a sick twist of revulsion and guilt in his belly. It had seemed naught but an amusing folly to keep a wild beast in his gardens. Now the creature had murdered a man, and Cat had once again been witness to the brutal reality of death.

"Oh God, Cat," he murmured into her hair. "I wish I could spare you what you saw, but I can't." His voice was raw and hoarse. "I'm not even sure I'd be willing to, if it were the only way to keep you alive. I couldn't bear to lose you."

Her body went rigid in his arms. She drew back, her eyes hot and accusing, and a painful ache seized his heart. She'd remembered they weren't on speaking terms. "I'm sure you'll get over your grief. Especially with Lady Amye to console you."

"Cat." He reached out, but she was already out of his lap and drawing further away. "It's not like that. I'm not in love with Amye, not anymore, not for a long time now!"

Cat scrubbed angrily at her eyes with the back of her hand. "Then why do you wear her ring close to your heart? I find it hard to believe that's out of simple fondness."

Nicholas blanched. He could either let Cat think he was still in love with Amye or he could tell her the truth and make her hate him. Either way, he was going to lose her.

"Cat—" His voice failed him, and he had to start over again. "Cat, I wear Amye's ring to remind me what I did to her, to remind me of my crime."

"Of what you did to her?" Her laugh was humorless. "She was the one who left you."

"That's nothing compared to what I did." A hot fist of shame clenched around his heart, squeezing away his courage and strength. "Cat, I murdered my own son."

For a long moment the only sounds were the nervous beating of his heart and the hiss of wind through the trees.

"You did what?"

"When Amye came to tell me that she was going to marry Heyward instead of me, I"—closing his eyes tightly, he forced himself to go on—"I struck her once. Across the cheek. Hard enough to send her reeling backward." Hearing her inhale sharply in shock, he opened his eyes to look at her. "Cat," he pleaded, "I was so angry, so hurt that she could leave me after everything I'd been through. I wasn't even thinking."

"And you struck her."

Head low, Nicholas nodded, unable to force anything else past the tight knot in his throat. He was losing her. He could feel it. He sat there, trembling in the dark, for what seemed hours before he had the courage to go on. "She took ill that night and early the next morning she lost the babe she was carrying. Our babe."

Cat shook her head furiously, unable to comprehend the horrible truth. "But you can't hold yourself to blame!" she protested. "There's no way to know why she lost the child!"

He cut her off abruptly. "It was *me*, Cat. In my anger, I murdered my own son." Then he lost the last remnants of his control and broke down into sobs of grief, not even knowing what he mourned the most, the son he never had, the woman he was about to lose, or the self-respect he'd lost forever.

Cat stared down at the wet remains of autumn leaves that had yet to entirely disintegrate beneath the snow. Her mind reeled in wild disorder. Nicholas held himself responsible for the death of his son. And he'd been trying to make amends ever since. He'd hoped that saving a thousand hearty Englishmen's lives might somehow counterbalance the one tiny life that had been lost.

Nicholas sat slumped on the ground, unconsciously rocking back and forth, surrendering to the grief he had fought to bury for seven years. In faith, could he be responsible for the loss of his son? Cat wondered. They would probably never know. But it was clear from the depth of Nicholas's remorse that he knew what he'd done was horribly wrong. And to lose a child . . . Could there be any punishment worse than that? Cat could find no answers to the questions that plagued her. She simply couldn't bear to see him suffer any more.

She crawled over to where he sat on the ground and took him into her arms, murmuring words of understanding and forgiveness, kissing him gently.

Twigs snapped and leaves crunched as someone hurried toward them. Nicholas seemed oblivious to the noise, his head burrowed against her chest. Cat looked up to see Jasper hovering at the edge of the orchard, his features wide with concern.

Silently she mouthed, "Leave us alone."

Jasper studied them both, assuring himself that neither of them were hurt. With a curt nod, he disappeared the way he'd come.

Cat continued to rock Nicholas in her arms. Slowly the tension eased from his body, and, still clinging to her, he began to return her kisses. But his own were awkward, almost shy, as if by sharing this darkest part of himself all familiarity, all confidence in one another were destroyed.

Cat's heart almost broke. Afraid that she too might collapse into helpless tears, she sought to convey with her hands, and mouth, and gaze that she could never turn him away. Hoping that the union of their bodies could say more of what was in her heart than all the pretty words in the world, she pushed him back toward the ground.

She kissed his eyes, cheeks, lips—anywhere tears lingered. She nuzzled his neck and the hollow under his chin. Remembering how he had kneaded away the tension in her neck, she did the same for him. Leaning close, she brushed back the tangled waves of his hair and murmured in his ear, "I don't care what happened in the past. You are the noblest, gentlest man I've ever known. You're my heart, my hero. I have no idea what I ever did to deserve you, Nicholas D'Avenant. But whatever it was," she continued, her voice husky with emotion, "'twas certainly my proudest moment."

A tremor ran the length of his frame, seeming to break through his stupor of misery. With a half-sob, Nicholas drew her into his arms, crushing her so tightly that she couldn't breathe. Just when her lungs began to scream for air, he rolled over so they were lying on their sides facing one another.

Cat drew in a breath of the cold night air and stared at him, fascinated. The moonlight drifted through the barren branches of the trees, casting his features in phantom patterns of light and shade. "Oh God, Cat, I love you."

A sudden warmth surged through Cat; a bottomless peace enfolded her. Before she could answer Nicholas's endearment, his mouth took hers in a long, absorbing kiss that scoured away any need for words. She took his hands in hers and encouraged him to explore. He caressed the lines of her waist and hip. His hands made love to the softness of her body. Dampness pooled between her legs, and she shivered with eagerness.

Sweet Mary, she needed this man, wanted him inside her. Unable to wait any longer, Cat untied the points of his doublet and raised her skirts. Bringing her top leg over his, she coaxed him to take her body the way he'd already claimed her heart. Nicholas shook with eagerness as he slid inside her. She gasped at his hard warmth of flesh.

They hovered there in a timeless moment. And what began as an act of tenderness became one of desperate passion inflamed by their mutual need to both comfort and grieve.

The next morning, Cat awoke before Nicholas. She lay on the slatted wooden floor of the tree house nestled in the orchard where cold had driven them for shelter. Her head resting atop Nicholas's chest, she listened to the deep, even beat of his heart, wishing she could linger forever in that moment. Nicholas had opened himself completely to her last night, shared his darkest secrets. She, in turn, had listened, accepted, and comforted. And, rousing from his grief, he had responded to her with all the pent-up tenderness and passion he'd never had a chance to share with another soul.

But now, in the light of day, she knew with painful certainty that tender moment of connection was all there could ever be between them. Nicholas's openness and generosity with himself had only served to illuminate how very little she had to give in return. Pensive, Cat traced a line across the noble arch of his brow.

He'd said he loved her . . .

Aye, the pleasure his body could win from hers was pure and explosive, overwhelming all thought of what stood irrevocably between the two of them. But she was nothing more than a cynical, bitter shell of a woman obsessed with seeing another man dead. There was nothing within her to share or give but bitterness.

Nay, Cat thought as she closed her eyes, the love that Nicholas had tried to share with her last night was something she could never have. Even if she longed for it with all her battered heart.

20

The queen's enormous Christmas table was stationed beneath the great candelabra. Lords and ladies were seated according to rank. Due to his status as the Lord of Misrule, Nicholas had been granted a place close to the salt cellar, which meant that Cat, as his guest, sat there as well. Aware of the curious glances coming her way, Cat twisted uncomfortably in her seat. Busy performing his various duties as Lord of Misrule, Nicholas had been forced to leave her side. Directly to her right was his empty chair, and, next to that, Laurence Heyward.

Careful not to meet his wrathful gaze, she looked instead at the precious carving knife a servant held across the table and wished wistfully that she could put it to good use.

Lady Amye Heyward had paid the queen's Master of Revels an enormous sum for the honor of bringing the peacock, the most royal of dishes, to the Christmas table. Waiting in the wings of the Great Hall, she eyed the bird with distaste.

Its large, silver tray rested on a table next to her. The creature's brilliant plumage was still intact if somewhat sodden from the pool of gravy in which it sat and from the egg yolk in which it was basted. Its gilded beak was stuffed with a sponge saturated in spirits that would be lit just before the grand entrance.

The bird was an abomination in culinary creation. The thought of bearing it on her shoulder into the Great Hall caused her stomach to lurch in revulsion. But it gave her a chance to talk to Nicholas alone.

As the royal retinue of servants bustled around Amye and Nicholas, she murmured out of the side of her mouth, "I thought you might like to know my husband recently received a letter from the rebel earls."

Nicholas shot her a glance. "Pray, what did it say?"

Amye didn't instantly respond. Rather, she watched the servants as if concerned they might overhear, and she let Nicholas stew at the delay. Finally she said, "It demands to know why they have not received the aid that was promised. Their man will be at Grey's Inn on Innocent's Day when Will Shakespeare's new play appears there." She ended it there, forcing him to ask for the last, vital pieces of information.

"How will the exchange occur?"

"My husband's man is to look for the gentlemen's Prince of Purple, their own Misrule"—she shot him an ironic look—"and deliver the note to him prior to the beginning of the show."

Nicholas took her hand in his and brought it briefly to his lips. "You have my everlasting thanks."

"Nay," Amye demurred absently. "It was the very least I could do." Thinking of how her husband would react when she and Nicholas entered the hall as the honored couple, Amye couldn't help but permit herself a small smile.

Horns blasted within the hall. Two men in the queen's livery, encircled by a company of minstrels, tugged the trunk of an apple tree, the Yule log, into the Great Hall.

The musicians broke into song:

> *Come bring, with a noise,*
> *My merry, merry boys*
> *The Christmas Log to the firing;*
> *While my good dame, she*
> *Bids ye all be free,*
> *And drink to your heart's desiring.*

> *With last year's Brand*
> *Light the new Block, and*
> *For good success in his spending,*
> *On your psalteries play,*
> *That sweet luck may*
> *Come while the log is a tending . . .*

A piece of last year's Yule log was kindled and thrown into the enormous fireplace, causing the new log to burst into flames.

Queen Elizabeth, dressed in a frothy gown of the purest white silk, rose and held her cup high. "This

Yule log burns. It destroys all old hatreds and misun-
derstandings."

For a second, Cat felt as if the monarch's gaze
rested on her and Heyward.

"Let your envies vanish, and let the spirit of good
fellowship reign supreme for this season and through
all the year!"

A hearty cheer rang out and everyone drank to the
monarch's toast.

Then the boar's head was brought to the table with
great state. First came Jasper, along with two pages,
carrying the bloody sword with which the holiday
boar had been slain. Nicholas, the Lord of Misrule,
resplendent in black velvet, was ushered in by the
Master of Revels, followed by an entourage of raucous choristers and minstrels.

The boar's head was dressed with garlands of rosemary and laurel, and a lemon, the symbol of plenty,
rested in its mouth. Nicholas brought the delicacy to
rest in front of the regal queen, then he retreated to
the side.

Next came Lady Amye Heyward, resplendent in
her Christmas gown and hat, bearing the peacock.
Whispers followed in her wake, but they were quickly
silenced by a quelling look from the queen. Lady
Amye placed the bird on the table.

Nicholas stepped forward into the silence. "Your
majesty, may I have the pleasure of making the first
vow?" His voice was gauged to reach the farthest corners of the hall.

The queen inclined her royal head. "By all means.
We are curious what pledge our Misrule might make
on this special day." Her small, rosy mouth formed
the faintest of smiles, as if she were privilege to some

secret amusement. Then she addressed her attention back to the hall at large. "Knights, you may line up for turn at the bird."

Chairs were heard squeaking backward as the men, Heyward included, left their seats.

Nicholas waited patiently until it was silent again. Placing his right hand on the peacock, he turned to look at the room as a whole. "I could vow to defend the virtue of all women, but some might have cause to question that one."

A ripple of laughter ran down the table.

"So instead"—his gray gaze rested on Cat—"let me pledge my life, my heart, and my soul to the two women I hold most dear." He inclined his head at Elizabeth. "First, of course, to my beloved queen who is always in my thoughts."

Elizabeth nodded, accepting the compliment.

"Second . . ." His voice broke, and he was forced to stop and clear his throat. "Second to my dear friend's cousin, Catrienne, who has taught me what it means to love."

Cat's heart leaped in surprise. The hall sat in stunned silence as Nicholas left Amye's side. He made his way to his own chair beside Cat. Sitting, he took her limp hand in his and slid something on her finger. She pulled her hand out from underneath the table. 'Twas his mother's ring.

"Be my wife, Catrienne," he murmured soft enough for only her to hear. "Make my most cherished dream come true."

Cat stared at him for a long moment in shock. Inside, the fragile remains of her heart withered and died. Unaware of the drama that played on at the table, knights stepped forward and proclaimed their peacock vows, each trying to outdo the last in loquacious audacity. Finally, Cat found the courage to look at him.

The resplendent glow faded from his face.

"Nay, Nicholas," she choked. "I cannot."

He nodded silently. "I understand."

The bitter tone of his words, however, told Cat the contrary. It was the first time he'd ever lied.

Miserably, she pulled the ring from her finger and slid it across the table to him.

Avoiding her tearful gaze, Nicholas picked it up with a trembling hand and tucked it into the left side of his doublet, next to the heart Cat sensed she'd just irreparably harmed.

Other than Nicholas's telling Cat in a hoarse whisper about the conversation with Amye, the trip home from Court was conducted in silence. Nicholas sat across from her, staring at his hands that lay in his lap. Cat's throat constricted in a tight ache and tears welled hot in her eyes. Sweet Mary, in front of all Court, he'd declared his love for her—a love that in another lifetime she would have accepted with all her heart.

But, in the cold realities of her world, it was a love that couldn't exist, a love she could never return, for there was nothing left in herself to give. What little that hadn't died with her family was devoted to the quest for vengeance. She owed them that.

Finally reaching Dacre House, Nicholas headed for the parlor while Cat retreated to her chambers upstairs. When she came back down an hour later, she found him slumped in the chair behind his worktable.

She dropped the forged letter in his lap before she could lose her nerve. "Here. I want you to have this." After what he'd asked of her at Court, she knew the gesture was laughably inadequate. But it was all she had to give.

He stared dumbly at the piece of paper. "What's this?"

"It's a replica of the stolen letter."

"But it was lost in the fire."

She swallowed uncomfortably. "I remembered enough from reading it to have a decent forgery made."

He looked at her sharply. "But you can't read."

Although she felt her chin tremble, Cat held his stare. "Yes, I can."

His wince of pain rocked Cat with another spasm of regret. She had played him false from the very beginning.

Carefully, Nicholas unfolded the letter. His lips moved slightly as he read the words. After reading it once, he looked up at her. He scanned it again, and his hand began to tremble. "Jesus, Cat, do you know what you have here?"

She nodded. "Aye, I think so. The meeting Amye mentioned—it's to set another time for an exchange, isn't it?"

"You're probably right, but that's not what I mean."

Running his hand along the edge of the carved table serving as his desk, Nicholas triggered a concealed lever. A secret compartment popped open on the top. With unsteady hands, he withdrew a pile of handwritten notes. Placing her forged letter on the table, he laid two others beside it. "Cat, are you certain you and your friend got the handwriting right?"

"Of course. I'm very good at remembering things like that. And Egan is . . . was . . . one of the best." She pointed at one of the other two letters. "See how well it matches your letter from Heyward."

"Mayhap you need to take a better look at that signature." The excitement in Nicholas's voice belied his cool words.

Drawing closer to the desk, Cat did, and her brow furrowed. "Wait a minute, this belongs to Essex, not Heyward."

"Don't you see?" he asked, coming to his feet. "I was right. He is the one dealing with the rebel earls. I can't believe he'd be so stupid as to put his treason in his own hand!"

Cat's puzzlement grew. The letter she'd stolen belonged to the earl? Then why did Heyward want it back so badly? She shook her head. "I don't understand."

Rocking on his heels with glee, Nicholas waved the forgery in front of her face. "Essex will have to send another letter to the rebel earls' man at Grey's Inn. If we gain the letter, a letter in his own hand, we'll have proof of his involvement! I can bring them both in—Heyward as the messenger and Essex as the head conspirator! Now all we need is a plan."

Cat watched Nicholas pace the room with frenetic energy. He seemed just as happy and alive as he had at the Christmas banquet. Aye, she thought sadly, she may not have given him her heart, but she'd unwittingly given him one last chance to catch Essex, one last chance to find peace.

Secretly, she hoped it would be enough. It had to be. For that was all she had to give.

21

Griffin finally built a fire. Hunched in his cloak, he stared into the flames and brooded over his recent defeat until nothing remained in the grate but evil red coals. Still his failure to capture the whore burned at him.

With an ugly grunt, he hurled another log into the hearth. Using the iron poker, he jarred the fire back to life. Burying the tip of the poker in the coals, Griffin grimaced. As Southwark's uprightman, stoking a fire should be a task well beneath him. But there no longer was anyone to take his orders. After the mauling of Heyward's servant by the lion, everyone except Teddar and Bodel had fled. Even they were seldom seen at the alehouse, for they were obeying orders to watch Dacre House and wait for the pretty little whore to move beyond the safety of the gates.

She won't be pretty much longer, Griffin thought, his face cracking into a smile. Slowly he drew the poker from the coals. Its red tip glowed in the dark.

Fascinated, he rotated the iron shaft one way, then another, allowing himself to dream of the magnificent damage it could do, pressed to the creamy flesh of Cat's face.

'Twas December 27th, St. John's Innocents, the day the martyr John had been plunged into burning oil. The saint had been swept to heaven uninjured, but Griffin hadn't been so fortunate.

But then, he thought with a wicked smile, no saint would ever dream of doing what he was going to do.

22

Grey's Inn, the largest of the Inns of Court, was a goodly-sized building at Holborn. The lane in which it sat held many other fair buildings and tenements, and it led toward the fields of Highgate and Hampstead. Even dusted with snow, the Inn's gardens did it proud.

The gallant gentlemen of Grey's Inn were known for their theatrical presentations and revels. When Cat, Nicholas, and Jasper arrived, a large number of people were packed in the hall beneath the giant hammerbeam roof. Word was out that most of Inner Temple, rivals of Grey's Inn, had been invited to the evening's entertainments.

Taking her hand in his, Nicholas barged his way through the press of overdressed Elizabethan elite to the end of the hall where a magnificent screen of Spanish chestnut stood. Light from the candles overhead cast the carving and Flemish strapwork in magnificent relief. Pretending to admire Lord

Howard of Effingham's gift to the Inn, Nicholas leaned over Cat and murmured in her ear, "Stay here. Jasper and I will go in search of the warhawk's man."

Cat nodded, but, made uncomfortable by the raucous crowd of people and terrified what might happen if things went wrong, she had to force herself to let go of his hand. Heading in the direction of the library, Nicholas and Jasper disappeared quickly into the crowd. Jasper was to assume the traitor's place and intercept the communication on the way from the warhawks to the rebel earls. The letter would provide proof of both Heyward's and Essex's involvement. If they got it.

Doing her best to keep to the shadows, Cat glanced nervously about the hall. Enormous portraits of the queen, Lord Burghley, and Francis Walsingham hung behind the dais and high table. Oriel windows looked out from both the north and south walls. Beribboned horses for the indoor jousts pranced and pawed in a gated corner of the hall.

The small stage that had been set up for the performers was rapidly disappearing under the growing press of people eager to see Will Shakespeare's latest comedy. The few costumed members of the Inn that were on the small platform did their best to urge people back, but there was nowhere for them to go. Hundreds of people each fought for enough room in which to stand. Someone elbowed Cat in the ribs.

A robust figure in moth-eaten purple velvet, curled-toe shoes, and outmoded paned trunk hose pushed his way through the crowd, drawing Cat's attention. The feather of his enormous hat bobbed to-

and-fro when he leapt onto the stage to join the other costumed gentlemen. The head of a gargoyle leered from his codpiece. 'Twas the Inn's Prince of Purple. A wave of apprehension swept through Cat. Had Nicholas and Jasper arrived too late?

The Prince of Purple turned to face the crowd, his protracted nose the only feature large enough to be seen past the floppy brim of his hat. The enormous wart on the end of it drew everyone's fascinated gaze. "Ladies. Gentlemen," he shouted, raising his hands. "I have the great honor of being your over-lord for this evening's entertainments." When a cheer struck up, he made a solemn bow. From behind the stage came a loud noise sounding suspiciously like a fart. The audience screamed with laughter.

Cat felt the first flutter of hope. No one but Jasper could make such an outrageous character seem charming.

Nicholas quietly reappeared at her side.

Cat stood on tiptoes and asked, "Did everything go well?"

He brought his mouth close to her ear. "It looks as though Savage has sunk to new depths in order to upstage a fellow member of the craft."

Something in his cold, ironic tone brought a shiver to her spine.

She mustn't have successfully masked her feeling of disquiet for he shot her a piercing look. "Nay, don't look at me so. We didn't kill the man. He's merely tied up in the chapel. I'm sure the gallant gentlemen of the Inn will find him soon enough."

Now that the novelty of the appearance of the Prince of Purple had worn off, the crowd began to grow restless again. It surged forward, forcing the costumed men on the stage flush against the far wall.

"This is bedlam," Nicholas muttered. "Has there been any sign of Heyward yet?"

"There," Cat whispered, her gaze locked on the small entourage headed toward them. At the forefront were Sir Laurence and his wife. Behind them came five heavily armed men.

"Why, darling, look who's here!" Amye cooed loudly. When her husband didn't instantly obey her order, she snapped him on the arm with her fan.

Rage twisted Nicholas's face. "You treacherous bitch! You set me up!"

Cat had just enough time to think the same thing before Heyward looked at Nicholas. The alderman's expression of polite indifference exploded into outrage. He pointed an accusatory finger at the two of them and bellowed to his men, "Seize them!"

Cat glanced wildly at the stage. She could tell from her line of view—straight up his enormous nose—that Jasper had seen them and was aware of their predicament.

"Let loose the horses!" the actor barked.

The young lawyer administering the corral looked at his commander as if he'd just gone completely daft.

"Do it! The Prince of Purple demands it!"

During the holiday season the mischief-maker's every whim was to be obeyed. The young man did as he'd been ordered. The horses, panicked by the crowd, reared and surged forward.

A hand was at the small of Cat's back. Nicholas pushed her through the crowd. He tread on feet and shoved to gain them space. From all about them came curses and shouts of outrage.

The horses' stampede seemed to be the final thing necessary to transform the irritable crowd into a mob. A fistfight broke out behind them. Off to their right a woman cried that she'd been knifed. Heyward's men were blocked by the confusion.

From the safety of the door, Cat glanced anxiously over her shoulder. "But what about Jasper?"

"Pray he's quick with his blade," Nicholas yelled in her ear, pushing her through the door into the cool night beyond. "Run, Cat, or we too shall be lost!"

It was over.

Nicholas lay slumped on the floor of the Great Hall with Cat and Savage. The actor had appeared at Dacre House shortly after they had. He'd managed to abandon his costume and slip away into the crowd. Disappointed and shaken, the three of them passed dwindling sacs of wine to one another.

After this night's fiasco at Grey's Inn, they'd certainly scared off Essex and his crew. The bitter knowledge twisted in his gut like the blade of a sword. Nicholas supposed he should be grateful that, due to the riot, it was doubtful they'd been able to establish a new drop-off for the stores and coin. But it vexed him that he would never be able to prove the earl's perfidy to the queen and that Heyward would go unpunished.

Nicholas was never quite certain exactly when Jasper had slunk back to his quarters at St. Mary's or when he summoned the energy to get himself and a drunken Cat—the alcohol allowing her to capitulate to tears—up the stairs and into bed. But somehow he managed to, and there they buried their misery in the dark oblivion of sleep.

"Say it! 'Twas you who told Dacre! For once in your life, don't lie to me, bitch!" Laurence Heyward's hand met his wife's face with a resounding slap. She flew back against her vanity, scattering gallipots of cosmetics. He permitted himself only the briefest of smiles; this was only the beginning of her punishment, for she'd cost him dearly.

There wouldn't be another chance to help the rebel earls in time for it to influence Spain's decision whether or not to intervene. And if Essex no longer had any use for the rebels, he also had no use for Laurence. Moreover, as badly as things had been botched, 'twas doubtful Laurence would receive any further assistance with advancement at Court.

There was nothing he could do to improve his situation so he indulged himself in beating his wife. It did little to vent his frustration. After the first slap, she ceased to cry out, taking his blows with all the liveliness of a sack of coal. Breathing heavily, he glared down at her half-crouched form.

From beneath the remnants of her elegant coiffure, she watched him with a mixture of disdain and caution, her right eye already swelling. "If you had an ounce of brains, darling," he hissed, "you'd be fearful for your life."

Slowly, wincing, she levered herself up to a sitting position. "Kill me then. But you'll lose something of great value."

"What could you possibly have that would interest me?"

She leaned back against the elegant parlor wall and smiled languorously. "I know how to get to the girl, Cat."

23

The letter came two days later:

Monseigneur,

I am pleased my tidings can finally bring you some good news. The rebels' despairing cries for aid have fallen on deaf ears! King Philip will not grant the subsidy and soldiers promised them two years ago by Sergeant Porres. England's battle will only be with the Catholic upstarts! Your loyal servant always.

Chateau Martin

Nicholas stared at the small piece of parchment, clenching then unclenching his hands. The head-on confrontation with Spain he'd fought so hard to prevent had been avoided. Whether his own actions had contributed to this favorable conclusion remained unclear. *But, damn it, shouldn't he be pleased just the same?*

Although he'd believed achieving this outcome might be his one chance for redemption, he felt no more or less the man he had been before receiving the good news. Victory proved hollow indeed.

Heyward had yet to pay for his crimes against Cat and her family, and suddenly that seemed to be the most important thing. For in her quest for justice, Cat had staked just as much of herself as Nicholas had on his own goal. Their failure at Grey's Inn had come as a devastating blow. It had taken all of Maris and Jonah's coaxing to get Cat to eat, let alone leave the dark confines of her newly claimed chambers.

Nicholas sighed heavily and raked a hand through his tangled hair. Cat had a death hold on the past and wouldn't let go until she felt justice had been served. And her tenacity was killing her just as surely as a deep wound could bleed her dry. Until Cat let go of the past, there could be no healing, no future—for her or for them.

Picking up the letter, Nicholas rose from behind his writing cabinet. He was going to feel like the lowest sort of cad sharing his good news with Cat when she had none of her own. But just the same, he knew he had to tell her. She'd played at least as big a role in this as he had. And mayhap knowing that her theft of the treasonous letter might have had a part in saving hundreds of lives could bring her some small comfort.

But he didn't hold much hope for anything anymore.

*   *   *

Someone pushed open the heavy curtains enclosing the bed upon which Cat sat. Afternoon sunlight spilled through, violating the sanctity of her lair. She blinked several times to clear her eyes. Nicholas stood before her looking ragged and tired, his lips pressed in a grim line. He sat down on the edge of the bed and offered her the piece of parchment he held in his hand.

Cat read the few lines. So he'd achieved his goal after all. There would be no confrontation with Spain.

When she looked back up at him she tried to smile. "C-congratulations." The word caught in her throat.

"Cat . . ." Nicholas peered at her intently but failed to find whatever he'd hoped to see. He bowed his head and swallowed heavily. After several uncomfortable seconds, he took her hand in his. "Lives have been saved, and I think you had a part to play in it. I know it's not all you hoped, but it's something."

Cat made to answer, but could only nod. Aye, it was something. But it was nothing even close to what she'd hoped. She was to have made Laurence Heyward admit to her family's innocence. She was to have destroyed him for his crimes. Neither had come to pass.

The treasonous letter she had thought was his had belonged to Essex, and the alderman had refused to trade a confession for it. Their attempt to trap him at Grey's Inn had failed, and he'd be too wise to step into another. And running him through with a sword—as if she had the skill!—would not bring her family back. She could feel a sob rise from deep within, but, refusing to give it voice, she brought her arms tight across her chest and began to rock back and forth.

"I'm sorry." Nicholas tried to take her into his arms.

Cat jerked free. She didn't want tenderness. Or comfort. There could be no consolation for her failure.

"Jesus, Cat. Say something. Anything! Just don't draw away from me!"

"There is nothing left to say," she whispered hoarsely. "You won. I lost." At his ragged intake of breath, she recanted her cruel words. "I'm sorry. That wasn't fair. It isn't your fault Heyward goes unpunished."

He brought his hand under her jaw and gently raised it until she was forced to look into his gray eyes. "Nor is it yours."

Saying nothing, Cat let him draw her into his arms. But it was more to comfort him than herself, for nothing could change the fact that she had failed her family. Irrevocably.

The pantry of the Lady Rose was dry and fairly warm. The sacks of flour provided an adequate, if not comfortable, place to sleep. What Rafe took to eat, he was careful to pay for. As long as he was willing to run errands, assist the cook, and lace up the girls, Sophie permitted his nightly presence amongst her foodstuffs. In terms of their unspoken arrangement, Rafe had few complaints. Other madames would have far less scruples about how they used a young boy in need of shelter.

It being New Year's Eve, the patrons and women of the Lady Rose were particularly raucous tonight. Wine and coin flowed freely as men sought to celebrate the beginning of the new year or obliterate memory of the old.

As he lacked the desire to do either and the hour was growing late, Rafe had shuffled off to his makeshift quarters. He was half asleep when the two roughly clothed men appeared at the door of the pantry. A woven bag was over his head before he could put up much of a fight. But, pride being one of his few possessions, fight them he did.

Not that it made any difference.

24

For the first time in a long while, the Great Hall of Dacre House was warm and filled with laughter. Candlelight flickered off polished wood, dousing the room in golden hues. An enormous trestle table was laden with a wealth of food. In the center of the culinary excess sat the wassail bowl, nestled amidst branches of greenery. The servants crowded around it, refilling their glasses and heartily toasting to one another's health.

Wishing she felt an equal measure of their good cheer, Cat forced a weak smile and nestled closer to Nicholas's side. His arm tightened around her waist. His smile was wide and filled with pleasure as he bent down to kiss her check. Her heart warmed slightly in relief. She and Maris had schemed the New Year's Eve celebration. It had been a long time since either of them had experienced a holiday like this, and perhaps a change could help them forget the past.

Lowering his head again, Nicholas murmured in her ear, "You've been busy, dearling."

Casually, Cat took a sip from her cup of warm, spiced ale. "Aren't I always?"

Nicholas beamed down at her. "Yes, but usually I'm not so pleased with the results."

Thinking of her former scheming and her reasons for it, Cat stiffened, the recent wound of failure still a tender thing.

A sudden draft of cold air issued from the front entry into the Great Hall, rousing Cat from her melancholy musings. Following in its wake came a diminutive, red-cloaked form. The happy burble of conversation quieted. When Nicholas failed to notice the new arrival, Cat squeezed his arm and nodded in the stranger's direction.

The cloaked figure hesitated, facing every eye in the room. But then the blonde-haired pixie shrugged back her cloak with an air of defiance. 'Twas Sophie, Cat realized with a start, the mistress of the Lady Rose.

A faint, disgruntled murmur rippled through the room. Granted, their master might have a slightly tarnished reputation, but it was nothing compared to that of this woman of the night. Slowly, the speculative gazes turned from the unwelcome visitor to Cat, curious to see how she meant to react.

"Sophie?" Nicholas exclaimed, careful to hide his surprise.

Cat supposed she ought to feel a sudden lurch of jealousy, but she didn't. She knew that whatever might or might not have been between Nicholas and the lovely woman was long past. Moreover, she judged the feisty mistress of the Lady Rose worthy of friendship for the kindness she'd demonstrated time and again. Yet, something did not feel right.

"Nicholas, my apologies for intruding, but this couldn't wait."

The vaporous feeling of dread that had been coalescing in the pit of Cat's stomach suddenly took on the weight of a rock. "What is it?" Cat cried. What's wrong?"

Slowly, Sophie turned to face her. "I'm so sorry. Rafe's been taken."

As soon as his wherry touched dock at Paris Garden, Nicholas was off at a dead run through the streets, shoving past anyone who dared to be in his way. London's finest gentry and heavily painted Winchester geese were but a blur of garish color as he passed.

One of Sophie's women had seen the coach Rafe had been shoved into. 'Twas Heyward's. Once again, the alderman had proved his treachery knew no bounds. If Heyward proposed a trade, Nicholas knew that Cat would sell her very soul if she thought it might save Rafe's life. Moreover, the boy would be cast aside, in God knows what condition, as soon as the alderman had what he wanted. Cat.

Slipping on muck-ridden cobblestones, Nicholas rounded the corner of the alley alongside the Lady Rose. He came to a stop in front of an angry crowd of Italians, awaiting him with blades drawn.

Don Antonio Carranza stepped forward from the crowd. The youth grinned widely as if he were welcoming an old friend. Only the narrowness of his eyes betrayed his true feelings. "Ah, *Signore* D'Avenant," he purred. "What a pleasant surprise. And just when I began to doubt we'd have a chance to settle our disagreement."

Like a pack of rabid hounds, the men stepped forward on their master's heels, ready to do violence.

Nicholas had just enough time to draw his blade before the second group of men, lounging behind wreckage in the alley he'd just run through, converged from behind.

He'd stepped right into the middle of an ambush.

Cat, along with Jonah and Maris, maintained an uneasy vigil in the kitchen, praying for Nicholas's and Rafe's safety. But the first day of the new year dawned without Nicholas's return. When the servants began to trickle in to prepare the New Year's Day feast, Maris turned them away. They had no cause to celebrate until they were certain of their lord's safety.

The fear that Nicholas might have caught up with the men who had taken Rafe and been overpowered began to gnaw at Cat's flagging confidence. Not wanting to give sway to such thoughts, she rose from her stool and paced the length of the small room. Sweet Mary, where was he? And what had happened to Rafe?

Suddenly, the silence in the kitchen was disrupted by the sound of hooves crunching on gravel beyond the side door. Someone was approaching the house! Cat's heart began pounding madly. All three of them hurried toward the door.

"Hello and good tidings to all. Happy New Year!" Jasper chirped, bounding through the door.

Noting his half-hearted reception, the crimson-

garbed actor raised his brow. "Such sorrowful coun-
tenances. Surely I'm not so terrible an omen for the year
as all that!" Leaning casually against the door frame he
added, "After all, I am male, single, handsome, and an
extraordinarily skilled lover—as many a woman can
happily attest." When that failed to get a rise out of
them, his wicked smile faded and he straightened.
"What is it? Somebody tell me what's wrong."

Cat fought hard to keep raw emotion in check.
"Last night someone captured Rafe."

"That little lifter?"

Unable to speak, Cat nodded.

The actor stepped forward and took her hands in
his and squeezed them tightly. "Who would want the
boy? Griffin?"

"No, 'twas Heyward. Nicholas went after the men
who took him, and he hasn't returned."

Jasper released his grip to run one of his hands nervously through his black mop of hair. "How long has
he been gone?"

"Most of the night."

"Too long," Jonah grumbled.

Jasper's gaze darted back and forth between her
and the aging butler. His expression turned grim.
"Where was he headed? I'll go looking for them
myself."

"The Lady Rose," Cat said, but—"

Distracted, she broke off to gape at a young boy in
beggar's rags who hovered uneasily in the doorway.
The others followed her stare.

Realizing he'd gained the room's attention, the boy
shifted from foot to foot and stammered. "Er, pardon
me, miss. Ye wouldn't happen to be, ah . . . Mistress
Lyly, would ye?"

Cat inhaled sharply. Lyly. He'd used her family's name.

Jasper stepped closer to Cat. "Who wants to know?"

The boy hunched into himself and ducked his head. "I have a message for 'er, sir, that's all."

"A message?" Cat's gaze darted to the small piece of parchment he clutched in his dirty hands. "Please, give it to me." A soon as the paper touched her palm, he snatched away his hand. Turning, he took off in a run. Cat unsteadily unfolded the paper. A tawny curl of hair fell out and drifted to the floor. It was Rafe's. There were only three lines scrawled on the page and they weren't from Nicholas:

> *'Twould be in both our interests to make an exchange. The boy for the letter. Be in your alehouse in an hour's time. Come alone.*

Could Heyward have Nicholas, too? No. He would have mentioned that, hoping to use it as a further lure to draw her in. But Heyward definitely had Rafe, and the blackguard would think nothing of harming the boy. He'd ordered the death of her own brothers. At that painful memory, a maelstrom of grief and terror began to whirl within. Sweet Mary, it was happening all over again. Someone had been put in danger because of her. If she didn't come forward . . .

Stop it, Cat ordered silently. She was panicking and that would only get them both killed. It was obvious, especially after Cheapside, that Heyward meant to trap her in the alehouse and seize the letter. He'd never allow Rafe and her to leave unharmed. Unless she forced him to.

The beginnings of a plan began to form. Heyward believed she really had the letter, and he wanted it back very badly. What if she were to hide the forgery away from the alehouse and refuse to tell him where it was until Rafe was safely set free?

"Cat, what does it say?" Jasper asked, breaking her concentration.

It was clear he wasn't about to allow her to go anywhere without some answers first. Sighing in defeat, Cat looked pointedly at Maris and Jonah. They took the hint and quickly found reasons to be in another room. As briefly as possible, she told Jasper what was going on. All the while, she mentally probed her plan for holes.

By the time he'd finished reading the letter, Jasper's expression had grown solemn and dangerous. "Give me this letter and I'll go in your place," he said curtly. "Better the bastard face a very angry man with a sword."

"No, Jas. I've inadvertently put too many people in danger already. Any more risks will be taken by me."

He glowered at her for a long moment. She did the same back to him.

Finally, he shrugged and said gruffly, "Well, you're not going alone."

She'd be fine on her own. She didn't need anyone else's help. The familiar retort rose instantly to her lips, but, for once, she held back. Studying the intensity on her friend's face, she began to wonder if Nicholas had been right when he suggested she would refuse anyone's help out of foolish pride. It was one thing to value her independence, 'twas something else to endanger Rafe's life out of misplaced pride. She acknowledge her defeat with a half-hearted smile.

"Very well. I could probably use someone to watch my back."

Jasper accepted his victory soberly. "So what's the plan?"

25

All that remained of the White Hart was the burned-out husk of the first floor. Taking a deep breath, Cat pushed open the rickety door and stepped inside. The smell of mildew and rot, mixed with that of human offal, was heavy in the air. Scaly-tailed rats slithered through the rushes at her feet. From the direction of the kitchen came the sound of dripping water. It struck an arrhythmic cadence with her own uneasy heartbeat.

Sea coals flamed in the hearth, coloring the rushes blood-red. As she wound her way through the wreckage, she was glad she'd taken time to change into the boots and trunk hose Nicholas had given her. Skirts would all too easily trip her up. Cat clutched her knife beneath the folds of her cloak and peered into the shadows. Although she'd come exactly at the time Heyward had requested, no one was readily visible. Finely honed instinct, however, told her she was not alone.

Her suspicions were confirmed when Heyward's voice floated out of the darkness. "So good of you to come, Catrienne."

She spun in the direction of the sound. "You bastard! Where is he?"

Slowly, the alderman stepped into the uncertain light, pushing Rafe before him. Wide-eyed and pale, hands trussed, the boy stared beseechingly at Cat.

Heyward maintained a steady grasp on the boy's shoulder. "Bring me the letter."

"Let him go first."

"I think not," he snapped. "Bring me the letter."

"I don't have it."

"Now that isn't very smart, is it?"

Nervously, she swallowed. "I hid it in the City. When Rafe's free, I'll tell you where."

"That isn't what we agreed."

"Do you want the letter or not, Heyward?" Raising her chin stubbornly, she added, "It's still of value to others."

Her threat lingered in the air.

After a long moment, the alderman responded. "Very well. You may have the boy. But you must come and get him yourself."

Cat studied Rafe and the alderman's position. Ruffin, they were too far away from the door. It could very easily be a trap. She remained unmoving, her senses straining in an effort to detect if others lurked amongst the wreckage.

Sighing, Heyward drew his poniard and applied the sharp edge to Rafe's throat. "Well, Catrienne, do you want the boy or not? I fear he means nothing to me."

No, innocent children meant nothing to the man.

Stark images of her brothers Richard and Edmund's crumpled forms rose unbidden, along with a wave of nausea. She had no choice but to act.

Slowly, she stepped forward, her gaze darting quickly from one side to the other. Heyward lowered his blade slightly, but Rafe looked even more alarmed. Just as Cat reached them, two figures converged on her from her periphery.

Whirling to face the closer man, whom she recognized as Teddar, she flung back the folds of her cloak and raised her blade. He lunged with a snarl. Stepping wide, she still managed to score a strike, neatly slicing open the palm of his hand. There was no time, however, to appreciate the small victory. A heavy blow took her in the chin. In a flash of brilliant light, pain shot down the length of her spine, stealing the strength from her legs. She crumpled to the floor, darkness engulfing her.

The next thing she was aware of was someone—probably Teddar—twisting the knife from her grip and, searching her for any other weapons, pulling her spare knife from her boot. Then she was hauled back to her feet and her arms were wrenched behind her back. The pain gave her enough incentive to force open her eyes.

"Now yer mine, whore," rasped a chilling voice. Like some misshapen, foul-smelling wraith, Griffin's cowled form emerged from the shadows to loom in front of her.

Panic welled inside Cat. Sweet Mary, what was *he* doing here? Had he and the alderman joined forces? "No!"

The uprightman reached out with a blackened finger to trace her features. "Oh yes, sweet Cat, yer all mine." His hooded head turned in Heyward's direction. "Isn't that so?"

The alderman's gaze narrowed. "Have you brought what I asked?"

"Aye."

A hint of pleasure gleamed in Heyward's eyes. "Very well, we shall make a trade. I'll throw in the boy as a bonus." Dispassionately, the alderman thrust Rafe forward.

"B-but you can't!" Cat cried, fighting back an overwhelming sense of despair. "You still don't have the letter. Let us go or a friend will see it reaches the queen's hands afore dark, I swear it!"

"Ah yes, the letter," Heyward murmured. "That could prove inconvenient"—a smile spread over his features—"if it hadn't have burned in the fire that happened here, hmm?"

Shock hit Cat like a fist in the stomach.

"The letter burned in the fire?" Griffin asked, sounding almost regretful. "No matter." He fished for something beneath the cloak, then thrust forward a bottle full of dark liquid. "Here's the nightshade. Be on your way."

Heyward frowned at the bottle. "You say all I need to do is put some on the point of my blade?"

"Aye. Mark him but once and he's a dead man."

Heyward took the bottle carefully in a gloved hand but still looked dubious. "It'd better not take more than once. Dacre's a deadly fighter."

Cat gasped in shock. He meant to murder Nicholas!

"Trust me. It'll work." Griffin turned to Cat. "I only nicked Skinner. Did a good enough job, eh, *mort*?" Taking in her look of abject horror, the uprightman wheezed a chuckle that degenerated into a coughing fit.

Cat stared at the uprightman's cloaked figure in sick hatred. "It really was you. You murdered Skinner!"

"Did ye ever have a doubt?"

No, she never had. But poison? And now Heyward meant to do the same with Nicholas. An image of Nicholas crouched over Crassus, smiling in pleasure for the first time, burst forth in her mind. The realization that she might never see him again froze her heart. "What makes you think Nicholas will fight you, Heyward?" Cat challenged desperately. "If he meant to humble you, he'd have done it long afore now."

"He'll fight me because he'll think it the only way to make me tell what I've done with you. Don't you see, little one? You're the bait."

Cat stared at him, mute with shock. Heyward was right. Nicholas would fight if he thought it might save her. He'd fall unsuspecting into the trap.

Drawing on bravado, she sneered at Heyward. "You overestimate my value to Dacre, sirrah. He only wanted the letter I'd stolen."

"Oh, I think there's more to it than that. But even if I'm mistaken on that account, I suspect he'll be ready to fight once my darling wife is through spewing the rest of her venom."

The ice that had stolen her heart spread to her limbs. Nicholas had to be warned! Seeking a route of escape, her gaze flew toward the back door.

Bodel staggered through the door with Jasper's limp form in his arms. "The cove tried to sneak in the back way," he said to Heyward. "Good hap I was on his blind side. Caught him good with me fist." The rogue let the actor's unconscious form slump to the floor.

"Oh God," Cat croaked, "Jas—"

Bodel smiled toothlessly at Cat. "Relax, *mort*, he's still alive."

Heyward looked from Bodel to Griffin. "You have a grudge with this man, don't you?" Not waiting for an answer, he drew away to the corner, unstopped the bottle, and set it on the ground.

Griffin watched him carefully. "Ye could say that."

"Good, then you won't mind taking him, too," the alderman murmured, dipping the point of his blade in the murky solution. With a flick of his wrist, he turned the blade one way and then the other over the hot coals in the hearth, allowing the poison to dry. Then he carefully sealed the bottle and pocketed it. "Remember, he said, looking at Griffin, "I must have enough time to get to the Exchange before you kill these bits of refuse."

Griffin gave a wheezing chuckle. "Aye, cove. There'll be plenty 'nough time for that. 'Specially with what I have in mind."

Heyward's eyes crinkled as he smiled. Nodding a silent farewell to Cat and her captors, he passed through the door into the bright light of day. When the door slammed close behind him, the sound held a dread finality.

Casually, Griffin walked over to the open hearth and prodded at the coals with the iron poker.

Cat struggled in Teddar's grasp. "No! You can't let Heyward kill him! Nicholas has nothing to do with any of this! Griffin, I beg you. You've got to stop him!"

Griffin looked casually over his shoulder at her. "Better worry 'bout yerself, sweetmeat."

Teddar, now at her back again, wheezed in humor. In a rush of sour breath, he said, "Aye, we're all going to have a turn with you, pretty thing."

"After I'm done with her, cove, you won't want a turn." Slowly, Griffin pulled the poker from the coals and examined its glowing tip.

Cat's gaze was transfixed by the glowing piece of iron. Unconsciously, she stepped back into Teddar's waiting embrace.

"You don't mean to burn the girl, do ye?" Teddar's question held the smallest hint of rebellion.

"And why not?" With his free hand Griffin whipped back the cowled hood of his cloak, exposing his raw, savaged flesh. Only his pale blue eyes, sharp with demonic fervor, stood out as recognizable features. The uprightman took in the horror they could not disguise, and those merciless eyes narrowed. "This," he said with a sweep of his hand, "is what the whore's done to me. She will suffer all that I have. And more!"

"Very well. Just don't hurt the end that really counts. If yer know what I mean."

The heat issuing from the glowing tip of the poker seemed to burn the small space of air that stood between her and Griffin. Cat sucked in her breath and drew back, pressing into Teddar. The rogue's gnarled hands clamped around her upper arms, forcing her still.

With a guttural growl of pleasure, Griffin edged the poker closer until it hissed but inches from the tender skin of Cat's cheek. Her chest rose and fell in heavy, desperate pants. Sick with fear and aversion, she was unable to stop herself from turning her head away.

Intrigued by the prospect of torture, Bodel had turned his back on the actor so he could better watch the entertainment.

Cat caught a faint movement behind him. Sweet Mary! Jasper's right hand had curled into one of the familiar signs of her trade—one of the signs he'd had her teach him on a lark. The message in his fingers was unmistakable: "I am ready. Make your move."

Nicholas pounded furiously on the door of the Southwark alderman's town house. When he'd regained consciousness at the Lady Rose, bruised and beaten but alive, he knew with a sick certainty that Carranza's ambush had been a diversion to buy time for Heyward. Sure enough, by the time he'd reached Dacre House, Cat was already gone. Christ, he'd been a fool! Giving vent to some of his frustration, he pounded again on the heavy oak door.

The door opened. It wasn't one of the Heyward servants that hovered in the portal, but, rather the mistress of the house, Lady Amye. Her right eye was swollen shut and the flesh on that side of her face was mottled purple and blue. For a brief moment, Nicholas's fury was forgotten as he assessed the damage Heyward's fists had wrought.

His shock must have been evident, for Amye brought a hand to her face and smiled painfully. "He figured out who told you about Grey's Inn."

Despite her treachery, Nicholas might have offered her a word of condolence, but she turned and walked down the hall. Fists tightening, he followed her into the parlor. She motioned to a chair, but he ignored her offer. "What has he done with her, Amye?"

"Killed her, no doubt."

"You lie."

Her guarded expression softened into something akin to pity. Her voice was overly sweet. "Poor Nicholas, I know how much it must hurt to accept what I've told you. But 'pon my word, it's the truth."

But it wasn't the truth. It was poisonous treachery sweetened with honey in hopes of making him swallow it. "No more," he said. "I'll hear no more of your lies!"

Her eyes narrowed briefly before she forced them wide in mock horror. "But, Nicholas, how can you—"

Nicholas grabbed her by the arms and shook her silent. "Damn it, Amye, tell me where she is!"

Amye flopped like a rag doll, but the smile that formed on her lips was brittle as glass. "You'll have to do better than that if you're trying to threaten me. I fear I've had many opportunities to toughen myself to violence since our youth."

Aye, and he had provided the first such opportunity with his blow, Nicholas thought, shame piercing through the haze of rage. He loosened his grip but didn't retreat.

Amye stared at him appraisingly. Her smile slowly faded, revealing the face of an aging beauty who looked tired and pale. Perhaps she realized how fully her ploy had failed, that the self-worth he'd discovered in Cat's arms left him immune to her poisonous half-truths.

She brought her arms across her chest and turned to stare out the window. "I cannot say where my husband is now. But he said he had some business to finish at the Exchange within the hour."

Nicholas turned to go.

Amye's dead-calm voice stopped him. "Nicholas? Don't leave yet. There's something you need to know."

"And what would that be?" he asked dangerously.

She leaned against the frame of the window as if she needed something to give her the courage and strength to remain standing. "You aren't to blame for the loss of our child."

Nicholas's blood ran cold. Fighting to keep his expression neutral, he managed to say, "I struck you, and you lost the babe. There is nothing to question."

"But it wasn't your blow that caused me to miscarry."

The muscles of his jaw tightened involuntarily. "Perhaps not, but we'll never know."

"Yes, we will." She held up a hand to stay his angry retort. "Would you just listen to me? It wasn't you! Laurence slipped me a draught of abortifacient that evening in my tea. He didn't want his heir to be another man's babe."

Every instinct told him she spoke the truth. Nicholas stared at her in speechless horror. When he finally found his voice it was cracked and hoarse. "Nay, that cannot be. Even he could not be so foul."

Amye stepped forward. "He can and he was. My husband bragged about it to me just after the consummation of our marriage. He was sadly in his cups." She laughed bitterly. "You still don't believe me, do you? Tell me this, Nicholas, what do you think left me sterile? Many women lose a babe and can still have another. My dear husband, however, was a bit generous with the dose of tansy and rue he gave me. He murdered your son, Nicholas."

As the full weight of what she said settled on

Nicholas's shoulders, the wall of self-control he'd fought to build and maintain crumbled to dust. He knew his reaction was exactly what Amye had hoped for with her shocking confession, but it didn't matter. He could no sooner change what he felt than he could correct the injustices of the past. Heyward had murdered his son. And, undoubtedly, he meant to do the same with Cat.

Without a word, Nicholas exited the parlor. His blade was drawn before he cleared the front door. Cat's suspicions had been right. That single thought managed to penetrate the red-hazed torrent of his rage. Aye, the murderous fury, the need to punish Heyward, was still there. And it was far stronger than all his precious control.

As much as he'd tried to reform his soul, murder was in his heart.

26

The poker loomed nearer.

Cat writhed and strained against Teddar's bony grip, careful to show as much flesh as possible in hopes of capturing every man's attention.

"Hold her!" Griffin snarled.

Out of the corner of her eye, she saw Jasper bound to his feet. With a flourish of his hand, he unwrapped the garrote from around his wrist. The thin coil of gut was over Bodel's head and biting deep into his dissipated flesh before the man even suspected his danger.

Open-mouthed yet speechless, the rogue clawed ineffectually at the cord that severed away his breath and life. Jasper held on like a stubborn carrion bird as the larger man attempted to shake him off.

Teddar got a firm grab on the back of Cat's collar and thrust her closer to his master. Eyes heavy-lidded with pleasure, Griffin lowered the poker toward her cheek.

Too late, screamed a hysterical voice inside Cat. *Jasper's help will come too late.*

At the last moment, with a tear of fabric, Cat wrenched partially free from Teddar. The hot iron tip tangled in her hair, burning it with a sickening sizzle.

Cursing, Griffin tore the poker free.

Bodel's struggles finally ceased and his heavy form crashed to the floor, taking Jasper with it. At the sound, Griffin spun around. The actor was trying to free the blade belonging to the man he'd just killed. With a snarl, the uprightman drew his rapier.

"Jasper, watch out!" Cat cried.

Jasper glanced up, his color blanching. But he continued to tug at the sword. He must have realized he wouldn't have a chance without a blade.

Griffin advanced, brandishing both poker and sword. "Kill one of my men, will ye?"

Rafe, almost forgotten, dodged from his corner and butted into the uprightman's legs, sending him off-course.

Jasper pulled the blade free.

Griffin quickly recovered his balance. With a violent swat of his hand, he sent the boy hurling toward the wall. Rafe landed with an agonized cry, struggled for a moment, then lay still.

Sweet Christ, was he dead? Cat wondered sickly. Nay, she could do nothing but hope he wasn't.

Griffin's and Jasper's swords met with a clash of steel.

Cat arched backward and, using the concealed razors in the heels of her boots, she brought both feet down and sliced through the insides of Teddar's calves. He howled in pain and loosed his grip. Breaking free, she pivoted, yanked the man's knife from his belt before he could stop her, and plunged the blade into his abdomen.

Teddar muttered a curse and grabbed the hilt, but he seemed to lack the strength to pull it free. For a moment, Cat froze, locked in the horror of what she'd done. But as the hunchbacked man began to sink to his knees, she drew his sword from its sheath with her left hand. Realizing she might also need the knife, she pulled it from his abdomen with a grimace and turned to help Jasper.

From the shredded cloth and bloodstain on Griffin's right arm, Cat could tell her friend had scored at least one blow. But Griffin held an extra weapon and had backed the actor up against the wall.

She kept expecting Griffin to turn and confront her with each step she took closer. But he didn't. The two continued to thrust and parry. Then she was close enough to strike. She had to act before her luck changed. But she couldn't. Her legs were heavy, frozen. Her stomach twisted with nausea.

Once again, Griffin's thrust missed Jasper's chest. But this time, he snagged the actor's shirt, effectively pinning him to the wall and limiting his range of motion.

Jasper glanced wildly about the room for help. His eye widened as he noticed Cat's presence. His blade lowered slightly. Now, Cat, his gaze seemed to implore her. Do it now!

Shaking uncontrollably, Cat hesitated.

With a shout of triumph, Griffin brought the poker crashing down toward his prisoner's head. Jasper thrust his left arm up, stopping the blow before it met with his head.

Jasper's expression as he looked at Cat changed

from pleading to shocked betrayal. Then his eye closed and, his shirt tearing away from the blade that pinned it, he slid heavily to the floor.

The uprightman, intent on finishing the job, drew back his rapier for a cutting blow.

A cry of equal parts outrage and terror tore itself free from Cat's throat. She lunged without thought. Her blade sunk into the rogue's back, but catching on the start of a rib, it glanced off to the left.

With a curse, Griffin pivoted to face her. He studied her crouched form and the blade she held. The remnants of one golden brow arched in amusement. "Prepare to die, sweetmeat."

Cat's mouth went dry with terror. Everything Nicholas had taught her about swordplay flew from her head. Instead of a practiced lunge, she hovered uncertainly. Griffin prodded at her with his blade, testing to see what she'd do. At the last minute she raised the poniard and managed a clumsy parry.

Unthinking, she retreated backward. Griffin followed, stalking her. His blade met hers with bone-wrenching force. He committed to the assault, attacking hard, keeping her too busy with parries to make any counters of her own. But she managed to hold her ground.

Slowly the rhythm of the fight began to change as Cat added her own thrusts. Firelight glinted off their blades. Cat began to shorten her thrusts with her rapier, hoping Griffin would misjudge the length of her reach.

He brought the poker crashing down over her head. Cat dodged to the side and drove her poniard into his forearm. With a scream, the uprightman dropped the poker. But he backed away before Cat could recover her blade.

Some of the color left the uprightman's face as he stared down at the poniard protruding from his forearm. Then, gritting his teeth, he pulled the weapon out and grasped it loosely in his left hand. "You'll pay for that, you bloodthirsty bitch."

They continued to thrust and parry, retreat and circle, drawing close to where Teddar's body lay. Cat's boot hit a slippery patch of blood and she went down in a tangle. Her sword skidded beyond her grasp.

Cat scrambled across the dirty floor. She felt Griffin's fist clutch the back of her shirt. Mad with terror, she fought against his grasp, and the fabric ripped. Gaining a better hold, Griffin dragged her backward. Cat clawed wildly at the wooden floor, scrabbling for purchase.

Crouching, he hauled her back against his chest. She felt his fingers tangle in her hair and the cold kiss of steel at the base of her throat. "Say your good-byes, whore."

Suddenly, Cat's hand closed about something hard and sharp in the straw. It was a serving knife from the tavern. She jabbed it into Griffin's hand.

The uprightman howled in pain. His grip slackened from her hair and the poniard clattered to the ground.

With a sob of terror, Cat tore free and lunged for her sword on the ground. Grabbing it, she had just enough time to whirl around on her knees and hold it in front of her before Griffin charged. Her position was terrible, and the sword barely held in her trembling, sweat-slicked grasp. But it worked just the same.

The uprightman's momentum carried him right onto the end of the blade. In the shock of the impact, Cat's grip failed entirely. Both uprightman and sword went crashing to the floor.

Griffin's chest rose and fell in quick, shallow breaths. Weakly, he raised his head to examine the wound. Then his pain-glazed gaze shifted to her. "What are you lookin' at, whore?" he roared. "This ain't over yet." He rolled to his side with a hoarse curse and began to inch toward her. The hilt of the rapier grated along the wooden floor with every furious heave.

Cat's blood ran cold. This couldn't be happening. The wound was mortal! Despite what reason told her, she scrambled backward.

"Sweetmeat," Griffin snarled, "ye may mean to send me to Hell, but yer comin' with me!" He grabbed wildly for her ankle. Suddenly, his tortured body convulsed. Then it slumped forward, leaning heavily on the sword that still impaled it.

Cat stared down at the corpse. "Nay, Griffin," she whispered. "I've already spent my time in Hell. Now it's your turn." She stayed there for a long moment, watching him closely as she gasped for breath, not quite convinced that he was truly dead. Then, with a heavy shudder, she turned away.

Jasper was beginning to stir in the corner. She hurried to his side and knelt.

The actor groaned. Then his one eye opened slowly. "Cat?"

Cat sighed in relief, her throat thick with gratitude. "It's me. Everything's all right."

She helped him rise to a sitting position. His eyebrow jumped with surprise as he spotted the uprightman's corpse. "You killed him?"

She nodded.

"Christ," he muttered, a weak smile playing at his lips. "Now I have to make sure I don't piss Nicholas or you off. The City's getting too dangerous."

At the mention of Nicholas's name, Cat's sense of urgency returned. "Can you walk? We have to stop Heyward!"

With a grimace, Jasper gained his feet. "My arm may be broke but both legs work. Let's go."

"Rafe—" Cat turned to see the boy, pale but conscious, leaning heavily against the wall that separated the dining area from the kitchen.

Cat made to kneel by his side, but the boy waved her away.

"I'm well 'nough," he grumbled. "Go save yer Nick."

Jasper rested a hand on her shoulder. "Go! I'll cut his bonds."

Cat nodded, not needing any further encouragement. She flew through the door and ran faster than she ever had, for never had the stakes been so high. Having faced death in the form of the uprightman, she'd learned a stunning truth: Nicholas's life meant more to her than her own.

Rage. Blind, murderous rage. The breath in Nicholas's throat burned like fire as he stalked through the winter streets. Heyward had done the unspeakable. The bastard had taken two of the people he loved most—his son and Cat. The babe was lost forever, but he prayed there was still time left for Cat.

The Royal Exchange sat between Cornhill and

Threadneedle Street, a monument of Italian architecture. Although it was often judged a handsome place in the warmer months, the diffused light from the overcast winter sky cast the building's stones in sullen grays. It being the first day of the new year, only a handful of patrons milled about the open piazza flanked by colonnaded walks.

It didn't take long to spot Heyward on one of the covered paths. He was deep in conversation with a black-gowned merchant. The alderman was unaware of the danger behind him until Nicholas grabbed his cloak and hauled him backward.

Heyward straightened the costly fabric of his clothing and turned to face his attacker. His gaze shifted briefly to the blade Nicholas held ready, his expression remaining surprisingly bland. "What do you want, Dacre?"

Nicholas nearly choked on his fury. "Where is she, you bastard? What have you done with Cat?"

"I have no idea what you're talking about."

"You lie in your throat," Nicholas said with a growl. Quickly he unfastened his cloak and wrapped it around his right forearm.

Heyward took a step back, as if affronted. With the merchant at the alderman's back, Nicholas was the only one privy to his enemy's wide, dangerous smile. "What, sirrah, do you call me a liar?" Heyward demanded a little louder than necessary, drawing the beginnings of a crowd. He unfastened his cloak and began to wrap it around his left arm as Nicholas already had.

"Aye." Nicholas seethed. "A liar, a murderer, and one of the foulest creatures that's ever dared to show itself in the light of day!"

The lines of Heyward's face grew stern, his body rigid. "I call you out, sir."

"You needn't bother. I was already planning to kill you."

"What confidence," the alderman said dryly.

Nicholas's hand tightened on the hilt of his blade. "I have good reason to be confident. I am no longer a boy weakened by war."

Heyward ignored his reply. He eyed the blade Nicholas held close to his throat and said with great cool, "You seem to be leaning toward single rapiers. Very well, I shall fulfill your wish." Gracefully he took a step back. And, with a snick of steel, he drew a blade as sharp as an asp's fang.

The small crowd of curious businessmen forming about them took a hasty step back. Nicholas and Heyward began to circle around the walk, watching one another closely.

A fiery bloodlust coursed through Nicholas's veins. He had to force his words past gritted teeth. "You shall know such agony at my hand that you'll beg me to kill you. But I'll refuse you that mercy until you tell me where she is."

The deadly, calculating mask that had swallowed Heyward's features dropped momentarily, revealing something akin to pity. "She's already dead, you know."

With an animal cry of outrage and pain, Nicholas charged.

The alderman quickly parried and made a counter-attack. Wrapping his cloak tighter about his left arm, Laurence Heyward opted for a diagonal line deeper into the piazza, watching his enemy closely. He needed to draw blood. Dacre was a deadly duelist.

Only his weakened state had prevented him from winning the fight six years before. Without the lethal poison, Dacre would quickly kill him.

Better to make a sacrifice and get it over with.

When the next thrust came, Laurence stepped into it rather than away. Dacre's blade plowed up the unprotected flesh of his sword arm, rending a trail of burning agony. But the pain was of little importance, for the tip of his own blade pierced Dacre's chest. It wasn't a deep thrust, but as Laurence pulled back, blood welled through the baron's shirt.

Praise fortune, he'd scored a hit! Now it was a simple matter of waiting for the poison to act. From what the uprightman had told him, the deadly nightshade should make its way quickly through his opponent's system. Blurry vision and disorientation would rapidly give way to convulsions, coma, and then death. Of course, Laurence meant to kill Dacre before the convulsions hit. To do otherwise might be to draw suspicion on himself.

Dacre's black scowl and unblinking stare never wavered. His attacks came quick and fierce. His voice was a thunder of rage. "Where is she, you whoreson?"

Each time their blades met with a ring of steel, Laurence sought for any sign of his opponent weakening. If anything, though, Dacre's onslaught had grown more aggressive. In the following minutes, the baron's blade bit into Laurence two more times, and doubt began to gnaw away his confidence. Why was it taking so damn long?

Crouching low and tightening his grip on the hilt made slick by blood trailing from his arm wound, Laurence studied his opponent. Aye, his eyes were dilated and he was breathing hard. But was it from the poison or merely the exertion of the fight?

Laurence lunged. Dacre parried well enough, but he was forced to blink heavily, as if trying to clear his vision before he could make a return thrust. His attack was awkward, unbalanced. The cloak began to unwind from around his arm.

The poison was beginning to do its job. Dacre would continue to weaken; soon Laurence would have the upper hand. Although the onlookers were certain to think it strange, he permitted himself a triumphant smile.

Dacre was a dead man, and he didn't even know it.

Nicholas began to feel as though he were fighting through seawater. Every movement required enormous effort and his vision was blurry. The sounds around him were strangely muffled by the rapid pounding of his heart. Apparently, Carranza's ambush had taken even more out of him than he thought. But he couldn't stop. Cat's life was in danger.

"Tell me what you've done with Cat!" He emphasized his order with a quick thrust toward the abdomen which Heyward barely managed to elude.

At the close call, the alderman's features blanched. "If you kill me, you'll never discover where she is."

Nicholas's anger became scalding fury. The strange calm that normally overtook him in a fight was pointedly absent. "Your wife told me what you did to my son. I'll kill you unless you tell me where Cat is."

Heyward retreated toward the walkway.

Nicholas matched him step for step, allowing him no room for escape. Noting that his opponent's sword had drifted sloppily to the right, he made a thrust to the outside line. Again Heyward was forced to retreat—right into a pillar. Nicholas's blade sank deeply into the alderman's midriff.

Heyward's blade clattered noisily to the tile. Shaken, he looked down to where the sharp piece of metal pierced his body. His pale blue eyes widened noticeably and his face turned ashen.

"Have you no mercy?" the alderman gasped weakly.

"Mercy?" Nicholas sneered. "Aye, I'll grant you as much mercy as you gave my son, as you've given Cat." He spat in Heyward's face and pushed the blade even deeper.

Nicholas dispassionately watched him writhe and twist around the blade. "Where is she, Laurence?"

Heyward's eyes were rimmed with white. "I don't know. I swear I don't know!"

The blade advanced a third time, reducing the man to tears.

Finally, head low, he found his voice. "I left her with Griffin. At that pathetic alehouse of hers. But it doesn't matter. That rogue hated her. I-I've never seen such malevolence. By now she's dead."

Nicholas stepped back on unsteady legs and allowed his enemy to slide from his blade. Heyward collapsed onto the tile. Then, without conscious thought, Nicholas's legs buckled, and he sank down beside his enemy. He was vaguely aware that the faint frost of snow on which they lay was rapidly turning red with their blood. "There may still be time," he muttered. "I have to find her."

One of Heyward's golden brows, handsome even in the throes of death, arched. "Don't be a fool, Dacre. It's over."

"No, it cannot be!" Nicholas grabbed him by the shirt and shook him hard.

A fit of heavy coughing seized Heyward, causing the man to clutch at his wounded side and grimace in pain. When he was able to speak again, his voice was a watery rasp. As the words left his mouth, so did a trail of blood. "She's dead, and soon you will be, too. There was poison on my blade."

A timorous smirk fought at the corners of the alderman's mouth; then it faded. His blue eyes rolled backward, and the dead weight of his body sagged toward the ground. The rich fabric of his shirt slid through Nicholas's numbed fingers, and the corpse dropped to the tiles.

Poison. . . . Whispers of Heyward's treachery swept through the small crowd.

Nicholas barely heard them. Instead, it was Heyward's final, heartrending pronouncement of Cat's fate that repeated over and over in his unsteady thoughts. Cat was dead. That cold, bitter reality pierced his heart like the sharp point of a rapier. He'd found the one woman in the world he was capable of truly loving only to lose her.

The world about him reeled and spun even more wildly. This time, he didn't fight it, for there was nothing left for him here. *Soon, my love,* Nicholas thought as he surrendered to the darkness that meant to swallow him whole. *We'll be together again. Soon.*

As he crumpled on top of Heyward's corpse, the last thing he heard was a heart-rending shriek. Thinking it must have come from one of the demons that had waited patiently for his soul, only to be cheated in the last moments by true love, he smiled faintly.

Then there was nothing.

27

From across the piazza, Cat watched in horror as Nicholas collapsed on top of Heyward and went as still as the alderman's lifeless form. "Nooooo!" The denial rent its way from her throat.

Discovering renewed strength in her legs, she bolted across the courtyard. Relentlessly shoving away curious onlookers, she reached her love's crumpled form and dropped next to him in the crimson-flecked snow. Panting, she rolled Nicholas off of Heyward and onto his back.

His body trembled under her hand, and she exhaled the breath she hadn't realized she was holding. He was alive, but for how long? Blood coursed from a single wound in his chest. By now the poison must be flowing through his veins.

Cradling him in her arms, she choked out, "Nicholas, can you hear me?"

His tremors only worsened. When his eyes fluttered briefly open, the pupils were dark, gaping pits.

Cat brought an unsteady hand to his forehead. It was hot and dry. A sheer, black fright swept through her. The nightshade had begun its deadly work.

Biting her lip to stop the tears of helplessness threatening to blind her, she ripped away part of Nicholas's shirt and used it in an attempt to staunch the flow of blood. But what about the poison? Skinner had lived only minutes from the time she'd found him.

Swallowing the despair in her throat, Cat glanced up at the handful of people milling about. "Is there a physician here? Anyone who knows something about medicine?"

"Is it poison then, miss?" a tradesman asked softly. "His alderman said as much but it's hard to credit such a thing."

"Aye," Cat choked. "He dipped his blade in deadly nightshade. Does anyone know what to do?"

"Can you make him vomit?" someone asked.

"Aye, make him drink warm beer and butter!" someone else suggested.

"But it's in his blood not his stomach," Cat protested.

"Then bleed 'im."

"Aye, bleed him!" several others joined in.

Cat winced at the raucous chorus. How much blood would she have to take to get the poison out of his system? she wondered in consternation. More likely, she'd kill him. Helplessly, she looked down at Nicholas, feeling bereft and desolate.

Desperation flamed into irrational anger.

"Dacre, you cowardly whoreson, don't you dare leave me. Not now!" She shook his shoulders. He was dead weight in her arms.

No. This couldn't be happening. In disbelief, Cat scanned the crowd. "Please! Can't anyone help us?"

"Make way, you sluggards. Make way!" Jasper, pale and sweaty, broke through the circle of onlookers.

Cat looked up at him. She could no longer fight the tears. "Oh, Jas, he's dying."

Her friend dropped beside her and leaned to check Nicholas's breathing. As Jasper sat back up, Nicholas's tremors began to escalate into a full convulsion. "Christ, he's worse than when I found him in Flanders."

Cat frowned for a moment in confusion, then realized what he meant. "That's right," she said, scarcely daring to hope. "You were with him when he was poisoned before! What do we do, Jas?"

"Christ, Cat, I'm no physician."

"But you were there," she persisted. "You must have seen what the physician did!"

The actor's one-eyed gaze darted nervously between her and Nicholas. Then he shook his head. "No, it was a different poison. It might not work. We should wait for Guerau."

"What might not work?" she demanded. "Jesu, I can't just sit here and watch him die!"

Jasper studied her for a long moment. "All right. First we need to clean out the wound in case any of the poison lingers. Then, we try to get some tea down him."

"Aye, make him vomit!" someone shouted.

Jasper looked up and shook his head. "Nay, vomiting will do no good. The tea is to help flush the poison through his system."

"Water and tea," muttered the tradesman hovering

near. "I'll find ye some, man." He was halfway across the piazza before Cat or Jasper even had time to thank him.

"While we're waiting for those, we need to get his amulet off."

Cat looked at him sharply. What did any of this have to do with Nicholas's superstitious trinket? "Jasper, we need something better than his foolish magic!"

Jasper didn't reply. Rather, he wrapped his good arm around Nicholas's twitching body and lifted his torso off the ground. "Take it off, Cat," he grunted.

Cat did as he'd asked. Once he'd lowered Nicholas back to the ground, she surrendered the leather pouch without protest.

Bringing the bag up to his mouth, Jasper used his teeth to bite through the knotted string that sealed it. Then he turned it upside down, dumping out the contents into Cat's palm.

She stared down at two tiny vials. One was full of a yellow-brown powder, the other a purple liquid. "What are those?"

"One of these might work as an antidote." Jasper hesitated, frowning. "If only I can remember which is which."

Cat stared at him in horror. "Don't tell me you can't—"

"All right. I think I got it now," Jasper murmured to himself. "His heart is racing like a frightened hare's. We need to slow it down. That means we use the liquid."

"What will that do?"

"Heyward's sword was coated with nightshade. That quickens the humors. Listen. You can hear his heart beating from five paces away. The apothecary in Flanders said this does the opposite. It should slow his heart as if he were sleeping."

Cat smiled tremulously. "Then what are you waiting for? Give it to him," she urged.

"First the water and tea." Jasper peered uneasily in the direction of where the tradesman had disappeared. Slowly, he dragged his gaze back to hers. Now he was crying, too.

The flutter of hope Cat had just begun to feel stilled inside. "What is it, Jas? What aren't you telling me?"

"The tincture's foxglove."

Cat stared at him. "Foxglove is poison. Nicholas told me that's what almost killed him in Flanders."

"It is."

She shook her head vehemently. "No. There has to be something else we can do to help him."

"If there is, I don't know it." His one-eyed stare bore into her. "Cat, I love him just as much as you. But we have no choice. It's the only thing that has a chance of counteracting the nightshade. And if it fails, his death may come quicker."

"Oh, God, please don't ask this of me," Cat sobbed. "Not this . . . "

"Make way! Make way!" The tradesman huffed to their side. "I got yer tea!" He waved a heavy sack of liquid triumphantly. There was a hearty cheer from the increasing crowd. Then they went silent.

"Well, Cat? Are we agreed?" Jasper looked at her expectantly.

Cat looked to where Nicholas lay racked with convulsions. He was already slipping further and further from their grasp. But, sweet Mary, what if she were to lose him all that much sooner?

Then even the actor's faint control slipped. "It's our only hope," he croaked.

Unable to speak, Cat nodded weakly.

But when the moment came, when Jasper brought the vial of the second poison to Nicholas's lips, a cry of pure anguish and heartbreak escaped Cat, and the crowd had to forcibly restrain her from stopping him.

With the help of a few of the onlookers, Cat and Jasper brought Nicholas back to his chambers at Dacre House, not knowing if his beloved four-post bed was to be where he would recover or die. Guerau tried another lavage with tea, then admitted there was nothing left to be done but wait and see if God would prove merciful.

For two torturous days Cat watched and waited. When even Jasper submitted to having his own wound tended to, and later to his body's demands for food and sleep, she remained at Nicholas's side, fearing that if she left, even for a moment, he would slip entirely from her reach.

At first, when his convulsions stopped, she'd been encouraged. But instead of reviving, Nicholas only seemed to retreat into a deeper sleep. Was it the foxglove or a coma that presaged death from nightshade poisoning? No matter. Time was running out, for he would take no sustenance.

As Cat sat with him through the dark hours of the night, she discovered vengeance to be a brittle, empty thing, no more substantial than a faded autumn leaf crushed to dust. Heyward was dead, but it didn't bring her family back. It didn't erase their suffering. It hadn't even cleared their name of the taint of treason. And, as painful as that was, she'd come to realize that it was history, part of the past.

Here, right now, she was losing Nicholas. 'Twas as if her marvelous, battle-scarred duelist had lost the will to fight. And after two days of watching him slowly die before her eyes, the pain in her heart was beyond simple tears, the exhaustion too great to fight. Even realizing that she'd missed her monthly courses and what that implied failed to rouse her.

But some strong, inviolable part of her could not accept the possibility of his dying, of a life bereft of his presence. If Nicholas died, so would the rest of her. For she loved him. Aye. She loved him. She knew that now. She could no longer resist what she'd fought so hard to deny. And she might never have the chance to see that knowledge reflected in her lover's eyes.

So she crawled into the large bed they might never share beyond sunrise the next morn. And she began to beg, cajole, and threaten him not to leave her. But he remained as still, and perfect, and cold as the marble effigy that might soon grace his grave. In despair, she began to list her sins and failings as if God might take pity on her if she made a full confession. But at some dark hour of the night she ran out of words to describe her fear, her guilt, the wisdom that had cost too much and come too late. She ran out of promises and threats.

So she simply told Nicholas of her love. She told him of the child she carried. "Come back to me," she begged. "I need you. I love you. Believe me. Please believe me." Murmuring dreams of what might have been, she finally slipped into the weary oblivion of sleep she'd fought so hard against. But even there she was alone.

Nicholas was discovering there were many degrees of death, just like the infinite shades of gray that stretched between shadow and light. First, at the piazza he'd lost the ability to move his poison-numbed body. Then he was swallowed into darkness. Finally, even the fiery pain in his gut subsided. Occasionally, some sense of motion or a snippet of someone's words would drift down to the cozy little nook he'd carved in oblivion. But as he continued to drift further and further away, such moments came less often. He meant to shun them entirely so that he might go to his poor, dead Cat, but some force kept pulling him back.

Nay, it was not a force. Rather, a relentless demon that fought to drag him back into the hell of life he wanted to flee. And when he struggled, it whispered horrible, torturous lies. It told him of a sable-haired beauty that waited for him in life, of a babe that soon would be.

If he still had hands, he would have drawn them over his ears. If he had a voice he would have screamed. But he had neither, and the assault raged on. Slowly, what little will and strength he had left drained away. And the treacherous demon dragged him back to a place he'd prayed never to see again. Back into a world that held nothing for him.

Light pierced his nest of darkness. First as a single ray, then as a searing beam that burnt to the farthest reaches of his mind, cutting away his mental armor, leaving him naked and vulnerable in the light of morning.

He took stock of his surroundings. He was laying on his back, nude except for a single sheet. The familiar canopy of his bed hovered overhead as it had any other morning. Nicholas tried to draw his hands into fists and discovered they were twined in the mass of curls of the woman who slumbered on his chest.

He blinked, scarcely able to credit his eyes. "Cat?" The question came out as a hoarse croak.

The apparition before him stirred. A heart-shaped face emerged from the sable mane. Dark lashes fluttered; green eyes widened. "Nicholas?" Familiar, delicate fingers sank deeply into his arm, as if she were trying to convince herself that he was really there.

"In the flesh," he murmured, too tired to make more than that feeble attempt at humor.

With a strangled sob, she wrapped her arms tightly around his neck, pressing her cheek close to his. "My love? You've come back? Oh, thank you, God. Thank you!"

My love? Even as deathly tired as he was, his ears caught the endearment.

Her hands cradled his head. "Thank Mary, I thought I'd lost you . . ."

Nicholas raised his head slightly so he could look into the lovely eyes he thought he'd never see again. "After all the trouble you put me through, do you really think I'd leave when you finally came to your senses? I may still be lacking in honor, but certainly not stubbornness."

Cat's deathhold tightened. Her tears gave way to full-fledged sobs. Nicholas wasn't certain, but he thought he joined her.

28

Jasper, who'd been slumped in an oak caquetoire with his splint resting on the arm of the chair, awoke soon after their tears began. His good eye squinted at the two of them in bed, then widened. He stood up stiffly and moved to the edge of the mattress. "Why, you tough-skinned old bastard," he said, moisture leaking down one cheek.

Nicholas managed a weak smile. "Good to see you, too, Savage."

"And here I thought you were just bragging about being unkillable—" The actor broke off with something sounding suspiciously like a sniffle.

Cat drew her devoted friend into their tight embrace. "Thank you, Jas. Thank you for saving him."

When the actor made to protest, Cat brought a finger to his lips. "Wouldst that I could have done the same for you with Lenore."

Jasper managed a pained smile. "You did what you could, Cat. At least fortune was kind enough to make me a tough-skinned old bastard, too. I'm a survivor, Cat. All of us are."

The three friends sat together for a long time in silence, their simple closeness speaking more eloquently than any words. Finally, with much coaxing from Cat and Nicholas, Jasper permitted Jonah and Maris to usher him away to a proper bed where he could rest and begin his own road to healing.

Soon after Nicholas regained consciousness, his strength began to return. By Twelfth Night, he was recovered enough to do what he longed to do since their first fateful meeting at St. Paul's—make love to Cat in all the glory of leisure. Their presents to one another had been hastily dispatched in favor of a day-long idyll amidst the feathered comfort of his four-post bed.

Their lovemaking was tender and soft, hard and demanding, curious and bashful. Slowly, with their mouths, and hands, and skin they learned every inch of one another's bodies. The valleys and curves of their flesh mated together in untold pleasure.

When Nicholas's strength flagged, Cat made use of her own, crawling on top and renewing the rhythm with shameless abandon.

Wave after wave of rapture enfolded them until she too collapsed, tired and breathless. At some point in the late afternoon, they fell into a lazy slumber in each other's arms.

Nicholas had just awoken and begun to suckle at Cat's breasts in an attempt to wake her as well when he heard feet upon the main stair. He chose to ignore them.

Drowsily, Cat opened her eyes and smiled at him.

"Ah, you return to me, *mia cara*," Nicholas whispered. He trailed delicate kisses from her throat down to the sensitive skin of her stomach which caused Cat to giggle and twine her fingers in his hair.

A pounding at the door interrupted their play.

Tossing back the covers, Nicholas glared angrily at the portal. "Go away!" he shouted.

The knocks immediately stopped, and he returned to the pleasurable task of properly ravishing the beauty who shared his bed.

It was only a moment before the pounding renewed. That, in turn, was followed by several over-loud coughs. Nicholas would have ignored that too, but the gilt handle began to turn. As the heavy door swung inward, he cursed his idiocy for not locking the door—his commands had always been obeyed so he'd never had the need—and groaned in frustration.

Her face flushed with lovemaking and embarrassment, Cat sunk deeper into the covers and snickered faintly in amusement.

Jonah's balding head poked through the opening. He was careful to keep his eyes downcast as he said timidly, "Begging your pardon, my lord, but there is a visitor downstairs who wishes to speak to you."

Cat's fit of giggling overtook her. She buried her head under the covers in a futile attempt to muffle the sound.

Nicholas, both furious and amused, was inclined to join her, but somehow managed only the disdainful raise of an eyebrow. "Then tell them I am, er"—he slanted a hungry glance at the curvaceous mound shifting under the covers beside him—"indisposed at the moment and that they should come back another time."

Jonah's brows drew together in solemn urgency. "Nay, my lord, I'm afraid I cannot."

Beneath the covers, Cat began to do decidedly delectable and immodest things to him with her hands, causing Nicholas to become more impatient than he might otherwise have been. "Jonah," he said with a growl, "either tell whoever it is to go away or bring me my sword so I can kill you."

The elderly servant paled but didn't retreat. "But, my lord, it's the queen and her entourage."

Not even on the field of battle had Nicholas donned clothes more quickly than in the wake of Jonah's news. There was barely enough time for him to pull on his stockings and trunks and for Jonah to pin on his sleeves, before he lost his nerve to keep his sovereign waiting any longer. He laced his shirt with clumsy fingers as he made his way to the stairs.

Elizabeth, richly garbed in ruby velvet and gems to match, was waiting for him at the landing in the very place he had ravished Cat not long before. She snapped her feather fan irritably.

The entourage of courtiers and guards stood at a polite distance by the far side of the hall. Nicholas noted with distaste that William Cecil, garbed in his traditional solemn robes, stood at the queen's side. No doubt by now the statesman had shared all the intelligence they'd garnered with the monarch, and had taken the lion's share of the credit.

It was with greater pleasure that Nicholas recognized the earl of Essex's significant absence. They may have failed to convince the queen of the lord's involvement in a treasonous plot, but it was clear that some measure of doubt had been cast her favorite's way.

Reaching the bottom of the stairs, Nicholas bowed as deeply as his leg permitted.

Elizabeth acknowledged his presence dryly. "Nicholas."

He rose slowly, careful to meet her gaze. "I cry your mercy, my queen, for my tardy appearance. I fear my recent infirmity has made me sadly inattentive of my duties."

Elizabeth brushed away his apology. "Nonsense," she snapped, her dark mood disappearing as quickly as it came. "I'd rather see you well and late than not see you at all." She scanned him appraisingly. "It gladdens me to see you recovered so quickly. It would have grieved me dearly to have lost my Misrule."

Nicholas managed a tight smile at the hated nickname. "Thank you, your majesty."

The queen's voice lost some of its breezy quality as she continued. "I could scarce credit the tales as to the depth of the alderman's treachery. I must say, it casts many of your youthful actions in a different light. I would have it known that from now on I *expect*"—she shot a purposeful look at her entourage—"you will be treated as a most welcome member of my court."

Nicholas began another reluctant thank you but heard footsteps on the stairs behind him. Turning, he saw 'twas Cat. She had struggled into a gown of some elegance, but she wore no stockings or shoes. Her clear, bright eyes, swollen lips, and wild disarray of hair spoke elegantly of their activities of the day.

A murmur made its way around the Great Hall.

As all eyes turned upon her, Cat made a hasty bow and murmured, "Your majesty."

Elizabeth's dark gaze raked coldly over Cat, taking in her state of dishabille. The monarch's starkly plucked brow furrowed beneath her garish wig. For one second she was transformed into little more than a judgmental and possessive old woman.

Then, the hint of displeasure disappeared, and England's queen returned. "Mistress Catrienne. I was hoping we would have a chance to speak." Elizabeth motioned her forward.

Cat did as she was bade.

"My good statesman, Burghley, has told me who you are. Nay, do not panic. He also told me of the crimes committed against your family."

Nicholas glanced sharply at his former ally. Burghley's expression was a careful mask of diplomacy. Aye, now that Heyward was dead, the statesman could tell the queen of Heyward's crimes of twelve years ago without fear of being implicated.

"I am greatly grieved by your loss," Elizabeth went on, "for I know what it is to lose a family member. Let this gift be of some small comfort."

The queen watched impassively as her solemn statesman stepped forward and presented Cat with a piece of rolled parchment.

When Burghley returned to her side, she said, "It's a royal pardon clearing the Lyly name of treason. Your lands in Oxford have been returned to you."

"Your majesty," Cat choked, her hands clutching the parchment. "I have no idea how I can adequately express my thanks—"

With a faint frown, Elizabeth turned businesslike again. "There is no need. I wouldst have all my subjects treated fairly." She brought her attention back to Nicholas, dismissing Cat. "There is one more thing, Misrule."

"And what would that be, my queen?"

"You shall marry Catrienne in all due haste." Elizabeth paused to sniff haughtily. "It would never do to have a gentlewoman's honor tarnished by scandal."

Laughter rippled through the entourage, and the two lovers finally hazarded a glance at one another. Cat's eyes were wide with shock. Nicholas was also startled, but when Cat opened her mouth to protest, he stunned her with his most dazzling of smiles and replied before she had a chance.

"Why, of course, your majesty," Nicholas murmured, his throat thick with emotion. "There is nothing I'd rather do." Inwardly, his spirits soared, for he'd spoken the truth.

Hearing the sincerity in his voice and seeing the warmth in his eyes, Cat seemed to settle down, although Nicholas thought he glimpsed a glimmer of a tear in one eye.

Elizabeth didn't bother to ask Cat's consent. Rather, permitting herself the faintest royal smile, she announced, "The ceremony will be this Sunday at St. Paul's, two days hence."

St. Paul's?

Thinking back to the day they first met, Nicholas caught Cat's gaze. She was biting her lip hard so as not to laugh like the wild-spirited bandit she was. But her answer hovered on her features as well . . .

"Yes, your majesty," they chorused in unison.

*   *   *

After the queen had left, the two lovers returned to Nicholas's chambers and piled blankets on the floor next to the fireplace. There they sat, Cat nestled between Nicholas's legs with her back against his chest and his arms wrapped so tight around her that it seemed he meant to never let her go.

Branch by branch, they tossed the Christmas greens into the fire. With the rich scent of pine, the branches crackled and glowed, quickly burning into nothingness.

Neither she nor Nicholas said anything in the hour or so it took for the last ornaments of Christmas to take their leave. Instead, they let the steady beat of one another's heart say what they both knew. Nicholas's reign as Lord of Misrule had ended. Their life together, however, had just begun.

Finally, Nicholas rose and stretched. He took Cat's hand in his and, after bringing it to his lips, coaxed her to follow him back to the bed they would share for the rest of their lives.

From the Dacre gardens, a young urchin watched the silhouettes of the two lovers pass by the second-story window, then disappear from sight. Smiling to himself, Rafe ruffled the lion's mane one more time, then climbed the ladder to his sumptuous new quarters— the tree house in the orchard.

As the boy drifted off to sleep, beneath him came the deep rumble of a very content feline. The peaceful sound followed into his dreams.

Author's Note

By 1594, Robert Devereux, the earl of Essex, was at the peak of his political power. He was the queen's favorite and had cultivated a talented network of spies. Although England had been officially at war with Spain since 1586, the last serious confrontation had been the defeat of the Spanish Armada in 1588. The war party, headed by Essex, was forever urging the queen to decisively confront Spain on its own soil. The party had a remarkable talent for both uncovering and inventing fresh Spanish plots as ammunition for their position.

Sending money to the rebel Scottish earls is my own creation but certainly not beneath Essex's character. After 1594, the earl's favor began to decline with the queen—due in large part to failed military exploits. In 1601, he led a revolt against Elizabeth I and was tried and executed for treason.

Incidentally, on the night of December 28, 1594, there really was a riot at Grey's Inn, where the Chamberlain's Men were to act *The Comedy of Errors*. According to writer Michael Justin Davis in *The England of William Shakespeare*, "a disordered tumult arose, and even the sex of gentlewomen did not 'privilege them from violence.'" The incident became known to later history as "The Night of Errors." Unfortunately, the first written account of this event was not printed until 1688, and the cause of the riot was never determined.

I couldn't resist offering an explanation.

Let HarperMonogram Sweep You Away!

Once a Knight by Christina Dodd
Golden Heart and RITA Award–winning author. Though slightly rusty, once great knight Sir David Radcliffe agrees to protect Lady Alisoun for a price. His mercenary heart betrayed by passion, Sir David proves to his lady that he is still master of love—and his sword is as swift as ever.

Timberline by Deborah Bedford
Held captive in her mountain cabin by escaped convict Ben Pershall, Rebecca Woodburn realizes that the man's need for love mirrors her own. Even though Ben has taken her hostage, he ultimately sets her soul free.

Conor's Way by Laura Lee Guhrke
Desperate to save her plantation after the Civil War, beautiful Olivia Maitland takes in Irish ex-boxer Conor Branigan in exchange for help. Cynical Conor has no place for romance in his life, until the strong-willed belle shows him that the love of a lifetime is worth fighting for.

Lord of Misrule by Stephanie Maynard
Golden Heart Award Winner. Posing as a thief to avenge the destruction of her noble family, Catrienne Lyly must match wits with Nicholas D'Avenant, Queen Elizabeth's most mysterious agent. But Cat's bold ruse cannot protect her from the ecstasy of Nicholas's touch.

And in case you missed last month's selections . . .

Once Upon a Time by Constance O'Banyon
Over seven million copies of her books in print. To save her idyllic kingdom from the English, Queen Jilliana must marry Prince Ruyen and produce an heir. Both are willing to do anything to defeat a common enemy, but they are powerless to fight the wanton desires that threaten to engulf them.

The Marrying Kind by Sharon Ihle

Romantic Times *Reviewers' Choice Award–winning author.* Liberty Ann Justice has no time for the silver-tongued stranger she believes is trying to destroy her father's Wyoming newspaper. Donovan isn't about to let a little misunderstanding hinder her pursuit of happiness, however, or his pursuit of the tempestuous vixen who has him hungering for her sweet love.

Honor by Mary Spencer

Sent by King Henry V to save Amica of Lancaster from a cruel marriage, Sir Thomas of Reed discovers his rough ways are no match for Amica's innocent sensuality. A damsel in distress to his knight, she unleashes passions in Sir Thomas that leave him longing for her touch.

Wake Not the Dragon by Jo Ann Ferguson

As the queen's midwife, Gizela de Montpellier travels to Wales and meets Rhys ap Cynan—a Welsh chieftain determined to drive out the despised English. Captivated by the handsome warlord, Gizela must choose between her loyalty to the crown and her heart's desire.

$\mathcal{M}$*onogram* Harper